IRISH FAIRY
AND
FOLK TALES

The queen drove the children into the lake, and striking them with a wand, they turned into four white swans.—Page 3. *Irish Fairy Tales.*

IRISH FAIRY
AND
FOLK TALES

EDITED AND SELECTED BY

W. B. YEATS

PROFUSELY ILLUSTRATED

**BARNES
& NOBLE
BOOKS**

NEW YORK

This edition published by Barnes & Noble, Inc.

1993 Barnes & Noble Books

MC ISBN 0-88029-073-0
MP ISBN 1-56619-532-2

Printed and bound in the United States of America
MC   18 17 16
MP   10   9

INTRODUCTION.

Dr. Corbett, Bishop of Oxford and Norwich, lamented
long ago the departure of the English fairies. "In Queen
Mary's time" he wrote—

> "When Tom came home from labor,
>   Or Cis to milking rose,
> Then merrily, merrily went their tabor,
>   And merrily went their toes."

But now, in the times of James, they had all gone, for
"they were of the old profession," and "their songs were
Ave Maries." In Ireland they are still extant, giving
gifts to the kindly, and plaguing the surly. "Have you
ever seen a fairy or such like?" I asked an old man in
County Sligo. "Amn't I annoyed with them," was the
answer. "Do the fishermen along here know anything of
the mermaids?" I asked a woman of a village in County
Dublin. "Indeed, they don't like to see them at all," she
answered, "for they always bring bad weather." "Here
is a man who believes in ghosts," said a foreign sea-cap-
tain, pointing to a pilot of my acquaintance. "In every
house over there," said the pilot, pointing to his native
village of Rosses, "there are several." Certainly that
now old and much respected dogmatist, the Spirit of the
Age, has in no manner made his voice heard down there.
In a little while, for he has gotten a consumptive appearance of late, he will be covered over decently in his grave,
and another will grow, old and much respected, in his
place, and never be heard of down there, and after him
another and another and another. Indeed, it is a question

iii

whether any of these personages will ever be heard of
outside the newspaper offices and lecture-rooms and draw-
ing-rooms and ee-pie houses of the cities, or if the Spirit
of the Age is at any time more than a froth. At any
rate, whole troops of their like will not ehange the Celt
much. Giraldus Cambrensis found the people of the
western islands a trifle paganish. "How many gods are
there?" asked a priest, a little while ago, of a man from
the Island of Innistor. "There is one on Innistor; but
this seems a big place," said the man, and the priest held
up his hands in horror, as Giraldus had, just seven centuries before. Remember, I am not blaming the man; it
is very much better to believe in a number of gods than
in none at all, or to think there is only one, but that he is
a little sentimental and impracticable, and not constructed
for the nineteenth century. The Celt, and his cromlechs,
and his pillar-stones, these will not change much—indeed,
it is doubtful if anybody at all changes at any time. In
spite of hosts of deniers, and asserters, and wise-men, and
professors, the majority still are averse to sitting down to
dine thirteen at table, or being helped to salt, or walking
under a ladder, or seeing a single magpie flirting his
checkered tail. There are, of course, children of light
who have set their faces against all this, though even a
newspaper man, if you entice him into a cemetery at midnight, will believe in phantoms, for every one is a visionary if you scratch him deep enough. But the Celt is a
visionary without scratching.

Yet, be it noticed, if you are a stranger, you will not
readily get ghost and fairy legends, even in a western village. You must go adroitly to work, and make friends
with the children, and the old men, with those who have
not felt the pressure of mere daylight existence, and those
with whom it is growing less, and will have altogether
taken itself off one of these days. The old women are
most learned, but will not so readily be got to talk, for
the fairies are very secretive, and much resent being
talked of; and are there not many stories of old women

who were nearly pinched into their graves or numbed with fairy blasts?

At sea, when the nets are out and the pipes are lit, then will some ancient hoarder of tales become loquacious, telling his histories to the tune of the creaking of the boats. Holy-eve night, too, is a great time, and in old days many tales were to be heard at wakes. But the priests have set faces against wakes.

In the Parochial Survey of Ireland it is recorded how the story-tellers used to gather together of an evening, and if any had a different version from the others, they would all recite theirs and vote, and the man who had varied would have to abide by their verdict. In this way stories have been handed down with such accuracy, that the long tale of Dierdre was, in the earlier decades of this century, told almost word for word, as in the very ancient MSS. in the Royal Dublin Society. In one case only it varied, and then the MS. was obviously wrong—a passage had been forgotten by the copyist. But this accuracy is rather in the folk and bardic tales than in the fairy legends, for these vary widely, being usually adapted to some neighboring village or local fairy-seeing celebrity. Each county has usually some family, or personage, supposed to have been favored or plagued, especially by the phantoms, as the Hackets of Castle Hacket, Galway, who had for their ancestor a fairy, or John-o'-Daly of Lisadell, Sligo, who wrote " Eilleen Aroon," the song the Scotch have stolen and called " Robin Adair," and which Handel would sooner have written than all his oratorios,* and the " O'Donahue of Kerry." Round these men stories tended to group themselves, sometimes deserting more ancient heroes for the purpose. Round poets have they gathered especially, for poetry in Ireland has always been mysteriously connected with magic.

These folk-tales are full of simplicity and musical occurrences, for they are the literature of a class for whom

* He lived some time in Dublin, and heard it then.

vi INTRODUCTION.

every incident in the old rut of birth, love, pain, and death has cropped up unchanged for centuries : who have steeped everything in the heart : to whom everything is a symbol. They have the spade over which man has leant from the beginning. The people of the cities have the machine, which is prose and a *parvenu.* They have few events. They can turn over the incidents of a long life as they sit by the fire. With us nothing has time to gather meaning, and too many things are occurring for even a big heart to hold. It is said the most eloquent people in the world are the Arabs, who have only the bare earth of the desert and a sky swept bare by the sun. "Wisdom has alighted upon three things," goes their proverb; "the hand of the Chinese, the brain of the Frank, and the tongue of the Arab." This, I take it, is the meaning of that simplicity sought for so much in these days by all the poets, and not to be had at any price.

The most notable and typical story-teller of my acquaintance is one Paddy Flynn, a little, bright-eyed, old man, living in a leaky one-roomed cottage of the village of B——, "The most gentle—*i. e.*, fairy—place in the whole of the County Sligo," he says, though others claim that honor for Drumahair or Drumcliff. A very pious old man, too! You may have some time to inspect his strange figure and ragged hair, if he happen to be in a devout humor, before he comes to the doings of the gentry. A strange devotion! Old tales of Columkill, and what he said to his mother. "How are you to-day, mother?" "Worse!" "May you be worse to-morrow;" and on the next day, "How are you to-day, mother?" "Worse!" "May you be worse to-morrow;" and on the next, "How are you to-day, mother?" "Better, thank God." "May you be better to-morrow." In which undutiful manner he will tell you Columkill inculcated cheerfulness. Then most likely he will wander off into his favorite theme—how the judge smiles alike in rewarding the good and condemning the lost to unceasing flames. Very consoling does it appear to Paddy

Flynn, this melancholy and apocalyptic cheerfulness of
the Judge. Nor seems his own cheerfulness quite earthly
—though a very palpable cheerfulness. The first time I
saw him he was cooking mushrooms for himself; the next
time he was asleep under a hedge, smiling in his sleep.
Assuredly some joy not quite of this steadfast earth light-
ens in those eyes—swift as the eyes of a rabbit—among
so many wrinkles, for Paddy Flynn is very old. A melancholy there is in the midst of their cheerfulness—a
melancholy that is almost a portion of their joy, the visionary melancholy of purely instinctive natures and of all
animals. In the triple solitude of age and eccentricity and
partial deafness he goes about much pestered by children.

As to the reality of his fairy and spirit-seeing powers,
not all are agreed. One day we were talking of the
Banshee. "I have seen it," he said, "down there by the
water 'batting' the river with its hands." He it was
who said the fairies annoyed him.

Not that the Skeptic is entirely afar even from these
western villages. I found him one morning as he bound
his corn in a merest pocket-hankerchief of a field. Very
different from Paddy Flynn—Skepticism in every wrinkle
of his face, and a traveled man, too!—a foot-long Mohawk
Indian tatooed on one of his arms to evidence the matter.
"They who travel," says a neighboring priest, shaking his
head over him, and quoting Thomas Á'Kempis, "seldom
come home holy." I had mentioned ghosts to the Skeptic.
"Ghosts," said he; "there are no such things at all, at all,
but the gentry, they stand to reason; for the devil, when
he fell out of heaven, took the weak-minded ones with him,
and they were put into the waste places. And that's what
the gentry are. But they are getting scarce now, because
their time's over, ye see, and they're going back. But
ghosts, no! And I'll tell ye something more I don't
believe in—the fire of hell;" then, in a low voice, "that's
only invented to give the priests and the parsons something
to do." Thereupon this man, so full of enlightenment,
returned to his corn-binding.

The various collectors of Irish folk-lore have, from our point of view, one great merit, and from the point of view of others, one great fault. They have made their work literature rather than science, and told us of the Irish peasantry rather than of the primitive religion of mankind, or whatever else the folk-lorists are on the gad after. To be considered scientists they should have tabulated all their tales in forms like grocer's bills— item the fairy king, item the queen. Instead of this they have caught the very voice of the people, the very pulse of life, each giving what was most noticed in his day. Croker and Lover, full of the ideas of harum-scarum Irish gentility, saw everything humorized. The impulse of the Irish literature of their time came from a class that did not —mainly for political reasons—take the populace seriously, and imagined the country as a humorist's Arcadia; its passion, its gloom, its tragedy, they knew nothing of. What they did was not wholly false ; they merely magnified an irresponsible type, found oftenest among boatmen, carmen, and gentlemen's servants, into the type of a whole nation, and created the stage Irishman. The writers of ' Forty-eight, and the famine combined, burst their bubble. Their work had the dash as well as the shallowness of an ascendant and idle class, and in Croker is touched everywhere with beauty—a gentle Arcadian beauty. Carleton, a peasant born, has in many of his stories—I have been only able to give a few of the slightest—more especially in his ghost stories, a much more serious way with him, for all his humor. Kennedy, an old bookseller in Dublin, who seems to have had a something of genuine belief in the fairies, came next in time. He has far less literary faculty, but is wonderfully accurate, giving often the very words the stories were told in. But the best book since Croker is Lady Wilde's *Ancient Legends*. The humor has all given way to pathos and tenderness. We have here the innermost heart of the Celt in the moments he has grown to love through years of persecution, when, cushioning himself about with dreams, and hearing fairy-songs in

the twilight, he ponders on the soul and on the dead.
Here is the Celt, only it is the Celt dreaming.

Besides these are two writers of importance, who have
published, so far, nothing in book shape—Miss Letitia
Maclintock and Mr. Douglas Hyde. Miss Maclintock
writes accurately and beautifully the half Scotch dialect
of Ulster; and Mr. Douglas Hyde is now preparing a
volumn of folk tales in Gaelic, having taken them down,
for the most part, word for word among the Gaelic speakers
of Roscommon and Galway. He is, perhaps, most to be
trusted of all. He knows the people thoroughly. Others
see a phase of Irish life; he understands all its elements.
His work is neither humorous nor mournful; it is simply
life. I hope he may put some of his gatherings into
ballads, for he is the last of our ballad-writers of the school
of Walsh and Callanan—men whose work seems fragrant
with turf smoke. And this brings to mind the chap-books.
They are to be found brown with turf smoke on cottage
shelves, and are, or were, sold on every hand by the pedlers,
but cannot be found in any library of this city of the
Sassanach. "The Royal Fairy Tales," "The Hibernian
Tales," and "The Legends of the Fairies" are the fairy
literature of the people.

Several specimens of our fairy poetry are given. It is
more like the fairy poetry of Scotland than of England.
The personages of English fairy literature are merely, in
most cases, mortals beautifully masquerading. Nobody
ever believed in such fairies. They are romantic bubbles
from Provence. Nobody ever laid new milk on their
doorstep for them.

As to my own part in this book, I have tried to make
it representative, as far as so few pages would allow, of
every kind of Irish folk-faith. The reader will perhaps
wonder that in all my notes I have not rationalized a single
hobgoblin. I seek for shelter to the words of Socrates.*

"*Phœdrus.* I should like to know, Socrates, whether

* *Phœdrus.* Jowett's translation. (Clarendon Press.)

the place is not somewhere here at which Boreas is said to have carried off Orithyia from the banks of the Ilissus?

"*Socrates.* That is the tradition.

"*Phædrus.* And is this the exact spot? The little stream is delightfully clear and bright; I can fancy that there might be maidens playing near.

"*Socrates.* I believe the spot is not exactly here, but about a quarter-of-a-mile lower down, where you cross to the temple of Artemis, and I think that there is some sort of an altar of Boreas at the place.

"*Phædrus.* I do not recollect; but I beseech you to tell me, Socrates, do you believe this tale?

"*Socrates.* The wise are doubtful, and I should not be singular if, like them, I also doubted. I might have a rational explanation that Orithyia was playing with Pharmacia, when a northern gust carried her over the neighboring rocks; and this being the manner of her death, she was said to have been carried away by Boreas. There is a discrepancy, however, about the locality. According to another version of the story, she was taken from the Areopagus, and not from this place. Now I quite acknowledge that these allegories are very nice, but he is not to be envied who has to invent them; much labor and ingenuity will be required of him; and when he has once begun, he must go on and rehabilitate centaurs and chimeras dire. Gorgons and winged steeds flow in apace, and numberless other inconceivable and portentous monsters. And if he is skeptical about them, and would fain reduce them one after another to the rules of probability, this sort of crude philosophy will take up all his time. Now, I have certainly not time for such inquiries. Shall I tell you why? I must first know myself, as the Delphian inscription says; to be curious about that which is not my business, while I am still in ignorance of my own self, would be ridiculous. And, therefore, I say farewell to all this; the common opinion is enough for me. For, as I was saying, I want to know not about this, but about

myself. Am I, indeed, a wonder more complicated and
swollen with passion than the serpent Typho, or a creature
of gentler and simpler sort, to whom nature has given a
diviner and lowlier destiny ? "

I have to thank Messrs Macmillan, and the editors of
Belgravia, *All the Year Round* and *Monthly Packet*
for leave to quote from Patrick Kennedy's *Legendary
Fictions of the Irish Celts*, and Miss Maclintock's articles
respectively ; Lady Wilde, for leave to give what I would
from her *Ancient Legends of Ireland* (Ward & Downey) ;
and Mr. Douglas Hyde, for his three unpublished stories,
and for valuable and valued assistance in several ways ;
and also Mr. Allingham, and other copyright holders, for
their poems. Mr. Allingham's poems are from *Irish
Songs and Poems* (Reeves and Turner) ; Ferguson's,
from Sealey, Bryers, & Walker's shilling reprint ; my
own and Miss O'Leary's from *Ballads and Poems of
Young Ireland*, 1888, a little anthology published by Gill
& Sons, Dublin.

W. B. YEATS.

CONTENTS.

IRISH FAIRY
AND
FOLK TALES

THE FATE OF THE CHILDREN OF LIR.

IT happened that the five Kings of Ireland met to determine who should have the head kingship over them, and King Lir of the Hill of the White Field expected surely he would be elected. When the nobles went into council together they chose for head king, Dearg, son of Daghda, because his father had been so great a Druid and he was the eldest of his father's sons. But Lir left the assembly of the Kings and went home to the Hill of the White Field. The other kings would have followed after Lir to give him wounds of spear and wounds of sword for not yielding obedience to the man to whom they had given the over-lordship. But Dearg the king would not hear of it and said : " Rather let us bind him to us by the bonds of kinship, so that peace may dwell in the land. Send over to him for wife the choice of the three maidens of the fairest form and best repute in Erin, the three daughters of Oilell of Aran, my own three bosom-nurslings."

So the messengers brought word to Lir that Dearg the king would give him a foster-child of his foster-children.

1

Lir thought well of it, and set out next day with fifty
chariots from the Hill of the White Field. And he came
to the Lake of the Red Eye near Killaloe. And when
Lir saw the three daughters of Oilell, Dearg the king
said to him: "Take thy choice of the maidens, Lir." "I
know not," said Lir, "which is the choicest of them all;
but the eldest of them is the noblest, it is she I had best
take." "If so," said Dearg the king, "Ove is the eldest,
and she shall be given to thee, if thou willest." So Lir
and Ove were married and went back to the Hill of the
White Field.

And after this there came to them twins, a son and
a daughter, and they gave them for names Fingula and
Aod. And two more sons came to them, Fiachra and
Conn. When they came Ove died, and Lir mourned
bitterly for her, and but for his great love for his children
he would have died of his grief. And Dearg the king
grieved for Lir and sent to him and said: ' We grieve
for Ove for thy sake; but, that our friendship may not
be rent asunder, I will give unto thee her sister, Oifa, for
a wife." So Lir agreed, and they were united, and he
took her with him to his own house. And at first Oifa
felt affection and honor for the children of Lir and her
sister, and indeed every one who saw the four children
could not help giving them the love of his soul. Lir doted
upon the children, and they always slept in beds in front
of their father, who used to rise at early dawn every
morning and lie down among his children. But thereupon the dart of jealousy passed into Oifa on account of
this and she came to regard the children with hatred and
enmity. One day her chariot was yoked for her and she
took with her the four children of Lir in it. Fingula
was not willing to go with her on the journey, for she
had dreamed a dream in the night warning her against
Oifa: but she was not to avoid her fate. And when the
chariot came to the Lake of the Oaks, Oifa said to the
people: "Kill the four children of Lir and I will give
you your own reward of every kind in the world." But

they refused and told her it was an evil thought she had. Then she would have raised a sword herself to kill and destroy the children, but her own womanhood and her weakness prevented her ; so she drove the children of Lir into the lake to bathe, and they did as Oifa told them. As soon as they were upon the lake she struck them with a Drnid's wand of spells and wizardry and put them into the forms of four beautiful, perfectly white swans, and she sang this song over them :

> " Out with you upon the wild waves, children of the king !
> Henceforth your cries shall be with the flocks of birds."

And Fingula answered :

> " Thou witch ! we know thee by thy right name !
> Thou mayest drive us from wave to wave,
> But sometimes we shall rest on the headlands ;
> We shall receive relief, but thou punishment.
> Though our bodies may be upon the lake,
> Our minds at least shall fly homewards."

And again she spoke : " Assign an end for the ruin and woe which thou hast brought upon us."

Oifa laughed and said : " Never shall ye be free until the woman from the south be united to the man from the north, until Lairgnen of Connaught wed Deoch of Munster ; nor shall any have power to bring you out of these forms. Nine hundred years shall you wander over the lakes and streams of Erin. This only I will grant unto you : that you retain your own speech, and there shall be no music in the world equal to yours, the plaintive music you shall sing." This she said because repentance seized her for the evil she had done.

And then she spake this lay :

> " Away from me, ye children of Lir,
> Henceforth the sport of the wild winds
> Until Lairgnen and Deoch come together,
> Until ye are on the north-west of Red Erin.

> " A sword of treachery is through the heart of Lir,
>   Of Lir the mighty champion,
>   Yet though I have driven a sword.
>   My victory cuts me to the heart."

Then she turned her steeds and went on to the Hall of
Dearg the king. The nobles of the court asked her where
were the children of Lir, and Oifa said : " Lir will not
trust them to Dearg the king." But Dearg thought in
his own mind that the woman had played some treachery
upon them, and he accordingly sent messengers to the
Hall of the White Field.

Lir asked the messengers : " Wherefore are ye come ? "
" To fetch thy children, Lir," said they.
" Have they not reached you with Oifa ? " said Lir.
" They have not," said the messengers ; " and Oifa said
it was you would not let the children go with her;"

Then was Lir melancholy and sad at heart, hearing these
things, for he knew that Oifa had done wrong upon his
children, and he set out towards the Lake of the Red Eye.
And when the children of Lir saw him coming Fingula
sang the lay :

> " Welcome the cavalcade of steeds
>   Approaching the Lake of the Red Eye,
>   A company dread and magical
>   Surely seek after us.

> " Let us move to the shore, O Aod.
>   Fiachra and comely Conn,
>   No host under heaven can those horsemen be
>   But King Lir with his mighty household."

Now as she said this King Lir had come to the shores
of the lake and heard the swans speaking with human
voices. And he spake to the swans and asked them who
they were. Fingula answered and said : " We are thy
own children, ruined by thy wife, sister of our own mother,
though her ill mind and her jealousy." " For how long
is the spell to be upon you ? " said Lir. " None can relieve
us till the woman from the south and the man from the

north come together, till Lairgnen of Connaught wed
Deoch of Munster."

Then Lir and his people raised their shouts of grief,
crying, and lamentation, and they stayed by the shore of
the lake listening to the wild music of the swans until
the swans flew away, and King Lir went on to the Hall
of Dearg the king. He told Dearg the king what Oifa
had done to his children. And Dearg put his power upon
Oifa and bade her say what shape on earth she would
think the worst of all. She said it would be in the form
of an air-demon. " It is into that form I shall put you,"
said Dearg the king, and he struck her with a Druid's
wand of spells and wizardry and put her into the form of
an air-demon. And she flew away at once, and she is still
an air-demon, and shall be so forever.

But the children of Lir continued to delight the Milesian
clans with the very sweet fairy music of their songs, so
that no delight was ever heard in Erin to compare with
their music until the time came appointed for the leaving
the Lake of the Red Eye.

Then Fingula sang this parting lay :

> " Farewell to thee, Dearg the king,
> Master of all Druid's lore !
> Farewell to thee, our father dear,
> Lir of the Hill of the White Field !

> " We go to pass the appointed time
> Away and apart from the haunts of men
> In the current of the Moyle,
> Our garb shall be bitter and briny,

> "Until Deoch come to Lairgnen.
> So come, ye brothers of once ruddy cheeks ;
> Let us depart from this Lake of the Red Eye,
> Let us separate in sorrow from the tribe that has
>   loved us."

And after they took to flight, flying highly, lightly, aerially
till they reached the Moyle, between Erin and Albain.

The men of Erin were grieved at their leaving, and it

was proclaimed throughout Erin that henceforth no swan should be killed. Then they stayed all solitary, all alone, filled with cold and grief and regret, until a thick tempest came upon them and Fingula said : " Brothers, let us ap- point a place to meet again if the power of the winds separate us." And they said : " Let us appoint to meet, O sister, at the Rock of the Seals." Then the waves rose up and the thunder roared, the lightnings flashed, the sweeping tempest passed over the sea, so that the children of Lir were scattered from each other over the great sea. There came, however, a placid calm after the great tem- pest and Fingula found herself alone, and she said this lay.

> " Woe upon me that I am alive !
> My wings are frozen to my sides.
> O beloved three, O beloved three,
> Who hid under the shelter of my feathers,
> Until the dead come back to the living
> I and the three shall never meet again ! "

And she flew to the Lake of the Seals and soon saw Conn coming towards her with heavy step and drenched feathers, and Fiachra also, cold and wet and faint, and no word could they tell, so cold and faint were they : but she nestled them under her wings and said : " If Aod could come to us now our happiness would be complete." But soon they saw Aod coming towards them with dry head and preened feathers : Fingula put him under the feathers of her breast, and Fiachra under her right wing, and Conn under her left : and they made this lay :

> " Bad was our stepmother with us,
> She played her magic on us,
> Sending us north on the sea
> In the shapes of magical swans.

> " Our bath upon the shore's ridge
> Is the foam of the brine-crested tide,
> Our share of the ale feast
> Is the brine of the blue-crested sea."

One day they saw a splendid cavalcade of pure white steeds coming towards them, and when they came near they were the two sons of Dearg the king who had been seeking for them to give them news of Dearg the king and Lir their father. "They are well," they said, "and live together happy in all except that ye are not with them, and for not knowing where ye have gone since the day ye left the Lake of the Red Eye." "Happy are not we," said Fingula, and she sang this song :

> "Happy this night the household of Lir,
>   Abundant their meat and their wine.
>   But the children of Lir—what is their lot?
>   For bed-clothes we have our feathers,
>   And as for our food and our wine—
>   The white sand and the bitter brine,
>   Fiachra's bed and Conn's place
>   Under the cover of my wings on the Moyle,
>   Aod has the shelter of my breast,
>   And so side by side we rest."

So the sons of Dearg the king came to the Hall of Lir and told the king the condition of his children.

Then the time came for the children of Lir to fulfil their lot, and they flew in the current of the Moyle to the Bay of Erris, and remained there till the time of their fate, and then they flew to the Hill of the White Field and found all desolate and empty, with nothing but unroofed green raths and forests of nettles—no house, no fire, no dwelling-place. The four came close together, and they raised three shouts of lamentation aloud, and Fingula sang this lay :

> "Uchone ! it is bitterness to my heart
>   To see my father's place forlorn—
>   No hounds, no packs of dogs,
>   No women, and no valiant kings

> "No drinking-horns, no cups of wood,
>   No drinking in its lightsome halls.
>   Uchone ! I see the state of this house
>   That its lord our father lives no more.

> " Much have we suffered in our wandering years,
>   By winds buffeted, by cold frozen ;
>   Now has come the greatest of our pain—
>   There lives no man who knoweth us in the house
>   where we were born."

So the children of Lir flew away to the Glory Isle of
Brandan the saint, and they settled upon the Lake of the
Birds until the holy Patrick came to Erin and the holy
Mac Howg came to Glory Isle.

And the first night he came to the island the children
of Lir heard the voice of his bell ringing for matins, so
that they started and leaped about in terror at hearing it;
and her brothers left Fingula alone. " What is it, beloved
brothers ? " said she. " We know not what faint, fearful voice it is we have heard." Then Fingula recited this
lay :

> " Listen to the Cleric's bell,
>   Poise your wings and raise
>   Thanks to God for his coming,
>   Be grateful that you hear him,
>
> " He shall free you from pain,
>   And bring you from the rocks and stones.
>   Ye comely children of Lir
>   Listen to the bell of the Cleric."

And Mac Howg came down to the brink of the shore
and said to them: " Are ye the children of Lir ? " " We
are indeed," said they. " Thanks be to God ! " said the
saint ; " it is for your sakes I have come to this Isle beyond every other island in Erin. Come ye to land now
and put your trust in me." So they came to land, and
he made for them chains of bright white silver, and put a
chain between Aod and Fingula and a chain between
Conn and Fiachra.

It happened at this time that Lairgnen was prince of
Connaught and he was to wed Deoch the daughter of the
king of Munster. She had heard the account of the birds
and she became filled with love and affection for them,

and she said she would not wed till she had the wondrous birds of Glory Isle. Lairgnen sent for them to the Saint Mac Howg. But the Saint would not give them, and both Lairgnen and Deoch went to Glory Isle. And Lairgnen went to seize the birds from the altar: but as soon as he had laid hands on them their feathery coats fell off, and the three sons of Lir became three withered bony old men, and Fingula, a lean withered old woman without blood or flesh. Lairgnen started at this and left the place hastily, but Fingula chanted this lay :

> " Come and baptise us, O Cleric,
> Clear away our stains !
> This day I see our grave—
> Fiachra and Conn on each side,
> And in my lap, between my two arms,
> Place Aod, my beauteous brother."

After this lay, the children of Lir were baptised. And they died, and were buried as Fingula had said, Fiachra and Conn on either side, and Aod before her face. A cairn was raised for them, and on it their names were written in runes. And that is the fate of the children of Lir.

THE TROOPING FAIRIES.

THE Irish word for fairy is *sheehogue* [*sidheóg*], a diminutive of "shee" in *banshee.* Fairies are *deenee shee* [*daoine sidhe*] (fairy people).

Who are they? "Fallen angels who were not good enough to be saved, nor bad enough to be lost," say the peasantry. "The gods of the earth," says the Book of Armagh. "The gods of pagan Ireland," say the Irish antiquarians, "the *Tuatha De Danān*, who, when no longer worshiped and fed with offerings, dwindled away in the popular imagination, and now are only a few spans high."

And they will tell you, in proof, that the names of fairy chiefs are the names of old *Danān* heroes, and the places where they especially gather together, *Danān* burying-places, and that the *Tuath De Danān* used also to be called the *slooa-shee* [*sheagh sidhe*] (the fairy host), or *Marcra shee* (the fairy cavalcade).

On the other hand, there is much evidence to prove them fallen angels. Witness the nature of the creatures, their caprice, their way of being good to the good and evil, to the evil having every charm but conscience—consistency. Beings so quickly offended that you must not speak much about them at all, and never call them anything but the "gentry," or else *daoine maithe*, which in English means good people, yet so easily pleased, they will do their best to keep misfortune away from you, if you leave a little milk for them on the window-sill over night. On the whole, the popular belief tells us most about them, telling us how they fell, and yet were not lost, because their evil was wholly without malice.

10

Are they "the gods of the earth?"* Perhaps! Many
poets, and all mystic and occult writers, in all ages and
countries, have declared that behind the visible are chains
on chains of conscious beings, who are not of heaven but
of the earth, who have no inherent form but change according to their whim, or the mind that sees them. You
cannot lift your hand without influencing and being in-
fluenced by hoards. The visible world is merely their
skin. In dreams we go amongst them, and play with
them, and combat with them. They are, perhaps, human
souls in the crucible—these creatures of whim.

Do not think the fairies are always little. Everything
is capricious about them, even their size. They seem to
take what size or shape pleases them. Their chief occu-
pations are feasting, fighting, and making love, and playing the most beautiful music. They have only one industrious person amongst them, the *lepra-caun*—the shoemaker. Perhaps they wear their shoes out with dancing. Near the village of Ballisodare is a little woman
who lived amongst them seven years. When she came
home she had no toes—she had danced them off.

They have three great festivals in the year—May
Eve, Midsummer Eve, November Eve. On May Eve,
every seventh year, they fight all round, but mostly on
the "Plain-a-Bawn" (wherever that is), for the harvest,
for the best ears of grain belong to them. An old man
told me he saw them fight once; they tore the thatch off

* Occultists, from Paracelsus to Elephas Levi, divide the nature spirits into gnomes, sylphs, salamanders, undines; or earth,
air, fire, and water spirits. Their emperors, according to Elephas, are named Cob, Paralda, Djin, Hicks respectively. The
gnomes are covetous, and of the melancholic temperament.
Their usual height is but two spans, though they can elongate
themselves into giants. The sylphs are capricious, and of the
bilious temperament. They are in size and strength much
greater than men, as becomes the people of the winds. The
salamanders are wrathful, and in temperament sanguine. In
appearance they are long, lean, and dry. The undines are soft,
cold, fickle, and phlegmatic. In appearance they are like man.
The salamanders and sylphs have no fixed dwellings.

a house in the midst of it all. Had any one else been
near they would merely have seen a great wind whirling everything into the air as it passed. When the
wind makes the straws and leaves whirl as it passes,
that is the fairies, and the peasantry take off their hats
and say, " God bless them."

On Midsummer Eve. when the bonfires are lighted
on every hill in honor of St. John, the fairies are at their
gayest, and sometimes steal away beautiful mortals to be
their brides.

On November Eve they are at their gloomiest, for, according to the old Gaelic reckoning, this is the first night
of winter. This night they dance with the ghosts, and
the *pooka* is abroad, and witches make their spells, and
girls set a table with food in the name of the devil, that
the fetch of their future lover may come through the
window and eat of the food. After November Eve the
blackberries are no longer wholesome, for the *pooka* has
spoiled them.

When they are angry they paralyze men and cattle
with their fairy darts.

When they are gay they sing. Many a poor girl has
heard them, and pined away and died, for love of that
singing. Plenty of the old beautiful tunes of Ireland are
only their music, caught up by eavesdroppers. No wise
peasant would hum " The Pretty Girl milking the Cow "
near a fairy rath, for they are jealous, and do not like to
hear their songs on clumsy mortal lips. Carolan, the last
of the Irish bards, slept on a rath, and ever after the fairy
tunes ran in his head, and made him the great man he
was.

Do they die? Blake saw a fairy's funeral; but in
Ireland we say they are immortal.

THE FAIRIES.

WILLIAM ALLINGHAM.

Up the airy mountain,
    Down the rushy glen,
We daren't go a hunting
    For fear of little men;
Wee folk, good folk,
    Trooping all together;
Green jacket, red cap,
    And white owl's feather!

Down along the rocky shore
    Some make their home,
They live on crispy pancakes
    Of yellow tide-foam;
Some in the reeds
    Of the black mountain lake,
With frogs for their watch-dogs,
    All night awake.

High on the hill-top
    The old King sits;
He is now so old and gray
    He's nigh lost his wits.
With a bridge of white mist
    Columbkill he crosses,
On his stately journeys
    From Slieveleague to Rosses;
Or going up with music
    On cold starry nights,
To sup with the Queen
    Of the gay Northern Lights.

They stole little Bridget
    For seven years long;

When she came down again
    Her friends were all gone.
They took her lightly back,
    Between the night and morrow,
They thought that she was fast asleep,
    But she was dead with sorrow.
They have kept her ever since
    Deep within the lake,
On a bed of flag-leaves,
    Watching till she wake.

By the craggy hill-side,
    Through the mosses bare,
They have planted thorn-trees
    For pleasure here and there.
Is any man so daring
    As dig them up in spite,
He shall find their sharpest thorns
    In his bed at night.

Up the airy mountain,
    Down the rushy glen,
We daren't go a-hunting
    For fear of little men;
Wee folk, good folk,
    Trooping all together;
Green jacket, red cap,
    And white owl's feather!

FRANK MARTIN AND THE FAIRIES.

WILLIAM CARLETON.

MARTIN was a thin pale man, when I saw him, of a sickly look, and a constitution naturally feeble. His hair was a light auburn, his beard mostly unshaven, and his hands of a singular delicacy and whiteness, owing, I dare say, as much to the soft and easy nature of his employment as to his infirm health. In everything else he was as sensible, sober, and rational as any other man; but on the topic of fairies, the man's mania was peculiarly strong and immovable. Indeed, I remember that the expression of his eyes was singularly wild and hollow, and his long narrow temples sallow and emaciated.

Now, this man did not lead an unhappy life, nor did the malady he labored under seem to be productive of either pain or terror to him, although one might be apt to imagine otherwise. On the contrary, he and the fairies maintained the most friendly intimacy, and their dialogues—which I fear were wofully one-sided ones— must have been a source of great pleasure to him, for they were conducted with much mirth and laughter, on his part at least.

" Well, Frank, when did you see the fairies?"

" Whist! there's two dozen of them in the shop (the weaving shop) this minute. There's a little ould fellow sittin' on the top of the sleys, an' all to be rocked while I'm weavin'. The sorrow's in them, but they're the greatest little skamers alive, so they are. See, there's another of them at my dressin' noggin.* Go out o' that, you *shingawn;* or, bad cess to me, if you don't, but I'll lave you a mark. Ha! cut, you thief you!"

" Frank, arn't you afeard o' them?"

" Is it me! Arra, what ud' I be afeard o' them for? Sure they have no power over me."

" And why haven't they, Frank?"

" Because I was baptized against them."

" What do you mean by that?"

" Why, the priest that christened me was tould by my father, to put in the proper prayer against the fairies— an' a priest can't refuse it when he's asked—an' he did so.

* The dressings are a species of sizy flummery, which is brushed into the yarn to keep the thread round and even, and to prevent it from being frayed by the friction of the reed.

Begorra, it's well for me that he did—(let the tallow alone, you little glutton—see, there's a weeny thief o' them aitin' my tallow)—becaise, you see, it was their intention to make me king o' the fairies."

" Is it possible ? "

" Devil a lie in it. Sure you may ax them, an' they'll tell you."

" What size are they, Frank ? "

" Oh, little wee fellows, with green coats, an' the purtiest little shoes ever you seen. There's two of them—both ould acquaintances o' mine—runnin' along the yarn-beam. That ould fellow with the bob-wig is called Jim Jam, an' the other chap, with the three-cocked hat, is called Nickey Nick. Nickey plays the pipes. Nickey, give us a tune, or I'll malivogue you—come now, ' Lough Erne Shore.' Whist, now—listen ! "

The poor fellow, though weaving as fast as he could all the time, yet bestowed every possible mark of attention to the music, and seemed to enjoy it as much as if it had been real.

But who can tell whether that which we look upon as a privation may not after all be a fountain of increased happiness, greater, perhaps, than any which we ourselves enjoy ? I forget who the poet is who says—

> " Mysterious are thy laws ;
> The vision's finer than the view ;
> Her landscape Nature never drew
> So fair as Fancy draws."

Many a time, when a mere child, not more than six or seven years of age, have I gone as far as Frank's weaving-shop, in order, with a heart divided between curiosity and fear, to listen to his conversation with the good people. From morning till night his tongue was going almost as incessantly as his shuttle ; and it was well known that at night, whenever he awoke out of his sleep, the first thing he did was to put out his hand, and push them, as it were, off his bed.

" Go out o' this, you thieves, you—go out o' this now, an' let me alone. Nickey, is this any time to be playing the pipes, and me wants to sleep? Go off, now—troth if yez do, you'll see what I'll give yez to-morrow. Sure I'll be makin' new dressin's; and if yez behave decently, maybe I'll lave yez the scrapin' o' the pot. There now. Och! poor things, they're dacent crathurs. Sure they're all gone, barrin' poor Red-cap, that doesn't like to lave me." And then the harmless monomaniac would fall back into what we trust was an innocent slumber.

About this time there was said to have occurred a very remarkable circumstance, which gave poor Frank a vast deal of importance among the neighbors. A man named Frank Thomas, the same in whose house Mickey M'Rorey held the first dance at which I ever saw him, as detailed in a former sketch; this man, I say, had a child sick, but of what complaint I cannot now remember, nor is it of any importance. One of the gables of Thomas's house was built against, or rather into, a Forth or Rath, called Towny, or properly Tonagh Forth. It was said to be haunted by the fairies, and what gave it a character peculiarly wild in my eyes was, that there were on the southern side of it two or three little green mounds, which were said to be the graves of unchristened children, over which it was considered dangerous and unlucky to pass. At all events, the season was mid-summer; and one evening about dusk, during the illness of the child, the noise of a hand-saw was heard upon the Forth. This was considered rather strange and, after a little time, a few of those who were assembled at Frank Thomas's went to see who it could be that was sawing in such a place, or what they could be sawing at so late an hour, for every one knew that nobody in the whole country about them would dare to cut down the few white-thorns that grew upon the Forth. On going to examine, however, judge of their surprise, when, after surrounding and searching the whole place, they could discover no trace of either saw or sawyer. In fact, with the exception of themselves, there was no one, either natural or supernatural, visible. They then returned to the house, and had scarcely sat down, when it was heard again within ten yards of them. Another examination of the premises took place, but with equal success. Now, however, while standing on the Forth, they heard the sawing in a little hollow, about a hundred and fifty yards below them, which was completely exposed to their view, but they could see nobody. A party of them immediately went down to ascertain, if possible, what this singular noise and invisible labor could mean; but on arriving at the spot, they heard the sawing, to which were now added hammering, and the driving of nails upon the Forth above, whilst those who stood on the Forth continued to hear it in the hollow. On comparing notes, they resolved to send down to Billy Nelson's for Frank Martin, a distance of only about eighty or ninety yards. He was soon on the spot, and without a moment's hesitation solved the enigma.

" 'Tis the fairies," said he. " I see them, and busy crathurs they are."

" But what are they sawing, Frank ? "

" They are makin' a child's coffin," he replied; " they have the body-already made, an' they're now nailin' the lid together."

That night the child died, and the story goes that on the second evening afterwards, the carpenter who was called upon to make the coffin brought a table out from Thomas's house to the Forth, as a temporary bench; and, it is said, that the sawing and hammering necessary for the completion of his task were precisely the same which had been heard the evening but one before—neither more nor less. I remember the death of the child myself, and the making of its coffin, but I think the story of the supernatural carpenter was not heard in the village for some months after its interment.

Frank had every appearance of a hypochondriac about him. At the time I saw him, he might be about thirty-four years of age, but I do not think, from the debility of his frame and infirm health, that he has been alive for several years. He was an object of considerable interest and curiosity, and often have I been present when he was pointed out to strangers as "the man that could see the good people."

THE PRIEST'S SUPPER.

T. CROFTON CROKER.

It is said by those who ought to understand such things, that the good people, or the fairies, are some of the angels who are turned out of heaven, and who landed on their feet in this world, while the rest of their companions, who had more sin to sink them, went down farther to a worse place. Be this as it may, there was a merry troop of the fairies, dancing and playing all manner of wild pranks, on a bright moonlight evening towards the end of September. The scene of their merriment was not far distant from Inchegeela, in the west of the county Cork—a poor village, although it had a barrack for soldiers; but great mountains and barren rocks, like those round about it, are enough to strike poverty into any place : however, as the fairies can have everything they want for wishing, poverty does not trouble them much, and all their care is to seek out unfrequented nooks and places where it is not likely any one will come to spoil their sport.

On a nice green sod by the river's side were the little fellows dancing in a ring as gaily as may be, with their red caps wagging about at every bound in the moonshine, and so light were these bounds that the lobs of dew, although they trembled under their feet, were not disturbed by their capering. Thus did they carry on their gambols, spinning round and round, and twirling and bobbing and diving, and going through all manner of figures, until one of them chirped out,

"Cease, cease, with your drumming,
Here's an end to our mumming;
By my smell
I can tell
A priest this way is coming!"

And away every one of the fairies scampered off as hard as they could, concealing themselves under the green leaves of the lusmore, where, if their little red caps should happen to peep out, they would only look like its crimson bells; and more hid themselves at the shady side of stones and brambles, and others under the bank of the river, and in holes and crannies of one kind or another.

The fairy speaker was not mistaken; for along the road, which was within view of the river, came Father Horrigan on his pony, thinking to himself that as it was so late he would make an end of his journey at the first cabin he came to. According to this determination, he stopped at the dwelling of Dermod Leary, lifted the latch, and entered with " My blessing on all here."

I need not say that Father Horrigan was a welcome guest wherever he went, for no man was more pious or better beloved in the country. Now it was a great trouble to Dermod that he had nothing to offer his reverence for supper as a relish to the potatoes, which " the old woman," for so Dermod called his wife, though she was not much past twenty, had down boiling in a pot over the fire; he thought of the net which he had set in the river, but as it had been there only a short time, the chances were against his finding a fish in it. " No matter," thought Dermod, " there can be no harm in stepping down to try; and maybe, as I want the fish for the priest's supper, that one will be there before me."

Down to the river-side went Dermod, and he found in the net as fine a salmon as ever jumped in the bright waters of " the spreading Lee;" but as he was going to take it out, the net was pulled from him, he could not tell how or by whom, and away got the salmon, and went swimming along with the current as gaily as if nothing had happened.

Dermod looked sorrowfully at the wake which the fish had left upon the water, shining like a line of silver in the moonlight, and then, with an angry motion of his right hand, and a stamp of his foot, gave vent to his feelings by muttering, " May bitter bad luck attend you night and day for a blackguard schemer of a salmon, wherever you go! You ought to be ashamed of yourself, if there's any shame in you, to give me the slip after this fashion! And I'm clear in my own mind you'll come to no good, for some kind of evil thing or other helped you—did I not feel it pull the net against me as strong as the devil himself ? "

" That's not true for you," said one of the little fairies who had scampered off at the approach of the priest, coming up to Dermod Leary with a whole throng of companions at his heels ; " there was only a dozen and a half of us pulling against you."

Dermod gazed on the tiny speaker with wonder, who continued, " Make yourself noways uneasy about the priest's supper ; for if you will go back and ask him one question from us, there will be as fine a supper as ever was put on a table spread out before him in less than no time."

" I'll have nothing at all to do with you," replied Dermod in a tone of determination; and after a pause he added, " I'm much obliged to you for your offer, sir, but I know better than to sell myself to you, or the like of you, for a supper; and more than that, I know Father Horrigan has more regard for my soul than to wish me to pledge it for ever, out of regard to anything you could put before him—so there's an end of the matter."

The little speaker, with a pertinacity not to be repulsed by Dermod's manner, continued, " Will you ask the priest one civil question for us ? "

Dermod considered for some time, and he was right in doing so, but he thought that no one could come to harm out of asking a civil question. "I see no objection to do that same, gentlemen," said Dermod; "but I will have nothing in life to do with your supper—mind that."

"Then," said the little speaking fairy, whilst the rest came crowding after him from all parts, "go and ask Father Horrigan to tell us whether our souls will be saved at the last day, like the souls of good Christians; and if you wish us well, bring back word what he says without delay."

Away went Dermod to his cabin, where he found the potatoes thrown out on the table, and his good woman handing the biggest of them all, a beautiful laughing red apple, smoking like a hard-ridden horse on a frosty night, over to Father Horrigan.

"Please your reverence," said Dermod, after some hesitation, "may I make bold to ask your honour one question?"

"What may that be?" said Father Horrigan.

"Why, then, begging your reverence's pardon for my freedom, it is, If the souls of the good people are to be saved at the last day?"

"Who bid you ask me that question, Leary?" said the priest, fixing his eyes upon him very sternly, which Dermod could not stand before at all.

"I'll tell no lies about the matter, and nothing in life but the truth," said Dermod. "It was the good people themselves who sent me to ask the question, and there they are in thousands down on the bank of the river, waiting for me to go back with the answer."

"Go back by all means," said the priest, "and tell them, if they want to know, to come here to me themselves, and I'll answer that or any other question they are pleased to ask with the greatest pleasure in life."

Dermod accordingly returned to the fairies, who came swarming round about him to hear what the priest had said in reply; and Dermod spoke out among them like a bold man as he was; but when they heard that they must go to the priest, away they fled, some here and more

there, and some this way and more that, whisking by
poor Dermod so fast and in such numbers that he was
quite bewildered.

When he came to himself, which was not for a long
time, back he went to his cabin, and ate his dry potatoes
along with Father Horrigan, who made quite light of the
thing ; but Dermod could not help thinking it a mighty
hard case that his reverence, whose words had the power
to banish the fairies at such a rate, should have no sort of
relish to his supper, and that the fine salmon he had in
the net should have been got away from him in such a
manner.

THE FAIRY WELL OF LAGNANAY.

BY SAMUEL FERGUSON.

MOURNFULLY, sing mournfully—
 " O listen, Ellen, sister dear ;
Is there no help at all for me,
  But only ceaseless sigh and tear ?
  Why did not he who left me here,
With stolen hope steal memory ?
  O listen, Ellen, sister dear,
(Mournfully, sing mournfully)—
  I'll go away to Sleamish hill,
I'll pluck the fairy hawthorn-tree,
  And let the spirits work their will ;
  I care not if for good or ill,
So they but lay the memory
  Which all my heart is haunting still !
(Mournfully, sing mournfully)—
  The Fairies are a silent race,
And pale as lily flowers to see ;
  I care not for a blanched face,
  For wandering in a dreaming place,

So I but banish memory :—
   I wish I were with Anna Grace ! "
Mournfully, sing mournfully !

Hearken to my tale of woe—
   "Twas thus to weeping Ellen Con,
Her sister said in accents low,
    Her only sister, Una bawn :
    'Twas in their bed before the dawn,
And Ellen answered sad and slow,—
   "Oh Una, Una, be not drawn
(Hearken to my tale of woe)—
   To this unholy grief I pray,
Which makes me sick at heart to know,
    And I will help you if I may :
    —The Fairy Well of Lagnanay—
Lie nearer me, I tremble so,—
   Una, I've heard wise women say
(Hearken to my tale of woe)—
   That if before the dews arise,
True maiden in its icy flow
    With pure hand bathe her bosom thrice,
    Three lady-brackens pluck likewise,
And three times round the fountain go,
   She straight forgets her tears and sighs."
Hearken to my tale of woe !

All, alas ! and well-away !
   "Oh, sister Ellen, sister sweet,
Come with me to the hill I pray,
    And I will prove that blessed freet ! "
    They rose with soft and silent feet,
They left their mother where she lay,
   Their mother and her care discreet,
(All, alas ! and well-away !
   And soon they reached the Fairy Well,
The mountain's eye, clear, cold, and gray,

Wide open in the dreary fell:
How long they stood 'twere vain to tell,
At last upon the point of day,
Bawn Una bares her bosom's swell,
(All, alas! and well-away!)
Thrice o'er her shrinking breasts she laves
The gliding glance that will not stay
Of subtly-streaming fairy waves:—
And now the charm three brackens craves,
She plucks them in their fring'd array:—
Now round the well her fate she braves,
All, alas! and well-away!

Save us all from Fairy thrall!
Ellen sees her face the rim
Twice and thrice, and that is all—
Fount and hill and maiden swim
All together melting dim!
" Una! Una!" thou may'st call,
Sister sad! but lith or limb
(Save us all from Fairy thrall!)
Never again of Una bawn,
Where now she walks in dreamy hall,
Shall eye of mortal look upon!
Oh! can it be the guard was gone,
The better guard than shield or wall?
Who knows on earth save Jurlagh Daune?
(Save us all from Fairy thrall!)
Behold the banks are green and bare,
No pit is here within to fall:
Aye—at the fount you well may stare,
But nought save pebbles smooth is there,
And small straws twirling one and all.
Hie thee home, and be thy pray'r,
Save us all from Fairy thrall.

TEIG O'KANE (TADHG O CÁTHÁN) AND THE CORPSE.*

LITERALLY TRANSLATED FROM THE IRISH BY DOUGLAS HYDE.

[I FOUND it hard to place Mr. Douglas Hyde's magnificent story. Among the ghosts or the fairies? It is among the fairies on the grounds that all these ghosts and bodies were in no manner ghosts and bodies, but *pishogues*— fairy spells. One often hears of these visions in Ireland. I have met a man who had lived a wild life like the man in the story, till a vision came to him in County —— one dark night—in no way so terrible a vision as this, but sufficient to change his whole character. He will not go out at night. If you speak to him suddenly he trembles. He has grown timid and strange. He went to the bishop and was sprinkled with holy water. "It may have come as a warning," said the bishop; "yet great theologians are of opinion that no man ever saw an apparition, for no man would survive it."—ED.]

THERE was once a grown-up lad in the County Leitrim, and he was storng and lively, and the son of a rich farmer. His father had plenty of money, and he did not spare it on the son. Accordingly, when the boy grew up he liked sport better than work, and, as his father had no other children, he loved this one so much that he allowed him to do in everything just as it pleased himself. He was very extravagant, and he used to scatter the gold money as another person would scatter the white. He was seldom to be found at home, but if there was a fair, or a race, or a gathering within ten miles of him, you were dead certain to find him there. And he seldom

* None of Mr. Hyde's stories here given have been published before. They will be printed in the original Irish in his forth-coming *Leabhar Sgeulaigheachta* (Gill, Dublin).

spent a night in his father's house, but he used to be always out rambling, and like Shawn Bwee long ago, there was

> " grádh gach cailin i mbrollach a léine,"

" the love of every girl in the breast of his shirt," and it's many's the kiss he got and he gave, for he was very handsome, and there wasn't a girl in the country but would fall in love with him, only for him to fasten his two eyes on her, and it was for that some one made this *rann* on on him—

> "Feuch an rógaire 'g irraidh póige,
> Ni h-iongantas móré a bheith mar atá
> Ag leanamhaint a gcómhnuidhe d'àrnán na gráineóige
> Anuas 's anois 's nna chodladh 'sa' lá."

i. e.—" Look at the rogue, it's for kisses he's rambling,
> It isn't much wonder, for that was his way ;
> He's like an old hedgehog, at night he'll be scrambling
> From this place to that, but he'll sleep in the day."

At last he became very wild and unruly. He wasn't to be seen day nor night in his father's house, but always rambling on his *kailee* (night-visit) from place to place and from house to house, so that the old people used to shake their heads and say to one another, " it's easy seen what will happen to the land when the old man dies; his son will run through it in a year, and it won't stand him that long itself.

He used to be always gambling and card-playing and drinking, but his father never minded his bad habits, and never punished him. But it happened one day that the old man was told that the son had ruined the character of a girl in the neighborhood, and he was greatly angry, and he called the son to him, and said to him, quietly and sensibly—" Avic," says he, " you know I loved you greatly up to this, and I never stopped you from doing your choice thing whatever it was, and I kept plenty of money with you, and I always hoped to leave you the house and land, and all I had after myself would be gone ; but I

heard a story of you to-day that has disgusted me with
you. I cannot tell you the grief .that I felt when I heard
such a thing of you, and I tell you now plainly that unless you marry that girl I'll leave house and land and
everything to my brother's son. I never could leave it to
any one who would make so bad a use of it as you do yourself, deceiving women and coaxing girls. Settle with
yourself now whether you'll marry that girl and get my
land as a fortune with her, or refuse to marry her and
give up all that was coming to you; and tell me in the
morning which of the two things you have chosen."

"Och! *Domnoo Sheery!* father, you wouldn't say that
to me, and I such a good son as I am. Who told you I
wouldn't marry the girl? " says he.

But his father was gone, and the lad knew well enough
that he would keep his word too; and he was greatly
troubled in his mind, for as quiet and as kind as the father
was, he never went back of a word that he had once said,
and there wasn't another man in the country who was
harder to bend than he was.

The boy did not know rightly what to do. He was in
love with the girl indeed, and he hoped to marry her
sometime or other, but he would much sooner have remained another while as he was, and follow on at his old
tricks—drinking, sporting, and playing cards ; and, along
with that, he was angry that his father should order him
to marry, and should threaten him if he did not do it.

"Isn't my father a great fool," says he to himself. "I
was ready enough, and only too anxious, to marry Mary·;
and now since he threatened me, faith I've a great mind
to let it go another while."

His mind was so much excited that he remained between two notions as to what he should do. He walked
out into the night at last to cool his heated blood, and
went on to the road. He lit a pipe, and as the night was
fine he walked and walked on, until the quick pace made
him begin to forget his trouble. The night was bright,
and the moon half full. There was not a breath of wind

blowing, and the air was calm and mild. He walked on for nearly three hours, when he suddenly remembered that it was late in the night, and time for him to turn. "Musha! I think I forgot myself," says he; "it must be near twelve o'clock now."

The word was hardly out of his mouth, when he heard the sound of many voices, and the trampling of feet on the road before him. "I don't know who can be out so late at night as this, and on such a lonely road," said he to himself.

He stood listening, and he heard the voices of many people talking through other, but he could not understand what they were saying. "Oh, wirra!" says he, "I'm afraid. It's not Irish or English they have; it can't be they're Frenchmen!" He went on a couple of yards further, and he saw well enough by the light of the moon a band of little people coming towards him, and they were carrying something big and heavy with them. "Oh, murder!" says he to himself, "sure it can't be that they're the good people that's in it!" Everp *rib* of hair that was on his head stood up, and there fell a shaking on his bones, for he saw that they were coming to him fast.

He looked at them again, and perceived that there were about twenty little men in it, and there was not a man at all of them higher than about three feet or three feet and a half, and some of them were gray, and seemed very old. He looked again, but he could not make out what was the heavy thing they were carrying until they came up to him, and then they all stood round about him. They threw the heavy thing down on the road, and he saw on the spot that it was a dead body.

He became as cold as the Death, and there was not a drop of blood running in his veins when an old little gray *maneen* came up to him and said, "Isn't it lucky we met you, Teig O'Kane?"

Poor Teig could not bring out a word at all, nor open his lips, if he were to get the world for it, and so he gave no answer.

"Teig O'Kane," said the little gray man again, "isn't it timely you met us?"

Teig could not answer him.

"Teig O'Kane," says he, "the third time, isn't it lucky and timely that we met you?"

But Teig remained silent, for he was afraid to return an answer, and his tongue was as if it was tied to the roof of his mouth.

The little gray man turned to his companions, and there was joy in his bright little eye. "And now," says he, "Teig O'Kane hasn't a word, we can do with him what we please. Teig, Teig," says he, "you're living a bad life, and we can make a slave of you now, and you cannot withstand us, for there's no use in trying to go against us. Lift that corpse."

Teig was so frightened that he was only able to utter the two words, "I won't;" for as frightened as he was, he was obstinate and stiff, the same as ever.

"Teig O'Kane won't lift the corpse," said the little *maneen*, with a wicked little laugh, for all the world like the breaking of a *lock* of dry *kippeens*, and with a little harsh voice like the striking of a cracked bell. "Teig O'Kane won't lift the corpse—make him lift it;" and before the word was out of his mouth they had all gathered round poor Teig, and they all talking and laughing through other.

Teig tried to run from them, but they followed him, and a man of them stretched out his foot before him as he ran, so that Teig was thrown in a heap on the road. Then before he could rise up the fairies caught him, some by the hands and some by the feet, and they held him tight, in a way that he could not stir, with his face against the ground. Six or seven of them raised the body then, and pulled it over to him, and left it down on his back. The breast of the corpse was squeezed against Teig's back and shoulders, and the arms of the corpse were thrown around Teig's neck. Then they stood back from him a couple of yards, and let him get up. He rose, foaming at the mouth and cursing, and he shook himself, thinking to throw the corpse off his back. But his fear and his wonder were great when he found that the two arms had a tight hold round his own neck, and that the two legs were squeezing his hips firmly, and that, however strongly he tried, he could not throw it off, any more than a horse can throw off its saddle. He was terribly frightened then, and he thought he was lost. "Ochone! forever," said he to himself, "it's the bad life I'm leading that has given the good people this power over me. I promise to God and Mary, Peter and Paul, Patrick and Bridget, that I'll mend my ways for as long as I have to live if I come clear out of this danger—and I'll marry the girl."

The little gray man came up to him again, and said he to him, "Now, Teig*een*," said he, "you didn't lift the body when I told you to lift it, and see how you were made to lift it; perhaps when I tell you to bury it you won't bury it until you're made to bury it!"

"Anything at all that I can do for your honor," said Teig, "I'll do it," for he was getting sense already, and if it had not been for the great fear that was on him, he never would have let that civil word slip out of his mouth.

The little man laughed a sort of laugh again. "You're getting quiet now, Teig," said he. "I'll go bail but you'll be quiet enough before I'm done with you. Listen to me now, Teig O'Kane, and if you don't obey me in all I'm telling you to do, you'll repent it. You must carry with you this corpse that is on your back to Teampoll-Démus, and you must bring it into the church with you, and make a grave for it in the very middle of the church, and you must raise up the flags and put them down again the very same way, and you must carry the clay out of the church and leave the place as it was when you came, so that no one could know that there had been anything changed. But that's not all. Maybe that the body won't be allowed to be buried in that church; perhaps some other man has the bed, and, if so, it's likely he won't share it with this one. If you don't get leave to bury it in Teampoll-Démus, you must carry it to Carrick-fhad-vic-Orus, and bury it in the churchyard there; and if you don't get it into that place, take it with you to Teampoll-Ronan; and if that churchyard is closed on you, take it to Imlogue-Fada; and if you're not able to bury it there, you've no more to do than to take it to Kill-Breedya, and you can bury it there without hindrance. I cannot tell you what one of those churches is the one where you will have leave to bury that corpse under the clay, but I know that it will be allowed you to bury him at some church or other of them. It you do this work rightly, we will be thankful to you, and you will have no cause to grieve; but if you are slow or lazy, believe me we shall take satisfaction of you."

When the gray little man had done speaking, his comrades laughed and clapped their hands together. "Glic! Glic! Hwee! Hwee!" they all cried; "go on, go on, you have eight hours before you till daybreak, and if you haven't this man buried before the sun rises, you're lost." They struck a fist and a foot behind on him, and drove him on in the road. He was obliged to walk, and to walk fast, for they gave him no rest.

He thought himself that there was not a wet path, or a dirty *boreen*, or a crooked contrary road in the whole country, that he had not walked that night. The night was at times very dark, and whenever there would come a cloud across the moon he could see nothing, and then he used often to fall. Sometimes he was hurt, and sometimes he escaped, but he was obliged always to rise on the moment and to hurry on. Sometimes the moon would break out clearly, and then he would look behind him and see the little people following at his back. And he heard them speaking amongst themselves, talking and crying out, and screaming like a flock of sea-gulls; and if he was to save his soul he never understood as much as one word of what they were saying.

He did not know how far he had walked, when at last one of them cried out to him, "Stop here!" He stood, and they all gathered round him.

"Do you see those withered trees over there?" said the old boy to him again. "Teampoll Démus is among those trees, and you must go in there by yourself, for we cannot follow you or go with you. We must remain here. Go on boldly."

Teig looked from him, and he saw a high wall that was in places half broken down, and an old gray church on the inside of the wall, and about a dozen withered old trees scattered here and there round it. There was neither leaf nor twig on any of them, but their bare crooked branches were stretched out like the arms of an angry man when he threatens. He had no help for it, but was obliged to go forward. He was a couple of hundred yards from the church, but he walked on, and never looked behind him until he came to the gate of the churchyard. The old gate was thrown down, and he had no difficulty in entering. He turned then to see if any of the little people were following him, but there came a cloud over the moon, and the night became so dark that he could see nothing. He went into the churchyard, and he walked up the old grassy pathway leading to the church. When he reached the door, he found it locked. The door was large and strong, and he did not know what to do. At last he drew out his knife with difficulty, and stuck it in the wood to try if it were not rotten, but it was not.

"Now," said he to himself, "I have no more to do; the door is shut, and I can't open it."

Before the words were rightly shaped in his own mind, a voice in his ear said to him, "Search for the key on the top of the door, or on the wall."

He started. "Who is that speaking to me?" he cried, turning round; but he saw no one. The voice said in his ear again, "Search for the key on the top of the door, or on the wall."

"What's that?" said he, and the sweat running from his forehead; "who spoke to me?"

"It's I, the corpse, that spoke to you!" said the voice.

"Can you talk?" said Teig.

"Now and again," said the corpse.

Teig searched for the key, and he found it on the top of the wall. He was too much frightened to say any more, but he opened the door wide, and as quickly as he could, and he went in, with the corpse on his back. It was as dark as pitch inside, and poor Teig began to shake and tremble.

"Light the candle," said the corpse.

Teig put his hand in his pocket, as well as he was able, and drew out a flint and steel. He struck a spark out of it, and lit a burnt rag he had in his pocket. He blew it until it made a flame, and he looked round him. The church was very ancient, and part of the wall was broken down. The windows were blown in or cracked, and the timber of the seats was rotten. There were six or seven old iron candlesticks left there still, and in one of these candlesticks Teig found the stump of an old candle, and he lit it. He was still looking round him on the strange and horrid place in which he found himself, when the cold corpse whispered in his ear, "Bury me now, bury me now; there is a spade and turn the ground." Teig looked from him, and he saw a spade lying beside the altar. He took it up, and he placed the blade under a flag that was in the middle of the aisle, and leaning all his weight on the handle of the spade, he raised it. When the first flag was raised it was not hard to raise the others near it, and he moved three or four of them out of their places. The clay that was under them was soft and easy to dig, but he had not thrown up more than three or four shovelfuls, when he felt the iron touch something soft like flesh. He threw up three of four more shovelfuls from around it, and then he saw that it was another body that was buried in the same place.

"I am afraid I'll never be allowed to bury the two

bodies in the same hole," said Teig, in his own mind.
"You corpse, there on my back," says he, "will you be
satisfied if I bury you down here?" But the corpse
never answered him a word.

"That's a good sign," said Teig to himself. "Maybe
he's getting quiet," and he thrust the spade down in the
earth again. Perhaps he hurt the flesh of the other
body, for the dead man that was buried there stood up in
the grave, and shouted an awful shout. "Hoo! hoo!!
hoo!!! Go! go!! go!!! or you're a dead, dead, dead
man!" And then he fell back in the grave again. Teig
said afterwards, that of all the wonderful things he saw
that night, that was the most awful to him. His hair
stood upright on his head like the bristles of a pig, the
cold sweat ran off his face, and then came a tremor over
all his bones, until he thought that he must fall.

But after a while he became bolder, when he saw that
the second corpse remained lying quietly there, and he
threw in the clay on it again, and he smoothed it overhead, and he laid down the flags carefully as they had
been before, "It can't be that he'll rise up any more,"
said he.

He went down the aisle a little further, and drew near
to the door, and began raising the flags again, looking for
another bed for the corpse on his back. He took up
three or four flags and put them aside, and then he dug
the clay. He was not long digging until he laid bare an
old woman without a thread upon her but her shirt. She
was more lively than the first corpse, for he had scarcely
taken any of the clay away from about her, when she sat
up and began to cry, "Ho, you *bodach* (clown)! Ha, you
bodach! Where has he been that he got no bed?"

Poor Teig drew back, and when she · found that she
was getting no answer, she closed her eyes gently, lost
her vigor, and fell back quietly and slowly under the
clay. Teig did to her as he had done to the man—he
threw the clay back on her, and left the flags down overhead.

He began digging again near the door, but before he had thrown up more than a couple of shovelfuls, he noticed a man's hand laid bare by the spade. "By my soul, I'll go no further, then," said he to himself; "what use is it for me?" And he threw the clay in again on it, and settled the flags as they had been before.

He left the church then, and his heart was heavy enough, but he shut the door and locked it, and left the key where he found it. He sat down on a tombstone that was near the door, and began thinking. He was in great doubt what he should do. He laid his face between his two hands, and cried for grief and fatigue, since he was dead certain at this time that he never would come home alive. He made another attempt to loosen the hands of the corpse that were squeezed round his neck, but they were as tight as if they were clamped; and the more he tried to loosen them, the tighter they squeezed him. He was going to sit down once more, when the cold, horrid lips of the dead man said to him, "Carrick-fhad-vic-Orus," and he remembered the command of the good people to bring the corpse with him to that place if he should be unable to bury it where he had been.

He rose up, and looked about him. "I don't know the way," he said.

He soon as he had uttered the word, the corpse stretched out suddenly its left hand that had been tightened round his neck, and kept it pointing out, showing him the road he ought to follow. Teig went in the direction that the fingers were stretched, and passed out of the churchyard. He found himself on an old rutty, stony road, and he stood still again, not knowing where to turn. The corpse stretched out its bony hand a second time, and pointed out to him another road—not the road by which he had come when approaching the old church. Teig followed that road and whenever he came to a path or road meeting, the corpse always stretched out its hand and pointed with its fingers, showing him the way he was to take.

Many was the cross-road he turned down, and many was the crooked *boreen* he walked, until he saw from him an old burying-ground at last, beside the road, but there was neither church nor chapel nor any other building in it. The corpse squeezed him tightly, and he stood. "Bury me, bury me in the burying-ground," said the voice.

Teig drew over towards the old burying-place, and he was not more than about twenty yards from it, when raising his eyes, he saw hundreds and hundreds of ghosts—men, women, and children—sitting on the top of the wall round about, or standing on the inside of it, or running backwards and forwards, and pointing at him, while he could see their mouths opening and shutting as if they were speaking, though he heard no word, nor any sound amongst them all.

He was afraid to go forward, so he stood where he was, and the moment he stood, all the ghosts became quiet, and ceased moving. Then Teig understood that it was trying to keep him from going in, that they were. He walked a couple of yards forwards, and immediately the whole crowd rushed together towards the spot to which he was moving, and they stood so thickly together that it seemed to him that he never could break through them, even though he had a mind to try. But he had no mind to try it. He went back broken and dispirited, and when he had gone a couple of hundred yards from the burying-ground, he stood again, for he did not know what way he was to go. He heard the voice of the corpse in his ear, saying "Teampoll-Ronan," and the skinny hand was stretched out again, pointing him out the road.

As tired as he was, he had to walk, and the road was neither short nor even. The night was darker than ever and it was difficult to make his way. Many was the toss he got, and many a bruise they left on his body. At last he saw Teampoll-Ronan from him in the distance, standing in the middle of the burying-ground. He moved over towards it, and thought he was all right and safe, when he

saw no ghosts nor anything else on the wall, and he
thought he would never be hindered now from leaving his
load off him at last. He moved over to the gate, but as
he was passing in, he tripped on the threshold. Before
he could recover himself, something that he could not see
seized him by the neck, by the hands and by the feet, and
bruised him, and shook him, and choked him, until he was
nearly dead ; and at last he was lifted up, and carried
more than a hundred yards from that place, and then
thrown down in an old dyke, with the corpse still clinging
to him.

He rose up, bruised and sore, but feared to go near the
place again, for he had seen nothing the time he was
thrown down and carried away.

"You corpse upon my back," said he, "shall I go over
again to the churchyard ? "—but the corpse never answered him. "That's a sign you don't wish me to try it
again," said Teig.

He was now in great doubt as to what he ought to do,
when the corpse spoke in his ear, and said "Imlogue-Fada."

"Oh, murder ! " said Teig, " must I bring you there?
If you keep me long walking like this, I tell you I'll fall
under you."

He went on, however, in the direction the corpse
pointed out to him. He could not have told, himself, how
long he had been going, when the dead man behind suddenly squeezed him, and said, " There ! "

Teig looked from him, and he saw a little low wall, that
was so broken down in places that it was no wall at all.
It was in a great wide field, in from the road ; and only
for three or four great stones at the corners, that were
more like rocks than stones, there was nothing to show
that there was either graveyard or burying-ground there.

"Is this Imlogue-Fada? Shall I bury you here ? " said
Teig.

" Yes," said the voice.

" But I see no grave or gravestone, only this pile of
stones," said Teig.

The corpse did not answer, but stretched out its long fleshless hand, to show Teig the direction in which he was to go. Teig went on accordingly, but he was greatly terrified, for he remembered what had happened to him at the last place. He went on, "with his heart in his mouth," as he said himself afterwards ; but when he came to within fifteen or twenty yards of the little low square wall, there broke out a flash of lightning, bright yellow and red, with blue streaks in it, and went round about the wall in one course, and it swept by as fast as the swallow in the clouds, and the longer Teig remained looking at it the faster it went, till at last it became like a bright ring of flame round the old graveyard, which no one could pass without being burnt by it. Teig never saw, from the time he was born, and never saw afterwards, so wonderful or so splendid a sight as that was. Round went the flame, white and yellow and blue sparks leaping out from it as it went, and although at first it had been no more than a thin, narrow line, it increased slowly until it was at last a great broad band, and it was continually getting broader and higher, and throwing out more brilliant sparks, till there was never a color on the ridge of the earth that was not to be seen in that fire ; and lightning never shone and flame never flamed that was so shining and so bright as that.

Teig was amazed ; he was half dead with fatigue, and he had no courage left to approach the wall. There fell a mist over his eyes, and there came a *soorawn* in his head, and he was obliged to sit down upon a great stone to recover himself. He could see nothing but the light, and he could hear nothing but the whirr of it as it shot round the paddock faster than a flash of lightning.

As he sat there on the stone, the voice whispered once more in his ear, "Kill-Breedya ; " and the dead man squeezed him so tightly that he cried out. He rose again, sick, tired, and trembling, and went forwards as he was directed. The wind was cold, and the road was bad, and the load upon his back was heavy, and the night was dark, and he himself was nearly worn out, and if he had had very much farther to go he must have fallen dead under his burden.

At last the corpse stretched out its hand, and said to him, "Bury me there."

"This is the last burying-place," said Teig in his own mind; "and the little gray man said I'd be allowed to bury him in some of them, so it must be this; it can't be but they'll let him in here."

The first faint streak of the *ring of day* was appearing in the east, and the clouds were beginning to catch fire, but it was darker than ever, for the moon was set, and there were no stars.

"Make haste, make haste!" said the corpse; and Teig hurried forward as well as he could to the graveyard, which was a little place on a bare hill, with only a few graves in it. He walked boldly in through the open gate, and nothing touched him, nor did he either hear or see anything. He came to the middle of the ground, and then stood up and looked round him for a spade or shovel to make a grave. As he was turning round and searching, he suddenly perceived what startled him greatly—a newly-dug grave right before him. He moved over to it, and looked down, and there at the bottom he saw a black coffin. He clambered down into the hole and lifted the lid, and found that (as he thought it would be) the coffin was empty. He had hardly mounted up out of the hole, and was standing on the brink, when the corpse, which had clung to him for more than eight hours, suddenly relaxed its hold of his neck, and loosened its shins from round his hips, and sank down with a *plop* into the coffin.

Teig fell down on his two knees at the brink of the grave, and gave thanks to God. He made no delay then, but pressed down the coffin lid in its place, and threw in the clay over it with his two hands; and when the grave was filled up, he stamped and leaped on it with his feet, until it was firm and hard, and then he left the place.

The sun was fast rising as he finished his work, and the

first thing he did was to return to the road, and look out for a house to rest himself in. He found an inn at last, and lay down upon a bed there, and slept till night. Then he rose up and ate a little, and fell asleep again till morning. When he awoke in the morning he hired a horse and rode home. He was more than twenty-six miles from home where he was, and he had come all that way with the dead body on his back in one night.

All the people at his own home thought that he must have left the country, and they rejoiced greatly when they saw him come back. Every one began asking him where he had been, and he would not tell anyone except his father.

He was a changed man from that day. He never drank too much ; he never lost his money over cards ; and especially he would not take the world and be out late by himself of a dark night.

He was not a fortnight at home until he married Mary, the girl he had been in love with ; and it's at their wedding the sport was, and it's he was the happy man from that day forward, and it's all I wish that we may be as happy as he was.

GLOSSARY.—*Rann*, a stanza ; *kailee* (*céilidhe*), a visit in the evening ; *wirra* (*a mhuire*), "Oh, Mary !" an exclamation like the French *dame ; rib*, a single hair (in Irish, *ribe*); *a lock* (*glac*), a bundle or wisp, or a little share of anything ; *kippeen* (*cipín*), a rod or twig ; *boreen* (*bóithrin*), a lane ; *bodach*, a clown ; *soor-awn* (*suarán*), vertigo. *Avic* (*a Mhic*) = my son, or rather, Oh, son. Mic is the vocative of Mac.

PADDY CORCORAN'S WIFE.

WILLIAM CARLETON.

PADDY CORCORAN'S wife was for several years afflicted with a kind of complaint which nobody could properly understand. She was sick, and she was not sick ; she was well, and she was not well ; she was as ladies wish to be who love their lords, and she was not as such ladies wish to be. In fact nobody could tell what the matter with her was. She had a gnawing at the heart which came heavily upon her husband; for, with the help of God, a keener appetite than the same gnawing amounted to could not be met with of a summer's day. The poor woman was delicate beyond belief, and had no appetite at all, so she hadn't, barring a little relish for a mutton-chop, or a " staik," or a bit o' mait, anyway, for sure, God help her! she hadn't the laist inclination for the dhry pratie, or the dhrop o' sour buttermilk along wid it, especially as she was so poorly; and, indeed, for a woman in her con- dition—for, sick as she was, poor Paddy always was made to believe her in *that* condition—but God's will be done! she didn't care. A pratie an' a grain o' salt was a wel- come to her—glory be to his name!—as the best roast an' boiled that ever was dressed; and why not? There was one comfort: she wouldn't be long wid him—long troub- lin' him; it matthered little what she got; but sure she knew herself, that from the gnawin' at her heart, she could never do good widout the little bit o' mait now and then; an', sure, if her own husband begridged it to her, who else had she a better right to expect it from?

Well, as we have said, she lay a bedridden invalid for long enough, trying doctors and quacks of all sorts, sexes, and sizes, and all without a farthing's benefit, until, at the long run, poor Paddy was nearly brought to the last pass, in striving to keep her in " the bit o' mait." The seventh year was now on the point of closing, when, one harvest day, as she lay bemoaning her hard condition, on her bed beyond the kitchen fire, a little weeshy woman, dressed in a neat red cloak, comes in, and, sitting down by the hearth, says :—

" Well, Kitty Corcoran, you've had a long lair of it there on the broad o' yer back for seven years, an' you're jist as far from bein' cured as ever."

" Mavrone, ay," said the other; " in throth that's what

I was this minnit thinkin' ov, and a sorrowful thought it's to me."

"It's yer own fau't, thin," says the little woman; "an', indeed, for that matter, it's yer fau't that ever you wor there at all."

"Arra, how is that?" asked Kitty; "sure I wouldn't be here if I could help it? Do you think it's a comfort or a pleasure to me to be sick and bedridden?"

"No," said the other, "I do not; but I'll tell you the truth: for the last seven years you have been annoying us. I am one o' the good people; an' as I have a regard for you, I'm come to let you know the raison why you've been sick so long as you are. For all the time you've been ill, if you'll take the thrubble to remimber, your childhre threwn out yer dirty wather afther dusk an' before sunrise, at the very time we're passin' yer door, which we pass twice a-day. Now, if you avoid this, if you throw it out in a different place, an' at a different time, the complaint you have will lave you: so will the gnawin' at the heart; an' you'll be as well as ever you wor. If you don't follow this advice, why, remain as you are, an' all the art o' man can't cure you." She then bade her good-bye, and disappeared.

Kitty, who was glad to be cured on such easy terms, immediately complied with the injunction of the fairy; and the consequence was, that the next day she found herself in as good health as ever she enjoyed during her life.

CUSHEEN LOO.

TRANSLATED FROM THE IRISH BY J. J. CALLANAN.

[This song is supposed to have been sung by a young bride, who was forcibly detained in one of those forts which are so common in Ireland, and to which the good people are very fond of resorting. Under pretence of hushing her child to rest, she retired to the outside margin of the fort,

and addressed the burthen of her song to a young woman
whom she saw at a short distance, and whom she requested to inform her husband of her condition, and to
desire him to bring the steel knife to dissolve the enchantment.

SLEEP, my child! for the rustling trees,
Stirr'd by the breath of summer breeze,
And fairy songs of sweetest note,
Around us gently float.

Sleep! for the weeping flowers have shed
Their fragrant tears upon thy head,
The voice of love hath sooth'd thy rest,
And thy pillow is a mother's breast.
                         Sleep, my child!

Weary hath pass'd the time forlorn,
Since to your mansion I was borne,
Tho' bright the feast of its airy halls,
And the voice of mirth resounds from its walls.
                         Sleep, my child!

Full many a maid and blooming bride
Within that splendid dome abide,—
And many a hoar and shrivel'd sage,
And many a matron bow'd with age.
                         Sleep, my child!

Oh! thou who hearest this song of fear,
To the mourner's home these tidings bear.
Bid him bring the knife of the magic blade,
At whose lightning-flash the charm will fade.
                         Sleep, my child!

Haste! for to-morrow's sun will see
The hateful spell renewed for me;
Nor can I from that home depart,
Till life shall leave my withering heart.
                         Sleep, my child!

Sleep, my child ! for the rustling trees,
Stirr'd by the breath of summer breeze,
And fairy songs of sweetest note,
Around us gently float.

THE WHITE TROUT; A LEGEND OF CONG.

BY S. LOVER.

THERE was wanst upon a time, long ago, a beautiful
lady that lived in a castle upon the lake beyant, and they
say she was promised to a king's son, and they wor to
be married, when all of a sudden he was murthered, the
crathur (Lord help us), and threwn into the lake above,
and so, of course, he couldn't keep his promise to the fair
lady,—and more's the pity.

Well, the story goes that she went out iv her mind,
bekase av loosin' the king's son—for she was tendher-
hearted, God help her, like the rest iv us ! and pined
away after him, until at last, no one about seen her, good
or bad ; and the story wint that the fairies took her
away.

Well, sir, in coorse o' time, the White Throut, God
bless it, was seen in the sthrame beyant, and sure the
people didn't know what to think av the crathur, seein' as
how a *white* throut was never heard av afor, nor since ;
and years upon years the throut was there, just where
you seen it this blessed minit, longer nor I can tell—aye
throth, and beyant the memory o' th' ouldest in the
village.

At last the people began to think it must be a fairy ;
for what else could it be ?—and no hurt nor harm was
iver put an the white throut, until some wicked sinners
of sojers kem to these parts, and laughed at all the people,
and gibed and jeered them for thinkin' o' the likes ; and
one o' them in partic'lar (bad luck to him ; God forgi' me

for saying it !) swore he'd catch the throut and ate it for his dinner—the blackguard !

Well, what would you think o' the villainy of the sojer ? Sure enough he cotch the throut, and away wid him home, and puts an the fryin'-pan, and into it he pitches the purty little thing. The throut squeeled all as one as a christian crathur, and, my dear, you'd think the sojer id split his sides laughin'—for he was a harden'd villain ; and when he thought one side was done, he turns it over to fry the other ; and, what would you think, but the divil a taste of a burn was an it at all at all ; and sure the sojer thought it was a *quare* throut that could not be briled. "But," says he, "I'll give it another turn by-and-by," little thinkin' what was in store for him, the haythen.

Well, when he thought that side was done he turns it agin, and lo and behould you, the divil a taste more done that side was nor the other. "Bad luck to me," says the sojer, "but that bates the world," says he ; "but I'll thry you agin, my darlint," says he, "as cunning as you think yourself ; " and so with that he turns it over and over, but not a sign of the fire was on the purty throut. "Well," says the desperate villain—(for sure, sir, only he was a desperate villain *entirely*, he might know he was doing a wrong thing, seein' that all his endeavors was no good)— "Well," says he, "my jolly little throut, maybe you're fried enough, though you don't seem over well dress'd ; but you may be better than you look, like a singed cat, and a tit-bit afther all," says he ; and with that he ups with his knife and fork to taste a piece o' the throut ; but, my jew'l, the minit he puts his knife into the fish, there was a murtherin' screech, that you'd think the life id lave you if you hurd it, and away jumps the throut out av the fryin'-pan into the middle o' the flure ; and an the spot where it fell, up riz a lovely lady—the beautifullest crathur that eyes ever seen, dressed in white, and a band o' goold in her hair, and a sthrame o' blood runnin' down her arm.

" Look where you cut me, you villain," says she, and she held out her arm to him—and, my dear, he thought the sight id lave his eyes.

" Couldn't you lave me cool and comfortable in the river where you snared me, and not disturb me in my duty ? " says she.

Well, he thrimbled like a dog in a wet sack, and at last he stammered out somethin', and begged for his life, and ax'd her ladyship's pardin, and said he didn't know she was on duty, or he was too good a sojer not to know betther nor to meddle wid her.

" I *was* on duty, then," says she lady ; " I was watchin' for my true love that is comin' by wather to me," says she, " an' if he comes while I'm away, an' that I miss iv him, I'll turn you into a pinkeen, and I'll hunt you up and down for evermore, while grass grows or wather runs."

Well the sojer thought the life id lave him, at the thoughts iv his bein' turned into a pinkeen, and begged for mercy ; and with that says the lady—

Renounce your evil coorses," says she, " you villain, or you'll repint it too late ; be a good man for the futhur, and go to your duty * reg'lar, and now," says she, " take me back and put me into the river again, where you found me."

" Oh, my lady," says the sojer, " how could I have the heart to drownd a beautiful lady like you ? "

But before he could say another word, the lady was vanished, and there he saw the little throut an the ground. Well he put it in a clean plate, and away he runs for the bare life, for fear her lover would come while she was away ; and he run, and he run, even till he came to the cave agin, and threw the throut into the river. The minit he did, the wather was as red as blood for a little while, by rayson av the cut, I suppose, until the sthrame washed

* The Irish peasant calls his attendance at the confessional " going to his duty."

the stain away; and to this day there's a little red mark
an the throut's side, where it was cut.*

Well, sir, from that day out the sojer was an altered
man, and reformed his ways, and went to his duty reg'lar,
and fasted three times a-week—though it was never fish
he tuk an fastin' days, for afther the fright he got, fish id
never rest an his stomach—savin' your presence.

But anyhow, he was an altered man, as I said before,
and in coorse o' time he left the army, and turned hermit
at last; and they say he *used to pray evermore for the
soul of the White Throut.*

[These trout stories are common all over Ireland.
Many holy wells are haunted by such blessed trout. There
is a trout in a well on the border of Lough Gill, Sligo,
that some paganish person put once on the gridiron. It
carries the marks to this day. Long ago, the saint who
sanctified the well put that trout there. Nowadays it is
only visible to the pious, who have done due penance.]

THE FAIRY THORN.

An Ulster Ballad.

SIR SAMUEL FERGUSON.

" GET up, our Anna dear, from the weary spinning-wheel;
　　For your father's on the hill, and your mother is asleep;
Come up above the crags, and we'll dance a highland-reel
　　Around the fairy thorn on the steep."

At Anna Grace's door 'twas thus the maidens cried,
　　Three merry maidens fair in kirtles of the green;
And Anna laid the rock and the weary wheel aside,
　　The fairest of the four, I ween.

They're glancing through the glimmer of the quiet eve,
　　Away in milky wavings of neck and ankle bare;

* The fish has really a red spot on its side.

The heavy-sliding stream in its sleepy song they leave,
   And the crags in the ghostly air ;

And linking hand in hand, and singing as they go,
   The maids along the hill-side have ta'en their fearless
      way,
Till they come to where the rowan trees in lonely beauty
      grow
   Beside the Fairy Hawthorn gray.

The Hawthorn stands between the ashes tall and slim,
   Like matron with her twin grand-daughters at her
      knee ;
The rowan berries cluster o'er her low head gray and dim
   In ruddy kisses sweet to see.

The merry maidens four have ranged them in a row,
   Between each lovely couple a stately rowan stem,
And away in mazes wavy, like skimming birds they go,
   Oh, never caroll'd bird like them !

But solemn is the silence of the silvery haze
   That drinks away their voices in echoless repose,
And dreamily the evening has still'd the haunted braes,
   And dreamier the gloaming grows.

And sinking one by one, like lark-notes from the sky
   When the falcon's shadow saileth across the open
      shaw,
Are hush'd the maiden's voices, as cowering down they
      lie
In the flutter of their sudden awe.

For, from the air above, and the grassy ground beneath,
   And from the mountain-ashes and the old Whitethorn
      between,
A Power of faint enchantment doth through their beings
      breathe,
   And they sink down together on the green.

They sink together silent, and stealing side by side,
    They fling their lovely arms o'er their drooping necks
        so fair,
Then vainly strive again their naked arms to hide,
    For their shrinking necks again are bare.

Thus clasp'd and prostrate all, with their heads together
        bow'd,
    Soft o'er their bosom's beating—the only human
        sound—
They hear the silky footsteps of the silent fairy crowd,
    Like a river in the air, gliding round.

No scream can any raise, no prayer can any say,
    But wild, wild, the terror of the speechless three—
For they feel fair Anna Grace drawn silently away,
    By whom they dare not look to see.

They feel their tresses twine with her parting locks of
        gold
    And the curls elastic falling as her head withdraws;
They feel her sliding arms from their tranced arms un-
        fold,
    But they may not look to see the cause:

For heavy on their senses the faint enchantment lies
    Through all that night of anguish and perilous amaze;
And neither fear nor wonder can ope their quivering eyes,
    Or their limbs from the cold ground raise,

Till out of night the earth has roll'd her dewy side,
    With every haunted mountain and streamy vale below;
When, as the mist dissolves in the yellow morning tide,
    The maidens' trance dissolveth so.

Then fly the ghastly three as swiftly as they may,
    And tell their tale of sorrow to anxious friends in
        vain—
They pined away and died within the year and day,
    And ne'er was Anna Grace seen again.

THE LEGEND OF KNOCKGRAFTON.

T. CROFTON CROKER.

THERE was once a poor man who lived in the fertile glen of Aherlow, at the foot of the gloomy Galtee mountains, and he had a great hump on his back : he looked just as if his body had been rolled up and placed upon his shoulders : and his head was pressed down with the weight so much that his chin, when he was sitting, used to rest upon his knees for support. The country people were rather shy of meeting him in any lonesome place, for though, poor creature, he was as harmless and as inoffensive as a new-born infant, yet his deformity was so great that he scarcely appeared to be a human creature, and some ill-minded persons had set strange stories about him afloat. He was said to have a great knowledge of herbs and charms ; but certain it was that he had a mighty skilful hand in plaiting straws and rushes into hats and baskets, which was the way he made his livelihood.

Lusmore, for that was the nickname put upon him by reason of his always wearing a sprig of the fairy cap, or lusmore (the foxglove), in his little straw hat, would ever get a higher penny for his plaited work than any one else, and perhaps that was the reason why some one, out of envy, had circulated the strange stories about him. Be that as it may, it happened that he was returning one evening from the pretty town of Cahir towards Cappagh, and as little Lusmore walked very slowly, on account of the great hump upon his back, it was quite dark when he came to the old moat of Knockgrafton, which stood on the right-hand side of the road. Tired and weary was he, and noways comfortable in his own mind at thinking how much farther he had to travel, and that he should be walking all the night ; so he sat down under the moat to rest himself, and began looking mournfully enough upon the moon, which—

> "Rising in clouded majesty, at length
> Apparent Queen, unveil'd her peerless light,
> And o'er the dark her silver mantle threw."

Presently there rose a wild strain of unearthly melody upon the ear of little Lusmore; he listened, and he thought that he had never heard such ravishing music before. It was like the sound of many voices, each mingling and blending with the other so strangely that they seemed to be one, though all singing different strains, and the words of the song were these—

Da Luan, Da Mort, Da Luan, Da Mort, Da Luan, Da Mort;

when there would be a moment's pause, and then the round of melody went on again.

Lusmore listened attentively, scarcely drawing his breath lest he might lose the slightest note. He now plainly perceived that the singing was within the moat; and though at first it had charmed him so much, he began to get tired of hearing the same round sung over and over so often without any change; so availing himself of the pause when *Da Luan, Da Mort,* had been sung three times, he took up the tune, and raised it with the words *augus Da Dardeen,* and then went on singing with the voices inside of the moat, *Da Luan, Da Mort,* finishing the melody, when the pause again came, with *augus Da Dardeen.*

The fairies within Knockgrafton, for the song was a fairy melody, when they heard this addition to the tune, were so much delighted that, with instant resolve, it was determined to bring the mortal among them, whose musical skill so far exceeded theirs, and little Lusmore was conveyed into their company with the eddying speed of a whirlwind.

Glorious to behold was the sight that burst upon him as he came down through the moat, twirling round and round, with the lightness of a straw, to the sweetest music that kept time to his motion. The greatest honor was then paid him, for he was put above all the musicians, and he had servants tending upon him, and everything to his heart's content, and a hearty welcome to all; and, in short, he was made as much of as if he had been the first man in the land.

Presently Lusmore saw a great consultation going forward among the fairies, and, notwithstanding all their civility, he felt very much frightened, until one stepping out from the rest came up to him and said—

> "Lusmore!   Lusmore!
> Doubt not, nor deplore,
> For the hump which you bore
> On your back is no more;
> Look down on the floor,
> And view it, Lusmore!"

When these words were said, poor little Lusmore felt himself so light, and so happy, that he thought he could have bounded at one jump over the moon, like the cow in the history of the cat and the fiddle; and he saw, with inexpressible pleasure, his hump tumble down upon the ground from his shoulders. He then tried to lift up his head, and he did so with becoming caution, fearing that he might knock it against the ceiling of the grand hall, where he was; he looked round and round again with the greatest wonder and delight upon everything, which appeared more and more beautiful; and, overpowered at beholding such a resplendent scene, his head grew dizzy, and his eyesight became dim. At last he fell into a sound sleep, and when he awoke he found that it was broad daylight, the sun shining brightly, and the birds singing sweetly; and that he was lying just at the foot of the moat of Knockgrafton, with the cows and sheep grazing peaceably round about. The first thing Lusmore did, after saying his prayers was to put his hand behind to feel for his hump, but no sign of one was there on his

back, and he looked at himself with great pride, for he
had now become a well-shaped dapper little fellow, and
more than that, found himself in a full suit of new clothes,
which he concluded the fairies had made for him.

Toward Cappagh he went, stepping out as lightly, and
springing up at every step as if he had been all his life a
dancing-master. Not a creature who met Lusmore knew
him without his hump, and he had a great work to persuade every one that he was the same man—in truth he
was not, so far as the outward appearance went.

Of course it was not long before the story of Lusmore's
hump got about, and a great wonder was made of it.
Through the country, for miles round, it was the talk of
every one, high and low.

One morning, as Lusmore was sitting contented enough
at his cabin door, up came an old woman to him, and asked
him if he could direct her to Cappagh.

"I need give you no directions, my good woman," said
Lusmore, "for this is Cappagh; and whom may you want
here?"

"I have come," said the woman, "out of Decie's
country, in the county of Waterford, looking after one
Lusmore, who -I have heard tell, had his hump taken off
by the fairies; for there is a son of a gossip of mine who
has got a hump on him that will be his death; and maybe, if he could use the same charm as Lusmore, the hump
may be taken off him. And now I have told you the
reason of my coming so far: 'tis to find out about this
charm if I can."

Lusmore, who was ever a good-natured little fellow, told
the woman all the particulars, how he had raised the tune
for the fairies at Knockgrafton, how his hump had been
removed from his shoulders, and how he had got a new
suit of clothes into the bargain.

The woman thanked him very much, and then went
away quite happy and easy in her own mind. When she
came back to her gossip's house, in the county of Waterford, she told her everything that Lusmore had said, and

they put the little hump-backed man, who was a peevish
and cunning creature from his birth, upon a car, and took
him all the way across the country. It was a long journey, but they did not care for that, so the hump was taken
from off him; and they brought him, just as nightfall,
and left him under the old moat of Knockgrafton.

Jack Madden, for that was the humpy man's name, had
not been sitting there long when he heard the tune going
on within the moat much sweeter than before; for the
fairies were singing it the way Lusmore had settled their
music for them, and the song was going on: *Da Luan,
Da Mort, Da Luan, Da Mort, Da Luan, Da Mort, augus
Da Dardeen*, without ever stopping. Jack Madden, who
was in a great hurry to get quit of his hump, never
thought of waiting until the fairies had done, or watching
for a fit opportunity to raise the tune higher again than
Lusmore had; so having heard them sing it over seven
times without stopping, out he bawls, never minding the
time or the humor of the tune, or how he could bring his
words in properly, *augus Da Dardeen, augus Da Hena*,
thinking that if one day was good, two were better; and
that if Lusmore had one new suit of clothes given him,
he should have two.

No sooner had the words passed his lips than he was
taken up and whisked into the moat with prodigious
force; and the fairies came crowding round about him
with great anger, screeching, and screaming, and roaring
out, " Who spoiled our tune? who spoiled our tune?"
and one stepped up to him above all the rest, and said—

> " Jack Madden ! Jack Madden !
> Your words came so bad in
> The tune we felt glad in ;—
> This castle you're had in,
> That your life we may sadden ;
> Here's two humps for Jack Madden ! "

And twenty of the strongest fairies brought Lusmore's
hump, and put it down upon poor Jack's back, over his
own, where it became fixed as firmly as if it was nailed

on with twelve-penny nails, by the best carpenter that
ever drove one. Out of their castle they then kicked
him; and in the morning, when Jack Madden's mother
and her gossip came to look after their little man, they
found him half dead, lying at the foot of the moat, with
the other hump upon his back. Well to be sure, how
they did look at each other! but they were afraid to say
anything, lest a hump might be put upon their own
shoulders. Home they brought the unlucky Jack Madden
with them, as downcast in their hearts and their looks as
ever two gossips were; and what through the weight of
his other hump, and the long journey, he died soon after,
leaving, they say, his heavy curse to any one who would
go to listen to fairy tunes again.

A DONEGAL FAIRY.

LETITIA MACLINTOCK.

Ay, it's a bad thing to displeasure the gentry, sure
enough—they can be unfriendly if they're angered, an'
they can be the very best o' gude neighbors if they're
treated kindly.

My mother's sister was her lone in the house one day,
wi' a' big pot o' water boiling on the fire, and ane o' the
wee folk fell down the chimney, and slipped wi' his leg
in the hot water.

He let a terrible squeal out o' him, an' in a minute the
house was full o' wee crathurs pulling him out o' the pot,
an' carrying him across the floor.

"Did she scald you?" my aunt heard them saying to
him.

"Na, na, it was mysel' scalded my ainsel'," quoth the
wee fellow.

"A weel, a weel," says they. "If it was your ainsel'
scalded yoursel', we'll say nothing, but if she had scalded
you, we'd ha' made her pay."

THE BLACK HORSE.

ONCE there was a king and he had three sons, and when the king died, they did not give a shade of anything to the youngest son, but an old white limping garron.

" If I get but this," quoth he, " it seems that I had best go with this same."

He was going with it right before him, sometimes walking, sometimes riding. When he had been riding a good while he thought that the garron would need a while of eating, so he came down to earth, and what should he see coming out of the heart of the western airt towards him but a rider riding high, well, and right well.

" All hail, my lad," said he.

" Hail, king's son," said the other.

" What's your news ? " said the king's son.

" I have got that," said the lad who came. " I am after breaking my heart riding this ass of a horse ; but will you give me the limping white garron for him ? "

" No," said the prince ; " it would be a bad business for me."

" You need not fear," said the man that came, " there is no saying but that you might make better use of him than I. He has one value, there is no single place that you can think of in the four parts of the wheel of the world that the black horse will not take you there."

So the king's son got the black horse, and he gave the limping white garron.

Where should he think of being when he mounted but in the Realm Underwaves. He went, and before sunrise on the morrow he was there. What should he find when he got there but the son of the King Underwaves holding a Court, and the people of the realm gathered to see if

there was any one who would undertake to go to seek
the daughter of the King of the Greeks to be the prince's
wife. No one came forward, when who should come up
but the rider of the black horse.

"You, rider of the black horse," said the prince, "I lay
you under crosses and under spells to have the daughter
of the King of the Greeks here before the sun rises to-
morrow."

He went out and he reached the black horse and leaned
his elbow on his mane, and he heaved a sigh.

"Sigh of a king's son under spells!" said the horse;
"but have no care; we shall do the thing that was set
before you." And so off they went.

"Now," said the horse, "when we get near the great
town of the Greeks, you will notice that the four feet of a
horse never went to the town before. The king's daughter will see me from the top of the castle looking out of a
window, and she will not be content without a turn of
a ride upon me. Say that she may have that, but the
horse will suffer no man but you to ride before a woman
on him."

They came near the big town, and he fell to horsemanship; and the princess was looking out of the windows,
and noticed the horse. The horsemanship pleased her,
and she came out just as the horse had come.

"Give me a ride on the horse, said she.

"You shall have that," said he, "but the horse will let
no man ride him before a woman but me."

"I have a horseman of my own, said she.

"If so, set him in front," said he.

Before the horseman mounted at all, when he tried to
get up, the horse lifted his legs and kicked him off.

"Come then yourself and mount before me," said she;
"I won't leave the matter so."

He mounted the horse and she behind him, and before
she glanced from her she was nearer sky than earth. He
was in Realm Underwaves with her before sunrise.

"You are come," said Prince Underwaves.

"I am come," said he.

"There you are, my hero," said the prince. "You are the son of a king, but I am a son of success. Anyhow, we shall have no delay or neglect now, but a wedding."

"Just gently," said the princess; "your wedding is not so short a way off as you suppose. Till I get the silver

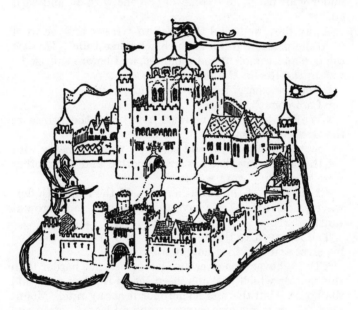

cup that my grandmother had at her wedding, and that my mother had as well, I will not marry, for I need to have it at my own wedding."

"You, rider of the black horse," said the Prince Under-waves, "I set you under spells and under crosses unless the silver cup is here before dawn to-morrow."

Out he went and reached the horse and leaned his elbow on his mane, and he heaved a sigh.

"Sigh of a king's son under spells!" said the horse; "mount and you shall get the silver cup. The people of

the realm are gathered about the king to-night, for he has
missed his daughter, and when you get to the palace go
in and leave me without; they will have the cup there
going round the company.   Go in and sit in their midst.
Say nothing, and seem to be as one of the people of the
place.   But when the cup comes round to you, take it
under your oxter, and come out to me with it, and we'll
go."

Away they went and they got to Greece, and he went
in to the palace and did as the black horse bade.   He took
the cup and came out and mounted, and before sunrise he
was in the Realm Underwaves.

" You are come," said Prince Underwaves.

" I am come," said he.

" We had better get married now," said the prince to
the Greek princess.

" Slowly and softly," said she.   " I will not marry till I
get the silver ring that my grandmother and my mother
wore when they were wedded."

" You, rider of the black horse," said the Prince Underwaves, " do that.   Let's have that ring here to-morrow at
sunrise."

The lad went to the black horse and put his elbow on
his crest and told him how it was.

" There never was a matter set before me harder than
this matter which has now been set in front of me," said
the horse, " but there is no help for it at any rate.   Mount
me.   There is a snow mountain and an ice mountain and
a mountain of fire between us and the winning of that
ring.   It is right hard for us to pass them."

Thus they went as they were, and about a mile from
the snow mountain they were in a bad case with cold.
As they came near it he struck the horse, and with the
bound he gave the black horse was on the top of the
snow mountain; at the next bound he was on the top of
the ice mountain; at the third bound he went through
the mountain of fire   When he had passed the mountains
he was dragging at the horse's neck, as though he were

The black horse rose in the middle of the water with one single spike in
him, and the ring on its end.—Page 61.　　　　*Irish Fairy Tales.*

about to lose himself. He went on before him down to a town below.

" Go down," said the black horse, " to a smithy ; make an iron spike for every bone end in me."

Down he went as the horse desired, and he got the spikes made, and back he came with them.

" Stick them, into me," said the horse, " every spike of them in every bone end that I have."

That he did ; he stuck the spikes into the horse.

" There is a loch here," said the horse, " four miles long and four miles wide, and when I go out into it the loch will take fire and blaze. If you see the Loch of Fire going out before the sun rises, expect me, and if not, go your way."

Out went the black horse into the lake, and the lake became flame. Long was he stretched about the lake, beating his palms and roaring. Day came, and the loch did not go out.

But at the hour when the the sun was rising out of the water the lake went out.

And the black horse rose in the middle of the water with one single spike in him, and the ring upon its end.

He came on shore, and down he fell beside the loch.

Then down went the rider. He got the ring, and he dragged the horse down to the side of a hill. He fell to sheltering him with his arms about him, and as the sun was rising he got better and better, till about midday, when he rose on his feet.

" Mount," said the horse, " and let us begone."

He mounted on the black horse, and away they went.

He reached the mountains, and he leaped the horse at the fire mountain and was on the top. From the mountain of fire he leaped to the mountain of ice, and from the mountain of ice to the mountain of snow. He put the mountains past him, and by morning he was in realm under the waves.

" You are come," said the prince.

" I am," said he.

"That's true," said Prince Underwaves. "A king's son are you, but a son of success am I. We shall have no more mistakes and delays, but a wedding this time."

"Go easy," said the princess of the Greeks. "Your wedding is not so near as you think yet. Till you make a castle, I won't marry you. Not to your father's castle nor to your mother's will I go to dwell; but make me a castle for which your father's castle will not make washing water."

"You, rider of the black horse, make that," said Prince Underwaves, "before the morrow's sun rises."

The lad went out to the horse and leaned his elbow on his neck and sighed, thinking that this castle never could be made forever.

"There never came a turn in my road yet that is easier for me to pass than this," said the black horse.

Glance that the lad give from him he saw all that there were, and ever so many wrights and stone masons at work, and the castle was ready before the sun rose.

He shouted at the Prince Underwaves, and he saw the castle. He tried to pluck out his eye, thinking that it was a false sight.

"Son of King Underwaves," said the rider of the black horse, "don't think that you have a false sight; this is a true sight."

"That's true," said the prince. "You are a son of success, but I am a son of success too. There will be no more mistakes and delays, but a wedding now."

"No," said she. "The time is come. Should we not go to look at the castle? There's time enough to get married before the night comes."

They went to the castle and the castle was without a "but"——

"I see one," said the prince. "One want at least to be made good. A well to be made inside, so that water may not be far to fetch when there is a feast or a wedding in the castle."

" That won't be long undone," said the rider of the black horse.

The well was made, and it was seven fathoms deep and two or three fathoms wide, and they looked at the well on the way to the wedding. ·

" It is very well made," said she, " but for one little fault yonder."

" Where is it ? " said Prince Underwaves.

" There," said she.

He bent him down to look. She came out, and she put her two hands at his back, and cast him in.

" Be thou there," said she. " If I go to be married, thou art not the man; but the man who did each exploit that has been done, and, if he chooses, him will I have."

Away she went with the rider of the little black horse to the wedding.

And at the end of three years after that so it was that he first remembered the black horse or where he left him.

He got up and went out, and he was very sorry for his neglect of the black horse. He found him just where he left him.

" Good luck to you, gentleman," said the horse. " You seem as if you had got something that you like better than me."

" I have not got that, and I won't; but it came over me to forget you," said he.

" I don't mind," said the horse, " it will make no difference. Raise your sword and smite off my head."

" Fortune will now allow that I should do that," said he.

" Do it instantly, or I will do it to you," said the horse.

So the lad drew his sword and smote off the horse's head ; then he lifted his two palms and uttered a doleful cry.

What should he hear behind him but " All hail, my brother-in-law."

He looked behind him, and there was the finest man he ever set eyes upon.

"What set you weeping for the black horse?" said he.

"This," said the lad, "that there never was born of man or beast a creature in this world that I was fonder of."

"Would you take me for him?" said the stranger.

"If I could think you the horse, I would; but if not, I would rather the horse," said the rider.

"I am the black horse," said the lad, "and if I were not, how should you have all these things that you went to seek in my father's house. Since I went under spells, many a man have I ran at before you met me. They had but one word amongst them: they could not keep me, nor manage me, and they never kept me a couple of days. But when I fell in with you, you kept me till the time ran out that was to come from the spells. And now you shall go home with me, and we will make a wedding in my father's house."

THE TROOPING FAIRIES.

CHANGELINGS.

SOMETIMES the fairies fancy mortals, and carry them away into their own country, leaving instead some sickly fairy child, or a log of wood so bewitched that it seems to be a mortal pining away, and dying, and being buried. Most commonly they steal children. If you "over look a child," that is look on it with envy, the fairies have it in their power. Many things can be done to find out in a child a changeling, but there is one infallible thing— lay it on the fire with this formula, "Burn, burn, burn— if of the devil, burn; but if of God and the saints, be safe from harm" (given by Lady Wilde). Then if it be a changeling it will rush up the chimney with a cry, for, according to Giraldus Cambrensis, "fire is the greatest of enemies to every sort of phantom, in so much that those who have seen apparitions fall into a swoon as soon as they are sensible of the brightness of fire."

Sometimes the creature is got rid of in a more gentle way. It is on record that once when a mother was leaning over a wizened changeling the latch lifted and a fairy came in, carrying home again the wholesome stolen baby. "It was the others," she said, "who stole it." As for her, she wanted her own child.

Those who are carried away are happy, according to some accounts, having plenty of good living and music and mirth. Others say, however, that they are continually longing for their earthly friends. Lady Wilde gives a gloomy tradition that there are two kinds of fairies—one kind merry and gentle, the other evil, and sacrificing every year a life to Satan, for which purpose they steal

65

mortals. No other Irish writer gives this tradition—if such fairies there be, they must be among the solitary spirits—Pookas, Fir Darrigs, and the like.

THE BREWERY OF EGG-SHELLS.

T. CROFTON CROKER.

MRS. SULLIVAN fancied that her youngest child had been exchanged by "fairies theft," and certainly appearances warranted such a conclusion : for in one night her healthy, blue-eyed boy had become shriveled up into almost nothing, and never ceased squalling and crying. This naturally made poor Mrs. Sullivan very unhappy ; and all the neighbors, by way of comforting her, said that her own child was, beyond any kind of doubt, with the good people, and that one of themselves was put in his place.

Mrs. Sullivan of course could not disbelieve what every one told her, but she did not wish to hurt the thing; for although its face was so withered, and its body wasted away to a mere skeleton, it had still a strong resemblance to her own boy. She, therefore, could not find it in her heart to roast it alive on the griddle, or to burn its nose off with the red-hot tongs, or to throw it out in the snow on the road-side, notwithstanding these, and several like proceedings, were strongly recommended to her for the recovery of her child.

One day who should Mrs. Sullivan meet but a cunning woman, well known about the country by the name of Ellen Leah (or Gary Ellen). She had the gift, however she got it, of telling where the dead were, and what was good for the rest of their souls ; and could charm away warts and wens, and do a great many wonderful things of the same nature.

" You're in grief this morning, Mrs. Sullivan," were the first words of Ellen Leah to her.

" You may say that, Ellen," said Mrs. Sullivan, " and good cause I have to be in grief, for there was my own fine child whipped off from me out of his cradle, without as much as ' by your leave ' or ' ask your pardon,' and an ugly dony bit of a shriveled-up fairy put in his place; no wonder, then, that you see me in grief, Ellen."

" Small blame to you, Mrs. Sullivan," said Ellen Leah, " but are you sure 'tis a fairy ? "

" Sure ! " echoed Mrs. Sullivan, " sure enough I am to my sorrow, and can I doubt my own two eyes?   Every mother's soul must feel for me ! "

" Will you take an old woman's advice ? " said Ellen Leah, fixing her wild and mysterious gaze upon the un-happy mother ; and, after a pause, she added, " but may-be you'll call it foolish ? "

" Can you get me back my child, my own child, Ellen ? " said Mrs. Sullivan with great energy.

" If you do as I bid you," returned Ellen Leah, " you'll know."   Mrs. Sullivan was silent in expectation, and Ellen continued, " Put down the big pot, full of water, on the fire, and make it boil like mad ; then get a dozen new-laid eggs, break them, and keep the shells, but throw away the rest ; when that is done, put the shells in the pot of boiling water, and you will soon know whether it is your own boy or a fairy.   If you find that it is a fairy in the cradle, take the red-hot poker and cram it down his ugly throat, and you will not have much trouble with him after that, I promise you."

Home went Mrs. Sullivan, and did as Ellen Leah de-sired.   She put the pot on the fire, and plenty of turf under it, and set the water boiling at such a rate, that if ever water was red-hot, it surely was.

The child was lying, for a wonder, quite easy and quiet in the cradle, every now and then cocking his eye, that would twinkle as keen as a star in a frosty night, over at the great fire, and the big pot upon it ; and he looked on with great attention at Mrs. Sullivan breaking the eggs and putting down the egg-shells to boil.   At last he asked, with the voice of a very old man, "What are you doing, mammy?"

Mrs. Sullivan's heart, as she said herself, was up in her mouth ready to choke her, at hearing the child speak, but she contrived to put the poker in the fire, and to answer, without making any wonder at the words, "I'm brewing, *a vick*" (my son).

"Aud what are you brewing, mammy?" said the little imp, whose supernatural gift of speech now proved beyond question that he was a fairy substitute.

"I wish the poker was red," thought Mrs. Sullivan; but it was a large one, and took a long time heating; so she determined to keep him in talk until the poker was in a proper state to thrust down his throat, and therefore repeated the question.

"Is it what I'm brewing, *a vick*," said she, "you want to know?"

"Yes, mammy: what are you brewing?" returned the fairy.

"Egg-shells, *a vick*," said Mrs. Sullivan.

"Oh!" shrieked the imp, starting up in the cradle, and clapping his hands together, "I'm fifteen hundred years in the world, and I never saw a brewery of egg-shells before!" The poker was by this time quite red, and Mrs. Sullivan, seizing it, ran furiously towards the cradle; but somehow or other her foot slipped, and she fell on the floor, and the poker flew out of her hand to the other end of the house. However, she got up without much loss of time and went to the cradle, intending to pitch the wicked thing that was in it into the pot of boiling water, when there she saw her own child in a sweet sleep, one of his soft round arms rested upon the pillow— his features were as placid as if their repose had never been disturbed, save the rosy mouth, which moved with gentle and regular breathing.

THE FAIRY NURSE.

BY EDWARD WALSH.

SWEET babe! a golden cradle holds thee,
And soft the snow-white fleece enfolds thee;
In airy bower I'll watch thy sleeping,
Where branchy trees to the breeze are sweeping.
      Shuheen, sho, lulo! lo!

When mothers languish broken-hearted,
When young wives are from husbands parted,
Ah! little think the keeners lonely,
They weep some time-worn fairy only.
      Shuheen sho, lulo lo!

Within our magic halls of brightness,
Trips many a foot of snowy whiteness;
Stolen maidens, queens of fairy—
And kings and chiefs a sluagh-shee airy.
      Shuheen sho, lulo lo!

Rest thee, babe! I love thee dearly,
And as thy mortal mother nearly;
Ours is the swiftest steed and proudest,
That moves where the tramp of the host is loudest.
      Shuheen sho, lulo lo!

Rest thee, babe! for soon thy slumbers
Shall flee at the magic's koelshie's * numbers;
In airy bower I'll watch thy sleeping,
Where branchy trees to the breeze are sweeping.
      Shuheen sho, lulo, lo!

* *Ceól-sidhe—i. e.*, fairy music.

JAMIE FREEL AND THE YOUNG LADY.

A Donegal Tale.

MISS LETITIA MACLINTOCK.

Down in Fannet, in times gone by, lived Jamie Freel and his mother. Jamie was the widow's sole support; his strong arm worked for her untiringly, and as each Saturday night came round, he poured his wages into her lap, thanking her dutifully for the halfpence which she returned him for tobacco.

He was extolled by his neighbors as the best son ever known or heard of. But he had neighbors, of whose opinion he was ignorant—neighbors who lived pretty close to him, whom he had never seen, who are, indeed, rarely seen by mortals, except on May eves and Halloweens.

An old ruined castle, about a quarter of a mile from his cabin, was said to be the abode of the " wee folk." Every Halloween were the ancient windows lighted up, and passers-by saw little figures flitting to and fro inside the building, while they heard the music of pipes and flutes.

It was well known that fairy revels took place; but nobody had the courage to intrude on them.

Jamie had often watched the little figures from a distance, and listened to the charming music, wondering what the inside of the castle was like; but one Halloween he got up and took his cap, saying to his mother, " I'm awa' to the castle to seek my fortune."

" What ! " cried she, " would you venture there ? you that's the poor widow's one son ! Dinna be sae venturesome an' foolitch, Jamie ! They'll kill you, an' then what'll come o' me ? "

70

"Never fear, mother; nae harm 'ill happen me, but I maun gae."

He set out, and as he crossed the potato-field, came in sight of the castle, whose windows were ablaze with light, that seemed to turn the russet leaves, still clinging to the crabtree branches, into gold.

Halting in the grove at one side of the ruin, he listened to the elfin revelry, and the laughter and singing made him all the more determined to proceed.

Numbers of little people, the largest about the size of a child of five years old, were dancing to the music of flutes and fiddles, while others drank and feasted.

"Welcome, Jamie Freel! welcome, welcome, Jamie!" cried the company, perceiving their visitor. The word "Welcome" was caught up and repeated by every voice in the castle.

Time flew, and Jamie was enjoying himself very much, when his hosts said, "We're going to ride to Dublin to-night to steal a young lady. Will you come too, Jamie Freel?"

"Ay, that will I!" cried the rash youth, thirsting for adventure.

A troop of horses stood at the door. Jamie mounted, and his steed rose with him into the air. He was presently flying over his mother's cottage, surrounded by the elfin troop, and on and on they went, over bold mountains, over little hills, over the deep Lough Swilley, over towns and cottages, when people were burning nuts, and eating apples, and keeping merry Halloween. It seemed to Jamie that they flew all round Ireland before they got to Dublin.

"This is Derry," said the fairies, flying over the cathedral spire; and what was said by one voice was repeated by all the rest, till fifty little voices were crying out, "Derry! Derry! Derry!"

In like manner was Jamie informed as they passed over each town on the rout, and at length he heard the silvery voices cry, "Dublin! Dublin!"

It was no mean dwelling that was to be honored by the fairy visit, but one of the finest houses in Stephen's Green.

The troop dismounted near a window, and Jamie saw a beautiful face, on a pillow in a splendid bed. He saw the young lady lifted and carried away, while the stick which was dropped in her place on the bed took her exact form.

The lady was placed before one rider and carried a short way, then given another, and the names of the towns were cried out as before.

They were approaching home. Jamie heard " Rath-mullan," " Milford," " Tamney," and then he knew they were near his own house.

" You've all had your turn at carrying the young lady," said he. " Why wouldn't I get her for a wee piece? "

" Ay, Jamie," replied they, pleasantly, " you may take your turn at carrying her, to be sure."

Holding his prize very tightly, he dropped down near his mother's door.

" Jamie Freel, Jamie Freel! is that the way you treat us? " cried they, and they too dropped down near the door.

Jamie held fast, though he knew not what he was hold-ing, for the little folk turned the lady into all sorts of strange shapes. At one moment she was a black dog, barking and trying to bite; at another, a glowing bar of iron, which yet had no heat; then, again, a sack of wool.

But still Jamie held her, and the baffled elves were turning away, when a tiny woman, the smallest of the party, exclaimed, " Jamie Freel has her awa' frae us, but he sall hae nae gude o' her, for I'll mak' her deaf and dumb," and she threw something over the young girl.

While they rode off disappointed, Jamie lifted the latch and went in.

" Jamie, man! " cried his mother, " you've been awa' all night; what have they done on you? "

" Naething bad, mother; I ha' the very best of gude

luck.   Here's a beautiful young lady I ha' brought you
for company."

"Bless us an' save us!" exclaimed the mother, and for
some minutes she was so astonished that she could not
think of anything else to say.

Jamie told his story of the night's adventure, ending
by saying, "Surely you wouldna have allowed me to let
her gang with them to be lost forever?"

"But a *lady*, Jamie! How can a lady eat we'er poor
diet, and live in we'er poor way? I ax you that, you
foolitch fellow?"

"Weel, mother, sure it's better for her to be here nor
over yonder," and he pointed in the direction of the
castle.

Meanwhile, the deaf and dumb girl shivered in her light
clothing, stepping close to the humble turf fire.

"Poor crathur, she's quare and handsome! Nae wonder
they set their hearts on her," said the old woman, gazing
at her guest with pity and admiration. "We maun dress
her first; but what, in the name o' fortune, hae I fit for
the likes o' her to wear?"

She went to her press in "the room," and took out her
Sunday gown of brown drugget; she then opened a drawer,
and drew forth a pair of white stockings, a long snowy
garment of fine linen, and a cap, her "dead dress," as she
called it.

These articles of attire had long been ready for a certain
triste ceremony, in which she would some day fill the
chief part, and only saw the light occasionally, when they
were hung out to air; but she was willing to give even
these to the fair trembling visitor, who was turning in
dumb sorrow and wonder from her to Jamie, and from
Jamie back to her.

The poor girl suffered herself to be dressed, and then
sat down on a "creepie" in the chimney corner, and
buried her face in her hands.

"What'll we do to keep up a lady like thou?" cried the
old woman.

"I'll work for you both, mother," replied the son.

"An' how could a lady live on we'er poor diet?" she repeated.

"I'll work for her," was all Jamie's answer.

He kept his word. The young lady was very sad for a long time, and tears stole down her cheeks many an evening while the old woman spun by the fire, and Jamie made salmon nets, an accomplishment lately acquired by him, in hopes of adding to the comfort of his guest.

But she was always gentle, and tried to smile when she perceived them looking at her; and by degrees she adapted herself to their ways and mode of life. It was not very long before she began to feed the pig, mash potatoes and meal for the fowls, and knit blue worsted socks.

So a year passed, and Halloween came round again. "Mother," said Jamie, taking down his cap, "I'm off to the ould castle to seek my fortune."

"Are you mad, Jamie?" cried his mother, in terror; "sure they'll kill you this time for what you done on them last year."

Jamie made light of her fears and went his way.

As he reached the crab-tree grove, he saw bright lights in the castle windows as before, and heard loud talking. Creeping under the window, he heard the wee folk say, "That was a poor trick Jamie Freel played us this night last year, when he stole the nice young lady from us."

"Ay," said the tiny woman, "an' I punished him for it, for there she sits, a dumb image by his hearth; but he does na' know that three drops out o' this glass I hold in my hand wad gie her her hearing and her speeches back again."

Jamie's heart beat fast as he entered the hall. Again he was greeted by a chorus of welcomes from the company—"Here comes Jamie Freel! welcome, welcome, Jamie!"

As soon as the tumult subsided, the little woman said, "You be to drink our health, Jamie, out o' this glass in my hand."

Jamie snatched the glass from her and darted to the door. He never knew how he reached his cabin, but he arrived there breathless, and sank on a stove by the fire.

"You're kilt surely this time, my poor boy," said his mother.

"No, indeed, better luck than ever this time!" and he gave the lady three drops of the liquid that still remained at the bottom of the glass, notwithstanding his mad race over the potato-field.

The lady began to speak, and her first words were words of thanks to Jamie.

The three inmates of the cabin had so much to say to one another, that long after cock-crow, when the fairy music had quite ceased, they were talking round the fire.

"Jamie," said the lady, "be pleased to get me paper and pen and ink, that I may write to my father, and tell him what has become of me."

She wrote, but weeks passed, and she received no answer. Again and again she wrote, and still no answer.

At length she said, "You must come with me to Dublin, Jamie, to find my father."

"I ha' no money to hire a car for you," he replied, "an' how can you travel to Dublin on your foot?"

But she implored him so much that he consented to set out with her, and walk all the way from Fannet to Dublin. It was not as easy as the fairy journey; but at last they rang the bell at the door of the house in Stephen's Green.

"Tell my father that his daughter is here," said she to the servant who opened the door.

"The gentleman that lives here has no daughter, my girl. He had one, but she died better nor a year ago."

"Do you not know me, Sullivan?"

"No, poor girl, I do not."

"Let me see the gentleman. I only ask to see him."

"Well, that's not much to ax; we'll see what can be done."

In a few moments the lady's father came to the door.

" Dear father," said she, " don't you know me? "

" How dare you call me your father?" cried the old gentleman, angrily. " You are an impostor. I have no daughter."

" Look in my face, father, and surely you'll remember me."

" My daughter is dead and buried. She died a long, long time ago." The old gentleman's voice changed from anger to sorrow. " You can go," he concluded.

" Stop, dear father, till you look at this ring on my finger. Look at your name and mine engraved on it."

" It certainly is my daughter's ring; but I do not know how you came by it. I fear in no honest way."

" Call my mother, *she* will be sure to know me," said the poor girl, who, by this time, was crying bitterly.

" My poor wife is beginning to forget her sorrow. She seldom speaks of her daughter now. Why should I renew her grief by reminding her of her loss ? "

But the young lady persevered, till at last the mother was sent for.

" Mother," she began, when the old lady came to the door, "don't *you* know your daughter ? "

" I have no daughter; my daughter died and was buried a long, long time ago.

" Only look in my face, and surely you'll know me."

The old lady shook her head.

" You have all forgotten me ; but look at this mole on my neck. Surely, mother, you know me now ? "

" Yes, yes," said the mother, " my Gracie had a mole on her neck like that; but then I saw her in her coffin, and saw the lid shut down upon her."

It became Jamie's turn to speak, and he gave the history of the fairy journey, of the theft of the young lady, of the figure he had seen laid in its place, of her life with his mother in Fannet, of last Halloween, and of the three drops that had released her from her enchantment.

She took up the story when he paused, and told how kind the mother and son had been to her.

The parents could not make enough of Jamie. They treated him with every distinction, and when he expressed his wish to return to Fannet, said they did not know what to do to show their gratitude.

But an awkward complication arose. The daughter would not let him go without her. " If Jamie goes, I'll go too," she said. " He saved me from the fairies, and has worked for me ever since. If it had not been for him, dear father and mother, you would never have seen me again. If he goes, I'll go too."

This being her resolution, the old gentleman said that Jamie should become his son-in-law. The mother was brought from Fannet in a coach and four, and there was a splendid wedding.

They all lived together in the grand Dublin house, and Jamie was heir to untold wealth at his father-in-law's death.

THE STOLEN CHILD.*

W. B. YEATS.

WHERE dips the rocky highland
　　Of Sleuth Wood in the lake,
There lies a leafy island
　　Where flapping herons wake
The drowsy water-rats.
There we've hid our fairy vats
Full of berries,
And of reddest stolen cherries.
Come away, O, human child !
To the woods and waters wild,

* The places mentioned are round about Sligo. Further Rosses is a very noted fairy locality. There is here a little point of rocks where, if any one falls asleep, there is danger of their waking silly, the fairies having carried off their souls.

With a fairy hand in hand,
For the world's more full of weeping than
      you can understand.

Where the wave of moonlight glosses
  The dim gray sands with light,
Far off by furthest Rosses
  We foot it all the night,
Weaving olden dances,
Mingling hands, and mingling glances,
  Till the moon has taken flight;
To and fro we leap,
  And chase the frothy bubbles,
  While the world is full of troubles.
And is anxious in its sleep.
Come away! O, human child!
To the woods and waters wild,
With a fairy hand in hand,
For the world's more full of weeping than
      you can understand.

Where the wandering water gushes
  From the hills above Glen-Car,
In pools among the rushes,
  That scarce could bathe a star,
We seek for slumbering trout,
  And whispering in their ears;
    We give them evil dreams,
Leaning softly out
  From ferns that drop their tears
    Of dew on the young streams.
Come! O, human child!
To the woods and waters wild,
With a fairy hand in hand,
For the world's more full of weeping than
      you can understand.

Away with us, he's going,
  The solemn-eyed;

He'll hear no more the lowing
  Of the calves on the warm hill-side.
Or the kettle on the hob
  Sing peace into his breast;
Or see the brown mice bob
  Round and round the oatmeal chest.
For he comes, the human child,
To the woods and waters wild,
With a fairy hand in hand,
For the world's more full of weeping than
       he can understand.

MORRAHA.

MORRAHA rose in the morning and washed his hands
and face, and said his prayers, and ate his food; and he
asked God to prosper the day for him. So, he went
down to the brink of the sea, and he saw a currach, short
and green, coming towards him; and in it there was but
one youthful champion, and he was playing hurly from
prow to stern of the currach. He had a hurl of gold and
a ball of silver; and he stopped not till the currach was
in on the shore; and he drew her up on the green grass,
and put fastenings on her for a year and a day, whether
he should be there all that time or should only be on land
for an hour by the clock. And Morraha saluted the
young man courteously; and the other saluted him in the
same fashion, and asked him would he play a game of
cards with him; and Morraha said that he had not the
wherewithal; and the other answered that he was never
without a candle or the making of it; and he put his
hand in his pocket and drew out a table and two chairs
and a pack of cards, and they sat down on the chairs and
went to card-playing. The first game Morraha won, and
the Slender Red Champion bade him make his claim;
and he asked that the land about him should be filled
with stock of sheep in the morning. It was well; and
he played no second game, but home he went.

The next day Morraha went to the brink of the sea,
and the young man came in the currach and asked him
would he play cards; they played, and Morraha won.
The young man bade him make his claim; and he asked
that the land above should be filled with cattle in the
morning. It was well; and he played no other game, but
went home.

On the third morning Morraha went to the brink of the sea, and he saw the young man coming. He drew up his boat on the shore and asked him would he play cards. They played, and Morraha won the game; and the young man bade him give his claim. And he said he would have a castle and a wife, the finest and fairest in the world; and they were his. It was well; and the Red Champion went away.

On the fourth day his wife asked him how he had found her. And he told her. "And I am going out," said he, "to play again to-day."

"I forbid you to go again to him. If you have won so much, you will lose more; have no more to do with him."

But he went against her will, and he saw the currach coming; and the Red Champion was driving his balls from end to end of the currach; he had balls of silver and a hurl of gold, and he stopped not till he drew his boat on the shore, and made her fast for a year and a day. Morraha and he saluted each other; and he asked Morraha if he would play a game of cards, and they played, and he won. Morraha said to him, "Give your claim now."

Said he, "You will hear it too soon. I lay on you bonds of the art of the Druid, not to sleep two nights in one house, nor finish a second meal at the one table, till you bring me the sword of light and news of the death of Anshgayliacht."

He went home to his wife and sat down in a chair, and gave a groan, and the chair broke in pieces.

"That is the groan of the son of a king under spells," said his wife; "and you had better have taken my counsel than that the spells should be on you."

He told her he had to bring news of the death of Anshgayliacht and the sword of light to the Slender Red Champion.

"Go out," said she, "in the morning of the morrow, and take the bridle in the window, and shake it; and whatever beast, handsome or ugly, puts its head in it; take that one with you. Do not speak a word to her till she speaks to you; and take with you three pint bottles of ale and three sixpenny loaves, and do the thing she tells you; and when she runs to my father's land, on a height above the castle, she will shake herself, and the bells will ring, and my father will say, ' Brown Allree is in the land. And if the son of a king or queen is there, bring him to me on your shoulders; but if it is the son of a poor man, let him come no further.' "

He rose in the morning, and took the bridle that was in the window, and went out and shook it; and Brown Allree came and put her head in it. He took the three loaves and three bottles of ale, and went riding; and when he was riding she bent her head down to take hold of her feet with her mouth, in hopes he would speak in ignorance; but he spoke not a word during the time, and the mare at last spoke to him, and told him to dismount and give her her dinner. He gave her the sixpenny loaf toasted, and a bottle of ale to drink.

" Sit up now riding, and take good heed of yourself: there are three miles of fire I have to clear at a leap."

She cleared the three miles of fire at a leap, and asked if he were still riding, and he said he was. Then they went on, and she told him to dismount and give her a meal; and he did so, and gave her a sixpenny loaf and a bottle; she consumed them and said to him there were before them three miles of hill covered with steel thistles, and that she must clear it. She cleared the hill with a leap, and she asked him if he were still riding, and he said he was. They went on, and she went not far before she told him to give her a meal, and he gave her the bread and the bottleful. She went over three miles of sea with a leap, and she came then to the land of the King of France; she went up on a height above the castle, and she shook herself and neighed, and the bells rang ; and the king said that it was Brown Allree was in the land.

"Go out," said he; "and if it is the son of a king or queen, carry him on your shoulders; if it is not, leave him there."

They went out; and the stars of the son of a king were on his breast; they lifted him high on their shoulders and bore him in to the king. They passed the night cheerfully, playing and drinking, with sport and with diversion, till the whiteness of the day came upon the morrow morning.

Then the young king told the cause of his journey, and he asked the queen to give him counsel and good luck, and she told him everything he was to do.

"Go now," said she, "and take with you the best mare in the stable, and go to the door of Rough Niall of the speckled Rock, and knock, and call on him to give you news of the death of Anshgayliacht and the sword of light: and let the horse's back be to the door, and apply the spurs, and away with you."

In the morning he did so, and took the best horse from the stable and rode to the door of Niall, and turned the horse's back to the door, and demanded news of the death of Anshgayliacht and the sword of light; then he applied the spurs, and away with him. Niall followed him hard, and, as he was passing the gate, cut the horse in two. His wife was there with a dish of puddings and flesh, and she threw it in his eyes and blinded him, and said, "Fool! whatever kind of man it is that's mocking you, isn't that a fine condition you have got your father's horse into?"

On the morning of the next day Morraha rose, and took another horse from the stable, and went again to the door of Niall, and knocked and demanded news of the death of Anshgayliacht and the sword of light, and applied the spurs to the horse and away with him. Niall followed, and as Morraha was passing, the gate cut the horse in two and took half the saddle with him; but his wife met him and threw flesh in his eyes and blinded him.

On the third day, Morraha went again to the door of Niall; and Niall followed him, and as he was passing

the gate, cut away the saddle from under him and the
clothes from his back. Then his wife said to Niall:

" The fool that's mocking you, is out yonder in the little
currach, going home; and take good heed to yourself, and
don't sleep one wink for three days."

For three days the little currach kept in sight, but then
Niall's wife came to him and said:

" Sleep as much as you want now. He is gone."

He went to sleep, and there was heavy sleep on him,
and Morraha went in and took hold of the sword that
was on the bed at his head. And the sword thought to
draw itself out of the hand of Morraha; but it failed.
Then it gave a cry, and it wakened Niall, and Niall said it
was a rude and rough thing to come into his house like
that; and said Morraha to him:

" Leave your much talking, or I will cut the head off
you. Tell me the news of the death of Anshgayliacht."

" Oh, you can have my head."

" But your head is no good to me; tell me the story."

" Oh," said Niall's wife, " you must get the story."

" Well," said Niall, " let us sit down together till I tell
the story. I thought no one would ever get it; but now
it will be heard by all."

THE STORY.

When I was growing up, my mother taught me the
language of the birds; and when I got married, I used to
be listening to their conversation; and I would be laughing; and my wife would be asking me what was the reason of my laughing, but I did not like to tell her, as
women are always asking questions. We went out walking one fine morning, and the birds were arguing with
one another. One of them said to another:

" Why should you be comparing yourself with me,
when there is not a king nor knight that does not come
to look at my tree? "

"What advantage has your tree over mine, on which there are three rods of magic mastery growing?"

When I heard them arguing, and knew that the rods were there, I began to laugh.

"Oh," asked my wife, "why are you always laughing? I believe it is at myself you are jesting, and I'll walk with you no more."

"Oh, it is not about you I am laughing. It is because I understand the language of the birds."

Then I had to tell her what the birds were saying to one another; and she was greatly delighted, and she asked me to go home, and she gave orders to the cook to have breakfast ready at six o'clock in the morning. I did not know why she was going out early, and breakfast was ready in the morning at the hour she appointed. She asked me to go out walking. I went with her. She went to the tree, and asked me to cut a rod for her.

"Oh, I will not cut it. Are we not better without it?"

"I will not leave this until I get the rod, to see if there is any good in it."

I cut the rod and gave it to her. She turned from me and struck a blow on a stone, and changed it; and she struck a second blow on me, and made of me a black raven, and she went home and left me after her. I thought she would come back; she did not come, and I had to go into a tree till morning. In the morning, at six o'clock, there was a bellman out, proclaiming that every one who killed a raven would get a fourpenny-bit. At last you could not find man or boy without a gun, nor, if you were to walk three miles, a raven that was not killed. I had to make a nest in the top of a parlor chimney, and hide myself all day till night came, and go out to pick up a bit to support me, till I spent a month. Here she is herself to say if it is a lie I am telling.

"It is not," said she.

Then I saw her out walking. I went up to her, and I thought she would turn me back to my own shape, and she struck me with the rod and made of me an old white horse, and she ordered me to be put to a cart with a man, to draw stones from morning till night. I was worse off then. She spread abroad a report that I had died suddenly in my bed, and prepared a coffin, and waked and buried me. Then she had no trouble. But when I got tired I began to kill every one who came near me, and I

used to go into the haggard every night and destroy the stacks of corn; and when a man came near me in the morning I would follow him till I broke his bones. Every one got afraid of me. When she saw I was doing mischief she came to meet me, and I thought she would change me. And she did change me, and made a fox of me. When I saw she was doing me every sort of damage

I went away from her. I knew there was a badger's hole in the garden, and I went there till night came, and I made great slaughter among the geese and ducks. There she is herself to say if I am telling a lie.

"Oh! you are telling nothing but the truth, only less than the truth."

When she had enough of my killing the fowl she came out into the garden, for she knew I was in the badger's hole. She came to me and made me a wolf. I had to be off, and go to an island, where no one at all would see me, and now and then I used to be killing sheep, for there were not many of them, and I was afraid of being seen and hunted ; and so I passed a year, till a shepherd saw me among the sheep and a pursuit was made after me. And when the dogs came near me there was no place for me to escape to from them ; but I recognized the sign of the king among the men, and I made for him, and the king cried out to stop the hounds. I took a leap upon the front of the king's saddle, and the woman behind cried out, "My king and my lord, kill him, or he will kill you!"

"Oh! he will not kill me. He knew me; he must be pardoned."

The king took me home with him, and gave orders I should be well cared for. I was so wise, when I got food, I would not eat one morsel until I got a knife and fork. The man told the king, and the king came to see if it was true, and I got a knife and fork, and I took the knife in one paw and the fork in the other, and I bowed to the king. The king gave orders to bring him drink, and it came ; and the king filled a glass of wine and gave it to me.

I took hold of it in my paw and drank it, and thanked the king.

"On my honor," said he, "it is some king or other has lost him, when he came on the island; and I will keep him, as he is trained; and perhaps he will serve us yet."

And this is the sort of king he was,—a king who had

not a child living.   Eight sons were born to him and three
daughters, and they were stolen the same night they
were born.   No matter what guard was placed over them,
the child would be gone in the morning.   A twelfth child
now came to the queen, and the king took me with him
to watch the baby.   The women were not satisfied with
me.

"Oh," said the king, "what was all your watching ever
good for?   One that was born to me I have not; I will
leave this one in the dog's care, and he will not let it go."

A coupling was put between me and the cradle, and
when every one went to sleep I was watching till the
person woke who attended in the daytime; but I was there
only two nights; when it was near the day, I saw a hand
coming down through the chimney, and the hand was so
big that it took round the child altogether, and thought to
take him away.   I caught hold of the hand above the wrist,
and as I was fastened to the cradle, I did not let go my
hold till I cut the hand from the wrist, and there was a
howl from the person without.   I laid the hand in the cradle
with the child, and as I was tired I fell asleep; and when
I awoke, I had neither child nor hand; and I began to
howl, and the king heard me, and he cried out that something was wrong with me, and he sent servants to see
what was the matter with me, and when the messenger
came he saw me covered with blood, and he could not see
the child; and he went to the king and told him the child
was not to be got.   The king came and saw the cradle
colored with the blood, and he cried out "where was
the child gone?" and every one said it was the dog had
eaten it.

The king said: "It is not; loose him, and he will get
the pursuit himself."

When I was loosed, I found the scent of the blood till I
came to a door of the room in which the child was.   I went
back to the king and took hold of him, and went back again
and began to tear at the door.   The king followed me and
asked for the key.   The servant said it was in the room of

I saw a hand coming down through the chimney, and it took the child, and thought to take him away.—Page 88.　　　　*Irish Fairy Tales.*

the stranger woman. The king caused search to be made
for her, and she was not to be found. " I will break the
door," said the king, " as I can't get the key." The king
broke the door, and I went in, and went to the trunk, and
the king asked for a key to unlock it. He got no key, and
he broke the lock. When he opened the trunk, the child
and the hand were stretched side by side, and the child
was asleep. The king took the hand and ordered a woman
to come for the child, and he showed the hand to every one
in the house. But the stranger woman was gone, and she
did not see the king ;—and here she is herself to say if I
am telling lies of her.

" Oh, it's nothing but the truth you have! "

The king did not allow me to be tied any more. He
said there was nothing so much to wonder at as that I cut
the hand off, as I was tied.

The child was growing till he was a year old. He was
beginning to walk, and no one cared for him more than I
did. He was growing till he was three, and he was
running out every minute ; so the king ordered a silver
chain to be put between me and the child, that he might
not go away from me. I was out with him in the garden
every day, and the king was as proud as the world of the
child. He would be watching him everywhere we went,
till the child grew so wise that he would loose the chain
and get off. But one day that he loosed it I failed to find
him ; and I ran into the house and searched the house but
there was no getting him for me. The king cried to go out
and find the child, that had got loose from the dog. They
went searching for him, but could not find him. When
they failed altogether to find him, there remained no more
favor with the king towards me, and every one disliked
me, and I grew weak, for I did not get a morsel to eat half
the time. When summer came, I said I would try and go
home to my own country. I went away one fine morning,
and I went swimming, and God helped me till I came home.
I went into the garden, for I knew there was a place in the
garden where I could hide myself, for fear my wife should

see me. In the morning I saw her out walking, and the
child with her, held by the hand. I pushed out to see the
child, and as he was looking about him everywhere, he saw
me and called out, "I see my shaggy papa. Oh!" said he;
"oh, my heart's love, my shaggy papa, come here till I see
you!"

I was afraid the woman would see me, as she was asking
the child where he saw me, and he said I was up in a
tree; and the more the child called me, the more I hid
myself. The woman took the child home with her but
I knew he would be up early in the morning.

I went to the parlor-window, and the child was within,
and he playing. When he saw me he cried out, "Oh!
my heart's love, come here till I see you, shaggy papa."
I broke the window and went in, and he began to kiss me.
I saw the rod in front of the chimney, and I jumped up
at the rod and knocked it down. "Oh! my heart's love,
no one would give me the pretty rod," said he. I hoped

he would strike me with the rod, but he did not. When
I saw the time was short I raised my paw, and I gave
him a scratch below the knee. " Oh ! you naughty, dirty,
shaggy papa, you have hurt me so much, I'll give you a
blow of the rod." He struck me a light blow, and so I
came back to my own shape again. When he saw a man
standing before him he gave a cry, and I took him up in
my arms. The servants heard the child. A maid came
in to see what was the matter with him. When she saw
me she gave a cry out of her, and she said, " Oh, if the
master isn't come to life again ! "

Another came in, and said it was he really. When the
mistress heard of it, she came to see with her own eyes,
for she would not believe I was there ; and when she saw
me she said she'd drown herself. But I said to her, "If
you yourself will keep the secret, no living man will ever
get the story from me until I lose my head." Here she is
herself to say if I am telling the truth. " Oh, it's nothing
but truth you are telling."

When I saw I was in a man's shape, I said I would
take the child back to his father and mother, as I knew
the grief they were in after him. I got a ship, and took
the child with me ; and as I journeyed I came to land on
an island, and I saw not a living soul on it, only a castle
dark and gloomy. I went in to see was there any one in
it. There was no one but an old hag, tall and frightful,
and she asked me, " What sort of person are you ? " I
heard some one groaning in another room, and I said I
was a doctor, and I asked her what ailed the person who
was groaning.

" Oh," said she, " it is my son, whose hand has been
bitten from his wrist by a dog."

I knew then that it was he who had taken the child
from me, and I said I would cure him if I got a good reward.

" I have nothing ; but there are eight young lads and
three young women, as handsome as any one ever laid
eyes on, and if you cure him I will give you them."

" Tell me first in what place his hand was cut from him ? "

" Oh, it was out in another country, twelve years ago."

" Show me the way, that I may see him."

She brought me into a room, so that I saw him, and his arm was swelled up to the shoulder. He asked me if I would cure him; and I said I would cure him if he would give me the reward his mother promised.

" Oh, I will give it; but cure me."

" Well, bring them out to me."

The hag brought them out of the room. I said I should burn the flesh that was on his arm. When I looked on him he was howling with pain. I said that I would not leave him in pain long. The wretch had only one eye in his forehead. I took a bar of iron, and put it in the fire till it was red, and I said to the hag, " He will be howling at first, but will fall asleep presently, and do not wake him till he has slept as much as he wants. I will close the door when I am going out." I took the bar with me, and I stood over him, and I turned it across through his eye as far as I could. He began to bellow, and tried to catch me, but I was out and away, having closed the door. The hag asked me, " Why is he bellowing? "

" Oh, he will be quiet presently, and will sleep for a good while, and I'll come again to have a look at him ; but bring me out the young men and the young women."

I took them with me, and I said to her, " Tell me where you got them."

" My son brought them with him, and they are all the children of one king."

I was well satisfied, and I had no wish for delay to get myself free from the hag, so I took them on board the ship, and the child I had myself. I thought the king might leave me the child I nursed myself; but when I came to land, and all these young people with me, the king and queen were out walking. The king was very aged, and the queen aged likewise. When I came to converse with them, and the twelve with me, the king

and queen began to cry. I asked, " Why are you crying ? "

" It is for good cause I am crying.   As many children
as these I should have, and now I am withered, gray, at
the end of my life, and I have not one at all."

I told him all I went through, and I gave him the child
in his hand, and " These are your other children who were
stolen from you, whom I am giving to you safe.   They
are gently reared."

When the king heard who they were he smothered
them with kisses and drowned them with tears, and dried
them with fine cloths silken and the hair of his own head,
and so also did their mother, and great was his welcome
for me, as it was I who found them all.   The king said
to me, " I will give you the last child, as it is you who
have earned him best; but you must come to my court
every year, and the child with you, and I will share with
you my possessions.

" I have enough of my own, and after my death I will
leave it to the child."

I spent a time, till my visit was over, and I told the king
all the troubles I went through, only I said nothing about
my wife.   And now you have the story.

And now when you go home, and the Slender Red
Champion asks you for news of the death of Anshgayliacht
and for the sword of light, tell him the way in which his
brother was killed, and say you have the sword ; and he
will ask the sword from you.   Say you to him, " If I
promised to bring it to you, I did not promise to bring it
for you ; " and then throw the sword into the air and it
will come back to me.

He went home, and he told the story of the death of
Anshgayliacht to the Slender Red Champion, " And here,"
said he, " is the sword."   The Slender Red Champion
asked for the sword ; but he said : " If I promised to bring
it to you, I did not promise to bring it for you ; " and he
threw it into the air and it returned to Blue Niall.

THE MERROW.

The *Merrow*, or if you write it in the Irish, *Moruadh* or *Murrúghach*, from *muir*, sea, and *oigh*, a maid, is not un-common, they say, on the wilder coasts. The fishermen do not like to see them, for it always means coming gales. The male *Merrows* (if you can use such a phrase—I have never heard the masculine of *Merrow*) have green teeth, green hair, pig's eyes, and red noses; but their women are beautiful, for all their fish tails and the little duck-like scale between their fingers. Sometimes they prefer, small blame to them, good-looking fishermen to their sea lovers. Near Bantry, in the last century, there is said to have been a woman covered all over with scales like a fish, who was descended from such a marriage. Sometimes they come out of the sea, and wander about the shore in the shape of little hornless cows. They have, when in their own shape, a red cap, called a *cohullen druith*, usually covered with feathers. If this is stolen, they cannot again go down under the waves.

Red is the color of magic in every country, and has been so from the very earliest times. The caps of fairies and magicians are well-nigh always red.

THE SOUL CAGES.

T. CROFTON CROKER.

JACK DOGHERTY lived on the coast of the county Clare. Jack was a fisherman, as his father and grandfather before him had been. Like them, too, he lived all alone (but for the wife), and just in the same spot. People used to wonder why the Dogherty family were so fond of that wild situation, so far away from all human kind, and in the midst of huge shattered rocks, with nothing but the wide ocean to look upon. But they had their own good reasons for it.

The place was just the only spot on that part of the coast where anybody could well live. There was a neat little creek, where a boat might lie as snug as a puffin in her nest, and out from this creek a ledge of sunken rocks ran into the sea. Now when the Atlantic, according to custom, was raging with a storm, and a good westerly wind was blowing strong on the coast, many a richly-laden ship went to pieces on these rocks; and then the fine bales of cotton and tobacco, and such like things, and the pipes of wine, and the puncheons of rum, and the casks of brandy, and the kegs of Hollands that used to come ashore! Dunbeg Bay was just like a little estate to the Doghertys.

Not but they were kind and humane to a distressed sailor, if ever one had the good luck to get to land; and many a time indeed did Jack put out in his little *corragh* (which, though not quite equal to honest Andrew Hennessy's canvas life-boat, would breast the billows like any gannet), to lend a hand towards bringing off the crew from a wreck. But when the ship had gone to pieces, and the crew were all lost, who would blame Jack for picking up all he could find?

"And who is the worse of it?" said he. "For as to the king, God bless him! everybody knows he's rich enough already without getting what's floating in the sea."

Jack, though such a hermit, was a good-natured, jolly fellow. No other, sure, could ever have coaxed Biddy Mahony to quit her father's snug and warm house in the middle of the town of Ennis, and to go so many miles off to live among the rocks, with the seals and sea-gulls for next-door neighbors. But Biddy knew that Jack was the man for a woman who wished to be comfortable and happy; for, to say nothing of the fish, Jack had the supplying of half the gentlemen's houses of the country with the *Godsends* that came into the bay. And she was right

in her choice; for no woman ate, drank, slept better, or
made a prouder appearance at chapel on Sundays, than
Mrs. Dogherty.

Many a strange sight, it may well be supposed, did Jack
see, and many a strange sound did he hear, but nothing
daunted him. So far was he from being afraid of Merrows,
or such beings, that the very first wish of his heart was to
fairly meet with one. Jack had heard that they were
mighty like Christians, and that luck had always come out
of an acquaintance with them. Never, therefore, did he
dimly discern the Merrows moving along the face of the
waters in their robes of mist, but he made direct for
them; and many a scolding did Biddy, in her own quiet
way, bestow upon Jack for spending his whole day out
at sea, and bringing home no fish. Little did poor Biddy
know the fish Jack was after !

It was rather annoying to Jack that, though living in a
place where the Merrows were as plenty as lobsters, he
never could get a right view of one. What vexed him
more was that both, his father and grandfather had
often and often seen them; and he even remembered hearing, when a child, how his grandfather, who was the first
of the family that had settled down at the creek, had been
so intimate with a Merrow that, only for fear of vexing
the priest, he would have had him stand for one of his
children. This, however, Jack did not well know how to
believe.

Fortune at length began to think that it was only right
that Jack should know as much as his father and grandfather did. Accordingly, one day when he had strolled a
little farther than usual along the coast to the northward,
just as he turned a point, he saw something, like to nothing he had ever seen before, perched upon a rock at a little
distance out to sea. It looked green in the body, as well
as he could discern at that distance, and he would have
sworn, only the thing was impossible, that it had a cocked
hat in its hand. Jack stood for a good half-hour straining
his eyes, and wondering at it, and all the time the thing

did not stir hand or foot. At last Jack's patience was quite worn out, and he gave a loud whistle and a hail, when the Merrow (for such it was) started up, put the cocked hat on its head, and dived down, head-foremost from the rock.

Jack's curiosity was now excited, and he constantly directed his steps towards the point: still he could never get a glimpse of the sea-gentleman with the cocked hat; and with thinking and thinking about the matter, he began at last to fancy he had been only dreaming. One very rough day, however, when the sea was running mountains high, Jack Dogherty determined to give a look at the Merrow's rock (for he had always chosen a fine day before), and then he saw the strange thing cutting capers upon the top of the rock, and then diving down, and then coming up, and then diving down again.

Jack had now only to choose his time (that is, a good blowing day) and he might see the man of the sea as often as he pleased. All this, however, did not satisfy him—"much will have more"; he wished now to get acquainted with the Merrows, and even in this he succeeded. One tremendous blustering day, before he got to the point whence he had a view of the Merrow's rock, the storm came on so furiously that Jack was obliged to take shelter in one of the caves which are so numerous along the coast; and there, to his astonishment, he saw sitting before him a thing with green hair, long green teeth, a red nose, and pig's eyes. It had a fish's tail, legs with scales on them, and short arms like fins. It wore no clothes, but had the cocked hat under its arm, and seemed engaged thinking very seriously about something.

Jack, with all his courage, was a little daunted; but now or never, thought he; so up he went boldly to the cogitating fishman, took off his hat, and made his best bow.

"Your servant, sir," said Jack.

"Your servant, kindly, Jack Dogherty," answered the Merrow.

"To be sure, then, how well your honor knows my name!" said Jack.

"Is it I not know your name, Jack Dogherty? Why, man, I knew your grandfather long before he was married to Judy Regan, your grandmother! Ah, Jack, Jack, I was fond of that grandfather of yours; he was a mighty worthy man in his time: I never met his match above or below, before or since, for sucking in a shellful of brandy. I hope, my boy," said the old fellow, with a merry twinkle in his eyes, " I hope you're his own grandson!"

"Never fear me for that," said Jack; "if my mother had only reared me on brandy, 'tis myself that would be a sucking infant to this hour!"

"Well, I like to hear you talk so manly; you and I must be better acquainted, if it were only for your grandfather's sake. But, Jack, that father of yours was not the thing! he had no head at all."

"I'm sure," said Jack, "since your honor lives down under the water, you must be obliged to drink a power to keep any heat in you in such a cruel, damp, *could* place. Well, I've often heard of Christians drinking like fishes; and might I be so bold as ask where you get the spirits?"

"Where do you get them yourself, Jack?" said the Merrow, twitching his red nose between his forefinger and thumb.

"Hubbubboo," cries Jack, "now I see how it is; but I suppose, sir, your honor has got a fine dry cellar below to keep them in."

"Let me alone for the cellar," said the Merrow, with a knowing wink of his left eye.

"I'm sure," continued Jack, "it must be mighty well worth the looking at."

"You may say that, Jack," said the Merrow; "and if you meet me here next Monday, just at this time of the day, we will have a little more talk with one another about the matter."

Jack and the Merrow parted the best friends in the

world. On Monday they met, and Jack was not a little surprised to see that the Merrow had two cocked hats with him, one under each arm.

"Might I take the liberty to ask, sir," said Jack, "why your honor has brought the two hats with you to day? You would not, sure, be going to give me one of them, to keep for the *curiosity* of the thing?"

"No, no, Jack," said he, "I don't get my hats so easily, to part with them that way; but I want you to come down and dine with me, and I brought you the hat to dine with."

"Lord bless and preserve us!" cried Jack, in amazement, "would you want me to go down to the bottom of the salt sea ocean? Sure, I'd be smothered and choked up with the water, to say nothing of being drowned! And what would poor Biddy do for me, and what would she say?"

"And what matter what she says, you *pinkeen?* Who cares for Biddy's squalling? It's long before your grandfather would have talked in that way. Many's the time he stuck that same hat on his head, and dived down boldly after me; and many's the snug bit of dinner and good shellful of brandy he and I have had together below, under the water."

"Is it really, sir, and no joke?" said Jack; "why, then, sorrow from me for ever and a day after, if I'll be a bit worse man nor my grandfather was! Here goes—but play me fair now. Here's neck or nothing!" cried Jack.

"That's your grandfather all over," said the old fellow; "so come along, then, and do as I do."

They both left the cave, walked into the sea, and then swam a piece until they got to the rock. The Merrow climbed to the top of it, and Jack followed him. On the far side it was as straight as the wall of a house, and the sea beneath looked so deep that Jack was almost cowed.

"Now, do you see, Jack," said the Merrow: "just put this hat on your head, and mind to keep your eyes wide

open. Take hold of my tail, and follow after me, and
you'll see what you'll see."

In he dashed, and in dashed Jack after him boldly.
They went and they went, and Jack thought they'd never
stop going. Many a time did he wish himself sitting at
home by the fireside with Biddy. Yet where was the use
of wishing now, when he was so many miles, as he thought,
below the waves of the Atlantic? Still he held hard by
the Merrow's tail, slippery as it was; and, at last, to
Jack's great surprise, they got out of the water, and he
actually found himself on dry land at the bottom of the
sea. They landed just in front of a nice house that was
slated very neatly with oyster shells! and the Merrow,
turning about to Jack, welcomed him down.

Jack could hardly speak, what with wonder, and what
with being out of breath with traveling so fast through
the water. He looked about him and could see no living
things, barring crabs and lobsters, of which there were
plenty walking leisurely about on the sand. Overhead
was the sea like a sky, and the fishes like birds swimming
about in it.

"Why don't you speak, man?" said the Merrow: "I
dare say you had no notion that I had such a snug little
concern here as this? Are you smothered, or choked, or
drowned, or are you fretting after Biddy, eh?"

"Oh! not myself, indeed," said Jack, showing his teeth
with a good-humored grin; "but who in the world would
ever have thought of seeing such a thing?"

"Well, come along, and let's see what they've got for
us to eat?"

Jack really was hungry, and it gave him no small
pleasure to perceive a fine column of smoke rising from
the chimney, announcing what was going on within.
Into the house he followed the Merrow, and there he saw
a good kitchen, right well provided with everything.
There was a noble dresser, and plenty of pots and pans,
with two young Merrows cooking. His host then led him
into the room, which was furnished shabbily enough. Not

a table or a chair was there in it; nothing but planks and logs of wood to sit on, and eat off. There was, however, a good fire blazing upon the hearth—a comfortable sight to Jack.

"Come now, and I'll show you where I keep—you know what," said the Merrow, with a sly look; and opening a little door, he led Jack into a fine cellar, well filled with pipes, and kegs, and hogsheads, and barrels.

"What do you say to that, Jack Dogherty? Eh! may be a body can't live snug under the water?"

"Never the doubt of that," said Jack, with a convincing smack of his under lip, that he really thought what he said.

They went back to the room, and found dinner laid. There was no tablecloth, to be sure—but what matter? It was not always Jack had one at home. The dinner would have been no discredit to the first house of the country on a fast day. The choicest of fish, and no wonder, was there. Turbots, and sturgeons, and soles, and lobsters, and oysters, and twenty other kinds, were on the planks at once, and plenty of the best of foreign spirits. The wines, the old fellow said, were too cold for his stomach.

Jack ate and drank till he could eat no more: then, taking up a shell of brandy, "Here's to your honor's good health, sir," said he; "though, begging your pardon, it's mighty odd that as long as we've been acquainted I don't know your name yet."

"That's true, Jack," replied he; "I never thought of it before, but better late than never. My name's Coomara."

"And a mighty decent name it is," cried Jack, taking another shellful: "here's to your good health, Coomara, and may ye live fifty years to come!"

"Fifty years!" repeated Coomara; "I'm obliged to you, indeed! If you had said five hundred, it would have been something worth the wishing."

"By the laws, sir," cries Jack, "*youz* live to a powerful

age here under the water! You knew my grandfather, and he's dead and gone better than these sixty years. I'm sure it must be a healthy place to live in."

" No doubt of it; but come, Jack, keep the liquor stirring."

Shell after shell did they empty, and to Jack's exceeding surprise, he found the drink never got into his head, owing, I suppose, to the sea being over them, which kept their noddles cool.

Old Coomara got exceedingly comfortable, and sung several songs; but Jack, if his life had depended on it, never could remember more than

> " *Rum fum boodle boo,*
> *Ripple dipple nitty dob ;*
> *Dumdoo doodle coo,*
> *Raffle taffle chittiboo !* "

It was the chorus to one of them; and, to say the truth, nobody that I know has ever been able to pick any particular meaning out of it; but that, to be sure, is the case with many a song nowadays.

At length said he to Jack, " Now, my dear boy, if you follow me, I'll show you my *curiosities!* " He opened a little door, and led Jack into a large room, where Jack saw a great many odds and ends that Coomara had picked up at one time or another. What chiefly took his attention, however, were things like lobster-pots ranged on the ground along the wall.

" Well, Jack, how do you like my *curiosities?* " said old Coo.

" Upon my *sowkins,** sir," said Jack, " they're mighty well worth the looking at; but might I make so bold as to ask what these things like lobster-pots are? "

" Oh! the Soul Cages, is it? "

" The what? sir! "

" These things here that I keep the souls in."

* *Sowkins,* diminutive of soul.

" *Arrah!* what souls, sir?" said Jack, in amazement; " sure the fish have no souls in them."

" Oh! no," replied Coo, quite coolly, " that they have not; but these are the souls of drowned sailors."

" The Lord preserve us from all harm!" muttered Jack, " how in the world did you get them?"

" Easily enough : I've only, when I see a good storm coming on, to set a couple of dozen of these, and then, when the sailors are drowned and the souls get out of them under the water, the poor things are almost perished to death, not being used to the cold ; so they make into my pots for shelter, and then I have them snug, and fetch them home, and keep them here dry and warm; and is it not well for them, poor souls, to get into such good quarters?"

Jack was so thunderstruck he did not know what to say, so he said nothing. They went back into the dining-room, and had a little more brandy, which was excellent, and then, as Jack knew that it must be getting late, and as Biddy might be uneasy, he stood up, and said he thought it was time for him to be on the road.

" Just as you like, Jack," said Coo, " but take a *ducan durrus* * before you go ; you've a cold journey before you."

Jack knew better manners than to refuse the parting glass. " I wonder," said he, " will I be able to make out my way home?"

" What should ail you," said Coo, " when I'll show you the way?"

Out they went before the house, and Coomara took one of the cocked hats, and put it upon Jack's head the wrong way, and then lifted him up on his shoulder that he might launch him up into the water.

" Now," says he, giving him a heave, " you'll come up just in the same spot you came down in ; and, Jack, mind and throw me back the hat."

He canted Jack off his shoulder, and up he shot like

* *Recte, deoch an dorrus*—door-drink or stirrup-cup.

a bubble—whirr, whirr, whiz—away he went up through the water, till he came to the very rock he had jumped off, where he found a landing-place, and then in he threw the hat, which sunk like a stone.

The sun was just going down in the beautiful sky of a calm summer's evening. *Feascor* was seen dimly twinkling in the cloudless heaven, a solitary star, and the waves of the Atlantic flashed in a golden flood of light. So Jack, perceiving it was late, set off home; but when he got there, not a word did he say to Biddy of where he had spent his day.

The state of the poor souls cooped up in the lobster-pots gave Jack a great deal of trouble, and how to release them cost him a great deal of thought. He at first had a mind to speak to the priest about the matter. But what could the priest do, and what did Coo care for the priest? Besides, Coo was a good sort of an old fellow, and did not think he was doing any harm. Jack had a regard for him, too, and it also might not be much to his own credit if it were known that he used to go dine with Merrows. On the whole, he thought his best plan would be to ask Coo to dinner, and to make him drunk, if he was able, and then to take the hat and go down and turn up the pots. It was, first of all, necessary, however, to get Biddy out of the way; for Jack was prudent enough, as she was a woman, to wish to keep the thing secret from her.

Accordingly, Jack grew mighty pious all of a sudden, and said to Biddy that he thought it would be for the good of both their souls if she was to go and take her rounds at Saint John's Well, near Ennis. Biddy thought so too, and accordingly off she set one fine morning at day-dawn, giving Jack a strict charge to have an eye to the place. The coast being clear, away went Jack to the rock to give the appointed signal to Coomara, which was throwing a big stone into the water. Jack threw, and up sprang Coo!

"Good morning, Jack," said he; "what do you want with me?"

"Just nothing at all to speak about, sir," returned Jack, "only to come and take a bit of dinner with me, if I might make so free as to ask you, and sure I'm now after doing so."

"It's quite agreeable, Jack, I assure you; what's your hour?"

"Any time that's most convenient to you, sir—say one o'clock, that you may go home, if you wish, with the daylight."

"I'll be with you," said Coo, "never fear me,"

Jack went home, and dressed a noble fish dinner, and got out plenty of his best foreign spirits, enough, for that matter, to make twenty men drunk. Just to the minute came Coo, with his cocked hat under his arm. Dinner was ready, they sat down, and ate and drank away manfully. Jack, thinking of the poor souls below in the pots, plied old Coo well with brandy, and encouraged him to sing, hoping to put him under the table, but poor Jack forgot that he had not the sea over his own head to keep it cool. The brandy got into it, and did his business for him, and Coo reeled off home, leaving his entertainer as dumb as a haddock on a Good Friday.

Jack never woke till the next morning, and then he was in a sad way. "'Tis to no use for me thinking to make that old Rapparee drunk," said Jack, "and how in this world can I help the poor souls out of the lobster-pots?" After ruminating nearly the whole day, a thought struck him. "I have it," says he, slapping his knee; "I'll be sworn that Coo never saw a drop of *poteen*, as old as he is, and that's the *thing* to settle him! Oh! then, is not it well that Biddy will not be home these two days yet; I can have another twist at him."

Jack asked Coo again, and Coo laughed at him for having no better head, telling him he'd never come up to his grandfather.

"Well, but try me again," said Jack, "and I'll be bail to drink you drunk and sober, and drunk again."

"Anything in my power," said Coo, "to oblige you."

At this dinner Jack took care to have his own liquor well watered, and to give the strongest brandy he had to Coo. At last says he, " Pray, sir, did you ever drink any poteen?—any real mountain dew?"

" No," says Coo; " what's that, and where does it come from?"

" Oh, that's a secret," said Jack, " but it's the right stuff —never believe me again, if 'tis not fifty times as good as brandy or rum either. Biddy's brother just sent me a present of a little drop, in exchange for some brandy, and as you're an old friend of the family, I kept it to treat you with."

" Well, let's see what sort of thing it is," said Coomara.

The *poteen* was the right sort. It was first-rate, and had the real smack upon it. Coo was delighted: he drank and he sung *Rum bum boodle boo* over and over again; and he laughed and he danced, till he fell on the floor fast asleep. Then Jack, who had taken good care to keep himself sober, snapt up the cocked hat—ran off to the rock—leaped in, and soon arrived at Coo's habitation.

All was as still as a churchyard at midnight—not a Merrow, old or young, was there. In he went and turned up the pots, but nothing did he see, only he heard a sort of a little whistle or chirp as he raised each of them. At this he was surprised, till he recollected what the priests had often said, that nobody living could see the soul, no more than they could see the wind or the air. Having now done all that he could do for them, he set the pots as they were before, and sent a blessing after the poor souls to speed them on their journey wherever they were going. Jack now began to think of returning; he put the hat on, as was right, the wrong way; but when he got out he found the water so high over his head that he had no hopes of ever getting up into it, now that he had not old Coomara to give him a lift. He walked about looking for a ladder, but not one could he find, and not a rock was there in sight. At last he saw a spot where the sea hung rather lower than anywhere else, so he resolved

to try there. Just as he came to it, a big cod happened
to put down his tail. Jack made a jump and caught hold
of it, and the cod, all in amazement, gave a bounce and
pulled Jack up. The minute the hat touched the water
away Jack was whisked, and up he shot like a cork, dragging the poor cod, that he forgot to let go, up with him
tail foremost. He got to the rock in no time, and without
a moment's delay hurried home, rejoicing in the good
deed he had done.

But, meanwhile, there was fine work at home; for our
friend Jack had hardly left the house on his soul-freeing
expedition, when back came Biddy from her soul-saving
one to the well. When she entered the house and saw
the things lying *thrie-na-helah* * on the table before her—
"Here's a pretty job!" said she ; "that blackguard of
mine—what ill-luck I had ever to marry him! He has
picked up some vagabond or other, while I was praying
for the good of his soul, and they've been drinking all the
poteen that my own brother gave him, and all the spirits,
to be sure, that he was to have sold to his honor." Then
hearing an outlandish kind of a grunt, she looked down,
and saw Coomara lying under the table. "The blessed
Virgin help me," shouted she, " if he has not made a real
beast of himself! Well, well, I've often heard of a man
making a beast of himself with drink! Oh hone, oh
hone!—Jack, honey, what will I do with you, or what
will I do without you? How can any decent woman
ever think of living with a beast?"

With such like lamentations Biddy rushed out of the
house, and was going she knew not where, when she heard
the well-known voice of Jack singing a merry tune. Glad
enough was Biddy to find him safe and sound, and not
turned into a thing that was like neither fish nor flesh.
Jack was obliged to tell her all, and Biddy, though she
had half a mind to be angry with him for not telling her
before, owned that he had done a great service to the

* *Tri-na-cheile, literally through other—i.e.,* higgledy-piggledy.

poor souls. Back they both went most lovingly to the
house, and Jack wakened up Coomara; and, perceiving
the old fellow to be rather dull, he bid him not to be cast
down, for 'twas many a good man's case; said it all came
of his not being used to the *poteen*, and recommended him,
by way of cure, to swallow a hair of the dog that bit him.
Coo, however, seemed to think he had had quite enough.
He got up, quite out of sorts, and without having the
manners to say one word in the way of civility, he sneaked
off to cool himself by a jaunt through the salt water.

Coomara never missed the souls. He and Jack continued the best friends in the world, and no one, perhaps,
ever equalled Jack for freeing souls from purgatory; for
he contrived fifty excuses for getting into the house below
the sea, unknown to the old fellow, and then turning up
the pots and letting out the souls. It vexed him, to be
sure, that he could never see them; but as he knew the
thing to be impossible, he was obliged to be satisfied.

Their intercourse continued for several years. However, one morning, on Jack's throwing in a stone as usual,
he got no answer. He flung another, and another, still
there was no reply. He went away, and returned the following morning, but it was to no purpose. As he was
without the hat, he could not go down to see what had
become of old Coo, but his belief was, that the old man, or
the old fish, or whatever he was, had either died, or had
removed from that part of the country.

FLORY CANTILLON'S FUNERAL.

T. CROFTON CROKER.

THE ancient burial-place of the Cantillon family was
on an island in Ballyheigh Bay. This island was situated
at no great distance from the shore, and at a remote period
was overflowed in one of the encroachments which the
Atlantic has made on that part of the coast of Kerry.

The fishermen declare they have often seen the ruined walls of an old chapel beneath them in the water, as they sailed over the clear green sea of a sunny afternoon. However this may be, it is well-known that the Cantillons were, like most other Irish families, strongly attached to their ancient burial-place; and this attachment led to the custom, when any of the family died, of carrying the corpse to the sea-side, where the coffin was left on the shore within reach of the tide. In the morning it had disappeared, being, as was traditionally believed, conveyed away by the ancestors of the deceased to their family tomb.

Connor Crowe, a county Clare man, was related to the Cantillons by marriage. " Connor Mac in Cruagh, of the seven quarters of Breintragh," as he was commonly called, and a proud man he was of the name. Connor, be it known, would drink a quart of salt water, for its medicinal virtues, before breakfast; and for the same reason, I suppose, double that quantity of raw whisky between breakfast and night, which last he did with as little inconvenience to himself as any man in the barony of Moyferta; and were I to add Clanderalaw and Ibrickan, I don't think I should say wrong.

On the death of Florence Cantillon, Connor Crowe was determined to satisfy himself about the truth of this story of the old church under the sea: so when he heard the news of the old fellow's death, away with him to Ardfert, where Flory was laid out in high style, and a beautiful corpse he made.

Flory had been as jolly and as rollicking a boy in his day as ever was stretched, and his wake was in every respect worthy of him. There was all kind of entertainment, and all sort of diversion at it, and no less than three girls got husbands there—more luck to them. Everything was as it should be; all that side of the country, from Dingle to Tarbert, was at the funeral. The Keen was sung long and bitterly; and, according to the family custom, the coffin was carried to Ballyheigh strand, where it

was laid upon the shore, with a prayer for the repose of
the dead.

The mourners departed, one group after another, and at
last Connor Crowe was left alone. He then pulled out
his whisky bottle, his drop of comfort, as he called it,
which he required, being in grief; and down he sat upon
a big stone that was sheltered by a projecting rock, and
partly concealed from view, to await with patience the
appearance of the ghostly undertakers.

The evening came on mild and beautiful. He whistled
an old air which he had heard in his childhood, hoping to
keep idle fears out of his head; but the wild strain of
that melody brought a thousand recollections with it,
which only made the twilight appear more pensive.

"If 'twas near the gloomy tower of Dunmore, in my
own sweet country, I was," said Connor Crowe, with a
sigh, "one might well believe that the prisoners, who
were murdered long ago there in the vaults under the
castle, would be the hands to carry off the coffin out of
envy, for never a one of them was buried decently, nor
had as much as a coffin amongst them all. 'Tis often,
sure enough, I have heard lamentations and great mourning coming from the vaults of Dunmore Castle; but,"
continued he, after fondly pressing his lips to the mouth
of his companion and silent comforter, the whisky bottle,
"didn't I know all the time well enough, 'twas the dismal
sounding waves working through the cliffs and hollows of
the rocks, and fretting themselves to foam. Oh, then,
Dunmore Castle, it is you that are the gloomy-looking
tower on a gloomy day, with the gloomy hills behind you;
when one has gloomy thoughts on their heart, and sees
you like a ghost rising out of the smoke made by the kelp
burners on the strand, there is, the Lord save us! as fearful a look about you as about the Blue Man's Lake at
midnight. Well, then, anyhow," said Connor, after a
pause, "is it not a blessed night, though surely the moon
looks mighty pale in the face? St. Senan himself between
us and all kinds of harm."

It was, in truth, a lovely moonlight night; nothing was to be seen around but the dark rocks, and the white pebbly beach, upon which the sea broke with a hoarse and melancholy murmur. Connor, notwithstanding his frequent draughts, felt rather queerish, and almost began to repent his curiosity. It was certainly a solemn sight to behold the black coffin resting upon the white strand. His imagination gradually converted the deep moaning of old ocean into a mournful wail for the dead, and from the shadowy recesses of the rocks he imaged forth strange and visionary forms.

As the night advanced, Connor became weary with watching. He caught himself more than once in the act of nodding, when suddenly giving his head a shake, he would look towards the black coffin. But the narrow house of death remained unmoved before him.

It was long past midnight, and the moon was sinking into the sea, when he heard the sound of many voices, which gradually became stronger, above the heavy and monotonous roll of the sea. He listened, and presently could distinguish a Keen of exquisite sweetness, the notes of which rose and fell with the heaving of the waves, whose deep murmur mingled with and supported the strain!

The Keen grew louder and louder, and seemed to approach the beach, and then fell into a low, plaintive wail. As it ended Connor beheld a number of strange and, in the dim light, mysterious-looking figures emerge from the sea, and surround the coffin, which they prepared to launch into the water.

" This comes of marrying with the creatures of earth," said one of the figures, in a clear, yet hollow tone.

" True," replied another, with a voice still more fearful, " our king would never have commanded his gnawing white-toothed waves to devour the rocky roots of the island cemetery, had not his daughter, Durfulla, been buried there by her mortal husband !"

" But the time will come," said a third bending over the coffin,

> " When mortal eye—our work shall spy,
> And mortal ear—our dirge shall hear."

"Then," said a fourth, "our burial of the Cantillons is at an end forever ! "

As this was spoken the coffin was borne from the beach by a retiring wave, and the company of sea people prepared to follow it ; but at the moment one chanced to discover Connor Crowe, as fixed with wonder and as motionless with fear as the stone on which he sat.

" The time is come," cried the unearthly being, " the time is come; a human eye looks on the forms of ocean, a human ear has heard their voices. Farewell to the Cantillions; the sons of the sea are no longer doomed to bury the dust of the earth ! "

One after the other turned slowly round, and regarded Connor Crowe, who still remained as if bound by a spell. Again arose their funeral song; and on the next wave they followed the coffin. The sound of the lamentation died away, and at length nothing was heard but the rush of waters. The coffin and the train of sea people sank over the old churchyard, and never since the funeral of old Flory Cantillon have any of the family been carried to the strand of Ballyheigh, for conveyance to their rightful burial-place, beneath the waves of the Atlantic.

THE GREEK PRINCESS AND THE YOUNG GARDENER.

THERE was once a king, but I didn't hear what country he was over, and he had one very beautiful daughter. Well, he was getting old and sickly, and the doctors found out that the finest medicine in the world for him was the apples of a tree that grew in the orchard just under his window. So you may be sure he had the tree well minded, and used to get the apples counted from the time they were the size of small marbles. One harvest, just as they were beginning to turn ripe, the king was awakened one night by the flapping of wings outside in the orchard; and when he looked out, what did he see but a bird among the branches of his tree. Its feathers were so bright that they made a light all round them, and the minute it saw the king in his night-cap and night-shirt it picked off an apple, and flew away. "Oh, botheration to that thief of a gardener!" says the king, "this is a nice way he's watching my precious fruit."

He didn't sleep a wink the rest of the night; and as soon as any one was stirring in the palace, he sent for the gardener, and abused him for his neglect.

"Please your Majesty!" says he, "not another apple you shall lose. My three sons are the best shots at the bow and arrow in the kingdom, and they and myself will watch in turn every night."

When the night came, the gardener's eldest son took his post in the garden, with his bow strung and his arrow between his fingers, and watched, and watched. But at the dead hour, the king, that was wide awake, heard the flapping of wings, and ran to the window. There was the

113

bright bird in the tree, and the boy fast asleep, sitting with his back to the wall, and his bow on his lap.

" Rise, you lazy thief ! " says the king, " there's the bird again, botheration to her ! "

Up jumped the poor fellow ; but while he was fumbling with the arrow and the string, away was the bird with the nicest apple on the tree. Well, to be sure, how the king fumed and fretted, and how he abused the gardener and the boy, and what a twenty-four hours he spent till midnight came again !

He had his eye this time on the second son of the gardener ; but though he was up and lively enough when the clock began to strike twelve, it wasn't done with the last bang when he saw him stretched like one dead on the long grass, and saw the bright bird again, and heard the flap of her wings, and saw her carry away the third apple. The poor fellow woke with the roar the king let at him, and even was in time enough to let fly an arrow after the bird. He did not hit her, you may depend ; and though the king was mad enough, he saw the poor fellows were under *pishtrogues*, and could not help it.

Well, he had some hopes out of the youngest, for he was a brave, active young fellow, that had everybody's good word. There he was ready, and there was the king watching him, and talking to him at the first stroke of twelve. At the last clang, the brightness coming before the bird lighted up the wall and the trees, and the rushing of the wings was heard as it flew into the branches ; but at the same instant the crack of the arrow on her side might be heard a quarter of a mile off. Down came the arrow and a large bright feather along with it, and away was the bird, with a screech that was enough to break the drum of your ear. She hadn't time to carry off an apple ; and bedad, when the feather was thrown up into the king's room it was heavier than lead, and turned out to be the finest beaten gold.

Well, there was great *cooramuch* made about the youngest boy next day, and he watched night after night

for a week, but not a mite of a bird or bird's feather was
to be seen, and then the king told him to go home and
sleep. Every one admired the beauty of the gold feather
beyond anything, but the king was fairly bewitched. He
was turning it round and round, and rubbing it against
his forehead and his nose the livelong day ; and at last
he proclaimed that he'd give his daughter and half his
kingdom to whoever would bring him the bird with the
gold feathers, dead or alive.

The gardener's eldest son had great conceit of himself,
and away he went to look for the bird. In the afternoon
he sat down under a tree to rest himself, and eat a bit of
bread and cold meat that he had in his wallet, when up
comes as fine a looking fox as you'd see in the burrow of
Munfin. "Musha, sir," says he, "would you spare a bit
of that meat to a poor body that's hungry?"

"Well," says the other, "you must have the divil's own
assurance, you common robber, to ask me such a question. Here's the answer," and he let fly at the *moddhereen rua.*

The arrow scraped from his side up over his back, as if
he was made of hammered iron, and stuck in a tree a
couple of perches off.

"Foul play," says the fox; "but I respect your young
brother, and will give a bit of advice. At nightfall you'll
come into a village. One side of the street you'll see a
large room lighted up, and filled with young men and
women, dancing and drinking. The other side you'll see
a house with no light, only from the fire in the front
room, and no one near it but a man and his wife, and their
child. Take a fool's advice, and get lodging there."
With that he curled his tail over his crupper, and trotted
off.

The boy found things as the fox said, but *begonies* he
chose the dancing and drinking, and there we'll leave
him. In a week's time, when they got tired at home
waiting for him, the second son said he'd try his fortune,
and off he set. He was just as ill-natured and foolish as

his brother, and the same thing happened to him. Well, when a week was over, away went the youngest of all, and as sure as the hearth-money, he sat under the same tree, and pulled out his bread and meat, and the same fox came up and saluted him. Well, the young fellow shared his dinner with the *moddhereen*, and he wasn't long beating about the bush, but told the other he knew all about his business.

"I'll help you," says he, "if I find you're biddable. So just at nightfall you'll come into a village. . . . . Good-bye till to-morrow."

It was just as the fox said, but the boy took care not to go near dancer, drinker, fiddler, or piper. He got welcome in the quiet house to supper and bed, and was on his journey next morning before the sun was the height of the trees.

He wasn't gone a quarter of a mile when he saw the fox coming out of a wood that was by the roadside.

"Good-morrow, fox," says one.

"Good-morrow, sir," says the other.

"Have you any notion how far you have to travel till you find the golden bird?"

"Dickens a notion have I ;—how could I ? "

"Well, I have. She's in the King of Spain's palace, and that's a good two hundred miles off."

"Oh, dear! we'll be a week going."

"No, we won't. Sit down on my tail, and we'll soon make the road short."

"Tail, indeed! that 'ud be the droll saddle, my poor *moddhereen*."

"Do as I tell you, or I'll leave you to yourself."

Well, rather than vex him he sat down on the tail that was spread out level like a wing, and away they went like thought. They overtook the wind that was before them, and the wind that came after didn't overtake them. In the afternoon, they stopped in a wood near the King of Spain's palace, and there they stayed till nightfall.

"Now," says the fox, "I'll go before you to make the

minds of the guards easy, and you'll have nothing to do but go from lighted hall to another lighted hall till you find the golden bird in the last. If you have a head on you, you'll bring himself and his cage outside the door, and no one then can lay hands on him or you. If you haven't a head I can't help you, nor no one else." So he went over to the gates.

In a quarter of an hour the boy followed, and in the first hall he passed he saw a score of armed guards standing upright, but all dead asleep. In the next he saw a dozen, and in the next half a dozen, and in the next three, and in the room beyond that there was no guard at all, nor lamp, nor candle, but it was as bright as day; for there was the golden bird in a common wood and wire cage, and on the table were the three apples turned into solid gold.

On the same table was the most lovely golden cage eye ever beheld, and it entered the boy's head that it would be a thousand pities not to put the precious bird into it, the common cage was so unfit for her. Maybe he thought of the money it was worth; anyhow he made the exchange, and he had soon good reason to be sorry for it. The instant the shoulder of the bird's wing touched the golden wires, he let such a *squawk* out of him as was enough to break all the panes of glass in the windows, and at the same minute the three men, and the half-dozen, and the dozen, and the score men, woke up and clattered their swords and spears, and surrounded the poor boy, and jibed, and cursed, and swore at hime, till he didn't know whether it's his foot or head he was standing on. They called the king, and told him what happened, and he put on a very grim face. " It's on a gibbet you ought to be this moment," says he, " but I'll give you a chance of your life, and of the golden bird, too. I lay you under prohibitions, and restrictions, and death, and destruction, to go and bring me the King of *Moroco's* bay filly that outruns the wind, and leaps over the walls of castle-bawns. When you fetch her into the bawn of this palace, you must get the golden bird, and liberty to go where you please."

Out passed the boy, very down-hearted, but as he went along, who should come out of a brake but the fox again.

"Ah, my friend," says he, "I was right when I sunpected you hadn't a head on you; but I won't rub your hair again' the grain. Get on my tail again, and when we

come to the King of Moroco's palace, we'll see what we can do."

So away they went like thought. The wind that was before them they would overtake; the wind that was behind them would not overtake them.

Well, the nightfall came on them in a wood near the palace, and says the fox, "I'll go and make things easy for you at the stables, and when you are leading out the filly, don't let her touch the door, nor doorposts, nor anything but the ground, and that with her hoofs ; and if you haven't a head on you once you are in the stable, you'll be worse off than before."

So the boy delayed for a quarter of an hour, and then he went into the big bawn of the palace. There were two rows of armed men reaching from the gate to the stable, and every man was in the depth of deep sleep, and through them went the boy till he got into the stable. There was the filly, as handsome a beast as ever stretched leg, and there was one stable-boy with a currycomb in his hand, and another with a bridle, and another with a sieve of oats, and another with an armful of hay, and all as if they were cut out of stone. The filly was the only live thing in the place except himself. She had a common wood and leather saddle on her back, but a golden saddle with the nicest work on it was hung from the post, and he thought it the greatest pity not to put it in place of the other. Well, I believe there was some *pishrogues* over it for a saddle ; anyhow, he took off the other, and put the gold one in its place.

Out came a squeal from the filly's throat when she felt the strange article, that might be heard from Tombrick to Bunclody, and all as ready were the armed men and the stable-boys to run and surround the *omadhan* of a boy, and the King of Moróco was soon there along with the rest, with a face on him as black as the sole of your foot. After he stood enjoying the abuse the poor boy got from everybody for some time, he says to him, " You deserve high hanging for your impudence, but I'll give you a chance for your life and the filly, too. I lay on you all sorts of prohibitions, and restrictions, and death, and destruction to go bring me Princess Golden Locks, the King of Greek's daughter. When you deliver her into my hand, you may have the ' daughter of the wind,' and welcome. Come in and take your supper and your rest, and be off at the flight of night."

The poor boy was down in the mouth, you may suppose, as he was walking away next morning, and very

much ashamed when the fox looked up in his face after
coming out of the wood.

"What a thing it is," says he, "not to have a head
when a body wants it worst; and here we have a fine
long journey before us to the King of Greek's palace.
The worse luck now, the same always. Here, get on my
tail, and we'll be making the road shorter."

So he sat on the fox's tail, and swift as thought they
went. The wind that was before them they would overtake it, the wind that was behind them would not overtake them, and in the evening they were eating their
bread and cold meat in the wood near the castle.

"Now," says the fox, when they were done, "I'll go
before you to make things easy. Follow me in a quarter
of an hour. Don't let Princess Golden Locks touch the
jambs of the doors with her hands, or hair, or clothes, and
if you're asked any favor, mind how you answer. Once
she's outside the door, no one can take her from you."

Into the palace walked the boy at the proper time, and
there were the score, and the dozen, and the half-dozen,
and the three guards all standing up or leaning on their
arms, and all dead asleep, and in the farthest room of all
was the Princess Golden Locks, as lovely as Venus herself. She was asleep in one chair, and her father, the
King of Greek, in another. He stood before her for ever
so long with the love sinking deeper into his heart every
minute, till at last he went down on one knee, and took
her darling white hand in his hand, and kissed it.

When she opened her eyes, she was a little frightened,
but I believe not very angry, for the boy, as I call him,
was a fine handsome young fellow, and all the respect and
love that ever you could think of was in his face. She
asked him what he wanted, and he stammered, and blushed,
and began his story six times, before she understood it.

"And would you give me up to that ugly black King
of Moroco?" says she.

"I am obliged to do so," says he, "by prohibitions, and
restrictions, and death, and destruction, but I'll have his

The Princess asked leave to kiss the old man; that wouldn't waken him, and then she'd go.—Page 121. *Irish Fairy Tales.*

life and free you, or lose my own. If I can't get you for
my wife, my days on the earth will be short."

" Well," says she, "let me take leave of my father at
any rate."

" Ah, I can't do that," says he, " or they'd all waken,
and myself would be put to death, or sent to some task
worse than any I got yet."

But she asked leave at any rate to kiss the old man;
that wouldn't waken him, and then she'd go. How could
he refuse her, and his heart tied up in every curl of
her hair? But, bedad the moment her lips touched her
father's, he let a cry, and every one of the score, the
dozen guards woke up, and clashed their arms, and were
going to make *gibbets* of the foolish boy.

But the king ordered them to hold their hands, till he'd
be *insensed* of what it was all about, and when he heard
the boy's story he gave him a chance for his life.

" There is," says he, " a great heap of clay in front of
the palace, that won't let the sun shine on the walls in
the middle of summer. Every one that ever worked at it
found two shovelfuls added to it for every one they threw
away. Remove it, and I'll let my daugher go with you.
If you're the man I suspect you to be, I think she'll be in
no danger of being wife to that yellow *Molott*."

Early next morning was the boy tackled to his work,
and for every shovelful he flung away two came back on
him, and at last he could hardly get out of the heap that
gathered round him. Well, the poor fellow scrambled
out some way, and sat down on a sod, and he'd have cried
only for the shame of it. He began at it in ever so many
places, and one was still worse than the other, and in the
heel of the evening, when he was sitting with his head
between his hands, who should be standing before him
but the fox.

" Well, my poor fellow," says he, " you're low enough.
Go in: I won't say anything to add to your trouble.
Take your supper and your rest: to-morrow will be a new
day."

"How is the work going off?" says the king, when they were at supper.

"Faith, your Majesty," says the poor boy, "it's not going off, but coming on it is. I suppose you'll have the trouble of digging me out at sunset to-morrow, and waking me."

"I hope not," says the princess, with a smile on her kind face; and the boy was as happy as anything the rest of the evening.

He was wakened up the next morning with voices shouting, and bugles blowing, and drums beating, and such a hullibulloo he never heard in his life before. He ran out to see what was the matter, and there, where the heap of clay was the evening before, were soldiers, and servants, and lords, and ladies, dancing like mad for joy that it was gone.

"Ah, my poor fox!" says he to himself, "this is your work."

Well there was little delay about his return. The king was going to send a great retinue with the princess and himself, but he wouldn't let him take the trouble.

"I have a friend," says he, "that will bring us both to the King of Moroco's palace in a day, d—— fly away with him!"——

There was great crying when she was parting from her father.

"Ah!" says he, "what a lonesome life I'll have now! Your poor brother in the power of that wicked witch, and kept away from us, and now you taken from me in my old age!"

Well, they both were walking on through the wood, and he telling her how much he loved her; out walked the fox from behind a brake, and in a short time he and she were sitting on the brush, and holding one another fast for fear of slipping off, and away they went like thought. The wind that was before them they would overtake it, and in the evening he and she were in the big bawn of the King of Moroco's castle.

" Well," says he to the boy, " you've done your duty
well ; bring out the bay filly. I'd give the full of the
bawn of such fillies, if I had them, for this handsome
princess. Get on your steed, and here is a good purse of
guineas for the road."

" Thank you," says he. " I suppose you'll let me shake
hands with the princess before I start."

" Yes, indeed, and welcome."

Well, he was some little time about the hand-shaking,
and before it was over he had her fixed snug behind him ;
and while you could count three, he, and she, and the
filly were through all the guards, and a hundred perches
away. On they went, and next morning they were in the
wood near the King of Spain's palace, and there was the
fox before them.

" Leave your princess here with me," says he, " and go
get the golden bird and the three apples. If you don't
bring us back the filly along with the bird, I must carry
you both home myself."

Well, when the King of Spain saw the boy and the filly
in the bawn, he made the golden bird, and the golden cage,

and the golden apples be brought out and handed to him, and was very thankful and very glad of his prize. But the boy could not part with the nice beast without petting it and rubbing it; and while no one was expecting such a thing, he was on its back, and through the guards, and a hundred perches away, and he wasn't long till he came to where he left his princess and the fox.

They hurried away till they were safe out of the King of Spain's land, and then they went on easier; and if I was to tell you all the loving things they said to one another, the story wouldn't be over till morning. When they were passing the village of the dance house they found his two brothers begging, and they brought them along. When they came to where the fox appeared first, he begged the young man to cut off his head and his tail. He would not do it for him; he shivered at the very thought, but the eldest brother was ready enough. The head and tail vanished with the blows, and the body changed into the finest young man you could see, and who was he but the princess's brother that was bewitched. Whatever joy they had before, they had twice as much now, and when they arrived at the palace bonfires were set blazing, oxes roasting, and puncheons of wine put out in the lawn. The young Prince of Greece was married to the king's daughter, and the prince's sister to the gardener's son. He and she went a shorter way back to her father's house, with many attendants, and the king was so glad of the golden bird and the golden apples, that he had sent a wagon full of gold and a wagon full of silver along with them.

THE SOLITARY FAÏRIES.*

LEPRACAUN.   CLURICAUN.   FAR DARRIG.

" THE name *Lepracaun*," Mr. Douglas Hyde writes to me, "is from the Irish *leith brog*—*i.e.*, the One-shoemaker, since he is generally seen working at a single shoe. It is spelt in Irish *leith bhrogan*, or *leith phrogan*, and is in some places pronounced Luchryman, as O'Kearney writes it in that very rare book, the *Feis Tigh Chonain*."

The *Lepracaun*, *Cluricaun*, and *Far Darrig*. Are these one spirit in different moods and shapes? Hardly two Irish writers are agreed. In many things these three fairies, if three, resemble each other. They are withered, old, and solitary, in every way unlike the sociable spirits of the first sections. They dress with all unfairy homeliness, and are, indeed, most sluttish, slouching, jeering, mischievous phantoms. They are the great practical jokers among the good people.

The *Lepracaun* makes shoes continually, and has grown very rich. Many treasure-crocks, buried of old in war-time, has he now for his own. In the early part of this century, according to Croker, in a newspaper office in

---

* The trooping fairies wear green jackets, the solitary ones red. On the red jacket of the Lepracaun, according to Mc-Anally, are seven rows of buttons—seven buttons in each row. On the western coast, he says, the red jacket is covered by a frieze one; and in Ulster the creature wears a cocked hat, and when he is up to anything unusually mischievous, leaps on to a wall and spins, balancing himself on the point of the hat with his heels in the air. McAnally tells how once a peasant saw a battle between the green jacket fairies and the red. When the green jackets began to win, so delighted was he to see the green above the red, he gave a great shout. In a moment all vanished and he was flung into the ditch.

125

Tipperary, they used to show a little shoe forgotten by a Lepracaun.

The *Cluricaun*, (*Clobhair-ceann*, in O'Kearney) makes himself drunk in gentlemen's cellars. Some suppose he is merely the Lepracaun on a spree. He is almost unknown in Connaught and the north.

The *Far Darring* (*fear dearg*), which means the Red Man, for he wears a red cap and coat, busies himself with practical joking, especially with gruesome joking. This he does, and nothing else.

The *Fear-Gorta* (Man of Hunger) is an emaciated phantom that goes through the land in famine time, begging an alms and bringing good luck to the giver.

There are other solitary fairies, such as the House-spirit and the *Water-sheerie*, own brother to the English Jack-o'-Lantern; the *Pooka* and the *Banshee*—concerning these presently; the *Dallahan*, or headless phantom—one used to stand in a Sligo street on dark nights till lately; the Black Dog, a form, perhaps, of the *Pooka*. The ships at the Sligo quays are haunted sometimes by this spirit, who announces his presence by a sound like the flinging of all "the tin porringers in the world" down into the hold. He even follows them to see.

The Leanhaun Shee (fairy mistress), seeks the love of mortals. If they refuse, she must be their slave; if they consent, they are hers, and can only escape by finding another to take their place. The fairy lives on their life, and they waste away. Death is no escape from her. She is the Gaelic muse, for she gives inspiration to those she persecutes. The Gaelic poets die young, for she is restless, and will not let them remain long on earth—this malignant phantom.

Besides these are divers monsters—the *Augh-iska*, the Water-horse, the Payshtha (*piast=bestia*), the Lake-dragon, and such like; but whether these be animals, fairies, or spirits, I know not.

THE LEPRACAUN; OR, FAIRY SHOEMAKER.

WILLIAM ALLINGHAM.

I.

LITTLE Cowboy, what have you heard,
　　Up on the lonely rath's green mound?
Only the plaintive yellow bird *
　　Sighing in sultry fields around,
Chary, chary, chary, chee-ee!—
Only the grasshopper and the bee?—
　　　　" Tip tap, rip-rap,
　　　　Tick-a-tack-too!
　　　Scarlet leather, sewn together,
　　　　This will make a shoe.
　　　Left, right, pull it tight;
　　　　Summer days are warm;
　　　Underground in winter,
　　　　Laughing at the storm!"
Lay your ear close to the hill.
Do you not catch the tiny clamor,
Busy click of an elfin hammer,
Voice of the Lepracaun singing shrill
　　　As he merrily plies his trade?
　　　　He's a span
　　　And a quarter in height.
Get him in sight, hold him tight,
　　　And you're a made
　　　　Man!

II.

You watch your cattle the summer day,
Sup on potatoes, sleep in the hay;

* " Yellow bird," the yellow-bunting, or *yorlin*.

How would you like to roll in your carriage,
  Look for a duchess's daughter in marriage?
Seize the Shoemaker—then you may!
    " Big boots a-hunting,
      Sandals in the hall,
    White for a wedding-feast,
      Pink for a ball.
    This way, that way,
      So we make a shoe;
    Getting rich every stitch,
      Tick-tack-too! "
Nine-and-ninety treasure-crocks
This keen miser-fairy hath,
Hid in mountains, woods, and rocks,
Ruin and round-tow'r, cave and rath,
  And where the cormorants build;
        From times of old
        Guarded by him;
        Each of them fill'd
        Full to the brim
          With gold!

                      III.

I caught him at work one day, myself,
  In the castle-ditch, where foxglove grows,—
A wrinkled, wizen d, and bearded Elf,
  Spectacles stuck on his pointed nose,
  Silver buckles to his hose,
  Leather apron—shoe in his lap—
      " Rip-rap, tip-tap,
        Tick-tack-too!
      (A grasshopper on my cap!
        Away the moth flew!)
      Buskins for a fairy prince,
        Brogues for his son,—
      Pay me well, pay me well,
        When the job is done! "

The rogue was mine, beyond a doubt.
I stared at him ; he stared at me ;
" Servant, Sir ! "   " Humph ! " says he,
   And pull'd a snuff-box out.
He took a long pinch, look'd better pleased,
   The queer little Lepracaun;
Offer'd the box with a whimsical grace,—
Pouf ! he flung the dust in my face,
     And, while I sneezed,
       Was gone !

MASTER AND MAN.

T. CROFTON CROKER.

BILLY MAC DANIEL was once as likely a young man as ever shook his brogue at a patron,* emptied a quart, or handled a shillelagh ; fearing for nothing but the want of drink ; caring for nothing but who should pay for it ; and thinking of nothing but how to make fun over it ; drunk or sober, a word and a blow was ever the way with Billy Mac Daniel ; and a mighty easy way it is of either getting into or of ending a dispute.   More is the pity that, through the means of his thinking, and fearing, and caring for nothing, this same Billy Mac Daniel fell into bad company ; for surely the good people are the worst of all company any one could come across.

It so happened that Billy was going home one clear frosty night not long after Christmas ; the moon was round and bright ; but although it was as fine a night as heart could wish for, he felt pinched with cold.   " By my word," chattered Billy, " a drop of good liquor would be no bad thing to keep a man's soul from freezing in him ; and I wish I had a full measure of the best."

" Never wish it twice, Billy," said a little man in a three-

---

* A festival held in honor of some patron saint.

cornered hat, bound all about with gold lace, and with
great silver buckles in his shoes, so big that it was a wonder how he could carry them, and he held out a glass as
big as himself, filled with as good liquor as ever eye looked
on or lip tasted.

" Success, my little fellow," said Billy Mac Daniel, nothing daunted, though well he knew the little man to belong
to the *good people;* " here's your health, any way, and
thank you kindly ; no matter who pays for the drink; "
and he took the glass and drained it to the very bottom
without ever taking a second breath to it.

" Success," said the little man ; and you're heartily
welcome, Billy ; but don't think to cheat me as you have
done others,—out with your purse and pay me like a gentleman."

" Is it I pay you ? " said Billy ; " could I not just take
you up and put you in my pocket as casily as a black-
berry ? "

"Billy Mac Daniel," said the little man, getting very
angry, " you shall be my servant for seven years and a
day, and that is the way I will be paid ; so make ready to
follow me."

When Billy heard this he began to be very sorry for
having used such bold words towards the little man ; and
he felt himself, yet could not tell how, obliged to follow
the little man the livelong night about the country, up
and down, and over hedge and ditch, and through bog and
brake, without any rest.

When morning began to dawn the little man turned
round to him and said, " You may now go home, Billy,
but on your peril don't fail to meet me in the Fort-field
to-night; or if you do it may be the worse for you in the
long run.   If I find you a good servant, you will find me
an indulgent master."

Home went Billy Mac Daniel ; and though he was tired
and weary, enough, never a wink of sleep could he get for
thinking of the little man ; but he was afraid not to do his
bidding, so up he got in the evening, and away he went to

the Fort-field. He was not long there before the little
man came towards him and said, "Billy, I want to go a
long journey to-night; so saddle one of my horses, and
you may saddle another for yourself, as you are to go along
with me, and may be tired after your walk last night."

Billy thought this very considerate of his master, and
thanked him accordingly : " But," said he, " if I may be so
bold, sir, I would ask which is the way to your stable, for
never a thing do I see but the fort here, and the old thorn
tree in the corner of the field, and the stream running at
the bottom of the hill, with the bit of bog over against
us."

" Ask no questions, Billy," said the little man, "but go
over to that bit of bog, and bring me two of the strongest
rushes you can find."

Billy did accordingly, wondering what the little man
would be at ; and he picked two of the stoutest rushes
he could find, with a little bunch of brown blossom stuck
at the side of each, and brought them back to his master.

" Get up, Billy," said the little man, taking one of the
rushes from him and striding across it.

" Where shall I get up, please your honor ? " said Billy.

" Why, upon horseback, like me, to be sure," said the
little man.

" Is it after making a fool of me you'd be," said Billy,
"bidding me get a horseback upon that bit of a rush ?
May be you want to persuade me that the rush I pulled
but a while ago out of the bog over there is a horse ? "

" Up! up! and no words," said the little man, looking
very angry; " the best horse you ever rode was but a fool
to it." So Billy, thinking all this was in joke, and fearing to vex his master, straddled across the rush. " Borram! Borram! Borram!" cried the little man three
times (which, in English, means to become great), and
Billy did the same after him ; presently the rushes
swelled up into fine horses, and away they went full
speed ; but Billy, who had put the rush between his legs,
without much minding how he did it, found himself

sitting on horseback the wrong way, which was rather
awkward, with his face to the horse's tail; and so quickly
had his steed started off with him that he had no power
to turn round, and there was therefore nothing for it but
to hold on by the tail.

At last they came to their journey's end, and stopped
at the gate of a fine house. "Now, Billy," said the little
man, "do as you see me do, and follow me close; but as
you did not know your horse's head from his tail, mind
that your own head does not spin round until you can't
tell whether you are standing on it or on your heels: for
remember that old liquor, though able to make a cat
speak, can make a man dumb.'

The little man then said some queer kind of words,
out of which Billy could make no meaning; but he contrived to say them after him for all that; and in they
both went through the key-hole of the door, and through
one key-hole after another, until they got into the wine-
cellar, which was well stored with all kinds of wine.

The little man fell to drinking as hard as he could, and
Billy, noway disliking the example, did the same. "The
best of masters are you, surely," said Billy to him; "no
matter who is the next; and well pleased will I be with
your service if you continue to give me plenty to drink."

"I have made no bargain with you," said the little man,
"and will make none; but up and follow me." Away
they went, through key-hole after key-hole; and each
mounting upon the rush which he left at the hall door,
scampered off, kicking the clouds before them like snow-
balls, as soon as the words, "Borram, Borram, Borram,"
had passed their lips.

When they came back to the Fort-field the little man
dismissed Billy, bidding him to be there the next night
at the same hour. Thus did they go on, night after night,
shaping their course one night here, and another night
there; sometimes north, and sometimes east, and sometimes south, until there was not a gentleman's wine-cellar
in all Ireland they had not visited, and could tell the

flavor of every wine in it as well, ay, better than the butler himself.

One night when Billy Mac Daniel met the little man as usual in the Fort-field, and was going to the bog to fetch the horses for their journey, his master said to him, " Billy, I shall want another horse to-night, for may be we may bring back more company than we take." So Billy, who now knew better than to question any order given to him by his master, brought a third rush, much wondering who it might be that would travel back in their company, and whether he was about to have a fellow-servant.   " If I have," thought Billy, "he shall go and fetch the horses from the bog every night; for I don't see why I am not, every inch of me, as good a gentleman as my master."

Well, away they went, Billy leading the third horse, and never stopped until they came to a snug farmer's house, in the county Limerick, close under the old castle of Carrigogunniel, that was built, they say, by the great Brian Boru.   Within the house there was great carousing forward, and the little man stopped outside for some time to listen; then turning round all of a sudden, said, " Billy, I will be a thousand years old to-morrow ! "

"God bless us, sir," said Billy ; " will you ? "

" Don't say these words again, Billy," said the little old man, " or you will be my ruin forever. Now, Billy, as I will be a thousand years in the world to-morrow, I think it is full time for me to get married."

" I think so too, without any kind of doubt at all," said Billy, " if ever you mean to marry."

" And to that purpose," said the little man, " have I come all the way to Carrigogunniel ; for in this house this very night, is young Darby Riley going to be married to Bridget Rooney ; and as she is a tall and comely girl, and has come of decent people, I think of marrying her myself, and taking her off with me."

" And what will Darby Riley say to that ? " said Billy.

" Silence ! " said the little man, putting on a mighty

severe look ; " I did not bring you here with me to ask
questions ; " and without holding further argument, he
began saying the queer words which had the power of
passing him through the key-hole as free as air, and
which Billy thought himself mighty clever to be able to
say after him.

In they both went; and for the better viewing the
company, the little man perched himself up as nimbly as
a cocksparrow upon one of the big beams which went
across the house over all their heads, and Billy did the
same upon another facing him ; but not being much accustomed to roosting in such a place, his legs hung down
as untidy as may be, and it was quite clear he had not taken
pattern after the way in which the little man had bundled himself up together.   If the little man had been a
tailor all his life he could not have sat more contentedly
upon his haunches.

There they were, both master and man, looking down
upon the fun that was going forward; and under them
were the priest and piper, and the father of Darby Riley,
with Darby's two brothers and his uncle's son; and there
were both the father and the mother of Bridget Rooney,
and proud enough the old couple were that night of their
daughter, as good right they had ; and her four sisters,
with bran new ribbons in their caps, and her three brothers
all looking as clean and as clever as any three boys in
Munster, and there were uncles and aunts, and gossips and
cousins enough besides to make a full house of it ; and
plenty was there to eat and drink on the table for every
one of them, if they had been double the number.

Now it happened, just as Mrs. Rooney had helped his
reverence to the first cut of the pig's head which was
placed before her, beautifully bolstered up with white
savoys, that the bride gave a sneeze, which made every
one at table start, but not a soul said " God bless us."   All
thinking that the priest would have done so, as he ought
if he had done his duty, no one wished to take the word
out of his mouth, which, unfortunately, was preoccupied

with pig's head and greens. And after a moment's pause the fun and merriment of the bridal feast went on without the pious benediction.

Of this circumstance both Billy and his master were no inattentive spectators from their exalted stations. "Ha!" exclaimed the little man, throwing one leg from under him with a joyous flourish, and his eye twinkled with a strange light, whilst his eyebrows became elevated into the curvature of Gothic arches; "Ha!" said he, leering down at the bride, and then up at Billy, "I have half of her now, surely. Let her sneeze but twice more, and she is mine, in spite of priest, mass-book, and Darby Riley."

Again the fair Bridget sneezed; but it was so gently, and she blushed so much, that few except the little man took, or seemed to take, any notice; and no one thought of saying "God bless us."

Billy all this time regarded the poor girl with a most rueful expression of countenance; for he could not help thinking what a terrible thing it was for a nice young girl of nineteen, with large blue eyes, transparent skin, and dimpled cheeks, suffused with health and joy, to be obliged to marry an ugly little bit of a man, who was a thousand years old, barring a day.

At this critical moment the bride gave a third sneeze, and Billy roared out with all his might, "God save us!" Whether this exclamation resulted from his soliloquy, or from the mere force of habit, he never could tell exactly himself; but no sooner was it uttered than the little man, his face glowing with rage and disappointment, sprung from the beam on which he had perched himself, and shrieking out in the shrill voice of a cracked bagpipe, "I discharge you from my service, Billy Mac Daniel—take *that* for your wages," gave poor Billy a most furious kick in the back, which sent his unfortunate servant sprawling upon his face and hands right in the middle of the supper-table.

If Billy was astonished, how much more so was every one of the company into which he was thrown with so little ceremony. But when they heard his story, Father Cooney laid down his knife and fork, and married the young couple out of hand with all speed; and Billy Mac Daniel danced the Rinka at their wedding, and plenty he did drink at it too, which was what he thought more of than dancing.

FAR DARRIG IN DONEGAL.

MISS LETITIA MACLINTOCK.

PAT DIVER, the tinker, was a man well-accustomed to a wandering life, and to strange shelters; he had shared the beggar's blanket in smoky cabins; he had crouched beside the still in many a nook and corner where poteen was made on the wild Innishowen mountains; he had even slept on the bare heather, or on the ditch, with no roof over him but the vault of heaven; yet were all his nights of adventure tame and commonplace when compared with one especial night.

During the day preceding that night, he had mended all the kettles and saucepans in Moville and Greencastle, and was on his way to Culdaff, when night overtook him on a lonely mountain road.

He knocked at one door after another asking for a night's lodging, while he jingled the halfpence in his pocket, but was everywhere refused.

Where was the boasted hospitality of Innishowen, which he had never before known to fail? It was of no use to be able to pay when the people seemed so churlish. Thus thinking, he made his way towards a light a little further on, and knocked at another cabin door.

An old man and woman were seated one at each side of the fire.

" Will you be pleased to give me a night's lodging, sir?" asked Pat respectfully.

" Can you tell a story?" returned the old man.

" No, then, sir, I canna say I'm good at story-telling,"
replied the puzzled tinker.

" Then you maun just gang further, for none but them
that can tell a story will get in here."

This reply was made in so decided a tone that Pat did
not attempt to repeat his appeal, but turned away reluctantly to resume his weary journey.

" A story, indeed," muttered he. " Auld wives, fables
to please the weans ! "

As he took up his bundle of tinkering implements, he
observed a barn standing rather behind the dwelling-house,
and, aided by the rising moon, he made his way towards it.

It was a clean, roomy barn, with a piled-up heap of straw
in one corner. Here was a shelter not to be despised; so
Pat crept under the straw, and was soon asleep.

He could not have slept very long when he was awakened
by the tramp of feet, and, peeping cautiously through a
crevice in his straw covering, he saw four immensely tall
men enter the barn, dragging a body, which they threw
roughly upon the floor.

They next lighted a fire in the middle of the barn, and
fastened the corpse by the feet with a great rope to a beam
in the roof. One of them then began to turn it slowly
before the fire. " Come on," said he, addressing a gigantic
fellow, the tallest of the four—" I'm tired ; you be to tak'
your turn."

" Faix an' troth, I'll no turn him," replied the big man.
" There's Pat Diver in under the straw, why wouldn't he
tak' his turn ? "

With hideous clamor the four men called the wretched
Pat, who seeing there was no escape, thought it was his
wisest plan to come forth as he was bidden.

" Now, Pat," said they, " you'll turn the corpse, but if
you let him burn you'll be tied up there and roasted in
his place."

Pat's hair stood on end, and the cold perspiration poured
from his forehead, but there was nothing for it but to perform his dreadful task.

Seeing him fairly embarked in it, the tall men went away.

Soon, however, the flames rose so high as to singe the rope, and the corpse fell with a great thud upon the fire, scattering the ashes and embers, and extracting a howl of anguish from the miserable cook, who rushed to the door, and ran for his life.

He ran on until he was ready to drop with fatigue, when, seeing a drain overgrown with tall, rank grass, he thought he would creep in there and lie hidden till morning.

But he was not many minutes in the drain before he heard the heavy tramping again, and the four men came up with their burthen, which they laid down on the edge of the drain.

"I'm tired," said one, to the giant; "it's your turn to carry him a piece now."

"Faix and troth, I'll no carry him," replied he, "but there's Pat Diver in the drain, why wouldn't he come out and tak' his turn?"

"Come out, Pat, come out," roared all the men, and Pat, almost dead with fright, crept out.

He staggered on under the weight of the corpse until he reached Kiltown Abbey, a ruin festooned with ivy, where the brown owl hooted all night long, and the forgotten dead slept around the walls under dense, matted tangles of brambles and ben-weed.

No one ever buried there now, but Pat's tall companions turned into the wild graveyard, and began digging a grave.

Pat, seeing them thus engaged, thought he might once more try to escape, and climbed up into a hawthorn tree in the fence, hoping to be hidden in the boughs.

"I'm tired," said the man who was digging the grave; "here, take the spade," addressing the big man, "it's your turn."

"Faix an' troth, it's no my turn," replied he, as before. "There's Pat Diver in the tree, why wouldn't he come down and tak' his turn?"

Pat came down to take the spade, but just then the cocks in the little farmyards and cabins round the abbey began to crow, and the men looked at one another.

"We must go," said they, "and well is it for you, Pat Diver, that the cocks crowed, for if they had not, you'd just ha' been bundled into that grave with the corpse."

Two months passed, and Pat had wandered far and wide over the county Donegal, when he chanced to arrive at Raphoe during a fair.

Among the crowd that filled the Diamond he came suddenly on the big man.

"How are you, Pat Diver?" said he, bending down to look into the tinker's face.

"You've the advantage of me, sir, for I havna' the pleasure of knowing you," faltered Pat,

"Do you not know me, Pat?"   Whisper—"When you go back to Innishowen, you'll have a story to tell!"

THE POOKA.

THE Pooka, *rectè* Púca, seems essentially an animal spirit. Some derive his name from *poc*, a he-goat; and speculative persons consider him the forefather of Shakespeare's "Puck." On solitary mountains and among old ruins he lives, " grown monstrous with much solitude," and is of the race of the nightmare. " In the M S. story, called ' Mac-na-Michomhairle,' of uncertain authorship," writes me Mr. Douglas Hyde, " we read that ' out of a certain hill in Leinster, there used to emerge as far as his middle, a plump, sleek, terrible steed, and speak in human voice to each person about November-day, and he was accustomed to give intelligent and proper answers to such as consulted him concerning all that would befall them until the November of next year. And the people used to leave gifts and presents at the hill until the coming of Patrick and the holy clergy. This tradition appears to be a cognate one which that of the Púca." Yes! unless it were merely an *augh-ishka* [*each-uisgè*], or Water-horse. For these, we are told, were common once, and used to come out of the water to gallop on the sands and in the fields, and people would often go between them and the marge and bridle them, and they would make the finest of horses if only you could keep them away from sight of the water; but if once they saw a glimpse of the water, they would plunge in with their rider, and tear him to pieces at the bottom. It being a November spirit, however, tells in favor of the Pooka, for November-day is sacred to the Pooka. It is hard to realize that wild, staring phantom grown sleek and civil.

He has many shapes—is now a horse, now an ass, now
140

a bull, now a goat, now an eagle. Like all spirits, he is only half in the world of form.

THE PIPER AND THE PUCA.

DOUGLAS HYDE.

Translated literally from the Irish of the *Leabbar Sgeulaighe-achta*.

IN the old times, there was a half fool living in Dunmore, in the county Galway, and although he was excessively fond of music, he was unable to learn more than one tune, and that was the " Black Rogue." He used to get a good deal of money from the gentlemen, for they used to get sport out of him. One night the piper was coming home from a house where there had been a dance, and he half drunk. When he came to a little bridge that was up by his mother's house, he squeezed the pipes on, and began playing the " Black Rogue " (an rógaire dubh). The Púca came behind him, and flung him up on his own back. There were long horns on the Púca, and the piper got a good grip of them, and then he said—

" Destruction on you, you nasty beast, let me home. I have a ten-penny piece in my pocket for my mother, and she wants snuff."

" Never mind your mother," said the Púca, " but keep your hold. If you fall, you will break your neck and your pipes." Then the Púca said to him, " Play up for me the 'Shan Van Vocht' (an t-seann-bhean bhocht)."

" I don't know it," said the piper.

" Never mind whether you do or you don't," said the Púca. " Play up, and I'll make you know."

The piper put wind in his bag, and he played such music as made himself wonder.

" Upon my word, you're a fine music-master," says the piper then ; " but tell me where you're for bringing me."

" There's a great feast in the house of the Banshee, on

the top of Croagh Patric to-night," says the Púca, "and I'm for bringing you there to play music, and, take my word, you'll get the price of your trouble."

"By my word, you'll save me a journey, then," says the piper, "for Father William put a journey to Croagh Patric on me, because I stole the white gander from him last Martinmas."

The Púca rushed him across hills and bogs and rough places, till he brought him to the top of Croagh Patric. Then the Púca struck three blows with his foot, and a great door opened, and they passed in together, into a fine room.

The piper saw a golden table in the middle of the room, and hundreds of old women (cailleacha) sitting round about it. The old women rose up, and said, "A hundred thousand welcomes to you, you Púca of November (na Samhna). Who is this you have with you?"

"The best piper in Ireland," says the Púca.

One of the old women struck a blow on the ground, and a door opened in the side of the wall, and what should the piper see coming out but the white gander which he had stolen from Father William.

"By my conscience, then," says the piper, "myself and my mother ate every taste of that gander, only one wing, and I gave that to Moy-rua (Red Mary), and it's she told the priest I stole his gander."

The gander cleaned the table, and carried it away, and the Púca said, "Play up music for these ladies."

The piper played up, and the old women began dancing, and they were dancing till they were tired. Then Púca said to pay the piper, and every old women drew out a gold piece, and gave it to him.

"By the tooth of Patric," said he, "I'm as rich as the son of a lord."

"Come with me," says the Púca, "and I'll bring you home."

They went out then, and just as he was going to ride on the Púca, the gander came up to him, and gave him a

new set of pipes. The Púca was not long until he brought
him to Dunmore, and he threw the piper off at the little
bridge, and then he told him to go home, and says to him,
" You have two things now that you never had before—
you have sense and music (ciall agus ceól).

The piper went home, and he knocked at his mother's
door, saying, " Let me in, I'm as rich as a lord, and I'm
the best piper in Ireland."

" You're drunk," said the mother.

" No, indeed," says the piper, "I haven't drunk a
drop."

The mother let him in, and he gave her the gold
pieces, and, " Wait now," says he " till you hear the music
I'll play."

He buckled on the pipes, but instead of music, there
came a sound as if all the geese and ganders in Ireland
were screeching together. He wakened the neighbors,
and they were all mocking him, until he put on the old
pipes, and then he played melodious music for them ;
and after that he told them all he had gone through that
night.

The next morning, when his mother went to look at
the gold pieces, there was nothing there but the leaves
of a plant.

The piper went to the priest, and told him his story,
but the priest would not believe a word from him, until
he put the pipes on him, and then the screeching of the
ganders and geese began.

" Leave my sight, you thief," says the priest.

But nothing would do the piper till he would put the
old pipes on him to show the priest that his story was
true.

He buckled on the old pipes, and he played melodious
music, and from that day till the day of his death, there
was never a piper in the county Galway was as good as he
was.

DANIEL O'ROURKE.

T. CROFTON CROKER.

PEOPLE may have heard of the renowned adventures of
Daniel O'Rourke, but how few are there who knew that
the cause of all his perils, above and below, was neither
more nor less than his having slept under the walls of
the Pooka's town. I knew the man well. He lived at
the bottom of Hungry Hill, just at the right-hand side
of the road as you go towards Bantry. An old man was
he, at the time he told me the story, with gray hair
and a red nose; and it was on the 25th of June, 1813,
that I heard it from his own lips, as he sat smoking hi
pipe under the old poplar tree, on as fine an evening as
ever shone from the sky. I was going to visit the caves
in Dursey Island, having spent the morning at Glen-
gariff.

"I am often *axed* to tell it, sir," said he, "so that this
is not the first time. The master's son, you see, had
come from beyond foreign parts in France and Spain as
young gentlemen used to go before Buonaparte or any
such was heard of; and sure enough there was a dinner
given to all the people on the ground, gentle and simple,
high and low, rich and poor. The *ould* gentlemen were
the gentlemen after all, saving your honor's presence.
They'd swear at a body a little, to be sure, and, may be,
give one a cut of a whip now and then, but we were no
losers by it in the end; and they were so easy and civil,
and kept such rattling houses, and thousands of welcomes;
and there was no grinding for rent, and there was hardly
a tenant on the estate that did not taste of his landlord's
bounty often and often in a year; but now it's another
thing. No matter for that, sir, for I'd better be telling
you my story.

"Well, we had everything of the best, and plenty of it; and we ate, and we drank, and we danced, and the young master by the same token danced with Peggy Barry, from the Bohereen—a lovely young couple they were, though they are both low enough now. To make a long story short, I got, as a body may say, the same thing as tipsy almost, for I can't remember ever at all, no ways, how it was I left the place; only I did leave it, that's certain. Well, I thought, for all that, in myself, I'd just step to Molly Cronohan's, the fairy woman, to speak a word about the bracket heifer that was bewitched; and so as I was crossing the stepping-stones of the ford of Ballyashenogh, and was looking up at the stars and blessing myself—for why? it was Lady-day—I missed my foot, and souse I fell into the water. 'Death alive!' thought I, 'I'll be drowned now!' However, I began swimming, swimming, swimming away for the dear life, till at last I got ashore, somehow or other, but never the one of me can tell how, upon a *dissolute* island.

" I wandered and wandered about there, without knowing where I wandered, until at last I got into a big bog. The moon was shining as bright as day, or your fair lady's eyes, sir (with your pardon for mentioning her), and I looked east and west, and north and south, and every way, and nothing did I see but bog, bog, bog—I could never find out how I got into it; and my heart grew cold with fear, for sure and certain I was that it would be my *berrin* place. So I sat down upon a stone which, as good luck would have it, was close by me, and I began to scratch my head, and sing the *Ullagone*—when all of a sudden the moon grew black, and I looked up, and saw something for all the world as if it was moving down between me and it, and I could not tell what it was. Down it came with a pounce, and looked at me full in the face; and what was it but an eagle? as fine a one as ever flew from the kingdom of Kerry. So he looked at me in the face, and says he to me, 'Daniel O'Rourke,' says he, 'how do you do?' 'Very well, I thank you, sir,' says I;

'I hope you're well;' wondering out of my senses all the time how an eagle came to speak like a Christian. 'What brings you here, Dan,' says he. 'Nothing at all, sir,' says I; 'only I wish I was safe home again.' 'Is it out of the island you want to go, Dan?' says he. ''Tis, sir,' says I: so I up and told him how I had taken a drop too much, and fell into the water; how I swam to the island; and how I got into the bog and did not know my way out of it. 'Dan,' says he, after a minute's thought, 'though it is very improper for you to get drunk on Lady-day, yet as you are a decent sober man, who 'tends mass well, and never fling stones at me or mine, nor cries out after us in the fields—my life for yours,' says he; 'so get up on my back, and grip me well for fear you'd fall off, and I'll fly you out of the bog.' 'I am afraid,' says I, 'your honor's making game of me; for who ever heard of riding a horseback on an eagle before?' ''Pon the honor of a gentleman,' says he, putting his right foot on his breast, 'I am quite in earnest: and so now either take my offer or starve in the bog—besides, I see that your weight is sinking the stone.'

"It was true enough as he said, for I found the stone every minute going from under me. I had no choice; so thinks I to myself, faint heart never won fair lady, and this is fair persuadance. 'I thank your honor,' says I, 'for the loan of your civility; and I'll take your kind offer.' I therefore mounted upon the back of the eagle, and held him tight enough by the throat, and up he flew in the air like a lark. Little I knew the trick he was going to serve me. Up—up—up, God knows how far up he flew. 'Why then,' said I to him—thinking he did not know the right road home—very civilly, because why? I was in his power entirely; 'sir,' says I, 'please your honor's glory, and with humble submission to your better judgment, if you'd fly down a bit, you're now just over my cabin, and I could be put down there, and many thanks to your worship.'

"'Arrah, Dan,' said he, 'do you think me a fool?

Look down in the next field, and don't you see two men
and a gun? By my word it would be no joke to be shot
this way, to oblige a drunken blackguard that I picked
up off a *could* stone in a bog.' 'Bother you,' said I to
myself, but I did not speak out, for where was the use?
Well, sir, up he kept, flying, flying, and I asking him
every minute to fly down, and all to no use. 'Where in
the world are you going, sir?' says I to him. 'Hold
your tongue, Dan,' says he: 'Mind your own business,
and don't be interfering with the business of other people.'
'Faith, this is my business, I think,' says I. 'Be quiet,
Dan,' says he: so I said no more.

"At last where should we come to, but to the moon
itself. Now you can't see it from this, but there is, or
there was in my time, a reaping-hook sticking out of the
side of the moon, this way (drawing the figure on the
ground with the end of his stick).

"'Dan,' said the eagle, 'I'm tired with this long fly; I
had no notion 'twas so far.' 'And my lord, sir,' said I,
'who in the world *axed* you to fly so far—was it I? did
not I beg and pray and beseech you to stop half an hour
ago?' 'There's no use talking, Dan,' said he: 'I'm tired
bad enough, so you must get off, and sit down on the
moon until I rest myself.' 'Is it sit down on the moon?'
said I; 'is it upon that little round thing, then? why,
then, sure I'd fall off in a minute, and be *kilt* and spilt,
and smashed all to bits; you are a vile deceiver—so you
are.' 'Not at all, Dan,' said he; 'you can catch fast hold
of the reaping-hook that's sticking out of the side of the
moon, and 'twill keep you up.' 'I won't then,' said I.
'May be not,' said he, quite quiet. 'If you don't, my man,
I shall just give you a shake, and one slap of my wing,
and send you down to the ground, where every bone in
your body shall be smashed as small as a drop of dew on
a cabbage-leaf in the morning.' 'Why, then, I'm in a
fine way,' said I to myself, 'ever to have come along with
the likes of you;' and so giving him a hearty curse in
Irish, for fear he'd know what I said, I got off his back

with a heavy heart, took hold of the reaping-hook, and
sat down upon the moon, and a mighty cold seat it was,
I can tell you that.

"When he had me there fairly landed, he turned about
on me, and said, 'Good morning to you, Daniel O'Rourke,'
said he; 'I think I've nicked you fairly now. You robbed
my nest last year ' ('was true enough for him, but how he
found it out is hard to say), 'and in return you are freely
welcome to cool your heels dangling upon the moon like
a cockthrow.'

"'Is that all, and is this the way you leave me, you
brute, you,' says I. 'You ugly unnatural *baste*, and is
this the way you serve me at last? Bad luck to yourself,
with your hook'd nose, and to all your breed, you blackguard.' 'Twas all to no manner of use; he spread out his
great big wings, burst out a laughing, and flew away like
lightning. I bawled after him to stop; but I might have
called and bawled forever, without his minding me.
Away he went, and I never saw him from that day to
this—sorrow fly away with him! You may be sure I
was in a disconsolate condition, and kept roaring out for
the bare grief, when all at once a door opened right in
the middle of the moon, creaking on its hinges as if it had
not been opened for a month before, I suppose they never
thought of greasing 'em, and out there walks,—who do
you think, but the man in the moon himself? I knew
him by his bush.

"'Good morrow to you, Daniel O'Rourke,' said he;
'how do you do?' 'Very well, thank your honor,' said
I. 'I hope your honor's well.' 'What brought you
here, Dan?' said he. So I told him how I was a little
overtaken in liquor at the master's, and how I was cast
on a *dissolute* island, and how I lost my way in the bog,
and how the thief of an eagle promised to fly me out of
it, and how, instead of that, he had fled me up to the
moon.

"'Dan,' said the man in the moon, taking a pinch of
snuff when I was done, 'you must not stay here.' 'In-

deed, sir,' says I, ' 'tis much against my will I'm here at
all; but how am I to go back?' 'That's your business,'
said he; 'Dan, mine is to tell you that here you must
not stay; so be off in less than no time.' 'I'm doing no
harm,' says I, 'only holding on hard by the reaping-hook,
lest I fall off.' 'That's what you must not do, Dan,' says
he. 'Pray, sir,' says I, 'may I ask how many you are in
family, that you would not give a poor traveler lodging:
I'm sure 'tis not so often you're troubled with strongers
coming to see you, for 'tis a long way.' 'I'm by myself,
Dan,' says he; 'but you'd better let go the reaping-hook.'
'Faith, and with your leave,' says I, 'I'll not let go the
grip, and the more you bids me, the more I won't let go;
—so I will.' 'You had better, Dan,' says he again. 'Why,
then, my little, fellow,' says I, taking the whole weight
of him with my eye from head to foot, 'there are two
words to that bargain; and I'll not budge, but you may
if you like.' 'We'll see how that is to be,' says he; and
back he went, giving the door such a great bang after
him (for it was plain he was huffed) that I thought the
moon and all would fall down with it.

"Well, I was preparing myself to try strength with him,
when back again he comes, with the kitchen cleaver in his
hand, and, without saying a word, he gives two bangs to
the handle of the reaping-hook that was keeping me up,
and *whap!* it came in two. 'Good morning to you, Dan,'
says the spiteful little old blackguard, when he saw me
cleanly falling down with a bit of the handle in my hand;
'I thank you for your visit, and fair weather after you,
Daniel.' I had not time to make any answer to him, for
I was tumbling over and over, and rolling and rolling, at
the rate of a fox-hunt. 'God help me!' says I, 'but this
is a pretty pickle for a decent man to be seen in at this
time of night: I am now sold fairly.' The word was not
out of my mouth when, whiz! what should fly by close
to my ear but a flock of wild geese, all the way from my
own bog of Ballyasheenogh, else how should they know
me? The *ould* gander, who was their general, turning

about his head, cried out to me, 'Is that you, Dan?'
'The same,' said I, not a bit daunted now at what he said,
for I was by this time used to all kinds of *bedevilment*,
and, besides, I knew him of *ould*. 'Good morrow to you,'
says he, 'Daniel O'Rourke; how are you in health this
morning?' 'Very well, sir,' says I, 'I thank you kindly,'
drawing my breath, for I was mightily in want of some.
'I hope your honor's the same.' 'I think 'tis falling you are,
Daniel,' says he. 'You may say that, sir,' says I. 'And
where are you going all the way so fast?' said the gander.
So I told him how I had taken the drop, and how I came
on the island, and how I lost my way in the bog, and how
the thief of an eagle flew me up to the moon, and how the
man in the moon turned me out. 'Dan,' said he, 'I'll
save you: put out your hand and catch me by the leg,
and I'll fly you home.' 'Sweet is your hand in a pitcher
of honey, my jewel,' says I, though all the time I thought
within myself that I don't much trust you; but there was
no help, so I caught the gander by the leg, and away I
and the other geese flew after him as fast as hops.

"We flew, and we flew, and we flew, until we came
right over the wide ocean. I knew it well, for I saw Cape
Clear to my right hand, sticking up out of the water.
'Ah, my lord,' said I to the goose, for I thought it best to
keep a civil tongue in my head any way, 'fly to land if
you pleose.' 'It is impossible, you see, Dan,' said he, 'for
a while, because you see we are going to Arabia.' 'To
Arabia!' said I; 'that's surely some place in foreign
parts, far away. Oh! Mr. Goose: why then, to be sure,
I'm a man to be pitied among you.' 'Whist, whist, you
fool,' said he, 'hold your tongue; I tell you Arabia is a
very decent sort of place, as like West Carbery as one egg
is like another, only there is a little more sand there.'

"Just as we were talking, a ship hove in sight, scudding
so beautiful before the wind. 'Ah! then, sir,' said I, 'will
you drop me on the ship, if you please?' 'We are not
fair over it,' said he; 'if I dropped you now you would go
splash into the sea.' 'I would not,' says I; 'I know

better than that, for it is just as clean under us, so let me drop now at once."

"'If you must, you must,' said he; 'there, take your own way;' and he opened his claw, and faith he was right —sure enough I came down plump into the very bottom of the salt sea! Down to the very bottom I went, and I gave myself up then forever, when a whale walked up to me, scratching himself after his night's sleep, and looked me full in the face, and never the word did he say, but lifting up his tail, he splashed me all over again with the cold salt water till there wasn't a dry stitch upon my whole carcass! and I heard somebody say—'twas a voice I knew, too—'Get up, you drunken brute, off o' that;' and with that I woke up, and there was Judy with a tub full of water, which she was splashing all over me—for, rest her soul! though she was a good wife, she never could bear to see me in drink, and had a bitter hand of her own.

"'Get up,' said she again: 'and of all places in the parish would no place *sarve* your turn to lie down upon but under the *ould* walls of Carrigapooka? an uneasy resting I am sure you had of it.' And sure enough I had: for I was fairly bothered out of my senses with eagles, and men of the moons, and flying ganders, and whales, driving me through bogs, and up to the moon, and down to the bottom of the green ocean. If I was in drink ten times over, long would it be before I'd lie down in the same spot again, I know that."

THE KILDARE POOKA.*

PATRICK KENNEDY.

MR. H—— R——, when he was alive, used to live a good deal in Dublin, and he was once a great while out of the country on account of the "ninety-eight" business. But the servants kept on in the big house at Rath—— all the same as if the family was at home. Well, they used to be frightened out of their lives after going to their beds with the banging of the kitchen-door, and the clattering of fire-irons, and the pots and plates and dishes. One evening they sat up ever so long, keeping one another in heart with telling stories about ghosts and fetches, and that when—what would you have of it?—the little scullery boy that used to be sleeping over the horses, and could not get room at the fire, crept into the hot hearth, and when he got tired listening to the stories, sorra fear him, but he fell dead asleep.

Well and good after they were all gone and the kitchen fire raked up, he was woke with the noise of the kitchen door opening, and the trampling of an ass on the kitchen floor. He peeped out, and what should he see but a big ass, sure enough, sitting on his curabingo and yawning before the fire. After a little he looked about him, and began scratching his ears as if he was quite tired, and says he, " I may as well begin first as last." The poor boy's teeth began to chatter in his head, for says he, " Now he's goin' to ate me ; " but the fellow with the long ears and tail on him had something else to do. He stirred the fire, and then he brought in a pail of water from the pump, and filled a big pot that he put on the fire before he went out. He then put in his hand—foot, I mean—into the hot hearth, and pulled out the little boy. He let a roar out of him with the fright, but the pooka only looked at

*Legendary Fictions of the Irish Celts.—Macmillan.

him, and thrust out his lower lip to show how little he valued him, and then he pitched him into his pew again.

Well, he then lay down before the fire till he heard the boil coming on the water, and maybe there wasn't a plate, or a dish, or a spoon on the dresser that he didn't fetch and put into the pot, and wash and dry the whole bilin' of 'em as well as e'er a kitchen-maid from that to Dublin town. He then put all of them up on their places on the shelves; and if he didn't give a good sweepin' to the kitchen, leave it till again. Then he comes and sits fornent the boy, let down one of his ears, and cocked up the other, and gave a grin. The poor fellow strove to roar out, but not a dheeg 'ud come out of his throat. The last thing the pooka done was to rake up the fire, and walk out, giving such a slap o' the door, that the boy thought the house couldn't help tumbling down.

Well, to be sure if there wasn't a hullabullo next morning when the poor fellow told his story! They could talk of nothing else the whole day. One said one thing, another said another, but a fat, lazy scullery girl said the wittiest thing of all. " Musha!" says she, " if the pooka docs be cleaning up everything that way when we are asleep, what should we be slaving ourselves for doing his work?" " *Shu gu dheine*,"* says another; "them's the wisest words you ever said, Kauth; it's meeself won't contradict you."

So said, so done. Not a bit of a plate or dish saw a drop of water that evening, and not a besom was laid on the floor, and every one went to bed soon after sundown. Next morning everything was as fine as fine in the kitchen, and the lord mayor might eat his dinner off the flags. It was great ease to the lazy servants, you may depend, and everything went on well till a foolhardy gag of a boy said he would stay up one night and have a chat with the pooka.

He was a little daunted when the door was thrown open and the ass marched up to the fire.

* Meant for *seadh go deimhin—i. e.,* yes, indeed.

"An then, sir," says he, at last, picking up courage, "if
it isn't taking a liberty, might I ax who you are, and why
you are so kind as to do half of the day's work for the
girls every night?" "No liberty at all," says the pooka,
says he: "I'll tell you, and welcome. I was a servant in
the time of Squire R.'s father, and was the laziest rogue
that ever was clothed and fed, and done nothing for it.
When my time came for the other world, this is the
punishment was laid on me—to come here and do all this
labor every night, and then go out in the cold. It isn't
so bad in the fine weather; but if you only knew what it
is to stand with your head between your legs, facing the
storm from midnight to sunrise, on a bleak winter night."
"And could we do anything for your comfort, my poor
fellow?" says the boy, "Musha, I don't know," says the
pooka; "but I think a good quilted frieze coat would
held to keep the life in me them long nights." Why
then, in troth, we'd be the ungratefullest of people if we
didn't feel for you."

To make a long story short, the next night but two the
boy was there again; and if he didn't delight the poor
pooka, holding up a fine warm coat before him, it's no
mather! Betune the pooka and the man, his legs was
got into the four arms of it, and it was buttoned down the
breast and the belly, and he was so pleased he walked up
to the glass to see how he looked. "Well," says he, "it's
a long lane that has no turning. I am much obliged to
you and your fellow-servants. You have made me happy
at last. Good-night to you."

So he was walking out, but the other cried, "Och! sure
your going too soon. What about the washing and
sweeping?' "Ah, you may tell the girls that they must
now get their turn. My punishment was to last till I
was thought worthy of a reward for the way I done my
duty. You'll see me no more." And no more they did,
and right sorry they were for having been in such a hurry
to reward the ungrateful pooka.

THE BANSHEE.

[THE *banshee* (from *ban* [*bean*], a woman, and *shee* [*sidhe*], a fairy) is an attendant fairy that follows the old families, and none but them, and wails before a death. Many have seen her as she goes wailing and clapping her hands. The keen [*caoine*], the funeral cry of the peasantry, is said to be an imitation of her cry. When more than one banshee is present, and they wail and sing in chorus, it is for the death of some holy or great one. An omen that sometimes accompanies the banshee is the *coach-a-bower* [*cóiste-bodhar*]—an immense black coach, mounted by a coffin, and drawn by headless horses driven by a *Dullahan*. It will go rumbling to your door, and if you open it, according to Croker, a basin of blood will be thrown in your face. These headless phantoms are found elsewhere than in Ireland. In 1807 two of the sentries stationed outside St. James's Park died of fright. A headless woman, the upper part of her body naked, used to pass at midnight and scale the railings. After a time the sentries were stationed no longer at the haunted spot. In Norway the heads of corpses were cut off to make their ghosts feeble. Thus came into existence the *Dullahans*,

* We have other omens beside the Banshee and the Dullahan and the Coach-a-Bower. I know one family where death is announced by the cracking of a whip. Some families are attended by phantoms of ravens or other birds. When McManus, of '48 celebrity, was sitting by his dying brother, a bird of vulture-like appearance came through the window and lighted on the breast of the dying man. The two watched in terror, not daring to drive it off. It crouched there, bright-eyed, till the soul left the body. It was considered a most evil omen. Lefanu worked this into a tale. I have good authority for tracing its origin to McManus and his brother,

perhaps; unless, indeed, they are descended from that
Irish giant who swam across the Channel with his head
in his teeth.—ED.]

HOW THOMAS CONNOLLY MET THE BANSHEE.

J. TODHUNTER.

Aw, the banshee, sir? Well, sir, as I was striving to
tell ye, I was going home from work one day, from Mr.
Cassidy's that I tould ye of, in the dusk o' the evening.
I had more nor a mile—aye, it was nearer two miles—to
thrack to, where I was lodgin' with a dacent widdy
woman I knew, Biddy Maguire be name, as to be near me
work.

It was the first week in November, an' a lonesome road
I had to travel, an' dark enough, wid threes above it; an'
about half-ways there was a bit of a brudge I had to cross,
over one o' them little sthrames that runs into the Dod-
dher. I walked on in the middle iv the road, for there
was no toe-path at that time, Misther Harry, nor for
many a long day afther that; but, as I was sayin', I
walked along till I come nigh upon the brudge, where the
road was a bit open, an' there, right enough, I seen the
hog's back o' the ould-fashioned brudge that used to be
there till it was pulled down, an' a white mist steamin'
up out o' the wather all around it.

Well, now, Misther Harry, often as I'd passed by the
place before, that night it seemed sthrange to me, an' like
a place ye might see in a dhrame; an' as I come up to it I
began to feel a could wind blowin' through the hollow o'
me heart. "Musha, Thomas," sez I to meself, "is it yer-
self that's in it?" sez I; "or, if it is, what's the matter
wid ye at all, at all?" sez I; so I put a bould face on it,
an' I made a sthruggle to set one leg afore the other, ontil
I came to the rise o' the brudge. And there, God be
good to us! in a cantle o' the wall I seen an ould woman,
as I thought, sittin' on her hunkers, all crouched together,

an' her head bowed down, seemin'ly in the greatest
affliction.

Well, sir, I pitied the ould craythur, an' though I wasn't
worth a thraneen, for the mortial fright I was in, I up an'
sez to her, " That's a cowld lodgin' for ye, ma'am." Well,
the sorra ha'porth she sez to that, nor tuk no more notice o'
me than if I hadn't let a word out o' me, but kep' rockin'
herself to an' fro, as if her heart was breakin'; so I sez to
her again, " Eh, ma'am, is there anythin' the matter wid
ye?" An' I made for to touch her on the shoulder, on'y
somethin' stopt me, for as I looked closer at her I saw she
was no more an ould woman nor she was an ould cat.
The first thing I tuk notice to, Misther Harry, was her
hair, that was sthreelin' down over her showldhers, an' a
good yard on the ground on aich side of her. O, be the
hoky farmer, but that was the hair! The likes of it I
never seen on mortial woman, young or ould, before nor
sense. It grew as sthrong out of her as out of e'er a young
slip of a girl ye could see; but the color of it was a mis-
thery to describe. The first squint I got of it I thought
it was silvery gray, like an ould crone's; but when I got
up beside her I saw, be the glance o' the sky, it was a
soart iv an Iscariot color, an' a shine out of it like floss
silk. It ran over her showldhers and the two shapely
arms she was lanin' her head on, for all the world like
Mary Magdalen's in a picther; and then I persaved that
the gray cloak and the green gownd undhernaith it was
made of no earthly matarial I ever laid eyes on. Now, I
needn't tell ye, sir, that I seen all this in the twinkle of a
bed-post—long as I take to make the narration of it. So
I made a step back from her, an' " The Lord be betune
us an' harm!" sez I, out loud, an' wid that I blessed meself. Well, Misther Harry, the word wasn't o' me mouth
afore she turned her face on me. Aw, Misther Harry, but
'twas that was the awfullest apparation ever I seen, the
face of her as she looked up at me! God forgive me for
sayin' it but 'twas more like the face of the " Axy Homo "
beyand in Marlboro' Sthreet Chapel nor like any face I

could mintion—as pale as a corpse, an' a most o' freckles
on it, like the freckles on a turkey's egg; an' the two eyes
sewn in wid red thread, from the terrible power o' crying
the' had to do; an' such a pair iv eyes as the' wor, Misther Harry, as blue as two forget-me-nots, an' as cowld as
the moon in a bog-hole of a frosty night, an' a dead-an'-
live look in them that sent a cowld shiver through the
marra o' me bones. Be the mortial! ye could ha' rung a
tay cupful o' cowld paspiration out o' the hair o' me head
that minute, so ye could. Well, I thought the life ud' lave
me intirely when she riz up from her hunkers, till, bedad!
she looked mostly as tall as Nelson's Pillar; an' wid the
two eyes gazing' back at me, an' her two arms stretched
out before her, an' a keine out of her that riz the hair o'
me scalp till it was as stiff as the hog's bristles in a new
hearth broom, away she glides—glides round the angle o'
the brudge, an' down with her into the sthrame that ran
undhernaith it. 'Twas then I began to suspect what she
was. " Wisha, Thomas! " says I to meself, sez I; an' I
made a great struggle to get me two legs into a throt, in
spite o' the spavin o' fright the pair o' them wor in; an'
how I brought meself home that same night the Lord in
heaven only knóws, for I never could tell; but I must ha'
tumbled agin the door, and shot in head foremost into the
middle o' the flure, where I lay in a dead swoon for mostly
an hour; and the first I knew was Mrs. Maguire stannin'
over me with a jorum o' punch she was pourin' down me
throath (throat), to bring back the life into me, an' me
head in a pool of cowld wather she dashed over me in her
first fright. " Arrah, Mister Connolly,!' shashee, " what
ails ye? " shashee, " to put the scare on a lone woman
like that? " shashee.   " Am I in this world or the next? "
sez I. " Musha! where else would ye be on'y here in my
kitchen? " shashee. " O, glory be to God! " sez I, " but
I thought I was in Purgathory at the laste, not to mintion
an uglier place," sez I, " only it's too cowld I find myself,
an' not too hot," sez I.   " Faix, an' maybe ye wor more nor
half-ways there, on'y for me," shashee; " but what's come

to you at all, at all ? Is it your fetch ye seen, Mister Connolly ? " " Aw, naboclish ! " * sez I. " Never mind what
I seen," sez I. So be degrees I began to come to a little ;
an' that's the way I met the banshee, Misther Harry !

" But how did you know it really was the banshee after
all, Thomas ? "

" Begor, sir, I knew the apparation of her well enough ;
but 'twas confirmed by a sarcumstance that occurred the
same time. There was a Misther O'Nales was come on a
visit, ye must know, to a place in the neighborhood—one
o' the ould O'Nales iv the county Tyrone, a rale ould Irish
family—an' the banshee was heard keening round the
house that same night, be more than one that was in it ;
an' sure enough, Misther Harry, he was found dead in his
bed the next mornin'. So if it wasn't the banshee I seen
that time, I'd like to know what else it could a' been."

A LAMENTATION.

*For the Death of Sir Maurice Fitzgerald, Knight, of
Kerry, who was killed in Flanders, 1642.*

FROM THE IRISH, BY CLARENCE MANGAN.

THERE was lifted up one voice of woe,
    One lament of more than mortal grief,
Through the wide South to and fro,
    For a fallen· Chief.
In the dead of night that cry thrilled through me,
    I looked out upon the midnight air !
My own soul was all as gloomy,
    As I knelt in prayer.

O'er Loch Gur, that night, once—twice—yea, thrice—
    Passed a wail of anguish for the Brave

No bac leis—i. e., don't mind it.

That half curled into ice
    Its moon-mirroring wave.
Then uprose a many-toned wild hymn in
    Choral swell from Ogra's dark ravine,
And Mogeely's Phantom Women
    Mourned the Geraldine!

Far on Carah Mona's emerald plains
    Shrieks and sighs were blended many hours,
And Fermoy in fitful strains
    Answered from her towers.
Youghal, Keenalmeaky, Eemokilly,
    Mourned in concert, and their piercing *keen*
Woke to wondering life the stilly
    Glens of Inchiqueen.

From Loughmoe to yellow Dunanore
    There was fear; the traders of Tralee
Gathered up their golden store,
    And prepared to flee;
For, in ship and hall from night till morning,
    Showed the first faint beamings of the sun,
All the foreigners heard the warning
    Of the Dreaded One!

" This," they spake, " portendeth death to us,
    If we fly not swiftly from our fate! "
Self-conceited idiots! thus
    Ravingly to prate!
Not for base-born higgling Saxon trucksters
    Ring laments like those by shore and sea!
Not for churls with souls like hucksters
    Waileth our Banshee!

For the high Milesian race alone
    Ever flows the music of her woe!
For slain heir to bygone throne,
    And for Chief laid low!

Hark! . . . Again, methinks, I hear her weeping
    Yonder! Is she near me now, as then?
Or was but the night-wind sweeping
    Down the hollow glen?

THE BANSHEE OF THE MAC CARTHYS.

T. CROFTON CROKER.

CHARLES MAC CARTHY was, in the year 1749, the only
surviving son of a very numerous family. His father died
when he was little more than twenty, leaving him the Mac
Carthy estate, not much encumbered, considering that it
was an Irish one. Charles was gay, handsome, unfettered
either by poverty, a father, or guardians, and therefore
was not, at the age of one-and-twenty, a pattern of regularity and virtue. In plain terms, he was an exceedingly dissipated—I fear I may say debauched, young man.
His companions were, as may be supposed, of the higher
classes of the youth in his neighborhood, and, in general,
of those whose fortunes were larger than his own, whose
dispositions to pleasure were, therefore, under still less
restrictions, and in whose example he found at once an
incentive and an apology for his irregularities. Besides,
Ireland, a place to this day not very remarkable for the
coolness and the steadiness of its youth, was then one of
the cheapest countries in the world in most of those
articles which money supplies for the indulgence of the
passions. The odious exciseman,—with his portentous
book in one hand, unrelenting pen held in the other, or
stuck beneath his hat-band, and the ink-bottle ('black
emblem of the informer') dangling from his waistcoat-
button—went not then from ale-house to ale-house de-
nouncing all those patriotic dealers in spirits, who pre-
ferred selling whisky, which had nothing to do with
English laws (but to elude them), to retailing that poison-
ous liquor, which derived its name from the British

"Parliament" that compelled its circulation among a re-
luctant people. Or if the gauger—recording angel of the
law—wrote down the peccadillo of a publican, he dropped
a tear upon the word, and blotted it out forever! For,
welcome to the tables of their hospitable neighbors, the
guardians of the excise, where they existed at all, scrupled
to abridge those luxuries which they freely shared; and
thus the competition in the market between the smuggler,
who incurred little hazard, and the personage ycleped
fair trader, who enjoyed little protection, made Ireland
a land flowing, not merely with milk and honey, but with
whisky and wine. In the enjoyments supplied by these,
and in the may kindred pleasures to which frail youth is
but too prone, Charles Mac Carthy indulged in such a degree, that just about the time when he had completed his
four-and-twentieth year, after a week of great excesses
he was seized with a violent fever, which, from its malig-
nity, and the weakness of his frame, left scarcely a hope
of his recovery. His mother, who had at first made many
efforts to check his vices, and at last had been obliged to
look on at his rapid progress to ruin in silent despair,
watched day and night at his pillow. The anguish of
parental feeling was blended with that still deeper misery
which those only know who have striven hard to rear in
virtue and piety a beloved and favorite child; have
found him grow up all that their hearts could desire, until he reached manhood; and then, when their pride was
highest, and their hopes almost ended in the fulfilment of
their fondest expectations, have seen this idol of their
affections plunge headlong into a course of reckless pro-
fligacy, and, after a rapid career of vice, hang upon the
verge of eternity, without the leisure or the power of
repentance. Fervently she prayed that, if his life could
not be spared, at least the delirium, which continued with
increasing violence from the first few hours of his disorder,
might vanish before death, and leave enough of light and
of calm for making his peace with offended Heaven.
After several days, however, nature seemed quite ex-

hausted, and he sunk into a state too like death to be
mistaken for the repose of sleep. His face had that pale,
glossy, marble look, which is in general so sure a symptom
that life has left its tenement of clay. His eyes were
closed and sunk ; the lids having that compressed and
stiffened appearance which seem to indicate that some
friendly hand had done its last office. The lips, half
closed and perfectly ashy, discovered just so much of the
teeth as to give to the features of death their most
ghastly, but most impressive look. He lay upon his back,
with his hands stretched beside him, quite motionless ;
and his distracted mother, after repeated trials, could discover not the least sympton of animation. The medical
man who attended, having tried the usual modes for as-
certaining the presence of life, declared at last his opinion
that it was flown, and prepared to depart from the house of
mourning. His horse was seen to come to the door. A
crowd of people who were collected before the windows,
or scattered in groups on the lawn in front, gathered
around when the door opened. These were   tenants,
fosters, and poor relations of the family, with others at-
tracted by affection, or by that interest which partakes of
curiosity, but is something more, and which collects the
lower ranks round a house where a human being is in
his passage to another world. They saw the professional
man come out from the hall door and approach his horse ;
and while slowly, and with a melancholy air, he prepared
to mount, they clustered round him with inquiring and
wistful looks. Not a word was spoken, but their meaning could not be misunderstood ; and the physician,
when he had got into his saddle, and while the servant
was still holding the bridle as if to delay him, and was
looking anxiously at his face as if expecting that he
would relieve the general suspense, shook his head and
said in a low voice, " It's all over, James ; " and moved
slowly away. The moment he had spoken the women
present, who were very numerous, uttered a shrill cry,
which, having been sustained for about half a minute,

fell suddenly into a full, loud, continued, and discordant but plaintive wailing, above which occasionally were heard the deep sounds of a man's voice, sometimes in deep sobs, sometimes in more distinct exclamations of sorrow. This was Charles's foster-brother, who moved about the crowd. now clapping his hands, now rubbing them together in an agony of grief. The poor fellow had been Charles's playmate and companion when a boy, and afterwards his servant; had always been distinguished by his peculiar regard, and loved his young master as much, at least, as he did his own life.

When Mrs. Mac Carthy became convinced that the blow was indeed struck, and that her beloved son was sent to his last account, even in the blossoms of his sin, she remained for some time gazing with fixedness upon his cold features; then, as if something had suddenly touched the string of her tenderest affections, tear after tear trickled down her cheeks, pale with anxiety and watching. Still she continued looking at her son, apparently unconscious that she was weeping, without once lifting her handkerchief to her eyes, until reminded of the sad duties which the custom of the country imposed upon her, by the crowd of females belonging to the better class of the peasantry, who now, crying audibly, nearly filled the apartment. She then withdrew, to give directions for the ceremony of waking, and for supplying the numerous visitors of all ranks with the refreshments usual on these melancholy occasions. Though her voice was scarcely heard, and though no one saw her but the servants and one or two old followers of the family, who assisted her in the necessary arrangements, everything was conducted with the greatest regularity; and though she made no effort to check her sorrows they never once suspended her attention, now more than ever required to preserve order in her household, which, in this season of calamity, but for her would have been all confusion.

The night was pretty far advanced; the boisterous lamentations which had prevailed during part of the day

in and about the house had given place to a solemn and
mournful stillness; and Mrs. Mac Carthy, whose heart,
notwithstanding her long fatigue and watching, was yet
too sore for sleep, was kneeling in fervent prayer in a
chamber adjoining that of her son. Suddenly her devo-
tions were disturbed by an unusual noise, proceeding from
the persons who were watching round the body. First
there was a low murmur, then all was silent, as if the
movements of those in the chamber were checked by a
sudden panic, and then a loud cry of terror burst from all
within. The door of the chamber was thrown open, and
all who were not overturned in the press rushed wildly
into the passage which led to the stairs, and into which
Mrs. Mac Carthy's room opened. Mrs. Mac Carthy made
her way through the crowd into her son's chamber, where
she found him sitting up in the bed, and looking vacantly
around, like one risen from the grave. The glare thrown
upon his sunk features and thin lathy frame gave an unearthly horror to his whole aspect. Mrs. Mac Carthy was
a woman of some firmness; but she was a woman, and
not quite free from the superstitions of her country. She
dropped on her knees, and, clasping her hands, began to
pray aloud. The form before her moved only its lips, and
barely uttered " Mother "; but though the pale lips moved,
as if there was a design to finish the sentence, the tongue
refused its office. Mrs. Mac Carthy sprung forward, and
catching the arm of her son, exclaimed, " Speak! in the
name of God and His saints, speak! are you alive? "

He turned to her slowly, and said, speaking still with
apparent difficulty, " Yes, my mother, alive, and—but sit
down and collect yourself; I have that to tell which will
astonish you still more than what you have seen." He
leaned back upon his pillow, and while his mother remained kneeling by the bedside, holding one of his hands
clasped in hers, and gazing on him with the look of one
who distrusted all her senses, he proceeded: " Do not in-
terrupt me until I have done. I wish to speak while the
excitement of returning life is upon me, as I know I shall

soon need much repose. Of the commencement of my illness I have only a confused recollection; but within the last twelve hours I have been before the judgment-seat of God. Do not stare incredulously on me—'tis as true as have been my crimes, and as, I trust, shall be repentance. I saw the awful Judge arrayed in all the terrors which invest him when mercy gives place to justice. The dreadful pomp of offended omnipotence, I saw—I remember. It is fixed here; printed on my brain in characters indelible; but it passeth human language. What I *can* describe I *will*—I may speak it briefly. It is enough to say, I was weighed in the balance, and found wanting. The irrevocable sentence was upon the point of being pronounced; the eye of my Almighty Judge, which had already glanced upon me, half spoke my doom; when I observed the guardian saint, to whom you so often directed my prayers when I was a child, looking at me with an expression of benevolence and compassion. I stretched forth my hands to him, and besought his intercession. I implored that one year, one month, might be given to be on earth to do penance and atonement for my transgressions. He threw himself at the feet of my Judge, and supplicated for mercy. Oh! never—not if I should pass through ten thousand successive states of being— never, for eternity, shall I forget the horrors of that moment, when my fate hung suspended—when an instant was to decide whether torments unutterable were to be my portion for endless ages! But Justice suspended its decree, and Mercy spoke in accents of firmness, but mildness, ' Return to that world in which thou hast lived but to outrage the laws of Him who made that world and thee. Three years are given thee for repentance; when these are ended, thou shalt again stand here, to be saved or lost forever.' I heard no more; I saw no more, until I awoke to life, the moment before you entered."

Charles's strength continued just long enough to finish these last words, and on uttering them he closed his eyes, and lay quite exhausted. His mother, though, as was before said, somewhat disposed to give credit to supernatural visitations, yet hesitated whether or not she should believe that, although awakened from a swoon which might have been the crisis of his disease, he was still under the influence of delirium. Repose, however, was at all events necessary, and she took immediate measures that he should enjoy it undisturbed. After some hours' sleep, he awoke refreshed, and thenceforward gradually but steadily recovered.

Still he persisted in his account of the vision, as he had at first related it; and his persuasion of its reality had an obvious and decided influence on his habits and conduct. He did not altogether abandon the society of his former associates, for his temper was not soured by his reformation; but he never joined in their excesses, and often endeavored to reclaim them. How his pious exertions succeeded, I have never learnt; but of himself it is recorded that he was religious without ostentation, and temperate without austerity; giving a practical proof that vice may be exchanged for virtue, without the loss of respectability, popularity, or happiness.

Time rolled on, and long before the three years were ended the story of his vision was forgotten, or, when spoken of, was usually mentioned as an instance proving the folly of believing in such things. Charles's health, from the temperance and regularity of his habits, became more robust than ever. His friends, indeed, had often occasion to rally him upon a seriousness and abstractedness of demeanor, which grew upon him as he approached the completion of his seven-and-twentieth year, but for the most part his manner exhibited the same animation and cheerfulness for which he had always been remarkable. In company he evaded every endeavor to draw from him a distinct opinion on the subject of the supposed prediction; but among his own family it was well known that he still firmly believed it. However, when the day had nearly arrived on which the prophecy was, if at all to be fulfilled, his whole appearance gave such promise of a long and healthy life, that he was persuaded by his friends to ask a large party to an entertainment at Spring House, to celebrate his birthday. But the occasion of this party, and the circumstances which attended it, will be best learned from a perusal of the following letters, which have been carefully preserved by some relations of his family. The first is from Mrs. Mac Carthy to a lady, a very near connection and valued friend of hers who lived in the country of Cork, at about fifty miles' distance from Spring House.

"TO MRS. BARRY, CASTLE BARRY.

" *Spring House, Tuesday morning,*
October 15*th*, 1752.

" MY DEAREST MARY,

" I am afraid I am going to put your affection for your old friend and kinswoman to a severe trial. A two days' journey at this season, over bad roads and through a troubled country, it will indeed require friendship such as yours to persuade a sober woman to encounter. But the truth is, I have, or fancy I have, more then usual cause for wishing you near me. You know my son's story. I can't tell you how it is, but as next Sunday approaches, when the prediction of his dream, or vision, will be proved false or true, I feel a sickening of the heart, which I cannot suppress, but which your presence, my dear Mary, will soften, as it has done so many of my sorrows. My nephew, James Ryan, is to be married to Jane Osborne (who, you know, is my son's ward), and the bridal entertainment will take place here on Sunday next, though Charles pleaded hard to have it postponed for a day or two longer. Would to God—but no more of this till we meet. Do prevail upon yourself to leave your good man for *one* week, if his farming concerns will not admit of his accompanying you ; and come to us, with the girls, as soon before Sunday as you can.

" Ever my dear Mary's attached cousin and friend,

" ANN MAC CARTHY."

Although this letter reached Castle Barry early on Wednesday, the messenger having traveled on foot over bog and moor, by paths impassable to horse or carriage, Mrs. Barry, who at once determined on going, had so many arrangements to make for the regulation of her domestic affairs (which, in Ireland, among the middle orders of the gentry, fall soon into confusion when the mistress of the family is away), that she and her two young daughters were unable to leave until late on the morning of Friday. The eldest daughter remained to keep her father company, and superintend the concerns of the household. As the travelers were to journey in an open one-horse vehicle, called a jaunting-car (still used in Ireland), and as the roads, bad at all times, were rendered still worse by the heavy rains, it was their design to make two easy stages —to stop about midway the first night, and reach Spring House early on Saturday evening. This arrangement was now altered, as they found that from the lateness of their departure they could proceed, at the utmost, no farther than twenty miles on the first day ; and they, therefore, purposed sleeping at the house of a Mr. Bourke, a friend of theirs, who lived at somewhat less than that distance from Castle Barry. They reached Mr. Bourke's in safety after a rather disagreeable ride. What befell them on their journey the next day to Spring House, and after their arrival there, is fully recounted in a letter from the second Miss Barry to her eldest sister.

Spring House, Sunday evening,
20th October, 1752.

" DEAR ELLEN,

" As my mother's letter, which encloses this, will announce to you briefly the sad intelligence which I shall here relate more fully, I think it better to go regularly through the recital of the extraordinary events of the last two days.

" The Bourkes kept us up so late on Friday night that yesterday was pretty far advanced before we could begin

our journey, and the day closed when we were nearly
fifteen miles distant from this place. The roads were
excessively deep, from the heavy rains of the last week,
and we proceeded so slowly that, at last, my mother resolved on passing the night at the house of Mr. Bourke's
brother (who lives about a quarter-of-a-mile off the road),
and coming here to breakfast in the morning. The day
had been windy and showery, and the sky looked fitful,
gloomy, and uncertain. The moon was full, and at times
shone clear and bright; at others it was wholly concealed
behind the thick, black, and rugged masses of clouds that
rolled rapidly along, and were every moment becoming
larger, and collecting together as if gathering strength for
a coming storm. The wind, which blew in our faces,
whistled bleakly along the low hedges of the narrow road,
on which we proceeded with difficulty from the number
of deep sloughs, and which afforded not the least shelter,
no plantation being within some miles of us. My mother,
therefore, asked Leary, who drove the jaunting-car, how
far we were from Mr. Bourke's? ' 'Tis about ten spades
from this to the cross, and we have then only to turn to the
left into the avenue, ma'am.' ' Very well, Leary ; turn up
to Mr. Bourke's as soon as you reach the cross roads.'
My mother had scarcely spoken these words, when a
shriek, that made us thrill as if our very hearts were
pierced by it, burst from the hedge to the right of our
way. If it resembled anything earthly it seemed the cry
of a female, struck by a sudden and mortal blow, and giving out her life in one long deep pang of expiring agony.
' Heaven defend us ! ' exclaimed my mother. ' Go you
over the hedge, Leary, and save that woman, if she is not
yet dead, while we run back to the hut we have just
passed, and alarm the village near it.' ' Woman ! ' said
Leary, beating the horse violently, while his voice trembled, ' that's no woman; the sooner we get on, ma'am, the
better ; ' and he continued his efforts to quicken the horse's
pace. We saw nothing. The moon was hid. It was
quite dark, and we had been for some time expecting a

heavy fall of rain.   But just as Leary had spoken, and
had succeeded in making the horse trot briskly forward,
we distinctly heard a loud clapping of hands, followed by
a succession of screams, that seemed to denote the last
excess of despair and anguish, and to issue from a person
running forward inside the hedge, to keep pace with our
progress.   Still we saw nothing ; until, when we were
within about ten yards of the place where an avenue
branched off to Mr. Bourke's to the left, and the road
turned to Spring House on the right, the moon started
suddenly from behind a cloud, and enabled us to see, as
plainly as I now see this paper, the figure of a tall, thin
woman, with uncovered head, and long hair that floated
round her shoulders, attired in something which seemed
either a loose white cloak or a sheet thrown hastily about
her.   She stood on the corner hedge, where the road on
which we were met that which leads to Spring House,
with her face towards us, her left hand pointing to this
place, and her right arm waving rapidly and violently as
if to draw us on in that direction.   The horse had stopped,
apparently frightened at the sudden presence of the figure, which stood in the manner I have described, still
uttering the same piercing cries, for about half a minute.
It then leaped upon the road, disappeared from our view
for one instant, and the next was seen standing upon a
high wall a little way up the avenue on which we purposed going, still pointing towards the road to Spring
House, but in an attitude of defiance and command, as if
prepared to oppose our passage up the avenue.   The figure
was now quite silent, and its garments, which had before
flown loosely in the wind, were closely wrapped around
it.   ' Go on, Leary, to Spring House, in God's name ! ' said
my mother ; ' whatever world it belongs to, we will pro-
voke it no longer.'   ' 'Tis the Banshee, ma'am,' said Leary ;
' and I would not, for what my life is worth, go anywhere this blessed night but to Spring House.   But I'm
afraid there's something bad going forward, or *she* would
not send us there.'   So saying, he drove forward ; and as

we turned on the road to the right, the moon suddenly
withdrew its light, and we saw the apparition no more;
but we heard plainly a prolonged clapping of hands, gradually dying away, as if it issued from a person rapidly
retreating. We proceeded as quickly as the badness of
the roads and the fatigue of the poor animal that drew us
would allow, and arrived here about eleven o'clock last
night. The scene which awaited us you have learned
from my mother's letter. To explain it fully, I must re-
count to you some of the transactions which took place
here during the last week.

"You are aware that Jane Osborne was to have been
married this day to James Ryan, and that they and
their friends have been here for the last week. On
Tuesday last, the very day on the morning of which cousin
Mac Carthy despatched the letter inviting us here, the
whole of the company were walking about the grounds a
little before dinner. It seems that an unfortunate creature, who had been seduced by James Ryan, was seen
prowling in the neighborhood in a moody, melancholy
state for some days previous. He had separated from her
for several months, and, they say, had provided for her
rather handsomely; but she had been seduced by the
promise of his marrying her; and the shame of her unhappy condition, uniting with disappointment and jealousy, had disordered her intellects. During the whole
forenoon of this Tuesday she had been walking in the
plantations near Spring House, with her cloak folded
tight round her, the hood nearly covering her face; and
she had avoided conversing with or even meeting any of
the family.

"Charles Mac Carthy, at the time I mentioned, was
walking between James Ryan and another, at a little
distance from the rest, on a gravel path, skirting a shrubbery. The whole party was thrown into the utmost consternation by the report of a pistol, fired from a thickly-
planted part of the shrubbery which Charles and his companions had just passed. He fell instantly, and it was

found that he had been wounded in the leg. One of the
party was a medical man. His assistance was immediately
given, and, on examining, he declared that the injury was
very slight, that no bone was broken, it was merely a flesh
would, and that it would certainly be well in a few days.
' We shall know more by Sunday," said Charles as he
was carried to his chamber. His wound was immediately
dressed, and so slight was the inconvenience which it
gave that several of his friends spent a portion of the
evening in his apartment.

  " On inquiry, it was found that the unlucky shot was
fired by the poor girl I just mentioned. It was also manifest that she had aimed, not at Charles, but at the des-
troyer of her innocence and happiness, who was walking
beside him. After a fruitless search for her through the
grounds, she walked into the house of her own accord,
laughing and dancing, and singing wildly, and every
moment exclaiming that she had at last killed Mr. Ryan.
When she heard that it was Charles, and not Mr. Ryan,
who was shot, she fell into a violent fit, out of which, after
working convulsively for some time, she sprung to the
door, escaped from the crowd that pursued her, and could
never be taken until last night, when she was brought
here, perfectly frantic, a little before our arrival.

  " Charles's wound was thought of such little consequence that the preparations went forward, as usual, for the
wedding entertainment on Sunday. But on Friday night
he grew restless and feverish, and on Saturday (yesterday)
morning felt so ill that it was deemed necessary to obtain
additional medical advice. Two physicans and a surgeon
met in consultation about twelve o'clock in the day, and
the dreadful intelligence was announced, that unless a
change, hardly hoped for, took place before night, death
must happen within twenty-four hours after. The wound,
it seems, had been too tightly bandaged, and otherwise
injudiciously treated. The physicians were right in their
anticipations. No favorable symptom appeared, and
long before we reached Spring House every ray of hope

had vanished. The scene we witnessed on our arrival
would have wrung the heart of a demon. We heard
briefly at the gate that Mr. Charles was upon his death-
bed. When we reached the house, the information was
confirmed by the servant who opened the door. But just
as we entered we were horrified by the most. appalling
screams issuing from the staircase. My mother thought
she heard the voice of poor Mrs. Mac Carthy, and sprung
forward. We followed, and on ascending a few steps of
the stairs, we found a young woman, in a state of frantic
passion, struggling furiously with two men-servants,
whose united strength was hardly sufficient to prevent
her rushing upstairs over the body of Mrs. Mac Carthy,
who was lying in strong hysterics upon the steps. This,
I afterwards discovered, was the unhappy girl I before
described, who was attempting to gain access to Charles's
room, to ' get his forgiveness,' as she said, ' before he went
away to accuse her for having killed him.' This wild
idea was mingled with another, which seemed to dispute
with the former possession of her·mind. In one sentence
she called on Charles to forgive her, in the next she would
denounce James Ryan as the murderer, both of Charles
and her. At length she was torn away ; and the last
words I heard her scream were, ' James Ryan, 'twas you
killed him, and not I—'twas you killed him, and not I.'

" Mrs. Mac Carthy, on recovering, fell into lhe arms of
my mother, whose presence seemed a great relief to her.
She wept—the first tears, I was told, that she had shed
since the fatal accident. She conducted us to Charles's
room, who, she said, had desired to see us the moment of
our arrival, as he found his end approaching, and wished
to devote the last hours of his existence to uninterrupted
prayer and meditation. We found him perfectly calm,
resigned, and even cheerful. He spoke of the awful event
which was at hand with courage and confidence, and
treated it as a doom for which he had been preparing ever
since his former remarkable illness, and which he never
once doubted was truly foretold to him. He bade us fare-

well with the air of one who was about to travel a short and easy journey; and we left him with impressions which, notwithstanding all their anguish, will, I trust, never entirely forsake us.

"Poor Mrs. Mac Carthy——but I am just called away. There seems a slight stir in the family; perhaps——"

The above letter was never finished.   The enclosure to which it more than once alludes told the sequel briefly, and it is all that I have further learned of the family of Mac Carthy. Before the sun had gone down upon Charles's seven-and-twentieth birthday, his soul had gone to render its last account to its Creator.

GHOSTS.

GHOSTS, or as they are called in Irish, *Thevshi* or *Tash* (*taidhbhse, tais*), live in a state intermediary between this life and the next. They are held there by some earthly longing or affection, or some duty unfulfilled, or anger against the living. " I will haunt you," is a common threat; and one hears such phrases as, " She will haunt him, if she has any good in her." If one is sorrowing greatly after a dead friend, a neighbor will say, " Be quiet now, you are keeping him from his rest;" or, in the Western Isles, according to Lady Wilde, they will tell you, " You are waking the dog that watches to devour the souls of the dead." Those who die suddenly, more commonly than others, are believed to become haunting Ghosts. They go about moving the furniture, and in every way trying to attract attention.

When the soul has left the body, it is drawn away, sometimes, by the fairies. I have a story of a peasant who once saw, sitting in a fairy rath, all who had died for years in his village. Such souls are considered lost. If a soul eludes the fairies, it may be snapped up by the evil spirits. The weak souls of young children are in especial danger. When a very young child dies, the western peasantry sprinkle the threshold with the blood of a chicken, that the spirits may be drawn away to the blood. A Ghost is compelled to obey the commands of the living. " The stable-boy up at Mrs. G——'s there," said an old countryman, " met the master going round the yards after he had been two days dead, and told him to be away with him to the lighthouse, and haunt that; and there he is far out to sea still, sir. Mrs. G—— was quite wild about it, and dismissed the boy." A very desolate light-
176

house poor devil of a Ghost! Lady Wilde considers it is only the spirits who are too bad for heaven, and too good for hell, who are thus plagued. They are compelled to obey some one they have wronged.

The souls of the dead sometimes take the shapes of animals. There is a garden at Sligo where the gardener sees a previous owner in the shape of a rabbit. They will sometimes take the forms of insects, especially of butterflies. If you see one fluttering near a corpse, that is the soul, and is a sign of its having entered upon immortal happiness. The author of the *Parochial Survey of Ireland*, 1814, heard a woman say to a child who was chasing a butterfly, " How do you know it is not the soul of your grandfather." On November eve the dead are abroad, and dance with the fairies.

As in Scotland, the fetch is commonly believed in. If you see the double, or fetch, of a friend in the morning, no ill follows; if at night, he is about to die.

A DREAM.

WILLIAM ALLINGHAM.

I HEARD the dogs howl in the moonlight night;
I went to the window to see the sight;
All the Dead that ever I knew
Going one by one and two by two.

On they pass'd, and on they pass'd;
Townsfellows all, from first to last;
Born in the moonlight of the lane,
Quench'd in the heavy shadow again.

Schoolmates, marching as when we play'd
At soldiers once—but now more staid;
Those were the strangest sight to me
Who were drown'd, I knew, in the awful sea.

Straight and handsome folk; bent and weak, too;
Some that I loved, and gasp'd to speak to;
Some but a day in their churchyard bed;
Some that I had not known were dead.

A long, long crowd—where each seem'd lonely,
Yet of them all there was one, one only,
Raised a head or look'd my way.
She linger'd a moment,—she might not stay.

How long since I saw that fair pale face!
Ah! Mother dear! might I only place
My head on thy breast, a moment to rest,
While thy hand on my tearful cheek were prest!

On, on, a moving bridge they made
Across the moon-stream, from shade to shade,
Young and old, women and men;
Many long-forgot, but remember'd then.

And first there came a bitter laughter;
A sound of tears the moment after;
And then a music so lofty and gay,
That every morning, day by day,
I strive to recall it if I may.

GRACE CONNOR.

MISS LETITIA MACLINTOCK.

THADY and Grace Connor lived on the borders of a large turf bog, in the parish of Clondevaddock, where they could hear the Atlantic surges thunder in upon the shore, and see the wild storms of winter sweep over the Muckish mountain, and his rugged neighbors. Even in summer the cabin by the bog was dull and dreary enough.

Thady Connor worked in the fields, and Grace made a livelihood as a pedler, carrying a basket of remnants of cloth, calico, drugget, and frieze about the country. The people rarely visited any large town, and found it convenient to buy from Grace, who was welcomed in many a lonely house, where a table was hastily cleared, that she might display her wares. Being considered a very honest woman, she was frequently entrusted with commissions to the shops in Letterkenny and Ramelton. As she set out towards home, her basket was generally laden with little gifts for her children.

"Grace, dear," would one of the kind housewives say, "here's a farrel * of oaten cake, wi' a taste o' butter on it; tak' it wi' you for the weans;" or, "Here's half-a-dozen of eggs; you've a big family to support."

Small Connors of all ages crowded round the weary mother, to rifle her basket of these gifts. But her thrifty, hard life came suddenly to an end. She died after an illness of a few hours, and was waked and buried as handsomely as Thady could afford.

Thady was in bed the night after the funeral, and the fire still burned brightly, when he saw his departed wife cross the room and bend over the cradle. Terrified, he muttered rapid prayers, covered his face with the blanket; and on looking up again the appearance was gone.

Next night he lifted the infant out of the cradle, and laid it behind him in the bed, hoping thus to escape his ghostly visitor; but Grace was presently in the room, and stretching over him to wrap up her child. Shrinking and shuddering, the poor man exclaimed, "Grace, woman, what is it brings you back? What is it you want wi' me?"

"I want naething fae you, Thady, but to put thon wean back in her cradle," replied the specter, in a tone of scorn. "You're too feared for me, but my sister Rose

* When a large, round, flat griddle cake is divided into triangular cuts, each of these cuts is called a farrel, farli, or parli.

willna be feared for me—tell her to meet me to-morrow evening, in the old wallsteads."

Rose lived with her mother, about a mile off, but she obeyed her sister's summons without the least fear, and kept the strange tryste in due time.

"Rose, dear," she said, as she appeared before her sister in the old wallsteads, "my mind's oneasy about them twa' red shawls that's in the basket. Matty Hunter and Jane Taggart paid me for them, an' I bought them wi' their money, Friday was eight days. Gie them the shawls the morrow. An' old Mosey McCorkell gied me the price o' a wiley coat; it's in under the other things in the basket. An' now farewell; I can get to my rest."

"Grace, Grace, bide a wee minute," cried the faithful sister, as the dear voice grew fainter, and the dear face began to fade—"Grace, darling! Thady? The children? One word mair!" but neither cries nor tears could further detain the spirit hastening to its rest!

A LEGEND OF TYRONE.

ELLEN O'LEARY.

CROUCHED round a bare hearth in hard, frosty weather,
Three lonely helpless weans cling close together;
Tangled those gold locks, once bonnie and bright—
There's no one to fondle the baby to-night.

"My mammie I want; oh! my mammie I want!"
The big tears stream down with the low wailing chant.
Sweet Eily's slight arms enfold the gold head:
"Poor weeny Willie, sure mammie is dead—

And daddie is crazy from drinking all day—
Come down, holy angels, and take us away!"
Eily and Eddie keep kissing and crying—
Outside, the weird winds are sobbing and sighing.

All in a moment the children are still,
Only a quick coo of gladness from Will.
The sheeling no longer seems empty or bare,
For, clothed in soft raiment, the mother stands there.

They gather around her, they cling to her dress;
She rains down soft kisses for each shy caress.
Her light, loving touches smooth out tangled locks,
And, pressed to her bosom, the baby she rocks.

He lies in his cot, there's a fire on the hearth;
To Eily and Eddy 'tis heaven on earth,
For mother's deft fingers have been everywhere;
She lulls them to rest in the low *suggaun* * chair.

They gaze open-eyed, then the eyes gently close,
As petals fold into the heart of a rose,
But ope soon again in awe, love, but no fear,
And fondly they murmur, " Our mammie is here."

She lays them down softly, she wraps them around ;
They lie in sweet slumbers, she starts at a sound,
The cock loudly crows, and the spirit's away—
The drunkard steals in at the dawning of day.

Again and again, 'tween the dark and the dawn,
Glides in the dead mother to nurse Willie Bawn :
Or is it an angel who sits by the hearth ?
An angel in heaven, a mother on earth.

* Chair made of twisted straw ropes.

THE BLACK LAMB.*

LADY WILDE.

It is a custom amongst the people, when throwing away water at night, to cry out in a loud voice, "Take care of the water ; " or literally, from the Irish, "Away with yourself from the water "—for they say that the spirits of the dead last buried are then wandering about, and it would be dangerous if the water fell on them.

One dark night a woman suddenly threw out a pail of boiling water without thinking of the warning words. Instantly a cry was heard, as of a person in pain, but no one was seen. However, the next night a black lamb entered the house, having the back all fresh scalded, and it lay down moaning by the hearth and died. Then they all knew that this was ·the spirit that had been scalded by the woman, and they carried the dead lamb out reverently, and buried it deep in the earth. Yet every night at the same hour it walked again into the house, and lay down, moaned, and died ; and after this had happened many times, the priest was sent for, and finally, by the strength of his exorcism, the spirit of the dead was laid to rest ; the black lamb appeared no more. Neither was the body of the lamb found in the grave when they searched for it, though it had been laid by their own hands deep in the earth, and covered with clay.

* Ancient Legends of Ireland.

SONG OF THE GHOST.

ALFRED PERCIVAL GRAVES.

WHEN all were dreaming
  But Pastheen Power,
A light came streaming
  Beneath her bower:
A heavy foot
  At her door delayed,
A heavy hand
  On the latch was laid.

" Now who dare venture,
  At this dark hour,
Unbid to enter
  My maiden bower?"
"Dear Pastheen, open
  The door to me,
And your true lover
  You'll surely see."

" My own true lover,
  So tall and brave,
Lives exiled over
  The angry wave."
" Your true love's body
  Lies on the bier,
His faithful spirit
  Is with you here."

"His look was cheerful,
  His voice was gay;
Your speech is fearful,
  Your face is gray;

And sad and sunken
    Your eye of blue,
But Patrick, Patrick,
    Alas! 'tis you!"

Ere dawn was breaking
    She heard below
The two cocks shaking
    Their wings to crow.
" Oh, hush you, hush you,
    Both red and gray,
Or you will hurry
    My love away.

" Oh, hush your crowing,
    Both gray and red,
Or he'll be going
    To join the dead ;
Or, cease from calling
    His ghost to the mould,
And I'll come crowning
    Your combs with gold."

When all were dreaming
    But Pasthèen Power,
A light went streaming
    From out her bower ;
And on the morrow,
    When they awoke,
They knew that sorrow
    Her heart had broke.

THE RADIANT BOY.

MRS. CROW.

CAPTAIN STEWART, afterwards Lord Castlereagh, when he was a young man, happened to be quartered in Ireland. He was fond of sport, and one day the pursuit of game carried him so far that he lost his way. The weather, too, had become very rough, and in this strait he presented himself at the door of a gentleman's house, and sending in his card, requested shelter for the night. The hospitality of the Irish country gentry is proverbial; the master of the house received him warmly; said he feared he could not make him so comfortable as he could have wished, his house being full of visitors already, added to which, some strangers, driven by the inclemency of the night, had sought shelter before him, but such accommodation as he could give he was heartily welcome to; whereupon he called his butler, and committing the guest to his good offices, told him he must put him up somewhere, and do the best he could for him. There was no lady, the gentleman being a widower.

Captain Stewart found the house crammed, and a very jolly party it was. His host invited him to stay, and promised him good shooting if he would prolong his visit a few days: and, in fine, he thought himself extremely fortunate to have fallen into such pleasant quarters.

At length after an agreeable evening, they all retired to bed, and the butler conducted him to a large room, almost divested of furniture, but with a blazing turf fire in the grate, and a shake-down on the floor, composed of cloaks and other heterogeneous materials.

Nevertheless, to the tired limbs of Captain Stewart, who had had a hard day's shooting, it looked very invit-

ing ; but before he lay down, he thought it advisable to
take off some of the fire, which was blazing up the chimney in what he thought an alarming manner. Having
done this, he stretched himself on his couch and soon fell
asleep.

He believed he had slept about a couple of hours when
he awoke suddenly, and was startled by such a vivid light
in the room that he thought it on fire, but on turning to
look at the grate he saw the fire was out, though it was
from the chimney the light proceeded. He sat up in bed,
trying to discover what it was, when he perceived the
form of a beautiful naked boy, surrounded by a dazzling
radiance. The boy looked at him earnestly, and then the
vision faded, and all was dark. Captain Stewart, so far
from supposing what he had seen to be of a spiritual
nature, had no doubt that the host, or the visitors, had
been trying to frighten him. Accordingly, he felt indig-
nant at the liberty, and on the following morning, when
he appeared at breakfast, he took care to evince his displeasure by the reserve of his demeanor, and by announcing his intention to depart immediately. The host
expostulated, reminding him of his promise to stay and
shoot. Captain Stewart coldly excused himself, and, at
length, the gentleman seeing something was wrong, took
him aside, and pressed for an explanation ; whereupon
Captain Stewart, without entering into particulars, said
he had been made the victim of a sort of practical joking
that he thought quite unwarrantable with a stranger.

The gentleman considered this not impossible amongst
a parcel of thoughtless young men, and appealed to them
to make an apology ; but one and all, on honor, denied
the impeachment. Suddenly a thought seemed to strike
him ; he clapt his hand to his forehead, uttered an exclamation, and rang the bell.

" Hamilton," said he to the butler ; " where did Captain
Stewart sleep last night ? "

" Well, sir," replied the man ; " you know every place
was full—the gentlemen were lying on the floor, three

or four in a room—so I gave him the *Boy's Room ;* but I lit a blazing fire to keep him from coming out."

" You were very wrong," said the host; " you know I have positively forbidden you to put any one there, and have taken the furniture out of the room to ensure its not being occupied." Then, retiring with Captain Stewart, he informed him, very gravely, of the nature of the phenomena he had seen ; and at length, being pressed for further information, he confessed that there *existed* a tradition in the family, that whoever the " Radiant boy " appeared to will rise to the summit of power ; and when he has reached the climax, will die a violent death, and I must say, he added, that the records that have been kept of his appearance go to confirm this persuasion.

THE FATE OF FRANK M'KENNA.

WILLIAM CARLETON.

THERE lived a man named M'Kenna at the hip of one of the mountainous hills which divide the county of Tyrone from that of Monaghan. This M'Kenna had two sons, one of whom was in the habit of tracing hares of a Sunday whenever there happened to be a fall of snow. His father, it seems, had frequently remonstrated with him upon what he considered to be a violation of the Lord's day, as well as for his general neglect of mass. The young man, however, though otherwise harmless and inoffensive, was in this matter quite insensible to paternal reproof, and continued to trace whenever the avocations of labor would allow him. It so happened that upon a Christmas morning, I think in the year of 1814, there was a deep fall of snow, and young M'Kenna, instead of going to mass, got down his cock-stick—which is a staff much thicker and heavier at one end than at the other—and prepared to set out on his favorite amuse-

ment.   His father, seeing this, reproved him seriously,
and insisted that he should attend prayers.   His enthusi-
asm for the sport, however, was stronger than his love of
religion, and he refused to be guided by his father's advice.   The old man during the altercation got warm; and
on finding that the son obstinately scorned his authority,
he knelt down and prayed that if the boy persisted in
following his own will, he might never return from the
mountains unless as a corpse.   The imprecation, which
was certainly as harsh as it was impious and senseless,
might have startled many a mind from a purpose that
was, to say the least of it, at variance with religion and
the respect due to a father.   It had no effect, however,
upon the son, who is said to have replied, that whether
he ever returned or not, he was determined on going; and
go accordingly he did.   He was not, however, alone, for it
appears that three or four of the neighboring young men
accompanied him.   Whether their sport was good or
otherwise, is not to the purpose, neither am I able to say;
but the story goes that towards the latter part of the day
they started a larger and darker hare than any they had
ever seen, and that she kept dodging on before them bit
by bit, leading them to suppose that every succeeding
cast of the cock-stick would bring her down.   It was
observed afterwards that she also led them into the recesses of the mountains, and that although they tried to
turn her course homewards, they could not succeed in
doing so.   As evening advanced, the companions of
M'Kenna began to feel the folly of pursuing her farther,
and to perceive the danger of losing their way in the
mountains should night or a snow-storm come upon them.
They therefore proposed to give over the chase and return home; but M'Kenna would not hear of it.   "If you
wish to go home, you may," said he; "as for me, I'll
never leave the hills till I have her with me."   They
begged and entreated of him to desist and return, but all
to no purpose; he appeared to be what the Scotch call
fey—that is, to act as if he were moved by some impulse

that leads to death, and from the influence of which a man cannot withdraw himself. At length, on finding him invincibly obstinate, they left him pursuing the hare directly into the heart of the mountains, and returned to their respective homes.

In the meantime one of the most terrible snow-storms ever remembered in that part of the country came on, and the consequence was, that the self-willed young man, who had equally trampled on the sanctities of religion and parental authority, was given over for lost. As soon as the tempest became still, the neighbors assembled in a body and proceeded to look for him. The snow, however, had fallen so heavily that not a single mark of a footstep could be seen. Nothing but one wide waste of white undulating hills met the eye wherever it turned, and of M'Kenna no trace whatever was visible or could be found. His father, now remembering the unnatural character of his imprecation, was nearly distracted; for although the body had not yet been found, still by every one who witnessed the sudden rage of the storm and who knew the mountains, escape or survival was felt to be impossible. Every day for about a week large parties were out among the hill-ranges seeking him, but to no purpose. At length there came a thaw, and his body was found on a snow-wreath, lying in a supine posture within a circle which he had drawn around him with his cock-stick. His prayer-book lay opened upon his mouth, and his hat was pulled down so as to cover it and his face. It is unnecessary to say that the rumor of his death, and of the circumstances under which he left home, created a most extraordinary sensation in the country—a sensation that was the greater in proportion to the uncertainty occasioned by his not having been found either alive or dead. Some affirmed that he had crossed the mountains, and was seen in Mona-ghan; others, that he had been seen in Clones, in Emyvale, in Five-mile-town; but despite of all these agreeable reports, the melancholy truth was at length made clear by the appearance of the body as just stated.

Now, it so happened that the house nearest the spot where he lay was inhabited by a man named Daly, I think —but of the name I am not certain—who was a herd or care-taker to Dr. Porter, then Bishop of Clogher. The situation of this house was the most lonely and desolate-looking that could be imagined. It was at least two miles distant from any human habitation, being surrounded by one wide and dreary waste of dark moor. By this house lay the route of those who had found the corpse, and I believe the door of it was borrowed for the purpose of conveying it home. Be this as it may, the family witnessed the melancholy procession as it passed slowly through the mountains, and when the place and circumstances are all considered, we may admit that to ignorant and superstitious people, whose minds, even upon ordinary occasions, were strongly affected by such matters, it was a sight calculated to leave behind it a deep, if not a terrible impression. Time soon proved that it did so.

An incident is said to have occurred at the funeral in fine keeping with the wild spirit of the whole melancholy event. When the procession had advanced to a place called Mullaghtinny, a large dark-colored hare, which was instantly recognized, by those who had been out with him on the hills, as the identical one that led him to his fate, is said to have crossed the roads about twenty yards or so before the coffin. The story goes, that a man struck it on the side with a stone, and that the blow, which would have killed any ordinary hare, not only did it no injury, but occasioned a sound to proceed from the body resembling the hollow one emitted by an empty barrel when struck.

In the meantime the interment took place, and the sensation began, like every other, to die away in the natural progress of time, when, behold, a report ran abroad like wild-fire that, to use the language of the people, " Frank M'Kenna was *appearing!* "

One night, about a fortnight after his funeral, the daughter of Daly, the herd, a girl about fourteen, while

lying in bed saw what appeared to be the likeness of
M'Kenna, who had been lost. She screamed out, and
covering her head with the bed-clothes, told her father
and mother that Frank M'Kenna was in the house. This
alarming intelligence naturally produced great terror;
still, Daly, who, notwithstanding his belief in such matters, possessed a good deal of moral courage, was cool
enough to rise and examine the house, which consisted of
only one apartment. This gave the daughter some courage, who, on finding that her father could not see him,
ventured to look out, and she *then* could see nothing of
him herself. She very soon fell asleep, and her father
attributed what she saw to fear, or some accidental com-
bination of shadows proceeding from the furniture, for it
was a clear moonlight night. The light of the following
day dispelled a great deal of their apprehensions, and com-
paratively little was thought of it until evening again advanced, when the fears of the daughter began to return.
They appeared to be prophetic, for she said when night
came that she knew he would appear again; and accordingly at the same hour he did so. This was repeated for
several successive nights, until the girl, from the very
hardihood of terror, began to become so far familiarized
to the specter as to venture to address it.

"In the name of God!" she asked, "what is troubling
you, or why do you appear to me instead of to some of
your own family or relations?"

The ghost's answer alone might settle the question involved in the authenticity of its appearance, being, as it
was, an account of one of the most ludicrous missions that
ever a spirit was despatched upon.

"I'm not allowed," said he, "to spake to any of my
friends, for I parted wid them in anger; but I'm come to
tell you that they are quarrelin' about my breeches—a new
pair that I got made for Christmas day; an' as I was
comin' up to thrace in the mountains, I thought the ould
one 'ud do betther, an' of coorse I didn't put the new pair
an me. My raison for appearin'," he added, "is, that you

may tell my friends that none of them is to wear them—
they must be given in charity."

This serious and solemn intimation from the ghost was
duly communicated to the family, and it was found that
the circumstances were exactly as it had represented them.
This, of course, was considered as sufficient proof of the
truth of its mission.   Their conversations now became not
only frequent, but quite friendly and familiar.   The girl
became a favorite with the specter, and the specter, on the
other hand, soon lost all his terrors in her eyes.   He told
her that whilst his friends were bearing home his body,
the handspikes or poles on which they carried him had
cut his back, and *occasioned him great pain!*   The cutting
of the back also was known to be true, and strengthened,
of course, the truth and authenticity of their dialogues.
The whole neighborhood was now in a commotion with
this story of the apparition, and persons incited by
curiosity began to visit the girl in order to satisfy themselves of the truth of what they had heard.   Everything,
however, was corroborated, and the child herself, without
any symptoms of anxiety or terror, artlessly related her
conversations with the spirit.   Hitherto their interviews
had been all nocturnal, but now that the ghost found his
footing made good, he put a hardy face on, and ventured
to appear by daylight.   The girl also fell into states of
syncope, and while the fits lasted, long conversations with
him upon the subject of God, the blessed Virgin, and
Heaven, took place between them.   He was certainly an
excellent moralist, and gave the best advice.   Swearing,
drunkenness, theft, and every evil propensity of our nature, were declaimed against with a degree of spectral
eloquence quite surprising.   Common fame had now a
topic dear to her heart, and never was a ghost made
more of by his best friends than she made of him.   The
whole country was in a tumult, and I well remember the
crowds which flocked to the lonely little cabin in the
mountains, now the scene of matters so interesting and
important.   Not a single day passed in which I should

think from ten to twenty, thirty, or fifty persons, were not present at these singular interviews. Nothing else was talked of, thought of, and, as I can well testify, dreamt of. I would myself have gone to Daly's were it not for a confounded misgiving I had, that perhaps the ghost might take such a fancy of appearing to *me*, as he had taken to cultivate an intimacy with the girl; and it so happens, that when I see the face of an individual nailed down in the coffin—chilling and gloomy operation !—I experience no particular wish to look upon it again.

The spot where the body of M'Kenna was found is now marked by a little heap of stones, which has been collected since the melancholy event of his death. Every person who passes it throws a stone upon the heap; but why this old custom is practised, or what it means, I do not know, unless it be simply to mark the spot as a visible means of preserving the memory of the occurrence.

Daly's house, the scene of the supposed apparition, is now a shapeless ruin, which could scarcely be seen were it not for the green spot that once was a garden, and which now shines at a distance like an emerald, but with no agreeable or pleasing associatious. It is a spot which no solitary schoolboy will ever visit, nor indeed would the unflinching believer in the popular nonsense of ghosts wish to pass it without a companion. It is, under any circumstances, a gloomy and barren place; but when looked upon in connection with what we have just re-cited, it is lonely, desolate, and awful.

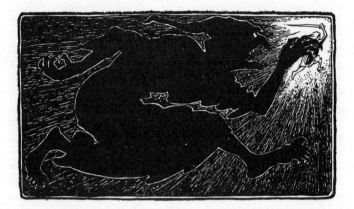

SMALLHEAD AND THE KING'S SONS.

Long ago there lived in Erin a woman who married a
man of high degree and had one daughter. Soon after
the birth of the daughter the husband died.

The woman was not long a widow when she married a
second time, and had two daughters. These two
daughters hated their half-sister, thought she was not so
wise as another, and nicknamed her Smallhead. When
the elder of the two sisters was fourteen years old their
father died. The mother was in great grief then, and began to pine away. She used to sit at home in the corner
and never left the house. Smallhead was kind to her
mother, and the mother was fonder of her eldest daughter
than of the other two, who were ashamed of her.

At last the two sisters made up in their minds to kill
their mother. One day, while their half-sister was gone,
they put the mother in a pot, boiled her, and threw the
bones outside. When Smallhead came home there was
no sign of the mother.

"Where is my mother?" asked she of the other two.

"She went out somewhere. How should we know
where she is?"

194

" Oh, wicked girls! you have killed my mother," said Smallhead.

Smallhead wouldn't leave the house now at all, and the sisters were very angry.

" No man will marry either one of us," said they, " if he sees our fool of a sister."

Since they could not drive Smallhead from the house they made up their minds to go away themselves. One fine morning they left home unknown to their half-sister and traveled on many miles. When Smallhead discovered that her sisters were gone she hurried after them and never stopped till she came up with the two. They had to go home with her that day, but they scolded her bitterly.

The two settled then to kill Smallhead, so one day they took twenty needles and scattered them outside in a pile of straw. " We are going to that hill beyond," said they, " to stay till evening, and if you have not all the needles that are in that straw outside gathered and on the tables before us, we'll have your life."

Away they went to the hill. Smallhead sat down, and was crying bitterly when a short gray cat walked in and spoke to her.

" Why do you cry and lament so ? " asked the cat.

" My sisters abuse me and beat me," answered Smallhead. " This morning they said they would kill me in the evening unless I had all the needles in the straw outside gathered before them."

" Sit down here," said the cat, " and dry your tears."

The cat soon found the twenty needles and brought them to Smallhead. " Stop there now," said the cat, " and listen to what I tell you. I am your mother; your sisters killed me and destroyed my body, but don't harm them; do them good, do the best you can for them, save them: obey my words and it will be better for you in the end."

The cat went away for herself, and the sisters came home in the evening. The needles were on the table before them. Oh, but they were vexed and angry when they saw the twenty needles, and they said some one was helping their sister !

One night when Smallhead was in bed and asleep they started away again, resolved this time never to return. Smallhead slept till morning. When she saw that the sisters were gone she followed, traced them from place to place, inquired here and there day after day, till one evening some person told her that they were in the house of an old hag, a terrible enchantress, who had one son and three daughters : that the house was a bad place to be in, for the old hag had more power of witchcraft than any one and was very wicked.

Smallhead hurried away to save her sisters, and facing the house knocked at the door, and asked lodgings for God's sake.

" Oh, then," said the hag, " it is hard to refuse any one lodgings, and besides on such a wild, stormy night. I wonder if you are anything to the young ladies who came the way this evening ? "

The two sisters heard this and were angry enough that Smallhead was in it, but they said nothing, not wishing the old hag to know their relationship. After supper the hag told the three strangers to sleep in a room on the right side of the house. When her own daughters were going to bed Smallhead saw her tie a ribbon around the neck of each one of them, and heard her say : " Do you sleep in the left-hand bed." Smallhead hurried and said to her sisters : " Come quickly, or I'll tell the woman who you are."

They took the bed in the left-hand room and were in it before the hag's daughters came.

"Oh," said the daughters, " the other bed is as good." So they took the bed in the right-hand room. When Smallhead knew that the hag's daughters were asleep she rose, took the ribbons off their necks, and put them on her sisters' necks and on her own. She lay awake and watched them. After a while she heard the hag say to her son :

THE BRIDGE OF BLOOD

Smallhead carried one sister over the bridge and then the other.—Page 197.
Irish Fairy Tales.

"Go, now, and kill the three girls; they have the clothes and money."

"You have killed enough in your life and so let these go," said the son.

But the old woman would not listen. The boy rose up, fearing his mother, and taking a long knife, went to the right-hand room and cut the throats of the three girls without ribbons. He went to bed then for himself, and when Smallhead found that the old hag was asleep she roused her sisters, told what had happened, made them dress quickly and follow her. Believe me, they were willing and glad to follow her this time.

The three traveled briskly and came soon to a bridge, called at that time "The Bridge of Blood." Whoever had killed a person could not cross the bridge. When the three girls came to the bridge the two sisters stopped: they could not go a step further. Smallhead ran across and went back again.

"If I did not know that you killed our mother," said she, "I might know it now, for this is the Bridge of Blood."

She carried one sister over the bridge on her back and then the other. Hardly was this done when the hag was at the bridge.

"Bad luck to you, Smallhead!" said she, "I did not know that it was you that was in it last evening. You have killed my three daughters."

"It wasn't I that killed them, but yourself," said Smallhead.

The old hag could not cross the bridge, so she began to curse, and she put every curse on Smallhead that she could remember. The sisters traveled on till they came to a king's castle. They heard that two servants were needed in the castle.

"Go now," said Smallhead to the two sisters, "and ask for service. Be faithful and do well. You can never go back by the road you came."

The two found employment at the King's castle.

Smallhead took lodgings in the house of a blacksmith near by.

"I should be glad to find a place as kitchen-maid in the castle," said Smallhead to the blacksmith's wife.

"I will go to the castle and find a place for you if I can," said the woman.

The blacksmith's wife found a place for Smallhead as kitchen-maid in the castle, and she went there next day.

"I must be careful," thought Smallhead, "and do my best. I am in a strange place. My two sisters are here in the King's castle. Who knows, we may have great fortune yet."

She dressed neatly and was cheerful. Every one liked her, liked her better than her sisters, though they were beautiful. The King had two sons, one at home and the other abroad. Smallhead thought to herself one day: "It is time for the son who is here in the castle to marry. I will speak to him the first time I can." One day she saw him alone in the garden, went up to him, and said:

"Why are you not getting married, it is high time for you?"

He only laughed and thought she was too bold, but then thinking that she was a simple-minded girl who wished to be pleasant, he said:

"I will tell you the reason: My grandfather bound my father by an oath never to let his oldest son marry until he could get the Sword of Light, and I am afraid that I shall be long without marrying."

"Do you know where the Sword of Light is, or who has it?" asked Smallhead.

"I do," said the King's son, "an old hag who has great power and enchantment, and she lives a long distance from this, beyond the Bridge of Blood. I cannot go there myself, I cannot cross the bridge, for I have killed men in battle. Even if I could cross the bridge I would not go, for many is the King's son that hag has destroyed or enchanted."

" Suppose some person were to bring the Sword of Light, and that person a woman, would you marry her?"

" I would, indeed," said the King's son.

" If you promise to marry my elder sister I will strive to bring the Sword of Light."

" I will promise most willingly," said the King's son.

Next morning early, Smallhead set out on her journey. Calling at the first shop she bought a stone weight of salt, and went on her way, never stopping or resting till she reached the hag's house at nightfall. She climbed to the gable, looked down, and saw the son making a great pot of stirabout for his mother, and she hurrying him. " I am as hungry as a hawk!" cried she.

Whenever the boy looked away, Smallhead dropped salt down, dropped it when he was not looking, dropped it till she had the whole stone of salt in the stirabout. The old hag waited and waited till at last she cried out: " Bring the stirabout. I am starving! Bring the pot. I will eat from the pot. Give the milk here as well."

The boy brought the stirabout and the milk, the old woman began to eat, but the first taste she got she spat out and screamed: " You put salt in the pot in place of meal!"

" I did not, mother."

" You did, and it's a mean trick that you played on me. Throw this stirabout to the pig outside and go for water to the well in the field."

" I cannot go," said the boy, "the night is too dark; I might fall into the well."

" You must go and bring the water; I cannot live till morning without eating."

" I am as hungry as yourself," said the boy, " but how can I go to the well without a light? I will not go unless you give me a light."

" If I give you the Sword of Light there is no knowing who may follow you; maybe that devil of a Smallhead is outside."

But sooner than fast till morning the old hag gave the

Sword of Light to her son, warning him to take good care of it. He took the Sword of Light and went out. As he saw no one when he came to the well he left the sword on the top of the steps going down to the water, so as to have good light. He had not gone down many steps when Smallhead had the sword, and away she ran over hills, dales, and valleys towards the Bridge of Blood.

The boy shouted and screamed with all his might. Out ran the hag. "Where is the sword?" cried she.

"Some one took it from the step."

Off rushed the hag, following the light, but she didn't come near Smallhead till she was over the bridge.

"Give me the Sword of Light, or bad luck to you," cried the hag.

"Indeed, then, I will not; I will keep it, and bad luck to yourself," answered Smallhead.

On the following morning she walked up to the King's son and said:

"I have the Sword of Light; now will you marry my sister?"

"I will," said he.

The King's son married Smallhead's sister and got the Sword of Light. Smallhead stayed no longer in the kitchen—the sister didn't care to have her in kitchen or parlor.

The King's second son came home. He was not long in the castle when Smallhead said to herself, "Maybe he will marry my second sister."

She saw him one day in the garden, went toward him; he said something, she answered, then asked: "Is it not time for you to be getting married like your brother?"

"When my grandfather was dying," said the young man, "he bound my father not to let his second son marry till he had the Black Book. This book used to shine and give brighter light than ever the Sword of Light did, and I suppose it does yet. The old hag beyond the Bridge of Blood has the book, and no one dares to go near her, for many is the King's son killed or enchanted by that woman."

"Would you marry my second sister if you were to get the Black Book?"

"I would, indeed; I would marry any woman if I got the Black Book with her. The Sword of Light and the Black Book were in our family till my grandfather's time, then they were stolen by that cursed old hag."

"I will have the book," said Smallhead, "or die in the trial to get it."

Knowing that stirabout was the main food of the hag, Smallhead settled in her mind to play another trick. Taking a bag she scraped the chimney, gathered about a stone of soot, and took it with her. The night was dark and rainy. When she reached the hag's house, she climbed up the gable to the chimney and found that the son was making stirabout for his mother. She dropped the soot down by degrees till at last the whole stone of soot was in the pot; then she scraped around the top of the chimney till a lump of soot fell on the boy's hand.

"Oh, mother," said he, "the night is wet and soft, the soot is falling."

"Cover the pot," said the hag. "Be quick with that stirabout, I am starving."

The boy took the pot to his mother.

"Bad luck to you," cried the hag the moment she tasted the stirabout, "this is full of soot; throw it out to the pig."

"If I throw it out there is no water inside to make more, and I'll not go in the dark and rain to the well."

"You must go!" screamed she.

"I'll not stir a foot out of this unless I get a light," said the boy.

"Is it the book you are thinking of, you fool, to take it and lose it as you did the sword? Smallhead is watching you."

"How could Smallhead, the creature, be outside all the

time ?   If you have no use for the water you can do without it."

Sooner than stop fasting till morning, the hag gave her
son the book, saying: " Do not put this down or let it
from your hand till you come in, or I'll have your life."

The boy took the book and went to the well.   Smallhead followed him carefully.   He took the book down
into the well with him, and when he was stooping to dip
water she snatched the book and pushed him into the
well, where he came very near drowning.

Smallhead was far away when the boy recovered, and
began to scream and shout to his mother.   She came in a
hurry, and finding that the book was gone, fell into such
a rage that she thrust a knife into her son's heart and
ran after Smallhead, who had crossed the bridge before
the hag could come up with her.

When the old woman saw Smallhead on the other side
of the bridge facing her and dancing with delight, she
screamed :

" You took the Sword of Light and the Black Book,
and your two sisters are married.   Oh, then, bad luck to
you.   I will put my curse on you wherever you go.   You
have all my children killed, and I a poor, feeble, old
woman."

" Bad luck to yourself," said Smallhead.   " I am not
afraid of a curse from the like of you.   If you had lived
an honest life you wouldn't be as you are to-day."

" Now, Smallhead," said the old hag, " you have me
robbed of everything, and my children destroyed.   Your
two sisters are well married.   Your fortune began with
my ruin.   Come, now, and take care of me in my old age.
I'll take my curse from you, and you will have good luck.
I bind myself never to harm a hair of your head."

Smallhead thought awhile, promised to do this, and
said: " If you harm me, or try to harm me, it will be the
worse for yourself."

The old hag was satisfied and went home.   Smallhead
went to the castle and was received with great joy.   Next

morning she found the King's son in the garden, and said : "If you marry my sister to-morrow, you will have the Black Book."

"I will marry her gladly," said the King's son.

Next day the marriage was celebrated and the King's son got the book.   Smallhead remained in the castle about a week, then she left good health with her sisters and went to the hag's house.   The old woman was glad to see her and showed the girl her work.   All Smallhead had to do was to wait on the hag and feed a large pig that she had.

"I am fatting that pig," said the hag; "he is seven years old now, and the longer you keep a pig the harder his meat is : we'll keep this pig a while longer, and then we'll kill and eat him."

Smallhead did her work ; the old hag taught her some things, and Smallhead learned herself far more than the hag dreamt of.   The girl fed the pig three times a day, never thinking that he could be anything but a pig.   The hag had sent word to a sister that she had in the Eastern World, bidding her come and they would kill the pig and have a great feast.   The sister came, and one day when the hag was going to walk with her sister she said to Smallhead :

"Give the pig plenty of meal to-day; this is the last food he'll have ; give him his fill."

The pig had his own mind and knew what was coming. He put his nose under the pot and threw it on Small-head's toes, and she barefoot.   With that she ran into the house for a stick, and seeing a rod on the edge of the loft, snatched it and hit the pig.

That moment the pig was a splendid young man.

Smallhead was amazed.

"Never fear," said the young man, "I am the son of a King that the old hag hated, the King of Munster.   She stole me from my father seven years ago and enchanted me—made a pig of me."

Smallhead told the King s son, then, how the hag had

treated her. "I must make a pig of you again," said she "for the hag is coming. Be patient and I'll save you, if you promise to marry me."

"I promise you," said the King's son.

With that she struck him, and he was a pig again. She put the switch in its place and was at her work when the two sisters came. The pig ate his meal now with a good heart, for he felt sure of rescue.

"Who is that girl you have in the house, and where did you find her?" asked the sister.

"All my children died of the plague, and I took this girl to help me. She is a very good servant."

At night the hag slept in one room, her sister in another, and Smallhead in a third. When the two sisters were sleeping soundly Smallhead rose, stole the hag's magic book, and then took the rod. She went next to where the pig was, and with one blow of the rod made a man of him

With the help of the magic book Smallhead made two doves of herself and the King's son, and they took flight through the air and flew on without stopping. Next morning the hag called Smallhead, but she did not come. She hurried out to see the pig. The pig was gone. She ran to her book. Not a sign of it.

"Oh!" cried she, "that villain of a Smallhead has robbed me. She has stolen my book, made a man of the pig, and taken him away with her."

What could she do but tell her whole story to the sister. "Go you," said she, "and follow them. You have more enchantment than Smallhead has."

"How am I to know them?" asked the sister.

"Bring the first two strange things that you find; they will turn themselves into something wonderful."

The sister then made a hawk of herself and flew away as swiftly as any March wind.

"Look behind," said Smallhead to the King's son some hours later; "see what is coming."

"I see nothing," said he, "but a hawk coming swiftly."

" That is the hag's sister. She has three times more enchantment than the hag herself. But fly down on the ditch and be picking yourself as doves do in rainy weather, and maybe she'll pass without seeing us."

The hawk saw the doves, but thinking them nothing wonderful, flew on till evening, and then went back to her sister.

" Did you see anything wonderful ? "

" I did not; I saw only two doves, and they picking themselves."

" You fool, those doves were Smallhead and the King's son. Off with you in the morning and don't let me see you again without the two with you."

Away went the hawk a second time, and swiftly as Smallhead and the King's son flew, the hawk was gaining on them. Seeing this Smallhead and the King's son dropped down into a large village, and, it being market-day, they made two heather brooms of themselves. The two brooms began to sweep the road without any one holding them, and swept toward each other. This was a great wonder. Crowds gathered at once around the two brooms.

The old hag flying over in the form of a hawk saw this and thinking that it must be Smallhead and the King's son were in it, came down, turned into a woman, and said to herself :

" I'll have those two brooms."

She pushed forward so quickly through the crowd that she came near knocking down a man standing before her. The man was vexed.

" You cursed old hag ! " cried he, " do you want to knock us down ? " With that he gave her a blow and drove her against another man, that man gave her a push that sent her spinning against a third man, and so on till between them all they came near putting the life out of her, and pushed her away from the brooms. A woman in the crowd called out then :

" It would be nothing but right to knock the head off

that old hag, and she trying to push us away from the
mercy of God, for it was God who sent the brooms to
sweep the road for us."

" True for you," said another woman. With that the
people were as angry as angry could be, and were ready
to kill the hag. They were going to take the head off
the hag when she made a hawk of herself and flew away,
vowing never to do another stroke of work for her sister.
She might do her own work or let it alone.

When the hawk disappeared the two heather brooms
rose and turned into doves. The people felt sure when
they saw the doves that the brooms were a blessing from
heaven, and it was the old hag that drove them away.

On the following day Smallhead and the King's son
saw his father's castle, and the two came down not too
far from it in their own forms. Smallhead was a very
beautiful woman now, and why not? She had the magic
and didn't spare it. She made herself as beautiful as
ever she could : the like of her was not to be seen in that
kingdom or the next one.

The King's son was in love with her that minute, and
did not wish to part with her, but she would not go with
him.

" When you are at your father's castle," said Smallhead,
"all will be overjoyed to see you, and the king will give
a great feast in your honor. If you kiss any one or let
any living thing kiss you, you'll forget me for ever."

" I will not let even my own mother kiss me," said he.

The King's son went to the castle. All were overjoyed;
they had thought him dead, had not seen him for seven
years. He would let no one come near to kiss him. " I
am bound by oath to kiss no one," said he to his mother.
At that moment an old greyhound came in, and with
one spring was on his shoulder licking his face : all that
the King's son had gone through in seven years was forgotten in one moment.

Smallhead went toward a forge near the castle. The
smith had a wife far younger than himself, and a step-

daughter. They were no beauties. In the rear of the
forge was a well and a tree growing over it. "I will go
up in that tree," thought Smallhead, "and spend the
night in it." She went up and sat just over the well.
She was not long in the tree when the moon came out
high above the hill tops and shone on the well. The
blacksmith's stepdaughter, coming for water, looked down
in the well, saw the face of the woman above in the tree,
thought it her own face, and cried:

"Oh, then, to have me bringing water to a smith, and
I such a beauty. I'll never bring another drop to him."
With that she cast the pail in the ditch and ran off to
find a king's son to marry.

When she was not coming with the water, and the
blacksmith waiting to wash after his day's work in the
forge, he sent the mother. The mother had nothing but
a pot to get the water in, so off she went with that, and
coming to the well saw the beautiful face in the water.

"Oh, you black, swarthy villain of a smith," cried she,
"bad luck to the hour that I met you, and I such a beauty.
I'll never draw another drop of water for the life of
you!"

She threw the pot down, broke it, and hurried away to
find some king's son.

When neither mother nor daughter came back with
water the smith himself went to see what was keeping
them. He saw the pail in the ditch, and, catching it,
went to the well; looking down, he saw the beautiful
face of a woman in the water. Being a man, he knew
that it was not his own face that was in it, so he looked
up, and there in the tree saw a woman. He spoke to her
and said:

"I know now why my wife and her daughter did not
bring water. They saw your face in the well, and, thinking themselves too good for me, ran away. You must
come now and keep the house till I find them."

"I will help you," said Smallhead. She came down,
went to the smith's house, and showed the road that the

women took. The smith hurried after them, and found
the two in the village ten miles away. He explained
their own folly to them, and they came home.

The mother and daughter washed fine linen for the
castle. Smallhead saw them ironing one day, and said:

"Sit down: I will iron for you."

She caught the iron, and in an hour had the work of
the day done.

The women were delighted. In the evening the
daughter took the linen to the housekeeper at the castle.

"Who ironed this linen?" asked the housekeeper.

"My mother and I."

"Indeed, then, you did not. You can't do the like of
that work, and tell me who did it."

The girl was in dread now and answered:

"It is a woman who is stopping with us who did the
ironing."

The housekeeper went to the Queen and showed her
the linen.

Send that woman to the castle," said the Queen.

Smallhead went: the Queen welcomed her, wondered
at her beauty; put her over all the maids in the castle.
Smallhead could do anything; everybody was fond of
her. The King's son never knew that he had seen her
before, and she lived in the castle a year; what the Queen
told her she did.

The King had made a match for his son with the
daughter of the King of Ulster. There was a great feast
in the castle in honor of the young couple, the marriage
was to be a week later. The bride's father brought many
of his people who were versed in all kinds of tricks and
enchantment.

The King knew that Smallhead could do many things,
for neither the Queen nor himself had asked her to do a
thing that she did not do in a twinkle.

"Now," said the King to the Queen, "I think she can
do something that his people cannot do." He summoned
Smallhead and asked:

" Can you amuse the strangers? "

" I can if you wish me to do so."

When the time came and the Ulster men had shown their best tricks, Smallhead came forward and raised the window, which was forty feet from the ground. She had a small ball of thread in her hand; she tied one end of the thread to the window, threw the ball out and over a wall near the castle; then she passed out the window, walked on the thread and kept time to music from players that no man could see. She came in; all cheered her and were greatly delighted.

" I can do that," said the King of Ulster's daughter, and sprang out on the string; but if she did she fell and broke her neck on the stones below. There were cries, there was lamentation, and, in place of a marriage, a funeral.

The King's son was angry and grieved and wanted to drive Smallhead from the castle in some way.

" She is not to blame," said the King of Munster, who did nothing but praise her.

Another year passed: the King got the daughter of the King of Connacht for his son. There was a great feast before the wedding day, and as the Connacht people are full of enchantment and witchcraft, the King of Munster called Smallhead and said:

" Now show the best trick of any."

" I will," said Smallhead.

When the feast was over and the Connacht men had shown their tricks the King of Munster called Smallhead.

She stood before the company, threw two grains of· wheat on the floor, and spoke some magic words. There was a hen and a cock there before her of beautiful plumage; she threw a grain of wheat between them; the hen sprang to eat the wheat, the cock gave her a blow of his bill, the hen drew back, looked at him, and said:

" Bad luck to you, you wouldn't do the like of that when I was serving the old hag and you her pig, and I made a man of you and gave you back your own form.

The King's son looked at her and thought, "There must be something in this."

Smallhead threw a second grain. The cock pecked the hen again. "Oh," said the hen, "you would not do that the day the hag's sister was hunting us, and we two doves."

The King's son was still more astonished.

She threw a third grain. The cock struck the hen, and she said, "You would not do that to me the day I made two heather brooms out of you and myself." She threw a fourth grain. The cock pecked the hen a fourth time. "You would not do that the day you promised not to let any living thing kiss you or kiss any one yourself but me—you let the hound kiss you and you forgot me."

The King's son made one bound forward, embraced and kissed Smallhead, and told the King his whole story from beginning to end.

"This is my wife," said he; "I'll marry no other woman."

"Whose wife will my daughter be?" asked the King of Connacht.

"Oh, she will be the wife of the man who will marry her," said the King of Munster, "my son gave his word to this woman before he saw your daughter, and he must keep it."

So Smallhead married the King of Munster's son.

"This is my wife," said the king's son. "I'll marry no other."—Page 210.

Irish Fairy Tales.

WITCHES,* FAIRY DOCTORS.

WITCHES and fairy doctors receive their power from opposite dynasties; the witch from evil spirits and her own malignant will; the fairy doctor from the fairies, and a something—a temperament—that is born with him or

* The last trial for witchcraft in Ireland—there were never very many—is thus given in MacSkimin's *History of Carrickfergus* :— "1711, March 31st, Janet Mean, of Braid-island ; Janet Latimer, Irish-quarter, Carrickfergus ; Janet Millar, Scotch-quarter, Carrickfergus ; Margaret Mitchel, Kilroot ; Catharine M'Calmond, Janet Liston, *alias* Seller, Elizabeth Seller, and Janet Carson, the four last from Island Magee, were tried here, in the County of Antrim Court, for witchcraft."
Their alleged crime was tormenting a young woman, called Mary Dunbar, about eighteen years of age, at the house of James Hattridge, Island Magee, and at other places to which she was removed. The circumstances sworn on the trial were as follows :—
"The afflicted person being, in the month of February, 1711, in the house of James Hattridge, Island Magee (which had been for some time believed to be haunted by evil spirits), found an apron on the parlor floor, that had been missing some time, tied with *five strange knots*, which she loosened.
" On the following day she was suddenly seized with a violent pain in her thigh, and afterwards fell into fits and ravings ; and, on recovering, said she was tormented by several women, whose dress and personal appearance she minutely described. Shortly after, she was again seized with the like fits, and on recovering she accused five other women of tormenting her, describing them also. The accused persons being brought from different parts of the country, she appeared to suffer extreme fear and additional torture as they approached the house.
" It was also deposed that strange noises, as of whistling, scratching, etc., were heard in the house, and that a sulphureous smell was observed in the rooms ; that stones, turf, and the like were thrown about the house, and the coverlets, etc., frequently taken off the beds and made up in the shape of a corpse ; and

211

her. The first is always feared and hated. The second is gone to for advice, and is never worse than mischievous. The most celebrated fairy doctors are sometimes people the fairies loved and carried away, and kept with them for seven years ; not that those the fairies' love are always carried off—they may merely grow silent and strange, and taken to lonely wanderings in the "gentle" places. Such will, in after-times, be great poets or musicians, or fairy doctors ; they must not be confused with those who have a *Lianhaun shee* [*leannán-sidhe*], for the *Lianhaun shee* lives upon the vitals of its chosen, and they waste and die.

that a bolster once walked out of a room into the kitchen with a night-gown about it ! It likewise appeared in evidence that in some of her fits three strong men were scarcely able to hold her in the bed ; that at times she vomited feathers, cotton yarn, pins, and buttons ; and that on one occasion she slid off the bed and was laid on the floor, as if supported and drawn by an invincible power. The afflicted person was unable to give any evidence on the trial, being during that time dumb, but had no violent fit during its continuance."

In defence of the accused, it appeared that they were mostly sober, industrious people, who attended public worship, could repeat the Lord's Prayer, and had been known to pray both in public and private ; and that some of them had lately received communion.

Judge Upton charged the jury, and observed on the regular attendance of accused at public worship ; remarking that he thought it improbable that real witches could so far retain the form of religion as to frequent the religious worship of God, both publicly and privately, which had been proved in favor of the accused. He concluded by giving his opinion "that the jury could not bring them in guilty upon the sole testimony of the afflicted person's visionary images." He was followed by Judge Macarthy, who differed from him in opinion, "and thought the jury might, from the evidence, bring them in guilty," which they accordingly did.

This trial lasted from six o'clock in the morning till two in the afternoon ; and the prisoners were sentenced to be imprisoned twelve months, and to stand four times in the pillory of Carrick-fergus.

Tradition says that the people were much exasperated against these unfortunate persons, who were severely pelted in the pillory with boiled cabbage stalks and the like, by which one of them had an eye beaten out.

She is of the dreadful solitary fairies. To her have belonged the greatest of the Irish poets, from Oisin down to
the last century.

Those we speak of have for their friends the trooping
fairies—the gay and sociable populace of raths and caves.
Great is their knowledge of herbs and spells. These
doctors; when the butter will not come on the milk, or
the milk will not come from the cow, will be sent for to
find out if the cause be in the course of common nature
or if there has been witchcraft. Perhaps some old hag in
the shape of a hare has been milking the cattle. Perhaps
some user of " the dead hand " has drawn away the butter
to her own churn. Whatever it be, there is the counter-
charm. They will give advice, too, in cases of suspected
changelings, and prescribe for the " fairy blast (when the
fairy strikes any one a tumor rises, or they become
paralyzed. This is called a " fairy blast " or a " fairy
stroke ") The fairies are, or course, visible to them, and
many a new-built house have they bid the owner pull
down because it lay on the fairies' road. Lady Wilde thus
describes one who lived in Innis Sark :—" He never
touched beer, spirits, or meat in all his life, but has lived
entirely on bread, fruit, and vegetables. A man who
knew him thus describes him—' Winter and summer his
dress is the same—merely a flannel shirt and coat, He
will pay his share at a feast, but neither eats nor drinks
of the food and drink set before him. He speaks no English, and never could be made to learn the English tongue,
though he says it might be used with great effect to curse
one's enemy. He holds a burial-ground sacred, and would
not carry away so much as a leaf of ivy from a grave.
And he maintains that the people are right to keep to their
ancient usages, such as never to dig a grave on a Monday,
and to carry the coffin three times round the grave,
following the course of the sun, for then the dead rest in
peace. Like the people, also, he holds suicides as accursed ;
for they believe that all its dead turn over on their faces
if a suicide is laid amongst them.

" ' Though well off, he never, even in his youth, thought
of taking a wife; nor was he ever known to love a woman.
He stands quite apart from life, and by this means holds
his power over the mysteries. No money will tempt him
to impart his knowledge to another, for if he did he would
be struck dead—so he believes. He would not touch a
hazel stick, but carries an ash wand, which he holds in
his hand when he prays, laid across his knees; and the
whole of his life is devoted to works of grace and charity,
and though now an old man, he has never had a day's
sickness. No one has ever seen him in a rage, nor heard
an angry word from his lips but once, and then being
under great irritation, he recited the Lord's Prayer backwards as an imprecation on his enemy. Before his death
he will reveal the mystery of his power, but not till the
hand of death is on him for certain.' " When he does
reveal it, we may be sure it will be to one person only —
his successor. There are several such doctors in County
Sligo, really well up in herbal medicine by all accounts,
and my friends find them in their own counties. All these
things go on merrily. The spirit of the age laughs in
vain, and is itself only a ripple to pass, or already passing,
away.

The spells of the witch are altogether different; they
smell of the grave. One of the most powerful is the
charm of the dead hand. With a hand cut from a corpse
they, muttering words of power, will stir a well and skim
from its surface a neighbor's butter.

A candle held between the fingers of the dead hand can
never be blown out. This is useful to robbers, but they
appeal for the suffrage of the lovers likewise, for they can
make love-potions by drying and grinding into powder
the liver of a black cat. Mixed with tea, and poured
from a black teapot, it is infallible. There are many
stories of its success in quite recent years, but, unhappily,
the spell must be continually renewed, or all the love may
turn into hate. But the central notion of witchcraft
everywhere is the power to change into some fictitious

form, usually in Ireland a hare or a cat.   Long ago a wolf
was the favorite.   Before Giraldus Cambrensis came to
Ireland, a monk wandering in a forest at night came upon
two wolves, one of whom was dying.   The other entreated
him to give the dying wolf the last sacrament.   He said
the mass, and paused when he came to the viaticum.
The other, on seeing this, tore the skin from the breast
of the dying wolf, laying bare the form of an old woman.
Thereon the monk gave the sacrament.   Years afterwards
he confessed the matter, and when Giraldus visited the
country, was being tried by the synod of the bishops.
To give the sacrament to an animal was a great sin.   Was
it a human being or an animal ?   On the advice of Giraldus
they sent the monk, with papers describing the matter,
to the Pope for his decision.   The result is not stated.

Giraldus himself was of opinion that the wolf-form was
an illusion, for, as he argued, only God can change the
form.   His opinion coincides with tradition, Irish and
otherwise.

It is the notion of many who have written about these
things that magic is mainly the making of such illusions.
Patrick Kennedy tells a story of a girl who, having in her
hand a sod of grass containing, unknown to herself, a
four-leaved shamrock, watched a conjurer at a fair.   Now,
the four-leaved shamrock guards its owner from all
pishogues (spells), and when the others were staring at a
cock carrying along the roof of a shed a huge beam in its
bill, she asked them what they found to wonder at in a
cock with a straw.   The conjurer begged from her the
sod of grass, to give to his horse, he said.   Immediately
she cried out in terror that the beam would fall and kill
somebody.

This, then, is to be remembered—the form of an enchanted thing is a fiction and a caprice.

BEWITCHED BUTTER (DONEGAL).

MISS LETITIA MACLINTOCK.

NOT far from Rathmullen lived, last spring, a family called Hanlon; and in a farm-house, some fields distant, people named Dogherty. Both families had good cows, but the Hanlons were fortunate in possessing a Kerry cow that gave more milk and yellower butter that the others.

Grace Dogherty, a young girl, who was more admired than loved in the neighborhood, took much interest in the Kerry cow, and appeared one night at Mrs. Hanlon's door with the modest request—

" Will you let me milk your Moiley cow ? "

" An' why wad you wish to milk wee Moiley, Grace, dear ? " inquired Mrs. Hanlon.

" Oh, just becase you're sae throng at the present time."

" Thank you kindly, Grace, but I'm no too throng to do my ain work.   I'll no trouble you to milk."

The girl turned away with a discontented air; but the next evening, and the next, found her at the cow-house door with the same request.

At length Mrs. Hanlon, not knowing well how to persist in her refusal, yielded, and permitted Grace to milk the Kerry cow.

She soon had reason to regret her want of firmness. Moiley gave no more milk to her owner.

When this melancholy state of things lasted for three days, the Hanlons applied to a certain Mark McCarrion, who lived near Binion.

" That cow has been milked by some one with an evil eye," said he. " Will she give you a wee drop, do you think?   The full of a pint measure wad do."

" Oh, ay, Mark, dear ; I'll get that much milk frae her, any way."

" Weel, Mrs. Hanlon, lock the door, an' get nine new pins that was never used in clothes, an' put them into a saucepan wi' the pint o' milk. Set them on the fire, an' let them come to the boil."

The nine pins soon began to simmer in Moiley's * milk.

Rapid steps were heard approaching the door, agitated knocks followed, and Grace Dogherty's high-toned voice was raised in eager entreaty.

"Let me in, Mrs. Hanlon!" she cried. "Tak off that cruel pot! Tak out them pins, for they're pricking holes in my heart, an' I'll never offer to touch milk of yours again."

[There is hardly a village in Ireland where the milk is not thus believed to have been stolen times upon times. There are many counter-charms. Sometimes the coulter of a plow will be heated red-hot, and the witch will rush in, crying out that she is burning. A new horse-shoe or donkey-shoe, heated and put under the churn, with three straws, if possible, stolen at midnight from over the witches' door, is quite infallible.—ED.]

A QUEEN'S COUNTY WITCH †

IT was about eighty years ago, in the month of May, that a Roman Catholic clergyman, near Rathdowney, in the Queen's County, was awakened at midnight to attend a dying man in a distant part of the parish. The priest obeyed without a murmur, and having performed his duty

* In Connaught called a "mweea" cow—i. e., a cow without horns. Irish *maol*, literally, blunt. When the new hammerless breechloaders came into use two or three years ago, Mr. Douglas Hyde heard a Connaught gentleman speak of them as the "mweeal" guns, because they had no cocks.

† *Dublin University Review*, 1889.

to the expiring sinner, saw him depart this world before
he left the cabin. As it was yet dark, the man who had
called on the priest offered to accompany him home, but
he refused, and set forward on his journey alone. The
gray dawn began to appear over the hills. The good
priest was highly enraptured with the beauty of the scene,
and rode on, now gazing intently at every surrounding
object, and again cutting with his whip at the bats and
big beautiful night-flies which flitted ever and anon from
hedge to hedge across his lonely way. Thus engaged, he
journeyed on slowly, until the nearer approach of sunrise
began to render objects completely discernible, when he
dismounted from his horse, and slipping his arm out of
the rein, and drawing forth his "Breviary" from his
pocket, he commenced reading his "morning office" as he
walked leisurely along.

He had not proceeded very far, when he observed his
horse, a very spirited animal, endeavoring to stop on the
road, and gazing intently into a field on one side of the
way where there were three or four cows grazing. However, he did not pay any particular attention to this circumstance, but went on a little farther, when the horse
suddenly plunged with great violence, and endeavored to
break away by force. The priest with great difficulty
succeeded in restraining him, and, looking at him more
closely, observed him shaking from head to foot, and
sweating profusely. He now stood calmly, and refused
to move from where he was, nor could threats or entreaty
induce him to proceed. The father was greatly astonished,
but recollecting to have often heard of horses laboring
under affright being induced to go by blindfolding them,
he took out his handkerchief and tied it across his eyes.
He then mounted, and, striking him gently, he went forward without reluctance, but still sweating and trembling
violently. They had not gone far, when they arrived
opposite a narrow path or bridle-way, flanked at either
side by a tall, thick hedge, which led from the high-road
to the field where the cows were grazing. The priest

happened by chance to look into the lane, and saw a spectacle which made the blood curdle in his veins. It was the legs of a man from the hips downwards, without head or body, trotting up the avenue at a smart pace. The good father was very much alarmed, but, being a man of strong nerve, he resolved, come what might, to stand, and be further acquainted with this singular specter. He accordingly stood, and so did the headless apparition, as if afraid to approach him. The priest, observing this, pulled back a little from the entrance of the avenue, and the phantom again resumed its progress. It soon arrived on the road, and the priest now had sufficient opportunity to view it minutely. It wore yellow buckskin breeches, tightly fastened at the knees with green ribbon; it had neither shoes nor stockings on, and its legs were covered with long, red hairs, and all full of wet, blood, and clay, apparently contracted in its progress through the thorny hedges. The priest, although very much alarmed, felt eager to examine the phantom, and for this purpose summoned all his philosophy to enable him to speak to it. The ghost was now a little ahead, pursuing its march at its usual brisk trot, and the priest urged on his horse speedily until he came up with it, and thus addressed it—

"Hilloa, friend! who art thou, or whither art thou going so early?"

The hideous specter made no reply, but uttered a fierce and superhuman growl, or "Umph."

"A fine morning for ghosts to wander abroad," again said the priest.

Another "Umph" was the reply.

"Why don't you speak?"

"Umph."

"You don't seem disposed to be very loquacious this morning."

"Umph," again.

The good man began to feel irritated at the obstinate silence of his unearthly visitor, and said, with some warmth—

"In the name of all that's sacred, I command you to answer me, Who art thou, or where art thou traveling?"

Another "Umph," more loud and more angry than before, was the only reply.

"Perhaps," said the father, "a taste of whipcord might render you a little more communicative;" and so saying, he struck the apparition a heavy blow with his whip on the breech.

The phantom uttered a wild and unearthly yell, and fell forward on the road, and what was the priest's astonishment when he perceived the whole place running over with milk. He was struck dumb with amazement; the prostrate phantom still continued to eject vast quantities of milk from every part; the priest's head swam, his eyes got dizzy; a stupor came all over him for some minutes, and on his recovering, the frightful specter had vanished, and in its stead he found stretched on the road, and half drowned in milk, the form of Sarah Kennedy, an old woman of the neighborhood, who had been long notorious in that district for her witchcraft and superstitious practices, and it was now discovered that she had, by infernal aid, assumed that monstrous shape, and was employed that morning in sucking the cows of the village. Had a volcano burst forth at his feet, he could not be more astonished; he gazed awhile in silent amazement— the old woman groaning, and writhing convulsively.

"Sarah," said he, at length, "I have long admonished you to repent of your evil ways, but you were deaf to my entreaties; and now, wretched woman, you are surprised in the midst of your crimes."

"Oh, father, father," shouted the unfortunate woman, "can you do nothing to save me? I am lost; hell is open for me, and legions of devils surround me this moment, waiting to carry my soul to perdition."

The priest had not power to reply; the old wretch's pains increased; her body swelled to an immense size; her eyes flashed as if on fire, her face was black as night, her entire form writhed in a thousand different contortions; her outcries were appalling, her face sunk, her eyes closed, and in a few minutes she expired in the most exquisite tortures.

The priest departed homewards, and called at the next cabin to give notice of the strange circumstances. The remains of Sarah Kennedy were removed to her cabin, situate at the edge of a small wood at a little distance. She had long been a resident in that neighborhood, but still she was a stranger, and came there no one knew from whence. She had no relation in that country but one daughter, now advanced in years, who resided with her. She kept one cow, but sold more butter, it was said, than any farmer in the parish, and it was generally suspected that she acquired it by devilish agency, as she never made a secret of being intimately acquainted with sorcery and fairyism. She professed the Roman Catholic religion, but never complied with the practices enjoined by that church, and her remains were denied Christian sepulture, and were buried in a sand-pit near her own cabin.

On the evening of her burial, the villagers assembled and burned her cabin to the earth. Her daughter made her escape, and never after returned.

THE WITCH HARE.

MR. AND MRS. S. C. HALL.

I was out thracking hares meeself, and I seen a fine puss of a thing hopping hopping in the moonlight, and whacking her ears about, now up, now down, and winking her great eyes, and—" Here goes," says I, and the thing was so close to me that she turned round and looked at me, and then bounced back, as well as to say, do your worst! So I had the least grain in life of *blessed powder* left, and I put it in the gun—and bang at her! My jewel, the scritch she gave would frighten a rigment, and a mist, like, came betwixt me and her, and I seen her no more; but when the mist wint off I saw blood on the spot where she had been, and I followed its track, and at last it led me—whist, whisper—right up to Katey MacShane's door; and when I was at the thrashold, I heerd a murnin' within, a great murnin', and a groanin', and I opened the door, and there she was herself, sittin' quite content in the shape of a woman, and the black cat that was sittin' by her rose up its back and spit at me; but I went on never heedin', and asked the ould —— how she was and what ailed her.

"Nothing," sis she.

"What's that on the floor?" sis I.

"Oh," she say, "I was cuttin' a billet of wood," she says, "wid the reaping hook," she says, "an' I've wounded me-self in the leg," she says, "and that's drops of my precious blood," she says.

BEWITCHED BUTTER (QUEEN'S COUNTY).*

About the commencement of the last century there lived in the vicinity of the once famous village of Agha-voe † a wealthy famer, named Bryan Costigan. This man kept an extensive dairy and a great many milch cows, and every year made considerable sums by the sale of milk and butter. The luxuriance of the pasture lands in this neighborhood has always been proverbial; and conse-quently, Bryan's cows were the finest and most produc-tive in the country, and his milk and butter the richest and sweetest, and brought the highest price at every market at which he offered these articles for sale.

*Dublin University Magazine, 1839.

†Aghavoe—"the field of kine,"—a beautiful and romantic vil-lage near Borris-in-Ossory, in the Queen's County. It was once a place of considerable importance, and for centuries the episcopal seat of the diocese of Ossory, but for ages back it has gone to decay, and is now remarkable for nothing but the magnificent runs of a priory of the Dominicans, erected here at an early period by St. Canice, the patron saint of Ossory.

Things contiuned to go on thus prosperously with Bryan Costigan, when, one season, all at once, he found his cattle declining in appearance, and his dairy almost entirely profitless. Bryan, at first, attributed this change to the weather, or some such cause, but soon found or fancied reasons to assign it to a far different source. The cows, without any visible disorder, daily declined, and were scarcely able to crawl about on their pasture : many of them, instead of milk, gave nothing but blood; and the scanty quantity of milk which some of them continued to supply was so bitter that even the pigs would not drink it; whilst the butter which it produced was of such a bad quality, and stunk so horribly, that the very dogs would not eat it. Bryan applied for remedies to all the quacks and " fairy-women" in the country—but in vain. Many of the impostors declared that the mysterious malady in his cattle went beyound *their* skill; whilst others, although they found no difficulty in tracing it to super-human agency, declared that they had no control in the matter, as the charm under the influence of which his property was made away with, was too powerful to be dissolved by anything less than the special interposition of Divine Providence. The poor farmer became almost distracted; he saw ruin staring him in the face; yet what was he to do? Sell his cattle and purchase others! No; that was out of the question, as they looked so miserable and emaciated, that no one would even take them as a present, whilst it was also impossible to sell to a butcher, as the flesh of one which he killed for his own family was as black as a coal, and stunk like any putrid carrion.

The unfortunate man was thus completely bewildered. He knew not what to do; he became moody and stupid; his sleep forsook him by night, and all day he wandered about the fields, amongst his " fairy-stricken" cattle like a maniac.

Affairs continued in this plight, when one very sultry evening in the latter days of July, Bryan Costigan's wife was sitting at her own door, spinning at her wheel, in a very gloomy and agitated state of mind. Happening to look down the narrow green lane which led from the high road to her cabin, she espied a little old woman barefoot, and enveloped in an old scarlet cloak, approaching slowly, with the aid of a crutch which she carried in one hand, and a cane or walking-stick in the other. The farmer's wife felt glad at seeing the odd-looking stranger; she smiled, and yet she knew not why, as she neared the house. A vague and indefinable feeling of pleasure crowded on her imagination; and, as the old woman gained the threshold, she bade her " welcome " with a warmth which plainly told that her lips gave utterance but to the genuine feelings of her heart.

"God bless this good house and all belonging to it," said the stranger as she entered.

" God save you kindly, and you are welcome, whoever you are," replied Mrs. Costigan.

" Hem, I thought so, said the old woman with a significant grin. "I thought so, or I wouldn't trouble you."

The farmer's wife ran, and placed a chair near the fire for the stranger; but she refused, and sat on the ground near where Mrs. C. had been spinning. Mrs. Costigan had now time to survey the old hag's person minutely. She appeared of great age; her countenance was extremely ugly and repulsive; her skin was rough and deeply embrowned as if from long exposure to the effects of some tropical climate; her forehead was low, narrow, and indented with a thousand wrinkles; her long gray hair fell in matted elf-locks from beneath a white linen skull-cap; her eyes were bleared, blood-shotten, and obliquely set in their sockets, and her voice was croaking, tremulous, and, at times, partially inarticulate. As she squatted on the floor, she looked round the house with an inquisitive gaze; she peered pryingly from corner to corner, with an earnestness of look, as if she had the faculty, like the Argonaut of old, to see through the very depths of the earth, whilst Mrs. C. kept watching her motions with mingled feelings of curiosity, awe, and pleasure.

"Mrs.," said the old woman, at length breaking silence, "I am dry with the heat of the day; can you give me a drink?"

"Alas!" replied the farmer's wife, "I have no drink to offer you except water, else you would have no occasion to ask me for it."

"Are you not the owner of the cattle I see yonder?" said the old hag, with a tone of voice and manner of gesticulation which plainly indicated her foreknowledge of the fact.

Mrs. Costigan replied in the affirmative, and briefly related to her every circumstance connected with the affair, whilst the old woman still remained silent, but shook her gray head repeatedly; and still continued gazing round the house with an air of importance and self-sufficiency.

When Mrs. C. had ended, the old hag remained a while as if in a deep reverie: at length she said—

"Have you any of the milk in the house?"

"I have," replied the other.

"Show me some of it."

She filled a jug from a vessel and handed it to the old sybil, who smelled it, then tasted it, and spat out what she had taken on the floor.

"Where is your husband?" she asked.

"Out in the fields," was the reply.

"I must see him."

A messenger was despatched for Bryan, who shortly after made his appearance.

"Neighbor," said the stranger, "your wife informs me that your cattle are going against you this season."

"She informs you right," said Bryan.

"And why have you not sought a cure?"

"A cure!" re-echoed the man; "why, woman, I have sought cures until I was heart-broken, and all in vain; they get worse every day."

"What will you give me if I cure them for you?"

"Anything in our power," replied Bryan and his wife, both speaking joyfully, and with a breath.

"All I will ask from you is a silver sixpence, and that you will do everything which I will bid you," said she.

The farmer and his wife seemed astonished at the moderation of her demand. They offered her a large sum of money.

"No," said she, "I don't want your money; I am no cheat, and I would not even take sixpence, but that I can do nothing till I handle some of your silver."

The sixpence was immediately given her, and the most implicit obedience promised to her injunctions by both Bryan and his wife, who already began to regard the old beldame as their tutelary angel.

The hag pulled off a black silk ribbon or fillet which encircled her head inside her cap, and gave it to Bryan, saying—

"Go, now, and the first cow you touch with this ribbon, turn her into the yard, but be sure don't touch the second, nor speak a word until you return; be also careful not to let the ribbon touch the ground, for, if you do, all is over."

Bryan took the talismanic ribbon, and soon returned, driving a red cow before him.

The old hag went out, and, approaching the cow, commenced pulling hairs out of her tail, at the same time singing some verses in the Irish language in a low, wild, and unconnected strain. The cow appeared restive and uneasy, but the old witch still continued her mysterious chant until she had the ninth hair extracted. She then ordered the cow to be drove back to her pasture, and again entered the house.

"Go, now, said she to the woman, "and bring me some milk from every cow in your possession."

She went, and soon returned with a large pail filled with a frightful-looking mixture of milk, blood, and corrupt matter. The old woman got it into the churn, and made preparations for churning.

"Now," she said, "you both must churn, make fast the door and windows, and let there be no light but from the fire; do not open your lips until I desire you, and by observing my directions, I make no doubt but, ere the sun goes down, we will find out the infernal villain who is robbing you."

Bryan secured the doors and windows, and commenced churning. The old sorceress sat down by a blazing fire which had been specially lighted for the occasion, and commenced singing the same wild song which she had sung at the pulling of the cow-hairs, and after a little time she cast one of the nine hairs into the fire, still singing her mysterious strain, and watching, with intense interest, the witching process.

A loud cry, as if from a female in distress, was now heard approaching the house; the old witch discontinued her incantations, and listened attentively. The crying voice approached the door.

"Open the door quickly," shouted the charmer.

Bryan unbarred the door, and all three rushed out in the yard, when they heard the same cry down the *boreheen*, but could see nothing.

"It is all over," shouted the old witch; "something has gone amiss, and our charm for the present is ineffectual."

They now turned back quite crestfallen, when, as they were entering the door, the sybil cast her eyes downwards, and perceiving a piece of horse-shoe nailed on the threshold,* she vociferated—

"Here I have it; no wonder our charm was abortive. The person that was crying abroad is the villain who has your cattle bewitched; I brought her to the house, but she was not able to come to the door on account of that horse-shoe. Remove it instantly, and we will try our luck again."

*It was once a common practice in Ireland to nail a piece of horse-shoe on the threshold of the door, as a preservative against the influence of the fairies, who, it is thought, dare not enter any house thus guarded. This custom, however, is much on the wane, but still it is prevalent in some of the more uncivilized districts of the country.

Bryan removed the horse-shoe from the doorway, and by
the hag's directions placed it on the floor under the churn,
having previously reddened it in the fire.

They again resumed their manual operations. Bryan
and his wife began to churn, and the witch again to sing
her strange verses, and casting her cow-hairs into the fire
until she had them all nearly exhausted. Her countenance now began to exhibit evident traces of vexation and
disappointment. She got quite pale, her teeth gnashed,
her hand trembled, and as she cast the ninth and last hair
into the fire, her person exhibited more the appearance of
a female demon than of a human being.

Once more the cry was heard, and an aged red-haired
woman * was seen approaching the house quickly.

" Ho, ho ! " roared the sorceress, " I knew it would be
so ; my charm has succeeded ; my expectations are
realized, and here she comes, the villain who has destroyed you."

" What are we to do now ? " asked Bryan.

" Say nothing to her," said the hag ; " give her whatever she demands, and leave the rest to me."

The woman advanced screeching vehemently, and
Bryan went out to meet her. She was a neighbor, and
she said that one of her best cows was drowning in a pool of
water—that there was no one at home but herself, and she
implored Bryan to go rescue the cow from destruction.

Bryan accompanied her without hesitation ; and having
rescued the cow from her perilous situation, was back
again in a quarter of an hour.

It was now sunset, and Mrs. Costigan set about preparing supper.

During supper they reverted to the singular transactions of the day. The old witch uttered many a fiendish
laugh at the success of her incantations, and inquired who
was the woman whom they had so curiously discovered.

Bryan satisfied her in every particular. She was the

---

* Red-haired people are thought to possess magic power.

wife of a neighboring farmer; her name was Rachel Higgins; and she had been long suspected to be on familiar terms with the spirit of darkness. She had five or six cows; but it was observed by her sapient neighbors that she sold more butter every year than other farmers' wives who had twenty. Bryan had, from the commencement of the decline in his cattle, suspected her for being the aggressor, but as he had no proof, he held his peace.

" Well," said the old beldame, with a grim smile, " it is not enough that we have merely discovered the robber ; all is in vain, if we do not take steps to punish her for the past, as well as to prevent her inroads for the future."

" And how will that be done ? " said Bryan.

" I will tell you ; as soon as the hour of twelve o'clock arrives to-night, do you go to the pasture, and take a couple of swift-running dogs with you ; conceal yourself in some place convenient to the cattle ; watch them carefully ; and if you see anything, whether man or beast, approach the cows, set on the dogs, and if possible make them draw the blood of the intruder; then ALL will be accomplished. If nothing approaches before sunrise, you may return, and we will try something else."

Convenient there lived the cow-herd of a neighboring squire. He was a hardy, courageous young man, and always kept a pair of very ferocious bull-dogs. To him Bryan applied for assistance, and he cheerfully agreed to accompany him, and, moreover, proposed to fetch a couple of his master's best greyhounds, as his own dogs, although extremely fierce and bloodthirsty, could not be relied on for swiftness. He promised Bryan to be with him before twelve o'clock and they parted.

Bryan did not seek sleep that night; he sat up anxiously awaiting the midnight hour. It arrived at last, and his friend, the herdsman, true to his promise, came at the time appointed. After some further admonitions from the *Collough*, they departed. Having arrived at the field, they consulted as to the best position they could choose for concealment. At last they pitched on a small brake of fern, situated at the extremity of the field, adjacent to the boundary ditch, which was thickly studded with large, old white-thorn bushes. Here they crouched themselves, and made the dogs, four in number, lie down beside them, eagerly expecting the appearance of their as yet unknown and mysterious visitor.

Here Bryan and his comrade continued a considerable time in nervous anxiety, still nothing approached, and it became manifest that morning was at hand; they were beginning to grow impatient, and were talking of returning home, when on a sudden they heard a rushing sound behind them, as if proceeding from something endeavoring to force a passage through the thick hedge in their rear. They looked in that direction, and judge of their astonishment, when they perceived a large hare in the act of springing from the ditch, and leaping on the ground quite near them. They were now convinced that this was the object which they had so impatiently expected, and they were resolved to watch her motions narrowly.

After arriving to the ground, she remained motionless for a few moments, looking around her sharply. She then began to skip and jump in a playful manner; now advancing at a smart pace towards the cows, and again retreating precipitately, but still dawing nearer and nearer at each sally. At length she advanced up to the next cow, and sucked her for a moment; then on to the next, and so respectively to every cow on the field—the cows all the time lowing loudly, and appearing extremely frightened and agitated. Bryan, from the moment the hare commenced sucking the first, was with difficulty restrained from attacking her; but his more sagacious companion suggested to him, that it was better to wait until she would have done, as she would then be much heavier, and more unable to effect her escape than at present. And so the issue proved; for being now done sucking them all, her belly appeared enormously distended, and she made her exit slowly and apparently with difficulty. She advanced towards the hedge where she had entered, and as she arrived just at the clump of ferns where her foes were couched, they started up with a fierce yell, and hallooed the dogs upon her path.

The hare started off at a brisk pace, squirting up the milk she had sucked from her mouth and nostrils, and the dogs making after her rapidly. Rachel Higgins's cabin appeared, through the gray of the morning twilight, at a little distance ; and it was evident that puss seemed bent on gaining it, although she made a considerable circuit through the fields in the rear. Bryan and his comrade, however, had their thoughts, and made towards the cabin by the shortest route, and had just arrived as the hare came up, panting and almost exhausted, and the dogs at her very scut. She ran round the house, evidently confused and disappointed at the presence of the men, but at length made for the door. In the bottom of the door was a small, semicircular aperture, resembling those cut in fowl-house doors for the ingress and egress of poultry. To gain this hole, puss now made a last and desperate effort, and had succeeded in forcing her head and shoulders through it, when the foremost of the dogs made a spring and seized her violently by the haunch. She uttered a loud and piercing scream, and struggled desperately to free herself from his gripe, and at last succeeded, but not until she left a piece of her rump in his teeth. The men now burst open the door ; a bright turf fire blazed on the hearth, and the whole floor was streaming with blood. No hare, however, could be found, and the men were more than ever convinced that it was old Rachel, who had, by the assistance of some demon, assumed the form of the hare, and they now determined to have her if she were over the earth. They entered the bedroom, and heard some smothered groaning, as if proceeding from some one in extreme agony. They went to the corner of the room from whence the moans proceeded, and there, beneath a bundle of freshly-cut rushes, found the form of Rachel Higgins, writhing in the most excruciating agony, and almost smothered in a pool of blood. The men were astounded ;

they addressed the wretched old woman, but she either could not, or would not answer them. Her wound still bled copiously ; her tortures appeared to increase, it was evident that she was dying. The aroused family thronged around her with cries and lamentations ; she did not seem to heed them, she got worse and worse, and her piercing yells fell awfully on the ears of the bystanders. At length she expired, and her corpse exhibited a most appalling spectacle, even before the spirit had well departed.

Bryan and his friend returned home. The old hag had been previously aware of the fate of Rachel Higgins, but it was not known by what means she aquired her super-natural knowledge. She was delighted at the issue of her mysterious operations. Bryan pressed her much to accept of some remuneration for her services, but she utterly rejected such proposals. She remained a few days at his house, and at length took her leave and de-parted, no one knew whither.

Old Rachel's remains were interred that night in the neighboring churchyard. Her fate soon became generally known, and her family, ashamed to remain in their native village, disposed of their property, and quitted the country forever. The story, however, is still fresh in the memory of the surrounding villagers ; and often, it is said, amid the gray haze of a summer twilight, may the ghost of Rachel Higgins, in the form of a hare, be seen scudding over her favorite and well-remembered haunts.

THE HORNED WOMEN.*

LADY WILDE.

A RICH woman sat up late one night carding and preparing wool, while all the family and servants were
asleep.	Suddenly a knock was given at the door, and a
voice called—" Open ! open ! "

" Who is there ? " said the woman of the house.

" I am the Witch of the one Horn," was answered.

The mistress, supposing that one of her neighbors had
called and required assistance, opened the door, and a
woman entered, having in her hand a pair of wool carders,
and bearing a horn on her forehead, as if growing there.
She sat down by the fire in silence, and began to card the
wool with violent haste.	Suddenly she paused, and said
aloud : " Where are the women ? they delay too long."

Then a second knock came to the door, and a voice
called as before, " Open ! open ! "

The mistress felt herself constrained to rise and open to
the call, and immediately a second witch entered, having
two horns on her forehead, and in her hand a wheel for
spinning wool.

" Give me place," she said, " I am the Witch of the two
Horns," and she began to spin as quick as lightning.

And so the knocks went on, and the call was heard, and
the witches entered, until at last twelve women sat round
the fire—the first with one horn, the last with twelve
horns.

And they carded the thread, and turned their spinning-
wheels, and wound and wove.

All singing together an ancient rhyme, but no word did
they speak to the mistress of the house.	Strange to hear,
and frightful to look upon, were these twelve women, with

* *Ancient Legends of Ireland.*

their horns and their wheels; and the mistress felt near to death, and she tried to rise that she might call for help, but she could not move, nor could she utter a word or a cry, for the spell of the witches was upon her.

Then one of them called to her in Irish, and said—

"Rise, woman, and make us a cake." Then the mistress searched for a vessel to bring water from the well that she might mix the meal and make the cake, but she could find none.

And they said to her, "Take a sieve and bring water in it."

And she took the sieve and went to the well; but the water poured from it, and she could fetch none for the cake, and she sat down by the well and wept.

Then a voice came by her and said, "Take yellow clay and moss, and bind them together, and plaster the sieve so that it will hold."

This she did, and the sieve held the water for the cake; and the voice said again—

"Return, and when thou comest to the north angle of the house, cry aloud three times and say, 'The mountain of the Fenian women and the sky over it is all on fire.'"

And she did so.

When the witches inside heard the call, a great and terrible cry broke from their lips, and they rushed forth with wild lamentations and shrieks, and fled away to Slievenamon,* where was their chief abode. But the Spirit of the Well bade the mistress of the house to enter and prepare her home against the enchantments of the witches if they returned again.

And first, to break their spells, she sprinkled the water in which she had washed her child's feet (the feet-water) outside the door on the threshold; secondly, she took the cake which the witches had made in her absence of meal mixed with the blood drawn from the sleeping family, and she broke the cake in bits, and placed a bit in the

* *Slidbh-na-mban—i.e.*, mountains of the women.

mouth of each sleeper, and they were restored; and she took the cloth they had woven and placed it half in and half out of the chest with the padlock; and lastly, she secured the door with a great crossbeam fastened in the jambs, so that they could not enter, and having done these things she waited.

Not long were the witches in coming back, and they raged and called for vengeance.

"Open! open!" they screamed, "open, feet-water!"

"I cannot," said the feet-water, "I am scattered on the ground, and my path is down to the Lough."

"Open, open, wood and trees and beam!" they cried to the door.

I cannot," said the door, "for the beam is fixed in the jambs and I have no power to move."

"Open, open, cake that we have made and mingled with the blood!" they cried again.

"I cannot," said the cake, "for I am broken and bruised, and my blood is on the lips of the sleeping children."

Then the witches rushed through the air with great cries, and fled back to Slivenamon, uttering strange curses on the Spirit of the Well, who had wished their ruin; but the woman and the house were left in peace, and a mantle dropped by one of the witches in her flight was kept hung up by the mistress as a sign of the night's awful contest; and this mantle was in possession of the same family from generation to generation for five hundred years after.

THE WITCHES' EXCURSION.*

PATRICK KENNEDY.

SHEMUS RUA † (Red James) awakened from his sleep one night by noises in his kitchen. Stealing to the door, he saw half-a-dozen old women sitting round the fire, jesting and laughing, his old housekeeper, Madge, quite frisky and gay, helping her sister cronies to cheering glasses of punch. He began to admire the impudence and imprudence of Madge, displayed in the invitation and the riot, but recollected on the instant her officiousness in urging him to take a comfortable posset, which she had brought to his bedside just before he fell asleep. Had he drunk it, he would have been just now deaf to the witches' glee. He heard and saw them drink his health in such a mocking style as nearly to tempt him to charge them, besom in hand, but he restrained himself.

The jug being emptied, one of them cried out, " Is it time to be gone ? " and at the same moment, putting on a red cap, she added—

> " By yarrow and rue,
>   And my red cap too,
>   Hie over to England."

Making use of a twig which she held in her hand as a steed, she gracefully soared up the chimney, and was rapidly followed by the rest. But when it came to the housekeeper, Shemus interposed. " By your leave, ma'am," said he, snatching twig and cap. " Ah, you desateful ould crocodile ! If I find you here on my return, there'll be wigs on the green—

* *Fictions of the Irish Celts.*

† Irish, *Séumus Ruadh.* The Celtic vocal organs are unable to pronounce the letter j, hence they make Shon or Shawn of John, or Shamus of James, etc.

' By yarrow and rue,
And my red cap too,
  Hie over to England.' ”

The words were not out of his mouth when he was soar-
ing above the ridge pole, and swiftly plowing the air.
He was careful to speak no word (being some what con-
versant with witch-lore), as the result would be a tumble,
and the immediate return of the expedition.

In a very short time they had crossed the Wicklow
hills, the Irish Sea, and the Welsh mountains, and were
charging, at whirlwind speed, the hall door of a castle.
Shemus, only for the company in which he found himself,
would have cried out for pardon, expecting to be a *mum-
my* against the hard oak door in a moment; but, all bewildered, he found himself passing through the keyhole,
along a passage, down a flight of steps, and through a
cellar-door key-hole before he could form any clear idea
of his situation.

Waking to the full consciousness of his position, he
found himself sitting on a stillion, plenty of lights glimmering round, and he and his companions, with full
tumblers of frothing wine in hand, hobnobbing and
drinking healths as jovially and recklessly as if the liquor
was honestly come by, and they were sitting in *Shemus's*
own kitchen.   The red birredh* had assimilated *Shemus's*
nature for the time being to that of his unholy companions.
The heady liquors soon got into their brains, and a period
of unconsciousness succeeded the ecstasy, the headache,
the turning round of the barrels, and the “ scattered
sight ” of Poor Shemus.   He woke up under the impression of being roughly seized and shaken, and dragged
upstairs, and subjected to a disagreeable examination by
the lord of the castle, in his state parlor.   There was
much derision among the whole company, gentle and
simple, on hearing Shemus's explanation, and, as the
thing occurred in the dark ages, the unlucky Leinster

---

* Ir., *Birreud—i. e.* a cap.

man was sentenced to be hung as soon as the gallows could be prepared for the occasion.

The poor Hibernian was in the cart proceeding on his last journey, with a label on his back, and another on his breast, announcing him as the remorseless villain who for the last month had been draining the casks in my lord's vault every night. He was surprised to hear himself addressed by his name, and in his native tongue, by an old woman in the crowd. "Ach, Shemus, alanna! is it going to die you are in a strange place without your *cappeen d'yarrag?*" * These words infused hope and courage into the poor victim's heart. He turned to the lord and humbly asked leave to die in his red cap, which he supposed had dropped from his head in the vault. A servant was sent for the headpiece, and Shemus felt lively hope warming his heart while placing it on his head. On the platform he was graciously allowed to address the spectators, which he proceeded to do in the usual formula composed for the benefit of flying stationers —"Good people all, a warning take by me;" but when he had finished the line, "My parents reared me tenderly," he unexpectedly added—"By yarrow and rue," etc., and the disappointed spectators saw him shoot up obliquely through the air in the style of a sky-rocket that had missed its aim. It is said that the lord took the circumstance much to heart, and never afterwards hung a man for twenty-four hours after his offense.

* Irish, *caipin dearg*—i. e., red cap.

THE CONFESSIONS OF TOM BOURKE.

T. CROFTON CROKER.

TOM ROURKE lives in a low, long farm-house, resembling in outward appearance a large barn, placed at the bottom of the hill, just where the new road strikes off from the old one, leading from the town of Kilworth to that of Lismore. He is of a class of persons who are a sort of black swans in Ireland: he is a wealthy farmer. Tom's father had, in the good old times, when a hundred pounds were no inconsiderable treasure, either to lend or spend, accommodated his landlord with that sum, at interest ; and obtained as a return for his civility a long lease, about half-a-dozen times more valuable than the loan which procured it. The old man died worth several hundred pounds, the greater part of which with his farm, he bequeathed to his son Tom. But besides all this, Tom received from his father, upon his death-bed, another gift, far more valuable than worldly riches, greatly as he prized and is still known to prize them. He was invested with the privilege, enjoyed by few of the sons of men, of communicating with those mysterious beings called "the good people."

Tom Bourke is a little, stout, healthy, active man, about fifty-five years of age. His hair is perfectly white, short and bushy behind, but rising in front erect and thick above his forehead, like a new clothes-brush. His eyes are of that kind which I have often observed with persons of a quick, but limited intellect—they are small, gray, and lively. The large and projecting eyebrows under, or rather within, which they twinkle, give them an expression of shrewdness and intelligence, if not of cunning. And this is very much the character of the man. If you want to make a bargain with Tom Bourke you must act

as if you were a general besieging a town, and make your
advances a long time before you can hope to obtain possession; if you march up boldly, and tell him at once
your object, you are for the most part sure to have the
gates closed in your teeth. Tom does not wish to part
with what you wish to obtain; or another person has
been speaking to him for the whole of the last week.
Or, it may be, your proposal seems to meet the most
favorable reception. "Very well, sir;" "That's true,
sir;" "I'm very thankful to your honor," and other ex-
pressions of kindness and confidence greet you in reply
to every sentence; and you part from him wondering
how he can have obtained the character which he univer-
sally bears, of being a man whom no one can make anything of in a bargain. But when you next meet him the
flattering illusion is dissolved: you find you are a great
deal further from your object than you were when you
thought you had almost succeeded; his eye and his
tongue express a total forgetfulness of what the mind
within never lost sight of for an instant; and you have
to begin operations afresh, with the disadvantage of
having put your adversary completely upon his guard.

Yet, although Tom Bourke is, whether from supernatural revealings, or (as many will think more probable)
from the tell-truth experience, so distrustful of mankind,
and so close in his dealings with them, he is no misan-
thrope. No man loves better the pleasures of the genial
board. The love of money, indeed, which is with him
(and who will blame him?) a very ruling propensity, and
the gratification which it has received from habits of
industry, sustained throughout a pretty long and success-
ful life, have taught him the value of sobriety, during
those seasons, at least, when a man's business requires
him to keep possession of his senses. He has, therefore,
a general rule, never to get drunk but on Sundays. But
in order that it should be a general one to all intents and
purposes, he takes a method which, according to better
logicians than he is, always proves the rule. He has many

exceptions ; among these, of course, are the evenings of all
the fair and market-days that happen in his neighborhood;
so also all the days in which funerals, marriages, and
christenings take place among his friends within many
miles of him. As to this last class of exceptions, it may
appear at first very singular, that he is much more punctual
in his attendance at the funerals than at the baptisms or
weddings of his friends. This may be construed as an
instance of disinterested affection for departed worth,
very uncommon is this selfish world. But I am afraid
that the motives which lead Tom Bourke to pay more
court to the dead than the living are precisely those which
lead to the opposite conduct in the generality of mankind
—a hope of future benefit and a fear of future evil.
For the good people, who are a race as powerful as they
are capricious, have their favorites among those who inhabit this world; often show their affection by easing
the objects of it from the load of this burdensome life ;
and frequently reward or punish the living according to
the degree of reverence paid to the obsequies and the
memory of the elected dead.

Some may attribute to the same cause the apparently
humane and charitable actions which Tom, and indeed the
other members of his family, are known frequently to
perform. A beggar has seldom left their farm-yard with
an empty wallet, or without obtaining a night's lodging,
if required, with a sufficiency of potatoes and milk to satisfy even an Irish beggar's appetite ; in appeasing which,
account must usually be taken of the auxiliary jaws of a
hungry dog, and of two or three still more hungry children,
who line themselves, well within, to atone for their naked-
ness without. If one of the neighboring poor be seized
with a fever, Tom will often supply the sick wretch with
some untenanted hut upon one of his two large farms (for
he has added one to his patrimony), or will send his
laborers to construct a shed at a hedge-side, and supply
straw for a bed while the disorder continues. His wife,
remarkable for the largeness of her dairy, and the goodness

of everything it contains, will furnish milk for whey ; and
their good offices are frequently extended to the family of
the patient, who are, perhaps, reduced to the extremity of
wretchedness, by even the temporary suspension of a
father's or a husband's labor.

If much of this arises from the hopes and fears to which
I above alluded, I believe much of it flows from a mingled
sense of compassion and of duty, which is sometimes seen
to break from an Irish peasant's heart, even where it happens to be enveloped in a habitual covering of avarice and
fraud ; and which I once heard speak in terms not to be
misunderstood : " When we get a deal, ' tis only fair we
should give back a little of it."

It is not easy to prevail on Tom to speak of those good
people, with whom he is said to hold frequent and intimate
communications. To the faithful, who believe in their
power, and their occasional delegation of it to him, he
seldom refuses, if properly asked, to exercise his high pre-
rogative when any unfortunate being is *struck* in his
neighborhood. Still he will not be won unsued ; he is
at first difficult of persuasion, and must be overcome by
a little gentle violence. On these occasions he is unusually solemn and mysterious, and if one word of reward
be mentioned he at once abandons the unhappy patient,
such a proposition being a direct insult to his supernatural
superiors. It is true that, as the laborer is worthy of his
hire, most persons gifted as he is do not scruple to receive
a token of gratitude from the patients or their friends
after their recovery. It is recorded that a very handsome
gratuity was once given to a female practitioner in this
occult science, who deserves to be mentioned, not only
because she was a neighbor and a rival of Tom's, but from
the singularity of a mother deriving her name from her
son. Her son's name was Owen, and she was always called
Owen sa vauher (Owen's mother). This person was, on
the occasion to which I have alluded, *persuaded* to give her
assistance to a young girl who had lost the use of her right
leg ; *Owen sa vauher* found the cure a difficult one. A

journey of about eighteen miles was essential for the purpose, probably to visit one of the good people who resided
at that distance ; and this journey could only be performed
by *Owen sa vauher* traveling upon the back of a white hen.
The visit, however, was accomplished ; and at a particular
hour, according to the prediction of this extraordinary
woman, when the hen and her rider were to reach their
journey's end, the patient was seized with an irresistible
desire to dance, which she gratified with the most perfect
freedom of the diseased leg, much to the joy of her anxious
family.   The gratuity in this case was, as it surely ought
to have been, unusually large, from the difficulty of pro-
curing a hen willing to go so long a journey with such a
rider.

To do Tom Bourke justice, he is on these occasions, as
I have heard from many competent authorities, perfectly
disinterested.   Not many months since he recovered a
young woman (the sister of a tradesman living near him),
who had been struck speechless after returning from a
funeral, and had continued so for several days.   He stead-
fastly refused receiving any compensation, saying that even
if he had not as much as would buy him his supper, he
could take nothing in this case, because the girl had
offended at the funeral of one of the *good people* belonging
to his own family, and though he would do her a kindness,
he could take none from her.

About the time this last remarkable affair took place, my
friend Mr. Martin, who is a neighbor of Tom's, had some
business to transact with him, which it was exceedingly
difficult to bring to a conclusion.   At last Mr. Martin,
having tried all quiet means, had recourse to a legal process, which brought Tom to reason, and the matter was
arranged to their mutual satisfaction, and with perfect
good-humor between the parties.   The accommodation
took place after dinner at Mr. Martin's house, and he invited Tom to walk into the parlor and take a glass of
punch, made of some excellent *poteen*, which was on the
table : he had long wished to draw out his highly-endowed

neighbor on the subject of his supernatural powers, and Mrs. Martin, who was in the room, was rather a favorite of Tom's, this seemed a good opportunity.

"Well, Tom," said Mr. Martin, "that was a curious business of Molly Dwyer's, who recovered her speech so suddenly the other day."

"You may say that, sir," replied Tom Bourke; "but I had to travel far for it; no matter for that now. Your health, ma'am," said he, turning to Mrs. Martin.

"Thank you, Tom. But I am told you had some trouble once in that way in your own family," said Mrs. Martin.

"So I had, ma'am; trouble enough: but you were only a child at that time."

"Come, Tom," said the hospitable Mr. Martin, interrupting him, "take another tumbler;" and he then added, "I wish you would tell us something of the manner in which so many of your children died. I am told they dropped off, one after another, by the same disorder, and that your eldest son was cured in a most extraordinary way, when the physicians had given him over."

"'Tis true for you, sir," returned Tom; "your father, the doctor (God be good to him, I won't belie him in his grave), told me, when my fourth boy was a week sick, that himself and Dr. Barry did all that man could do for him; but they could not keep him from going after the rest. No more they could, if the people that took away the rest wished to take him too. But they left him; and sorry to the heart I am I did not know before why they were taking my boys from me; if I did, I would not be left trusting to two of 'em now."

"And how did you find it out, Tom?" inquired Mr. Martin.

"Why, then, I'll tell you, sir," said Bourke. "When your father said what I told you, I did not know very well what to do. I walked down the little *bohereen**

---

* *Bohereen*, or *boghreen*, *i. e.*, a green lane.

you know, sir, that goes to the river-side near Dick
Heafy's ground ; for 'twas a lonesome place, and I wanted
to think of myself. I was heavy, sir, and my heart got weak
in me, when I thought I was to lose my little boy ; and I
did not well know how to face his mother with the news,
for she doated down upon him. Besides, she never got
the better of all she cried at his brother's *berrin* * the week
before. As I was going down the *bohereen* I met an old
bocough, that used to come about the place once or twice
a year, and used always to sleep in our barn while he staid
in the neighborhood. So he asked me how I was. 'Bad
enough, Shamous,' † says I. 'I'm sorry for your trouble,'
says he ; ' but you're a foolish man, Mr. Bourke. Your son
would be well enough if you would only do what you ought
with him.' ' What more can I do with him, Shamous ?'
says I ; ' the doctors give him over.' ' The doctors know no
more what ails him than they do what ails a cow when
she stops her milk,' says Shamous ; ' but go to such a
one,' telling me his name, ' and try what he'll say to you. ' "
    " And who was that, Tom ? " asked Mr. Martin.
    " I could not tell you that, sir," said Bourke, with a
mysterious look ; " howsomcver, you often saw him, and
he does not live far from this. But I had a trial of him
before ; and if I went to him at first, maybe I'd have now
some of them that's gone, and so Shamous often told me.
Well, sir, I went to this man, and he came with me to
the house. By course, I did everything as he bid me.
According to his order, I took the little boy out of the
dwelling-house immediately, sick as he was, and made a
bed for him and myself in the cow-house. Well, sir, I
lay down by his side in the bed, between two of the cows,
and he fell asleep. He got into a perspiration, saving
your presence, as if he was drawn through the river, and
breathed hard, with a great *impression* on his chest, and
was very bad—very bad entirely through the night. I
thought about twelve o'clock he was going at last, and I
was just getting up to go call the man I told you of ; but

---

    * *Berrin*, burying.   † *Shamous*, James.

there was no occasion. My friends were getting the
better of them that wanted to take him away from me.
There was nobody in the cow-house but the child and
myself. There was only one halfpenny candle lighting
it, and that was stuck in the wall at the far end of the
house. I had just enough of light where we were lying
to see a person walking or standing near us: and there
was no more noise than if it was a churchyard, except the
cows chewing the fodder in the stalls.

Just as I was thinking of getting up, as I told you—I
won't belie my father, sir, he was a good father to me—I
saw him standing at the bedside, holding out his right
hand to me, and leaning his other on the stick he used to
carry when he was alive, and looking pleasant and smiling at me, all as if he was telling me not to be afeard, for
I would not lose the child. 'Is that you, father?' says
I. He said nothing. 'If that's you,' says I again, 'for
the love of them that are gone, let me catch your hand.'
And so he did, sir; and his hand was as soft as a child's.
He stayed about as long as you'd be going from this to
the gate below at the end of the avenue, and then went
away. In less than a week the child was as well as if
nothing ever ailed him; and there isn't to-night a
healthier boy of nineteen, from this blessed house to the
town of Ballyporeen, across the Kilworth mountains."

"But I think, Tom," said Mr. Martin, "it appears as if
you are more indebted to your father than to the man
recommended to you by Shamous; or do you suppose it
was he who made favor with your enemies among the
good people, and that then your father——"

"I beg you pardon, sir," said Bourke, interrupting him;
"but don't call them my enemies. 'Twould not be wishing to me for a good deal to sit by when they are called so.
No offense to you, sir. Here's wishing you a good health
and long life."

"I assure you," returned Mr. Martin, "I meant no offense, Tom; but was it not as I say?"

"I can't tell you that, sir," said Bourke; "I'm bound

down, sir. Howsoever, you may be sure the man I spoke of and my father, and those they know, settled it between them."

There was a pause, of which Mrs. Martin took advantage to inquire of Tom whether something remarkable had not happened about a goat and a pair of pigeons, at the time of his son's illness—circumstances often mysteriously hinted at by Tom.

" See that, now," said he, turning to Mr. Martin, " how well she remembers it! True for you, ma'am. The goat I gave the mistress, your mother, when the doctors ordered her goats' whey ? "

Mrs. Martin nodded assent, and Tom Bourke continued, " Why, then, I'll tell you how that was. The goat was as well as e'er goat ever was, for a month after she was sent to Killaan, to your father's. The morning after the night I just told you of, before the child woke, his mother was standing at the gap leading out of the barn-yard into the road, and she saw two pigeons flying from the town of Kilworth off the church down towards her. Well, they never stopped, you see, till they came to the house on the hill at the other side of the river, facing our farm. They pitched upon the chimney of that house, and after looking about them for a minute or two, they flew straight across the river, and stopped on the ridge of the cow-house where the child and I were lying. Do you think they came there for nothing, sir ? "

" Certainly not, Tom," returned Mr. Martin.

" Well, the woman came in to me, frightened, and told me. She began to cry. " Whisht, you fool ? ' says I ; ' 'tis all for the better.' 'Twas true for me. What do you think, ma'am ; the goat that I gave your mother, that was seen feeding at sunrise that morning by Jack Cronin, as merry as a bee, dropped down dead without anybody knowing why, before Jack's face ; and at that very moment he saw two pigeons fly from the top of the house out of the town, toward Lismore road. 'Twas at the same time my woman saw them, as I just told you,"

" 'Twas very strange, indeed, Tom," said Mr. Martin;
"I wish you could give us some explanation of it."

"I wish I could, sir," was Tom Bourke's answer;
" but I'm bound down. I can't tell but what I'm allowed
to tell, any more than a sentry is let walk more than his
rounds."

" I think you said something of having had some former
knowledge of the man that assisted in the cure of your
son," said Mr. Martin.

" So I had, sir," returned Bourke. " I had a trial of
that man. But that's neither here nor there. I can't tell
you anything about that, sir. But would you like to know
how he got his skill?"

" Oh! very much, indeed," said Mr. Martin.

" But you can tell us his Christian name, that we may
know him better through the story," added Mrs. Martin.

Tom Bourke paused for a minute to consider this proposition.

" Well, I believe that I may tell you that, anyhow; his
name is Patrick. He was always a smart, 'cute * boy, and
would be a great clerk if he stuck to it. The first time I
knew him, sir, was at my mother's wake. I was in great
trouble, for I did not know where to bury her. Her
people and my father's people—I mean their friends, sir,
among the *good people*—had the greatest battle that was
known for many a year, at Dunmanwaycross, to see to
whose churchyard she'd be taken. They fought for three
nights, one after another, without being able to settle it.
The neighbors wondered how long I was before I buried
my mother; but I had my reasons, though I could not
tell them at that time. Well, sir, to make my story short,
Patrick came on the fourth morning and told me he settled the business, and that day we buried her in Kilcrumper churchyard, with my father's people."

" He was a valuable friend, Tom," said Mrs. Martin,
with difficulty suppressing a smile. " But you were about
to tell how he became so skilful."

* *Cute*, acute.

" So I will and welcome," replied Bourke. " Your
health, ma'am. I'm drinking too much of this punch,
sir; but to tell the truth, I never tasted the like of it; it
goes down one's throat like sweet oil. But what was I
going to say ? Yes—well—Patrick, many a long year ago,
was coming home from a *berrin* late in the evening, and
walking by the side of a river, opposite the big inch,*
near Ballyhefaan ford.   He had taken a drop, to be sure ;
but he was only a little merry, as you may say, and knew
very well what he was doing. The moon was shining,
for it was in the month of August, and the river was as
smooth and as bright as a looking-glass. He heard nothing for a long time but the fall of the water at the mill
weir about a mile down the river, and now and then the
crying of the lambs on the other side of the river. All
at once there was a noise of a great number of people
laughing as if they'd break their hearts, and of a piper
playing among them. It came from the inch at the other
side of the ford, and he saw, through the mist that hung
over the river, a whole crowd of people dancing on the
inch. Patrick was as fond of a dance, as he was of a
glass, and that's saying enough for him; so he whipped
off his shoes and stockings, and away with him across the
ford. After putting on his shoes and stockings at the
other side of the river he walked over to the crowd, and
mixed with them for some time without being minded.
He thought, sir, that he'd show them better dancing than
any of themselves, for he was proud of his feet, sir, and
a good right he had, for there was not a boy in the
same parish could foot a double or treble with him. But
pwah! his dancing was no more to theirs than mine
would be to the mistress' there. They did not seem as if
they had a bone in their bodies, and they kept it up as if
nothing could tire them. Patrick was 'shamed within
himself, for he thought he had not his fellow in all the
country round; and was going away, when a little old
man, that was looking at the company bitterly, as if he

* *Inch,* low meadow ground near a river.

did not like what was going on, came up to him. 'Patrick,' says he. Patrick started, for he did not think anybody there knew him. 'Patrick,' says he, 'you're dis-
couraged, and no wonder for you. But you have a friend
near you. I'm your friend, and your father's friend, and
and I think worse * of your little finger than I do of all
that are here, though they think no one is as good as
themselves. Go into the ring and call for a lilt. Don't
be afeard. I tell you the best of them did not do it as
well as you shall, if you will do as I bid you.' Patrick felt something within him as if he ought not to
gainsay the old man. He went into the ring, and called
the piper to play up the best double he had. And sure
enough, all that the others were able for was nothing to
to him! He bounded like an eel, now here and now there,
as light as a feather, although the people could hear the
music answered by his steps, that beat time to every turn
of it, like the left foot of the piper. He first danced a
hornpipe on the ground. Then they got a table, and he
danced a treble on it that drew down shouts from the
whole company. At last he called for a trencher; and
when they saw him, all as if he was spinning on it like
a top, they did not know what to make of him. Some
praised him for the best dancer that ever entered a ring;
others hated him because he was better than themselves;
although they had good right to think themselves better
than him or any other man that ever went the long
journey."

"And what was the cause of his great success?" inquired Mr. Martin.

"He could not help it, sir," replied Tom Bourke.
"They that could make him do more than that made him
do it. Howsomever, when he had done, they wanted him
to dance again, but he was tired, and they could not
persuade him. At last he got angry, and swore a big
oath, saving your presence, that he would not dance a step

* *Worse*, more.

more ; and the word was hardly out of his mouth when he found himself all alone, with nothing but a white cow grazing by his side."

" Did he ever discover why he was gifted with these extraordinary powers in the dance, Tom ? " said Mr. Martin.

" I'll tell you that too, sir," answered Bourke, " when I come to it. When he went home, sir, he was taken with a shivering, and went to bed ; and the next day they found he had got the fever, or something like it, for he raved like as if he was mad. But they couldn't make out what it was he was saying, though he talked constant. The doctors gave him over. But it's little they knew what ailed him. When he was, as you may say, about ten days sick, and everybody thought he was going, one of the neighbors came in to him with a man, a friend of his, from Ballinlacken, that was keeping with him some time before. I can't tell you his name either, only it was Darby. The minute Darby saw Patrick he took a little bottle, with the juice of herbs in it, out of his pocket, and gave Patrick a drink of it. He did the same every day for three weeks, and then Patrick was able to walk about, as stout and as hearty as ever he was in his life. But he was a long time before he came to himself ; and he used to walk the whole day sometimes by the ditchside, talking to himself, like as if there was some one along with him. And so there was, surely, or he wouldn't be the man he is to-day."

" I suppose it was from some such companion he learned his skill," said Mr. Martin.

" You have it all now, sir," replied Bourke. " Darby told him his friends were satisfied with what he did the night of the dance ; and though they couldn't hinder the fever, they'd bring him over it, and teach him. And so they did. For you see, all the people he met on the inch that night were friends of a different faction ; only the old man that spoke to him, he was a friend of Patrick's family, and it went again his heart, you see, that the

others were so light and active, and he was bitter in himself to hear 'em boasting how they'd dance with any set
in the whole country round. So he gave Patrick the
gift that night, and afterwards gave him the skill that
makes him the wonder of all that know him. And to
be sure it was only learning he was at that time when he
was wandering in his mind after the fever."

"I have heard many strange stories about that inch near
Ballyhefaan ford," said Mr. Martin. "'Tis a great place
for the good people, isn't it, Tom?"

"You may say that, sir," returned Bourke. "I could
tell you a great deal about it. Many a time I sat for as
good as two hours by moonlight, at th' other side of the
river, looking at 'em playing goal as if they'd break their
hearts over it; with their coats and waistcoats off, and
white handkerchiefs on the heads of one party, and red
ones on th' other, just as you'd see on a Sunday in Mr.
Simming's big field. I saw 'em one night play till the
moon set, without one party being able to take the ball
from th' other. I'm sure they were going to fight, only
'twas near morning. I'm told your grandfather, ma'am,
used to see 'em there too," said Bourke, turning to Mrs.
Martin.

"So I have been told, Tom," replied Mrs. Martin. "But
don't they say that the churchyard of Kilcrumper is just
as favorite a place with the good people as Ballyhefaan
inch?"

"Why, then, maybe you never heard, ma'am, what happened to Davy Roche in that same churchyard," said
Bourke; and turning to Mr. Martin, added, "'Twas a long
time before he went into your service, sir. He was walking home, of an evening, from the fair of Kilcumber, a
little merry, to be sure, after the day, and he came up with
a berrin. So he walked along with it, and thought it very
queer that he did not know a mother's soul in the crowd
but one man, and he was sure that man was dead many
years afore. Howsomever, he went on with the berrin till
they came to Kilcrumper churchyard; and, faith, he went

in and stayed with the rest, to see the corpse buried.   As
soon as the grave was covered, what should they do but
gather about a piper that *come* along with 'em, and fall to
dancing as if it was a wedding.   Davy longed to be among
'em (for he hadn't a bad foot of his own, that time, whatever he may now); but he was loth to begin, because they
all seemed strange to him, only the man I told you that
he thought was dead.   Well, at last this man saw what
Davy wanted, and came up to him.   'Davy,' says he,
'take out a partner, and show what you can do, but take
care and don't offer to kiss her.'   'That I won't,' says
Davy, 'although her lips were made of honey.'   And with
that he made his bow to the *purtiest* girl in the ring, and
he and she began to dance.   'Twas a jig they danced, and
they did it to th' admiration, do you see, of all that were
there.   'Twas all very well till the jig was over; but just
as they had done, Davy, for he had a drop in, and was
warm with the dancing, forgot himself, and kissed his
partner, according to custom.   The smack was no sooner off
of his lips, you see, than he was left alone in the churchyard,
without a creature near him, and all he could see was the
tall tombstones.   Davy said they seemed as if they were
dancing too, but I suppose that was only the wonder that
happened him, and he being a little in drink.   Howsomever, he found it was a great many hours later than he
thought it; 'twas near morning when he came home; but
they couldn't get a word out of him till the next day,
when he woke out of a dead sleep about twelve o'clock."

When Tom had finished the account of Davy Roche
and the berrin, it became quite evident that spirits, of some
sort, were working too strong within him to admit of his
telling many more tales of the good people.   Tom seemed
conscious of this.   He muttered for a few minutes broken
sentences concerning churchyards, river-sides, lepre-
chauns, and *dina magh*,* which were quite unintelligible,
perhaps, to himself, certainly to Mr. Martin and his lady.

* *Daoine maithe, i. e.*, the good people.

At length he made a slight motion of the head upwards, as if he would say, "I can talk no more;" stretched his arm on the table, upon which he placed the empty tumbler slowly, and with the most knowing and cautious air; and rising from his chair, walked, or rather rolled, to the parlor door. Here he turned round to face his host and hostess; but after various ineffectual attempts to bid them good-night, the words, as they rose, being always choked by a violent hiccup, while the door, which he held by the handle, swung to and fro, carrying his unyielding body along with it, he was obliged to depart in silence. The cow-boy, sent by Tom's wife, who knew well what sort of allurement detained him when he remained out after a certain hour, was in attendance to conduct his master home. I have no doubt that he returned without meeting any material injury, as I know that within the last month he was to use his own words, "as stout and hearty a man as any of his age in the county Cork."

THE PUDDING BEWITCHED.

WILLIAM CARLETON.

"MOLL ROE RAFFERTY was the son—daughter I mane—of ould Jack Rafferty, who was remarkable for a habit he had of always wearing his head undher his hat; but indeed the same family was a quare one, as everybody knew that was acquainted wid them. It was said of them—but whether it was thrue or not I won't undhertake to say, for 'fraid I'd tell a lie—that whenever they didn't wear shoes or boots they always went barefooted; but I heard afthervards that this was disputed, so rather than say anything to injure their character, I'll let that pass. Now, ould Jack Rafferty had two sons, Paddy and Molly —but! what are you all laughing at?—I mane a son and daughter, and it was generally believed among the neighbors that they were brother and sisther, which you know might be thrue or it might not: but that's a thing that, wid the help o' goodness, we have nothing to say to. Troth there was many ugly things put out on them that I don't wish to repate, such as that neither Jack nor his son Paddy ever walked a perch widout puttin' one foot afore the other like a salmon; an' I know it was whispered about, that whinever Moll Roe slep', she had an out-of-the-way custom of keepin' her eyes shut. If she did, however, for that matther the loss was her own; for sure we all know that when one comes to shut their eyes they can't see as far before them as another.

"Moll Roe was a fine young bouncin' girl, large and lavish, wid a purty head o' hair on her like scarlet, that bein' one of the raisons why she was called *Roe*, or red; her arms an' cheeks were much the color of the hair, an' her saddle nose was the purtiest thing of its kind that ever was on a face. Her fists—for, thank goodness, she was well sarved wid them too—had a strong simularity to two thumpin' turnips, reddened by the sun; an' to keep all right and tight, she had a temper as fiery as her head— for, indeed, it was well known that all the Rafferties were *warm*-hearted. Howandiver, it appears that God gives nothing in vain, and of coorse the same fists, big and red as they were, if all that is said about them is thrue, were not so much given to her for ornament as use. At laist, takin' them in connection wid her lively temper, we have it upon good authority, that there was no danger of their getting blue-moulded for want of practice. She had a twist, too in one of her eyes that was very becomin' in its way, and made her poor husband, when she got him, take it into his head that she could see round a corner. She found him out in many quare things, widout doubt; but whether it was owin' to that or not, I wouldn't undertake to say *for 'fraid I'd tell a lie*.

"Well, begad, anyhow it was Moll Roe that was the *dilsy*.* It happened that there was a nate vagabone in

* Perhaps from Irish *dilse—i. e.*, love.

the neighborhood, just as much overburdened wid beauty as herself, and he was named Gusty Gillespie. Gusty, the Lord guard us, was what they call a black-mouth Prosbytarian, and wouldn't keep Christmas-day, the blagard, except what they call 'ould style.' Gusty was rather goodlookin' when seen in the dark, as well as Moll herself; and, indeed, it was purty well known that—accordin' as talk went—it was in nightly meetings that they had an opportunity of becomin' detached to one another. The quensequence was, that in due time both families began to talk very seriously as to what was to be done. Moll's brother Pawdien O'Rafferty gave Gusty the best of two choices. What they were it's not worth spakin' about; but at any rate *one* of them was a poser, an' as Gusty knew his man, he soon came to his senses. Accordianly everything was deranged for their marriage, and it was appointed that they should be spliced by the Rev. Samuel M'Shuttle, the Prosbytarian parson, on the following Sunday.

"Now this was the first marriage that had happened for a long time in the neighborhood betune a black-mouth an' a Catholic, an' of coorse there was strong objections on both sides against it; an' begad, only for one thing, it would never 'a tuck place at all. At any rate, faix, there was one of the bride's uncles, ould Harry Connolly, a fairy-man, who could cure all complaints wid a secret he had, and as he didn't wish to see his niece married upon sich a fellow, he fought bittherly against the match. All Moll's friends, however, stood up for the marriage barrin' him, an' of coorse the Sunday was appointed, as I said, that they were to be dove-tailed together.

"Well, the day arrived, and Moll, as became her, went to mass, and Gusty to meeting, afther which they were to join one another in Jack Rafferty's, where the priest, Father M'Sorley, was to slip up afther mass to take his dinner wid them, and to keep Misther M'Shuttle, who was to marry them, company. Nobody remained at home but ould Jack Rafferty an' his wife, who stopped to dress the dinner, for, to tell the truth, it was to be a great let-out entirely. Maybe, if all was known, too, that Father M'Sorley was to give them a cast of his office over an' above the ministher, in regard that Moll's friends were not altogether satisfied at the kind of marriage which M'Shuttle could give them. The sorrow may care about that—splice here—splice there—all I can say is, that when Mrs. Rafferty was goin' to tie up a big bag pudden, in walks Harry Connolly, the fairy-man, in a rage, and shouts out,—'Blood and blunderbushes, what are yez here for?'

" 'Arrah why, Harry? Why, avick?'

" 'Why the sun's in the suds and the moon in the high Horicks; there's a clipstick comin' an, an' there you're both as unconsarned as if it was about to rain mether. Go out and cross yourselves three times in the name u' the four Mandromarvins, for as prophecy says :—Fill the pot, Eddy, supernaculum—a blazing star's a rare spectaculum. Go out both of you and look at the sun, I say, an' ye'll see the condition he's in—off !'

" Begad, sure enough, Jack gave a bounce to the door, and his wife leaped like a two-year-ould, till they were both got on a stile beside the house to see what was wrong in the sky.

" 'Arrah, what is it, Jack,' said she; ' can you see any-thing?'

" 'No,' says he, ' sorra the full o' my eye of anything I can spy, barrin' the sun himself, that's not visible in regard of the clouds. God guard us ! I doubt there's something to happen.'

" 'If there wasn't, Jack, what 'ud put Harry, that knows so much, in the state he's in?'

" 'I doubt it's this marriage,' said Jack : ' betune our-selves, it's not over an' above religious for Moll to marry a black-mouth, an' only for——; but it can't be helped now, though you see not a taste o' the sun is willin' to show his face upon it.'

" 'As to that,' says the wife, winkin' wid both her eyes,

'if Gusty's satisfied wid Moll, it's enough.   I know who'll
carry the whip hand, anyhow; but in the manetime let
us ax Harry 'ithin what ails the sun.'

"Well, they accordianly went in an' put the question to
him:

"'Harry, what's wrong, ahagur?   What is it now, for
if anybody alive knows, 'tis yourself?'"

"'Ah!' said Harry, screwin' his mouth wid a kind of
a dhry smile, 'the sun has a hard twist o' the cholic; but
never mind that, I tell you you'll have a merrier weddin'
than you think, that's all;' and havin' said this, he put
on his hat and left the house.

"Now, Harry's answer relieved them very much, and
so, afther calling to him to be back for the dinner, Jack
sat down to take a shough o' the pipe, and the wife lost
no time in tying up the pudden and puttin' it in the pot
to be boiled.

"In this way things went on well enough for a while,
Jack smokin' away, an' the wife cookin' and dhressin' at
the rate of a hunt.   At last, Jack, while sittin', as I said,
contentedly at the fire, thought he could persave an odd
dancin' kind of motion in the pot that puzzled him a good
deal.

"'Katty,' said he, 'what the dickens is in this pot on
the fire?'"

"'Nerra thing but the big pudden.   Why do you ax?'
says she.

"'Why,' said he, 'if ever a pot tuck it into its head to
dance a jig, and this did.   Thundher and sparbles, look
at it!'

"Begad, it was thrue enough; there was the pot bobbin'
up an' down and from side to side, jiggin' it away as merry
as a grig; an' it was quite aisy to see that it wasn't the
pot itself, but what was inside of it, that brought about
the hornpipe.

"'Be the hole o' my coat,' shouted Jack, 'there's something alive in it, or it would never cut sich capers!'

"'Be gorra, there is, Jack; something sthrange entirely has got into it. Wirra, man alive, what's to be done?'

"Jist as she spoke, the pot seemed to cut the buckle in prime style, and afther a spring that 'ud shame a dancin'-masther, off flew the lid, and out bounced the pudden itself, hoppin', as nimble as a pea on a drum-head, about the floor. Jack blessed himself, and Katty crossed herself. Jack shouted, and Katty screamed. 'In the name of goodness, keep your distance; no one here injured you!'

"The pudden, however, made a set at him, and Jack lepped first on a chair and then on the kitchen table to avoid it. It then danced-towards Kitty, who was now repating' her prayers at the top of her voice, while the cunnin' thief of a pudden was hoppin' and jiggin' it round her, as if it was amused at her distress.

"'If I could get the pitchfork,' said Jack, 'I'd dale wid it—by goxty I'd thry its mettle.'

"' No, no,' shouted Katty, thinkin' there was a fairy in it; ' let us spake it fair. Who knows what harm it might do? Aisy now,' said she to the pudden, 'aisy, dear; don't harm honest people that never meant to offend you. It wasn't us —no, in troth, it was ould Harry Connolly that bewitched you; pursue *him* if you wish, but spare a woman like me; for, whisper, dear, I'm not in a condition to be frightened— troth I'm not.

"The pudden, bedad, seemed to take her at her word, and danced away from her towards Jack, who, like the wife, believin' there was a fairy in it, an' that spakin' it fair was the best plan, thought he would give it a soft word as well as her.

"' Plase your honor,' said Jack, ' she only spaiks the truth; an,' upon my voracity, we both feels much obliged to your honor for your quietness. Faith, it's quite clear that if you weren't a gentlemanly pudden all out, you'd act otherwise. Ould Harry, the rogue, is your mark : he's jist gone down the road there, and if you go fast you'll overtake him. Be me song, your dancin' masther did his duty, anyhow. Thank your honor! God speed you, an' may you never meet wid a parson or alderman in your thravels!'

"Jist as Jack spoke the pudden appeared to take the hint, for it quietly hopped out, and as the house was directly on the road-side, turned down towards the bridge, the very way that ould Harry went. It was very natural of course, that Jack and Katty should go out to see how it intended to thravel; and, as the day was Sunday, it was but natural, too, that a greater number of people than usual were passin' the road. This was a fact; and when Jack and his wife were seen followin' the pudden, the whole neighborhood was soon up and after it.

"'Jack Rafferty, what is it? Katty, ahagur, will you tell us what it manes?'

"'Why,' replied Katty, 'it's my big pudden that's bewitched, an' it's now hot foot pursuin'——;' here she stopped, not wishin' to mention her brother's name— '*some one* or other that surely put *pishrogues* an it.' *

" This was enough; Jack, now seein' that he had assistance, found his courage comin' back to him; so says he to Katty, 'Go home,' says he, 'an' lose no time in makin' another pudden as good, an' here's Paddy Scanlan's wife, Bridget, says she'll let you boil it on her fire, as you'll want our own to dress the rest o' the dinner: and Paddy himself will lend me a pitchfork, for purshuin to the morsel of that same pudden will escape till I let the wind out of it, now that I've the neighbors to back an' support me,' says Jack.

"This was agreed to, and Katty went back to prepare a fresh pudden, while Jack an' half the townland pursued the other wid spades, graips, pitchforks, scythes, flails, and all possible description of instruments. On the pudden went however, at the rate of about six Irish miles an hour, an' such a chase never was seen. Catholics, Prodestants, an' Prosbytarians, were all afther it, armed, as I said, an' bad

* Put it under fairy influence.

end to the thing but its own activity could save it. Here it made a hop, and there a prod was made at it; but off it went, an' some one, as eager to get a slice at it on the other side, got the prod instead of the pudden. Big Frank Farrell, the miller of Ballyboulteen, got a prod backwards that brought a hullabaloo out of him you might hear at the other end of the parish. One got a slice of a scythe, another a whack of a flail, a third a rap of a spade that made him look nine ways at wanst.

"'Where is it goin'?' asked one. 'My life for you, it's on it's way to Meeting. Three cheers for it if it turns to Carntaul.' 'Prod the sowl out of it, if it's a Prodestan',' shouted the others; 'if it turns to the left, slice it into pancakes. We'll have no Prodestan' puddens here.'

"Begad, by this time the people were on the point of beginnin' to have a regular fight about it, when, very fortunately, it took a short turn down a little by-lane that led towards the Methodist praichin-house, an' in an instant all parties were in an uproar against it as a Methodist pudden. 'It's a Wesleyan,' shouted several voices; 'an' by this an' by that, into a Methodist chapel it won't put a foot to-day, or we'll lose a fall. Let the wind out of it. Come, boys, where's your pitchforks?'

"The divle purshuin to the one of them, however, ever could touch the pudden, an' jist when they thought they had it up against the gavel of the Methodist chapel, begad it gave them the slip, and hops over to the left, clane into the river, and sails away before all their eyes as light as an egg-shell.

"Now, it so happened that a little below this place, the demesne-wall of Colonel Bragshaw was built up to the very edge of the river on each side of its banks; and so findin' there was a stop put to their pursuit of it, they went home again, every man, woman, and child of them, puzzled to think what the pudden was at all, what it meant, or where it was goin'! Had Jack Rafferty an' his wife been willin' to let out the opinion they held about Harry Connolly bewitchin' it, there is no doubt of it but poor Harry might be badly trated by the crowd, when their blood was up. They had sense enough, howandiver, to keep that to themselves, for Harry bein' an' ould bachelor, was a kind friend to the Raffertys. So, of coorse, there was all kinds of talk about it—some guessin' this, and some guessin' that—one party sayin' the pudden was of their side, another party denyin' it, an' insistin' it belonged to them, an' so on.

" In the manetime, Katty Rafferty, for 'fraid the dinner might come short, went home and made another pudden much about the same size as the one that had escaped, and bringin' it over to their next neighbor, Paddy Scanlan's, it was put into a pot and placed on the fire to boil, hopin' that it might be done in time, espishilly as they were to have the ministher, who loved a warm slice of good pudden as well as e'er a gintleman in Europe.

" Anyhow, the day passed ; Moll and Gusty were made man an' wife, an' no two could be more lovin'. Their friends that had been asked to the weddin' were saunterin' about in pleasant little groups till dinner-time, chattin' an' laughin' ; but, above all things, sthrivin' to account for the figaries of the pudden ; for, to tell the truth, its adventures had now gone through the whole parish.

" Well, at any rate, dinner-time was dhrawin' near, and Paddy Scanlan was sittin' comfortably wid his wife at the fire, the pudden boilen before their eyes, when in walks Harry Connolly, in a flutter, shoutin'—' Blood an' blunderbushes, what are yez here for ? '

" ' Arra, why, Harry—why, avick ? ' said Mrs. Scanlan.

" Why,' said Harry, ' the sun's in the suds an' the moon in the high Horicks ! Here's a clipstick comin' an, an' there you sit as unconsarned as if it was about to rain mether ! Go out both of you, an' look at the sun, I say, and ye'll see the condition he's in—off ! '

" ' Ay, but, Harry, what's that rowled up in the tail of your cothamore* (big coat) ? '

* Irish, *cóta mór.*

" 'Out wid yez,' said Harry, 'an' pray aginst the clip-stick—the sky's fallin'!'

" Begad, it was hard to say whether Paddy or the wife got out first, they were so much alarmed by Harry's wild thin face an' piercin' eyes; so out they went to see what was wondherful in the sky, an' kep' lookin' an' lookin' in every direction, but not a thing was to be seen, barrin' the sun shinin' down wid great good-humor, an' not a single cloud in the sky.

" Paddy an' the wife now came in laughin', to scould Harry, who, no doubt, was a great wag in his way when he wished. 'Musha, bad scran to you, Harry——.' They had time to say no more, howandiver, for, as they were goin' into the door, they met him comin' out of it wid a reek of smoke out of his tail like a lime-kiln.

" 'Harry,' shouted Bridget, 'my sowl to glory, but the tail of your cothamore's a fire—you'll be burned. Don't you see the smoke that's out of it?'

" 'Cross yourselves three times,' said Harry, widout stoppin', or even lookin' behind him, 'for, as the prophecy says—Fill the pot, Eddy——' They could hear no more, for Harry appeared to feel like a man that carried some-thing a great deal hotter than he wished, as anyone might see by the liveliness of his motions, and the quare faces he was forced to make as he went along.

" 'What the dickens is he carryin' in the skirts of his big coat?" asked Paddy.

" 'My sowl to happiness, but maybe he has stole the pudden', said Bridget, 'for it's known that many a sthrange thing he does.'

" They immediately examined the pot, but found that the pudden was there as safe as tuppence, an' this puzzled them the more, to think what it was he could be carryin' about wid him in the manner he did. But little they knew what he had done while they were sky-gazin!

" Well, anyhow, the day passed and the dinner was ready, an' no doubt but a fine gatherin' there was to par-take of it. The Prosbytarian ministher met the Methodist praicher—a divilish stretcher of an appetite he had, in throth—on their way to Jack Rafferty's, an' as he knew he could take the liberty, why he insisted on his dinin' wid him; for, afther all, begad, in thim times the clargy of all descriptions lived upon the best footin' among one another, not all as one as now—but no matther. Well, they had nearly finished their dinner, when Jack Rafferty himself axed Katty for the pudden; but, jist as he spoke, in it came as big as a mess-pot.

" 'Gintlemen,' said he, 'I hope none of you will refuse tastin' a bit of Katty's pudden; I don't mane the dancin' one that tuck to its thravels to-day, but a good solid fellow that she med since.'

" 'To be sure we won't,' replied the priest; 'so, Jack, put a thrifle on them three plates at your right hand, and send them over here to the clargy, an' maybe,' he said, laughin'—for he was a droll good-humored man—'maybe, Jack, we won't set you a proper example.'

" 'Wid a heart an' a 'half, yer reverence an' gintlemen; in throth, it's not a bad example ever any of you set us at the likes, or ever will set us, I'll go bail. An' sure I only wish it was betther fare I had for you; but we're humble people, gintlemen, and so you can't expect to meet here what you would in higher places.'

" 'Betther a male of herbs,' said the Methodist praicher, 'where pace is——.' He had time to go no farther, however; for much to his amazement, the priest and the ministher started up from the table jist as he was goin' to swallow the first spoonful of the pudden, and before you could say Jack Robinson, started away at a lively jig down the floor.

" At this moment a neighbor's son came runnin' in, an' tould them that the parson was comin' to see the new-married couple, an' wish them all happiness; an' the words were scarcely out of his mouth when he made his appearance. What to think he knew not, when he saw the ministher footing it away at the rate of a weddin'. He had very little time, however, to think; for, before he could sit down, up starts the Methodist praicher, and clappin' his two fists in his sides chimes in in great style along wid him.

" 'Jack Rafferty,' says he—and, by the way, Jack was his tenant— 'what the dickens does all this mane ?' says he; 'I'm amazed!'"

" 'The not a particle o' me can tell you,' says Jack; 'but will your reverence jist taste a morsel o' pudden, merely that the young couple may boast that you ait at their weddin'; for sure if *you* wouldn't, *who* would?'"

" 'Well,' says he, 'to gratify them I will; so just a morsel. But, Jack, this bates Bannagher,' says he again, puttin' the spoonful o' pudden into his mouth; 'has there been dhrink here?'"

" 'Oh, the divle a *spudh*,' says Jack, 'for although there's plinty in the house, faith, it appears the gintlemen wouldn't wait for it. Unless they tuck it elsewhere, I can make nothin' of this.'

" He had scarcely spoken, when the parson, who was an active man, cut a caper a yard high, an' before you could bless yourself, the three clargy were hard at work dancin', as if for a wager. Begad, it would be unpossible for me to tell you the state the whole meetin' was in when they seen this. Some were hoarse wid laughin'; some turned up their eyes wid wondher; many thought them mad, an' others thought they had turned up their little fingers a thrifle too often.

" 'Be goxty, it's a burnin' shame,' said one, 'to see three black-mouth clargy in sich a state at this early hour!' 'Thundher an' ounze, what's over them at all?' says others; 'why, one would think they're bewitched. Holy Moses, look at the caper the Methodis cuts! An' as for the Recther, who would think he could handle his feet at such a rate! Be this an' be that, he cuts the buckle, and does the threblin' step aiquil to Paddy Horaghan, the dancin'-masther himself? An' see! Bad cess to the morsel of the parson that's not hard at *Peace upon a trancher*, an' it of a Sunday too! Whirroo, gintlemen, the fun's in yez afther all—whish! more power to yez!'

"The sorra's own fun they had, an' no wondher; but judge of what they felt, when all at once they saw ould Jack Rafferty himself bouncin' in among them, and footing it away like the best o' them. Bedad, no play could come up to it, an' nothin' could be heard but laughin', shouts of encouragement, and clappin' of hands like mad. Now the minute Jack Rafferty left the chair where he had been carvin' the pudden, ould Harry Connolly comes over and claps himself down in his place, in ordher to send it round, of coorse; an' he was scarcely sated, when who should make his appearance but Barney Hartigan, the piper. Barney, by the way, had been sent for early in the day, but bein' from home when the message for him went, he couldn't come any sooner.

"'Begorra,' said Barney, 'you're airly at the work, gintlemen! but what does this mane? But, divle may care, yez shan't want the music while there's a blast in the pipes, anyhow!' So sayin' he gave them *Jig Polthogue*, an' after that *Kiss my Lady*, in his best style.

"In the manetime the fun went on thick an' threefold, for it must be remimbered that Harry, the ould knave, was at the pudden; an' maybe he didn't sarve it about in double quick time too. The first he helped was the bride, and, before you could say chopstick, she was at it hard an' fast before the Methodist praicher, who gave a jolly spring before her that threw them into convulsions. Harry liked this, and made up his mind soon to find partners for the rest; so he accordianly sent the pudden about like lightnin'; an' to made a long story short, barrin' the piper an' himself, there wasn't a pair o' heels in the house but was as busy at the dancin' as if their lives depinded on it.

"'Barney,' says Harry, 'just taste a morsel o' this pudden; divle the such a bully of a pudden ever you ett; here, your sowl! thry a snig of it—it's beautiful.'

"'To be sure I will,' says Barney. 'I'm not the boy

to refuse a good thing; but, Harry, be quick, for you
know my hands is engaged, an' it would be a thousand
pities not to keep them in music, an' they so well inclined.
Thank you, Harry; begad that is a famous pudden; but
blood an' turnips, what's this for?'

"The word was scarcely out of his mouth when he
bounced up, pipes an' all, an' dashed into the middle of
the party. 'Hurroo, your sowls, let us make a night of
it! The Ballyboulteen boys forever! Go it, your reverence—turn your partner—heel an' toe, ministher. Good!
Well done again—Whish! Hurroo! Here's for Ballyboulteen, an' the sky over it!"

"Bad luck to the sich a set ever was seen together in
this world, or will again, I suppose. The worst, however,
wasn't come yet, for just as they were in the very heat
an' fury of the dance, what do you think comes hoppin'
in among them but another pudden, as nimble an' merry
as the first! That was enough; they all had heard of—
the ministhers among the rest—an' most o' them had seen
the other pudden, and knew that there must be a fairy
in it, sure enough. Well, as I said, in it comes to the
thick o' them; but the very appearance of it was enough.
Off the three clargy danced, and off the whole weddiners
danced afther them, every one makin' the best of their
way home; but not a sowl of them able to break out of
the step, if they were to be hanged for it. Throth it
wouldn't lave a laugh in you to see the parson dancin'
down the road on his way home, and the ministher and
Methodist praicher cuttin' the buckle as they went along
in the opposite direction. To make short work of it,
they all danced home at last, wid scarce a puff of wind
in them; the bride and bridegroom danced away to bed;
an' now, boys, come an' let us dance the *Horo Lheig* in
the barn 'idout. But you see, boys, before we go, an' in
ordher that I may make everything plain, I had as good
tell you that Harry, in crossing the bridge of Ballyboulteen, a couple of miles below Squire Bragshaw's demesne-
wall, saw the pudden floatin' down the river—the truth

is he was waitin' for it; but be this as it may, he took it
out, for the wather had made it as clane as a new pin,
and tuckin' it up in the tail of his big coat, contrived, as
you all guess, I suppose, to change it while Paddy Scanlan an' the wife were examinin' the sky; an' for the other,
he contrived to bewitch it in the same manner, by gettin'
a fairy to go into it, for, indeed, it was purty well known
that the same Harry was hand an' glove wid the *good
people*. Others will tell you that it was half a pound of
quicksilver he put into it; but that doesn't stand to raison.
At any rate, boys, I have tould you the adventures of the
Mad Pudden of Ballyboulteen; but I don't wish to tell
you many other things about it that happened—*for, fraid
I'd tell a lie*." *

* Some will insist that a fairy-man or fairy-woman has the
power to bewitch a pudding by putting a fairy into it; whilst
others maintain that a competent portion of quicksilver will
make it dance over half the parish.

T'YEER-NA-N-OGE.

[There is a country called Tír-na-n-Og, which means the Country of the Young, for age and death have not found it; neither tears nor loud laughter have gone near it. The shadiest boskage covers it perpetually. One man has gone there and returned. The bard, Oisen, who wandered away on a white horse, moving on the surface of the foam with his fairy Niamh, lived there three hundred years, and then returned looking for his comrades. The moment his foot touched the earth his three hundred years fell on him, and he was bowed double, and his beard swept the ground. He described his sojourn in the Land of Youth to Patrick before he died. Since then many have seen it in many places; some in the depths of lakes, and have heard rising therefrom a vague sound of bells; more have seen it far off on the horizon, as they peered out from the western cliffs. Not three years ago a fisherman imagined that he saw it. It never appears unless to announce some national trouble.

There are many kindred beliefs. A Dutch pilot, settled in Dublin, told M. De La Boullage Le Cong, who traveled in Ireland in 1614, that round the poles were many islands; some hard to be approached because of the witches who inhabit them and destroy by storms those who seek to land. He had once, off the coast of Greenland, in sixty-one degrees of latitude, seen and approached such an island only to see it vanish. Sailing in an opposite direction, they met with the same island, and sailing near, were almost destroyed by a furious tempest.

According to many stories, Tír-na-n-Og is the favorite

dwelling of the fairies. Some say it is triple—the island of the living, the island of victories, and an underwater land.]

THE LEGEND OF O'DONOGHUE. *

T. CROFTON CROKER.

In an age so distant that the precise period is unknown, a chieftain named O'Donoghue ruled over the country which surrounds the romantic Lough Lean, now called the Lake of Killarney. Wisdom, beneficence, and justice distinguished his reign, and the prosperity and happiness of his subjects were their natural results. He is said to have been as renowned for his warlike exploits as for his pacific virtues; and as a proof that his domestic administration was not the less rigorous because it was mild, a rocky island is pointed out to strangers, called, "O'Donoghue's Prison," in which this prince once confined his own son for some act of disorder and disobedience.

His end—for it cannot correctly be called his death— was singular and mysterious. At one of those splendid feasts for which his court was celebrated, surrounded by the most distinguished of his subjects, he was engaged in a prophetic relation of the events which were to happen in ages yet to come. His auditors listened, now wrapt in wonder, now fired with indignation, burning with shame, or melted into sorrow, as he faithfully detailed the heroism, the injuries, the crimes, and the miseries of their descendants. In the midst of his predictions he rose slowly from his seat, advanced with a solemn, measured, and majestic tread to the shore of the lake, and walked forward composedly upon its unyielding surface. When he had nearly reached the center he paused for a moment, then, turning slowly round, looked toward his friends, and

* *Fairy Legends of the South of Ireland.*

waving his arms to them with the cheerful air of one taking a short farewell, disappeared from their view.

The memory of the good O'Donoghue has been cherished by successive generations with affectionate reverence; and it is believed that at sunrise, on every May-day morning, the anniversary of his departure, he revisits his ancient domains : a favored few only are in general permitted to see him, and this distinction is always an omen of good fortune to the beholders ; when it is granted to many it is a sure token of an abundant harvest,—a blessing, the want of which during this prince's reign was never felt by his people.

Some years have elapsed since the last appearance of O'Donoghue. The April of that year had been remarkably wild and stormy; but on May-morning the fury of the elements had altogether subsided. The air was hushed and still ; and the sky, which was reflected in the serene lake, resembled a beautiful but deceitful countenance, whose smiles, after the most tempestuous emotions, tempt the stranger to believe that it belongs to a soul which no passion has ever ruffled.

The first beams of the rising sun were just gilding the lofty summit of Glenäa, when the waters near the eastern shore of the lake became suddenly and violently agitated, though all the rest of its surface lay smooth and still as a tomb of polished marble, the next morning a foaming wave darted forward, and, like a proud high-crested war-horse, exulting in his strength, rushed across the lake toward Toomies mountain. Behind this wave appeared a stately warrior fully armed, mounted upon a milk-white steed ; his snowy plume waved gracefully from a helmet of polished steel, and at his back fluttered a light blue scarf. The horse, apparently exulting in his noble burden, sprung after the wave along the water, which bore him up like firm earth, while showers of spray that glittered brightly in the morning sun were dashed up at every bound.

The warrior was O'Donoghue ; he was followed by numberless youths and maidens, who moved lightly and unconstrained over the watery plain, as the moonlight fairies glide through the fields of air ; they were linked together by garlands of delicious spring flowers, and they timed their movements to strains of enchanting melody. When O'Donoghue had nearly reached the western side of the lake, he suddenly turned his steed, and directed his course along the wood-fringed shore of Glenaa, preceded by the huge wave that curled and foamed up as high as the horse's neck, whose fiery nostrils snorted above it. The long train of attendants followed with playful deviations the track of their leader, and moved on with unabated fleetness to their celestial music, till gradually, as they entered the narrow strait between Glenaa and Dinis, they became involved in the mists which still partially floated over the lakes, and faded from the view of the wondering beholders : but the sound of their music still fell upon the ear, and echo, catching up the harmonious strains, fondly repeated and prolonged them in soft and softer tones, till the last faint repetition died away, and the hearers awoke as from a dream of bliss.

RENT-DAY.

" Oh, ullagone ! ullagone ! this is a wide world, but what will we do in it, or where will we go ? " muttered Bill Doody, as he sat on a rock by the Lake of Killarney. " What will we do ? To-morrow's rent-day, and Tim the Driver swears if we don't pay our rent, he'll cant ever *ha'perth* we have ; and then, sure enough, there's Judy and myself, and the poor *grawls.** will be turned out to starve on the high-road, for the never a halfpenny of rent have I !—Oh hone, that ever I should live to see this day ! "

Thus did Bill Doody bemoan his hard fate, pouring his

* Children.

sorrows to the reckless waves of the most beautiful of
lakes, which seemed to mock his misery as they rejoiced
beneath the cloudless sky of a May morning. That lake,
glittering in sunshine, sprinkled with fairy isles of rock
and verdure, and bounded by giant hills of ever-varying
hues, might, with its magic beauty, charm all sadness but
despair; for alas,

> " How ill the scene that offers rest
> And heart that cannot rest agree ! "

Yet Bill Doody was not so desolate as he supposed; there
was one listening to him he little thought of, and help was
at hand from a quarter he could not have expected.

" What's the matter with you, my poor man ? " said a
tall, portly-looking gentlman, at the same time stepping
out of a furze-brake. Now Bill was seated on a rock that
commanded the view of a large field. Nothing in the
field could be concealed from him, except this furze-brake,
which grew in a hollow near the margin of the lake. He
was, therefore, not a little surprised at the gentleman's
sudden appearance, and began to question whether the
personage before him belonged to this world or not. He,
however, soon mustered courage sufficient to tell him
how his crops had failed, how some bad member had
charmed away his butter, and how Tim the Driver
threatened to turn him out of the farm if he didn't pay
up every penny of the rent by twelve o'clock next day.

" A sad story, indeed," said the stranger; " but surely,
if you represented the case to your landlord's agent, he
won't have the heart to turn you out."

" Heart, your honor; where would an agent get a
heart ! " exclaimed Bill. " I see your honor does not
know him ; besides, he has an eye on the farm this long
time for a fosterer of his own; so I expect no mercy at
all at all, only to be turned out."

" Take this, my poor fellow, take this," said the
stranger, pouring a purse full of gold into Bill's old hat,
which in his grief he had flung on the ground. " Pay the

fellow your rent, but I'll take care it shall do him no good.
I remember the time when things went otherwise in this
country, when I would have hung up such a fellow in the
twinkling of an eye!"

These words were lost upon Bill, who was insensible to
everything but the sight of the gold, and before he could
unfix his gaze, and lift up his head to pour out his hundred
thousand blessings, the stranger was gone. The bewildered
peasant looked around in search of his benefactor, and at
last he thought he saw him riding on a white horse a long
way off on the lake.

"O'Donoghue, O'Donoghue!" shouted Bill; "the good,
the blessed O'Donoghue!" and he ran capering like a
madman to show Judy the gold, and to rejoice her heart
with the prospect of wealth and happiness.

The next day Bill proceeded to the agent's; not sneak-
ingly, with his hat in his hand, his eyes fixed on the
ground, and his knees bending under him; but bold and
upright, like a man conscious of his independence.

"Why don't you take off your hat, fellow? don't you
know you are speaking to a magistrate?" said the agent.

"I know I'm not speaking to the king, sir," said Bill;
"and I never takes off my hat but to them I can respect
and love. The Eye that sees all knows I've no right
either to respect or love an agent!"

"You scoundrel!" retorted the man in office, biting his
lips with rage at such an unusual and unexpected opposition, "I'll teach you how to be insolent again; I have
the power, remember."

"To the cost of the country, I know you have," said
Bill, who still remained with his head as firmly covered
as if he was the Lord Kingsale himself.

"But, come," said the magistrate; "have you got the
money for me? this is rent-day. If there's one penny of
it wanting, or the running gale that's due, prepare to turn
out before night, for you shall not remain another hour
in possession."

"There is your rent," said Bill, with an unmoved expression of tone and countenance; " you'd better count it, and give me a receipt in full for the running gale and all."

The agent gave a look of amazement at the gold; for it was gold—real guineas! and not bits of dirty ragged small notes, that are only fit to light one's pipe with. However willing the agent may have been to ruin, as he thought, the unfortunate tenant, he took up the gold, and handed the receipt to Bill, who strutted off with it as proud as a cat of her whiskers.

The agent going to his desk shortly after, was confounded at beholding a heap of gingerbread cakes instead of the money he had deposited there. He raved and swore, but all to no purpose; the gold had become gingerbread cakes, just marked like the guineas, with the king's head; and Bill had the receipt in his pocket; so he saw there was no use in saying anything about the affair, as he would only get laughed at for his pains.

From that hour Bill Doody grew rich; all his undertakings prospered; and he often blesses the day that he met with O'Donoghue, the great prince that lives down under the Lake of Killarney.

———

LOUGHLEAGH (LAKE OF HEALING).*

" Do you see that bit of a lake," said my companion, turning his eyes towards the acclivity that overhung Loughleagh. " Troth, and as little as you think of it, and as ugly as it looks with its weeds and its flags, it is the most famous one in all Ireland. Young and ould, rich and poor, far and near, have come to that lake to get cured of all kinds of scurvy and sores. The Lord keep us our limbs whole and sound, for it's a sorrowful thing not to have the use o' them. 'Twas but last week we had a great grand Frenchman here; and, though he came upon

* *Dublin and London Magazine*, 1825.

crutches, faith he went home sound as a bell; and well
he paid Billy Reily for curing him."

"And, pray, how did Billy Reily cure him?"

"Oh, well enough. He took his long pole, dipped it
down to the bottom of the lake, and brought up on the
top of it as much plaster as would do for a thousand
sores!"

"What kind of plaster?"

"What kind of plaster? why, black plaster to be sure;
for isn't the bottom of the lake filled with a kind of black
mud which cures all the world?"

"Then it ought to be a famous lake indeed."

"Famous, and so it is," replied my companion, "but it
isn't for its cures neather that it is famous; for, sure,
doesn't all the world know there is a fine beautiful city
at the bottom of it, where the good people live just like
Christians. Troth, it is the truth I tell you; for *Shemus-
a-sneidh* saw it all when he followed his dun cow that
was stolen."

"Who stole her?"

"I'll tell you all about it:—Shemus was a poor gossoon, who lived on the brow of the hill, in a cabin with
his ould mother. They lived by hook and by crook, one
way and another, in the best way they could. They had
a bit of ground that gave 'em the preaty, and a little dun
cow that gave 'em the drop o' milk; and, considering
how times go, they weren't badly off, for Shemus was a
handy gossoon to boot; and, while minden the cow, cut
heath and made brooms, which his mother sould on a
market-day, and brought home the bit o' tobaccy, the
grain of salt, and other nic-nackenes, which a poor body
can't well do widout. Once upon a time, however, Shemus
went farther than usual up the mountain, looken for long
heath, for town's-people don't like to stoop, and so like
long handles to their brooms. The little dun cow was
a'most as cunning as a .Christian sinner, and followed
Shemus like a lap-dog everywhere he'd go, so that she
required little or no herden. On this day she found nice

picken on a round spot as green as a leek; and, as poor
Shemus was weary, as a body would be on a fine summer's day, he lay down on the grass to rest himself, just
as we're resten ourselves on the cairn here. Begad, he
hadn't long lain there, sure enough, when, what should
he see but whole loads of ganconers * dancing about the
place. Some o' them were hurlen, some kicking a foot-
ball, and others leaping a kick-step-and-a-lep. They were
so soople and so active that Shemus was highly delighted
with the sport, and a little tanned-skinned chap in a red
cap pleased him better than any o' them, bekase he used
to tumble the other fellows like mushrooms. At one
time he kept the ball up for as good as half-an-hour, when
Shemus cried out, ' Well done, my hurler ! ' The word
wasn't well out of his mouth when whap went the ball
on his eye, and flash went the fire. Poor Shemus thought
he was blind, and roared out, ' Mille murdher ! ' † but the
only thing he heard was a loud laugh. ' Cross o' Christ
about us,' says he to himself, ' what is this for ? " and
after rubbing his eyes they came to a little, and he could
see the sun and the sky, and, by-and-by, he could see
everything but his cow and the mischievous ganconers.
They were gone to their rath or mote; but where was the

---

* Ir. *gean-canach*—*i.e.*, love-talker, a kind of fairy appearing
in lonesome valleys, a dudeen (tobacco-pipe) in his mouth, making love to milk-maids, etc, O'Kearney, a Louthman, deeply
versed in Irish lore, writes of the *gean-cānach* (love-talker) that
he is " another diminutive being of the same tribe as the Lepracaun, but, unlike him, he personated love and idleness, and
always appeared with a dudeen in his jaw in lonesome valleys-
and it was his custom to make love to shepherdesses and milk-
maids. It was considered very unlucky to meet him, and whoever was known to have ruined his fortune by devotion to the
fair sex was said to have met a *gean-cānach*. The dudeen, or
ancient Irish tobacco pipe, found in our raths, etc., is still popu-
larly called a *gean-cānach's* pipe."
The word is not to be found in dictionaries, nor does this spirit
appear to be well known, if known at all, in Connacht. The
word is pronounced *gánconágh*.
† A thousand murders.

little dun cow? He looked, and he looked, and he might
have looked from that day to this, bekase she wasn't to
be found, and good reason why—the ganconers took her
away with 'em.

"Shemus-a-sneidh, however, didn't think so, but ran
home to his mother.

"'Where is the cow, Shemus?' axed the ould woman.

"'Och, musha, bad luck to her,' said Shemus, 'I donna
where she is!'

"'Is that an answer, you big blaggard, for the likes o'
you to give your poor ould mother?' said she.

"'Och, musha," said Shemus, 'don't kick up saich a
bollhous about nothing. The ould cow is safe enough,
I'll be bail, some place or other, though I could find her
if I put my eyes upon *kippeens*,* and, speaking of eyes,
faith, I had very good luck o' my side, or I had never a
one to look after her.'

"'Why, what happened your eyes, agrah?' axed the
ould woman.

"'Oh! didn't the ganconers—the Lord save us from all
hurt and harm!—drive their hurlen ball into them both!
and sure I was stone blind for an hour.'

"'And may be,' said the mother, 'the good people took
our cow?'

"'No, nor the devil a one of them,' said Shemus, 'for,
by the powers, that same cow is as knowen as a lawyer,
and wouldn't be such a fool as to go with the ganconers
while she could get such grass as I found for her to-day.'

In this way, continued my informant, they talked about
the cow all that night, and next mornen both o' them set
off to look for her. After searching every place, high and
low, what should Shemus see sticking out of a bog-hole
but something very like the horns of his little beast!

"Oh, mother, mother," said he, "I've found her!"

"Where, alanna?" axed the ould woman.

"In the bog-hole, mother," answered Shemus.

---

* Ir. *cipin*—*i.e.*, a stick, a twig.

At this the poor ould creathure set up such a *pullallue*
that she brought the seven parishes about her ; and the
neighbors soon pulled the cow out of the bog-hole.
You'd swear it was the same, and yet it wasn't as you
shall hear by-and-by.

Shemus and his mother brought the dead beast home
with them ; and, after skinnen her, hung the meat up in
the chimney.   The loss of the drop o' milk was a sorrowful thing, and though they had a good deal of meat, that
couldn't last always ; besides, the whole parish *faughed*
upon them for eating the flesh of a beast that died without bleeden.   But the pretty thing was, they couldn't eat
the meat after all, for when it was boiled it was as tough
as carrion, and as black as a turf.   You might as well
think of sinking your teeth in an oak plank as into a
piece of it, and then you'd want to sit a great piece from
the wall for fear of knocking your head against it when
pulling it through your teeth.   At last and at long run
they were forced to throw it to the dogs, but the dogs
wouldn't smell to it, and so it was thrown into the ditch,
where it rotted.   This misfortune cost poor Shemus many
a salt tear, for he was now obliged to work twice as
hard as before, and be out cutten heath on the mountain
late and early.   One day he was passing by this cairn
with a load of brooms on his back, when what should he
see but the little dun cow and two red-headed fellows
herding her.

" That's my mother's cow," said Shemus-a-sneidh.

" No, it is not," said one of the chaps.

" But I say it is," said Shemus, throwing the brooms
on the ground, and seizing the cow by the horns.   At
that the red fellows drove her as fast as they could to
this steep place, and with one leap she bounced over, with
Shemus stuck fast to her horns.   They made only one
splash in the lough, when the waters closed over 'em, and
they sunk to the bottom.   Just as Shemus-a-sneidh
thought that all was over with him, he found himself before
a most elegant palace built with jewels, and all manner of

fine stones. Though his eyes were dazzled with the splendor of the place, faith he had gomsh * enough not to let go his holt, but in spite of all they could do, he held his little cow by the horns. He was axed into the place, but wouldn't go.

The hubbub at last grew so great that the door flew open, and out walked a hundred ladies and gentlemen, as fine as any in the land.

" What does this boy want? " axed one o' them, who seemed to be the masther.

" I want my mother's cow," said Shemus.

" That's not your mother's cow," said the gentleman.

" Bethershin ! " † cried Shemus-a-sneid ; " don't I know her as well as I know my right hand ? "

" Where did you lose her ? " axed the gentleman. And so Shemus up and tould him all about it : how he was on the mountain—how he saw the good people hurlen—how the ball was knocked in his eye, and his cow was lost.

" I believe you are right," said the gentleman, pulling out his purse, " and here is the price of twenty cows for you."

" No, no," said Shemus, " you'll not catch ould birds wid chaff. I'll have my cow and nothen else."

" You're a funny fellow," said the gentleman ; " stop here and live in a palace."

" I'd rather live with my mother."

" Foolish boy ! " said the gentleman ; " stop here and live in a palace."

" I'd rather live in my mother's cabin."

" Here you can walk through gardens loaded with fruit and flowers."

" I'd rather," said Shemus, " be cutting heath on the mountain."

" Here you can eat and drink of the best."

---

* Otherwise " gumshun "—*i. e.*, sense, cuteness.
† Ir. *B'éidir sin—i. e.*, " that is possible."

"Since I've got my cow, I can have milk once more with the praties."

"Oh!" cried the ladies, gathering round him, "sure you wouldn't take away the cow that gives us milk for our tea?"

"Oh!" said Shemus, "my mother wants milk as bad as any one, and she must have it; so there is no use in your palaver—I must have my cow."

At this they all gathered about him and offered him bushels of gould, but he wouldn't have anything but his cow. Seeing him as obstinate as a mule, they began to thump and beat him; but still he held fast by the horns, till at length a great blast of wind blew him out of the place, and in a moment he found himself and the cow standing on the side of the lake, the water of which looked as if it hadn't been disturbed since Adam was a boy—and that's a long time since.

Well, Shemus-a-sneidh drove home his cow, and right glad his mother was to see her; but the moment she said "God bless the beast," she sunk down like the *breesha** of a turf rick. That was the end of Shemus-a-sneid's dun cow.

"And, sure," continued my companion, standing up "it is now time for me to look after my brown cow, and God send the ganconers haven't taken her!"

Of this I assured him there could be no fear; and so we parted.

* Ir. *briseadh*—*i. e.*, breaking.

HY-BRASAIL—THE ISLE OF THE BLEST.

BY GERALD GRIFFIN.

On the ocean that hollows the rocks where ye dwell,
A shadowy land has appeared, as they tell;
Men thought it a region of sunshine and rest,
And they called it *Hy-Brasail*, the isle of the blest.
From year unto year on the ocean's blue rim,
The beautiful specter showed lovely and dim;
The golden clouds curtained the deep where it lay,
And it looked like an Eden, away, far away!

A peasant who heard of the wonderful tale,
In the breeze of the Orient loosened his sail;
From Ara the holy, he turned to the west,
For though Ara was holy, *Hy-Brasail* was blest.
He heard not the voices that called from the shore—
He heard not the rising wind's menacing roar;
Home, kindred, and safety, he left on that day,
And he sped to *Hy-Brasail*, away, far away!

Morn rose on the deep, and that shadowy isle,
O'er the faint rim of distance, reflected its smile;
Noon burned on the wave, and that shadowy shore
Seemed lovelily distant, and faint as before;
Lone evening came down on the wanderer's track,
And to Ara again he looked timidly back;
" Oh! far on the verge of the ocean it lay,
Yet the isle of the blest was away, far away!

Rash dreamer, return! O, ye winds of the main,
Bear him back to his own peaceful Ara again.
Rash fool! for a vision of fanciful bliss,
To barter thy calm life of labor and peace.

The warning of reason was spoken in vain ;
He never revisited Ara again !
Night fell on the deep, amidst tempest and spray,
And he died on the waters, away, far away !

THE PHANTOM ISLE.

GIRALDUS CAMBRENSIS.*

AMONG the other islands is one newly formed, which
they call the Phantom Isle, which had its origin in this
manner.   One calm day a large mass of earth rose to the
surface of the sea, where no land had ever been seen before, to the great amazement of islanders who observed it.
Some of them said that it was a whale, or other immense
sea-monster ; others, remarking that it continued motionless, said, " No ; it is land."   In order, therefore, to reduce
their doubts to certainty, some picked young men of the
island determined to approach nearer the spot in a boat.
When, however, they came so near to it that they thought
they should go on shore, the island sank in the water and
entirely vanished from sight.   The next day it re-ap-
peared, and again mocked the same youths with the like
delusion.   At length, on their rowing towards it on the
third day, they followed the advice of an older man, and
let fly an arrow, barbed with red-hot steel, against the
island ; and then landing, found it stationary and habit-
able.

This adds one to the many proofs that fire is the greatest of enemies to every sort of phantom ; in so much that
those who have seen apparitions, fall into a swoon as soon
as they are sensible of the brightness of fire.   For fire,

* " Giraldus Cambrensis " was born in 1146, and wrote a celebrated account of Ireland.

both from its position and nature, is the noblest of the elements, being a witness of the secrets of the heavens.

The sky is fiery; the planets are fiery; the bush burnt with fire, but was not consumed; the Holy Ghost sat upon the apostles in tongues of fire.

SAINTS, PRIESTS.

EVERYWHERE in Ireland are the holy wells. People as they pray by them make little piles of stones, that will be counted at the last day and the prayers reckoned up. Sometimes they tell stories. These following are their stories. They deal with the old times, whereof King Alfred of Northumberland wrote—

"I found in Innisfail the fair,
In Ireland, while in exile there,
Women of worth, both grave and gay men,
Many clericks and many laymen.

Gold and silver I found, and money,
Plenty of wheat, and plenty of honey;
I found God's people rich in pity,
Found many a feast, and many a city."

There are no martyrs in the stories. That ancient chronicler Giraldus taunted the Archbishop of Cashel because no one in Ireland had received the crown of martyrdom. "Our people may be barbarous," the prelate answered, "but they have never lifted their hands against God's saints; but now that a people have come amongst us who know how to make them (it was just after the English invasion), we shall have martyrs plentifully."

The bodies of saints are fastidious things. At a place called Four-mile-Water, in Wexford, there is an old graveyard full of saints. Once it was on the other side of the river, but they buried a rogue there, and the whole graveyard moved across in the night, leaving the rogue-corpse in solitude. It would have been easier to move merely the rogue-corpse, but they were saints, and had to do things in style.

THE PRIEST'S SOUL.*

LADY WILDE.

In former days there were great schools in Ireland, where every sort of learning was taught to the people, and even the poorest had more knowledge at that time than many a gentleman has now. But as to the priests, their learning was above all, so that the fame of Ireland went over the whole world, and many kings from foreign lands used to send their sons all the way to Ireland to be brought up in the Irish schools.

Now, at this time there was a little boy learning at one of them, who was a wonder to every one for his cleverness. His parents were only laboring people, and of course poor; but young as he was, and as poor as he was, no king's or lord's son could come up to him in learning. Even the masters were put to shame; for when they were trying to teach him he would tell them something they never heard of before, and show them their ignorance. One of his great triumphs was in argument; and he would go on till he proved to you that black was white, and then when you gave in, for no one could beat him in talk, he would turn around and show you that white was black, or maybe that there was no color at all in the world. When he grew up his poor father and mother were so proud of him that they resolved to make him a priest, which they did at last, though they nearly starved themselves to get the money. Well, such another learned man was not in Ireland, and he was as great in argument as ever, so that no one could stand before him. Even the bishops tried to talk to him, but he showed them at once they knew nothing at all.

Now, there were no schoolmasters in those times, but

* Ancient Legends of Ireland.

it was the priests taught the people; and as this man was the cleverest in Ireland, all the foreign kings sent their sons to him as long as he had house-room to give them. So he grew very proud, and began to forget how low he had been, and worst of all, even to forget God, who had made him what he was. And the pride of arguing got hold of him, so that from one thing to another he went on to prove that there was no Purgatory, and then no Hell, and then no Heaven, and then no God; and at last that men had no souls, but were no more than a dog or a cow, and when they died there was an end of them. "Whoever saw a soul?" he would say. "If you can show me one, I will believe." No one could make any answer to this; and at last they all come to believe that as there was no other world, every one might do what they liked in this; the priest setting the example, for he took a beautiful young girl to wife. But as no priest or bishop in the whole land could be got to marry them, he was obliged to read the service over for himself. It was a great scandal, yet no one dared to say a word, for all the king's sons were on his side, and would have slaughtered any one who tried to prevent his wicked goings-on. Poor boys; they all believed in him, and thought every word he said was the truth. In this way his notions began to spread about, and the whole world was going to the bad, when one night an angel came down from Heaven, and told the priest he had but twenty-four hours to live. He began to tremble, and asked for a little more time.

But the angel was stiff, and told him that could not be.

"What do you want time for, you sinner?" he asked.

"Oh, sir, have pity on my poor soul!" urged the priest.

"Oh, no! You have a soul, then," said the angel. "Pray, how did you find that out?"

"It has been fluttering in me ever since you appeared," answered the priest. "What a fool I was not to think of it before."

" A fool, indeed," said the angel. " What good was all your learning, when it could not tell you that you had a soul?"

" Ah, my lord," said the priest, " if I am to die, tell me how soon I may be in Heaven?"

" Never," replied the angel. " You denied there was a Heaven."

" Then, my lord, may I go to Purgatory?"

" You denied Purgatory also; you must go straight to Hell," said the angel.

" But, my lord, I denied Hell also," answered the priest, " so you can't send me there either."

The angel was a little puzzled.

" Well," said he, " I'll tell you what I can do for you. You may either live now on earth for a hundred years, enjoying every pleasure, and then be cast into Hell for ever ; or you may die in twenty-four hours in the most horrible torments, and pass through Purgatory, there to remain till the Day of Judgment, if only you can find some one person that believes, and through his belief mercy will be vouchsafed to you, and your soul will be saved."

The priest did not take five minutes to make up his mind.

" I will have death in the twenty-four hours," he said, " so that my soul may be saved at last."

On this the angel gave him directions as to what he was to do, and left him.

Then immediately the priest entered the large room where all the scholars and the kings' sons were seated, and called out to them—

" Now, tell me the truth, and let none fear to contradict me ; tell me what is your belief—have men souls?"

" Master," they answered, " once we believed that men had souls ; but thanks to your teaching, we believe so no longer. There is no Hell, and no Heaven, and no God. This is our belief, for it is thus you taught us."

Then the priest grew pale with fear, and cried out—

" Listen! I taught you a lie. There is a God, and man
has an immortal soul. I believe now all I denied before."

But the shouts of laughter that rose up drowned the
priest's voice, for they thought he was only trying them
for argument.

" Prove it, master," they cried. " Prove it. Who has
ever seen God? Who has ever seen the soul?"

And the room was stirred with their laughter.

The priest stood up to answer them, but no word could
he utter. All his eloquence, all his powers of argument
had gone from him; and he could do nothing but wring
his hands and cry out, " There is a God! there is a God!
Lord have mercy on my soul!"

And they all began to mock him! and repeat his own
words that he had taught them—

" Show him to us; show us your God." And he fled
from them, groaning with agony, for he saw that none
believed; and how, then, could his soul be saved?

But he thought next of his wife. " She will believe,"
he said to himself: " women never give up God."

And he went to her; but she told him that she believed
only what he taught her, and that a good wife should
believe in her husband first and before and above all things
in Heaven or earth.

Then despair came on him, and he rushed from the
house, and began to ask every one he met if they believed.
But the same answer came from one and all—" We believe only what you have taught us," for his doctrine had
spread far and wide through the country.

Then he grew half mad with fear, for the hours were
passing, and he flung himself down on the ground in a
lonesome spot, and wept and groaned in terror, for the
time was coming fast when he must die.

Just then a little child came by. " God save you
kindly," said the child to him.

The priest started up.

"Do you believe in God?" he asked.

" I have come from a far country to learn about him,"
said the child. " Will your honor direct me to the best
school they have in these parts ? "

" The best school and the best teacher is close by," said
the priest, and he named himself.

" Oh, not to that man," answered the child, " for I am
told he denies God, and Heaven, and Hell, and even that
man has a soul, because he cannot see it ; but I would
soon put him down."

The priest looked at him earnestly. " How? " he inquired.

" Why," said the child, " I would ask him if he believed
he had life to show me his life."

" But he could not do that, my child," said the priest.
" Life cannot be seen ; we have it, but it is invisible."

" Then if we have life, though we cannot see it, we may
also have a soul, though it is invisible," answered the
child.

When the priest heard him speak these words, he fell
down on his knees before him, weeping for joy, for now he
knew his soul was safe ; he had met one at last that believed. And he told the child his whole story—all his
wickedness, and pride, and blasphemy against the great
God ; and how the angel had come to him, and told him of
the only way in which he could be saved, through the
faith and prayers of some one that believed.

" Now, then," he said to the child, " take this penknife
and strike it into my breast, and go on stabbing the flesh
until you see the paleness of death on my face. Then
watch—for a living thing will soar up from my body as
I die, and you will then know that my soul has ascended to
the presence of God. And when you see this thing, make
haste and run to my school, and call on all my scholars
to come and see that the soul of their master has left the
body, and that all he taught them was a lie, for that there
is a God who punishes sin, and a Heaven, and a Hell, and
that man has an immortal soul destined for eternal happiness or misery."

"I will pray," said the child, "to have courage to do this work."

And he kneeled down and prayed. Then when he rose up he took the penknife and struck it into the priest's heart, and struck and struck again till all the flesh was lacerated; but still the priest lived, though the agony was horrible, for he could not die until the twenty-four hours had expired.

At last the agony seemed to cease, and the stillness of death settled on his face. Then the child, who was watching, saw a beautiful living creature, with four snow-white wings, mount from the dead man's body into the air and go fluttering round his head.

So he ran to bring the scholars; and when they saw it, they all knew it was the soul of their master; and they watched with wonder and awe until it passed from sight into the clouds.

And this was the first butterfly that was ever seen in Ireland; and now all men know that the butterflies are the souls of the dead, waiting for the moment when they may enter Purgatory, and so pass through torture to purification and peace.

But the schools of Ireland were quite deserted after that time, for people said, What is the use of going so far to learn, when the wisest man in all Ireland did not know if he had a soul till he was near losing it, and was only saved at last through the simple belief of a little child.

THE PRIEST OF COLOONY.

W. B. YEATS.

Good Father John O'Hart *
    In penal days rode out
To a *shoneen* in his freelands,
    With his snipe marsh and his trout.

In trust took he John's lands,
    —*Sleiveens* were all his race—
And he gave them as dowers to his daughters,
    And they married beyond their place.

But Father John went up,
    And Father John went down;
And he wore small holes in his shoes,
    And he wore large holes in his gown.

All loved him, only the *shoneen*,
    Whom the devils have by the hair,
From their wives and their cats and their children,
    To the birds in the white of the air.

* Father O'Rourke is the priest of the parishes of Ballysadare and Kilvarnet, and it is from his learnedly and faithfully and sympathetically written history of these parishes that I have taken the story of Father John, who had been priest of these parishes, dying in the year 1739. Coloony is a village in Kilvarnet.

Some sayings of Father John's have come down. Once when he was sorrowing greatly for the death of his brother, the people said to him, " Why do you sorrow so for your brother when you forbid us to keen?" " Nature," he answered, " forces me, but ye force nature." His memory and influence survives, in the fact that to the present day there has been no keening in Coloony.

He was a friend of the celebrated poet and musician, Carolan.

† *Shoneen*—i.e., upstart. ‡ *Sleiveen*—i.e., mean fellow,

The birds, for he opened their cages,
    As he went up and down ;
And he said with a smile, " Have peace, now,"
    And went his way with a frown.

But if when any one died,
    Came keeners hoarser than rooks,
He bade them give over their keening,
    For he was a man of books.

And these were the works of John,
    When weeping score by score,
People came into Coloony,
    For he'd died at ninety-four.

There was no human keening ;
    The birds from Knocknarea,
And the world round Knocknashee,
    Came keening in that day,—

Keening from Innismurry,
    Nor stayed for bit or sup ;
This way were all reproved
    Who dig old customs up.

[Coloony is a few miles south of the town of Sligo. Father
O'Hart lived there in the last century, and was greatly beloved.
These lines accurately record the tradition. No one who has
held the stolen land has prospered. It has changed owners
many times.]

THE STORY OF THE LITTLE BIRD.*

T. CROFTON CROKER.

MANY years ago there was a very religious and holy man, one of the monks of a convent, and he was one day kneeling at his prayers in the garden of his monastery, when he heard a little bird singing in one of the rose-trees of the garden, and there never was anything that he had heard in the world so sweet as the song of that little bird.

And the holy man rose up from his knees where he was kneeling at his prayers to listen to its song ; for he thought he never in all his life heard anything so heavenly.

And the little bird, after singing for some time longer on the rose-tree, flew away to a grove at some distance from the monastery, and the holy man followed it to listen to its singing, for he felt as if he would never be tired of listening to the sweet song it was singing out of its throat.

And the little bird after that went away to another distant tree, and sung there for a while, and then to another tree, and so on in the same manner, but ever further and further away from the monastery, and the holy man still following it farther, and farther, and farther, still listening delighted to its enchanting song.

But at last he was obliged to give up, as it was growing late in the day, and he returned to the convent ; and as he approached it in the evening, the sun was setting in the west with all the most heavenly colors that were ever seen in the world, and when he came into the convent, it was nightfall.

And he was quite surprised at everything he saw, for they were all strange faces about him in the monastery that he had never seen before, and the very place itself, and everything about it, seemed to be strangely altered ; and,

* *Amulet*, 1827. T. C. Croker wrote this, he says, word for word as he heard it from an old woman at a holy well.

altogether, it seemed entirely different from what it was when he had left in the morning ; and the garden was not like the garden where he had been kneeling at his devotion when he first heard the singing of the little bird.

And while he was wondering at all he saw, one of the monks of the convent came up to him, and the holy man questioned him, " Brother, what is the cause of all these strange changes that have taken place here since the morning ? "

And the monk that he spoke to seemed to wonder greatly at his question, and asked him what he meant by the change since morning ? for, sure, there was no change ; that all was just as before. And then he said, " Brother, why do you ask these strange questions, and what is your name ? for you wear the habit of our order, though we have never seen you before."

So upon this the holy man told his name, and said that he had been at mass in the chapel in the morning before he had wandered away from the garden listening to the song of a little bird that was singing among the rose-trees, near where he was kneeling at his prayers.

And the brother, while he was speaking, gazed at him very earnestly, and then told him that there was in the convent a tradition of a brother of his name, who had left it two hundred years before, but that what was become of him was never known.

And while he was speaking, the holy man said, " My hour of death is come ; blessed be the name of the Lord for all his mercies to me, through the merits of his only-begotten Son."

And he kneeled down that very moment, and said, " Brother, take my confession, for my soul is departing."

And he made his confession, and received his absolution, and was anointed, and before midnight he died.

The little bird, you see, was an angel, one of the cherubims or seraphims ; and that was the way the Almighty was pleased in His mercy to take to Himself the soul of that holy man.

CONVERSION OF KING LAOGHAIRE'S
DAUGHTERS.

ONCE when Patrick and his clericks were sitting beside
a well in the Rath of Croghan, with books open on their
knees, they saw coming towards them the two young
daughters of the King of Connaught. 'Twas early morning, and they were going to the well to bathe.

The young girls said to Patrick, " Whence are ye, and
whence come ye ? " and Patrick answered, " It were better
for you to confess to the true God than to inquire concerning our race."

" Who is God ? " said the young girls, " and where is
God, and of what nature is God, and where is His dwelling-place? Has your God sons and daughters, gold and
silver? Is he everlasting? Is he beautiful? Did Mary
foster her son? Are His daughters dear and beauteous
to men of the world ? Is He in heaven, or on earth, in
the sea, in rivers, in mountainous places, in valleys ? "

Patrick answered them, and made known who God was,
and they believed and were baptized, and a white garment
put upon their heads; and Patrick asked them would they
live on, or would they die and behold the face of Christ?
They chose death, and died immediately, and were buried
near the well Clebach.

KING O'TOOLE AND HIS GOOSE.

S. LOVER.

" By Gor, I thought all the world, far and near, heerd o'
King O'Toole—well, well, but the darkness of mankind is
ontellible! Well, sir, you must know, as you didn't hear it
afore, that there was a king, called King O'Toole, who was
a fine ould king in the ould ancient times, long ago; and
it was him that owned the churches in the early days.
The king, you see, was the right sort; he was the rale
boy, and loved sport as he loved his life, and huntin' in
partic'lar; and from the risin' o' the sun, up he got, and
away he wint over the mountains beyant afther the deer;
and the fine times them wor.

" Well, it was all mighty good, as long as the king had
his health; but, you see, in coorse of time the king grew
ould, by raison he was stiff in his limbs, and when he got
sthriken in years, his heart failed him, and he was lost
intirely for want o' divarshin, bekase he couldn't go
a huntin' no longer; and, by dad, the poor king was
obleeged at last for to get a goose to divart him. Oh, you
may laugh, if you like, but it's truth I'm tellin' you; and
the way the goose divarted him was this-a-way: You see,
the goose used for to swim acrass the lake, and go divin'
for throut, and cotch fish on a Friday for the king, and
flew every other day round about the lake, divartin' the
poor king. All went on mighty well, antil, by dad, the
goose got sthriken in years like her master, and couldn't
divart him no longer, and then it was that the poor king
was lost complate. The king was walkin' one mornin'
by the edge of the lake, lamentin' his cruel fate, and
thinkin' o' drownin' himself, that could get no divarshun
in life, when all of a suddint, turnin' round the corner

beyant, who should he meet but a mighty dacent young man comin' up to him.

" 'God save you,' says the king to the young man.

" 'God save you kindly, King O'Toole,' says the young man. 'Thrue for you,' says the king. 'I am King O'Toole,' says he, 'prince and plennypennytinchery o' these parts,' says he ; 'but how kem ye to know that?' says he. 'Oh, never mind,' says St. Kavin

" You see it was Saint Kavin, sure enough—the saint himself in disguise, and nobody else. 'Oh, never mind,' says he, 'I know more than that. May I make bowld to ax how is your goose, King O'Toole?' says he. 'Bluran-agers, how kem ye to know about my goose?' says the king. 'Oh, no matther ; I was given to understand it,' says Saint Kavin. After some more talk the king says, 'What are you?' 'I'm an honest man,' says Saint Kavin. 'Well, honest man,' says the king, 'and how is it you make your money so aisy?' 'By makin' ould things as good as new,' says Saint Kavin. 'Is it a tinker you are?' says the king. 'No,' says the saint ; 'I'm no tinker by thrade, King O'Toole ; I've a betther thrade than a tinker,' says he—'what would you say,' says he, 'if I made your ould goose as good as new?'

" My dear, at the word o' making his goose as good as new, you'd think the poor ould king's eyes was ready to jump out iv his head. With that the king whistled, and down kem the poor goose, all as one as a hound, waddlin' up to the poor cripple, her masther, and as like him as two pays. The minute the saint clapt his eyes on the goose, 'I'll do the job for you,' says he, 'King O'Toole.' 'By *Jaminee!*' says King O'Toole, ' if you do, bud I'll say you're the cleverest fellow in the sivin parishes.' 'Oh, by dad,' says St. Kavin, 'you must say more nor that—my horn's not so soft all out,' says he, ' as to repair your ould goose for nothin' ; what'll you gi' me if I do the job for you?—that's the chat,' says St. Kavin. 'I ll give you whatever you ax,' says the king ; 'isn't that fair?' 'Divil a fairer,' says the saint ; ' that's the way to do business. Now,' says he, 'this

is the bargain I'll make with you, King O'Toole : will
you gi' me all the ground the goose flies over, the first offer,
afther I make her as good as new ?' 'I will,' says the king.
'You won't go back o' your word?' says St. Kavin.
'Honor bright!' says King O'Toole, howldin' out his fist.
'Honor bright!' says St. Kavin, back agin, 'it's a bargain.
Come here!' says he to the poor ould goose—'come here,
you unfort'nate ould cripple, and it's I that'll make you the
sportin' bird.' With that, my dear, he took up the goose by
the two wings—'Criss o' my crass an you,' says he, markin'
her to grace with the blessed sign at the same minute—and
throwin' her up in the air, 'whew,' says he, jist givin' her a
blast to help her ; and with that, my jewel, she tuk to her
heels, flyin' like one o' the aigles themselves and cuttin'
as many capers as a swallow before a shower of rain.

"Well, my dear, it was a beautiful sight to see the
king standin' with his mouth open, lookin' at his poor
ould goose flyin' as light as a lark, and betther nor ever
she was : and when she lit at his fut, patted her an the
head, and, ' *Ma vourneen*,' says he, ' but you are the *darlint* o' the world.' 'And what do you say to me,' says
Saint Kavin, 'for makin' her the like?' 'By gor,' says
the king, 'I say nothin' bates the art o' man, barrin' the
bees.' 'And do you say no more nor that?' says Saint
Kavin. 'And that I'm behoulden to you,' says the king.
'But will you give me all the ground the goose flew
over?' says Saint Kavin. 'I will,' says King O'Toole, 'and
you're welkim to it,' says he, 'though it's the last acre I
have to give.' 'But you'll keep your word thrue?' says the
saint. 'As thrue as the sun,' says the king. 'It's well
for you, King O'Toole, that you said that word,' says he ;
'for if you didn't say that word, *the devil receave the bit
o' your goose id ever fly agin.*' Whin the king was as
good as his word, Saint Kavin was *plazed* with him, and
thin it was that he made himself known to the king. 'And,'
says he, 'King O'Toole, you're a decent man, for I only
kem here to *thry you*. You don't know me,' says he,
'bekase I'm disguised.' 'Musha! thin,' says the king,

'who are you? 'I'm Saint Kavin,' said the Saint, blessin'
himself. 'Oh, queen iv heaven!' says the king makin'
the sign o' the crass betune his eyes, and fallin' down on
his knees before the saint; 'is it the great Saint Kavin,'
says he, 'that I've been discoorsin' all this time without
knowin' it,' says he, 'all as one as if he was a lump iv a
gosson?—and so you're a saint?' says the king. 'I am,'
says Saint Kavin. 'By gor, I thought I was only talking
to a dacent boy,' says the king. 'Well, you know the
differ now,' says the saint. 'I'm Saint Kavin,' says he,
'the greatest of all the saints.' And so the king had his
goose as good as new, to divart him as long as he lived:
and the saint supported him afther he kem into his property, as I tould you, until the day iv his death—and that
was soon afther; for the poor goose thought he was
ketchin' a throut one Friday; but, my jewel, it was a
mistake he made—and instead of a throut, it was a thievin'
horse-eel; and by gor, instead iv the goose killin' a throut
for the king's supper,—by dad, the eel killed the king's
goose—and small blame to him; but he didn't ate her,
bekase he darn't ate what Saint Kavin had laid his
blessed hands on."

THE LEECHING OF KAYN'S LEG.

THERE were five hundred blind men, and five hundred deaf men, and five hundred limping men, and five hundred dumb men, and five hundred cripple men. The five hundred deaf men had five hundred wives, and the five hundred limping men had five hundred wives, and the five hundred dumb men had five hundred wives, and the five hundred cripple men had five hundred wives. Each five hundred of these had five hundred children and five hundred dogs. They were in the habit of going about in one band, and were called the Sturdy Strolling Beggarly Brotherhood. There was a knight in Erin called O'Cronicert, with whom they spent a day and a year; and they ate up all that he had, and made a poor man of him, till he had nothing left but an old tumble-down black house, and an old lame white horse. There was a king in Erin called Brian Boru; and O'Cronicert went to him for help. He cut a cudgel of gray oak on the outskirts of the wood, mounted the old lame white horse, and set off at speed through wood and over moss and rugged ground, till he reached the king's house. When he arrived he went on his knees to the king; and the king said to him, " What is your news, O'Cronicert ? "

" I have but poor news for you, king."

" What poor news have you ? " said the king.

" That I have had the Sturdy Strolling Beggarly Brotherhood for a day and a year, and they have eaten all that I had, and made a poor man of me," said he.

" Well ! " said the king, " I am sorry for you ; what do you want ? "

" I want help," said O'Cronicert ; " anything that you may be willing to give me."

The king promised him a hundred cows. He went to the queen, and made his complaint to her, and she gave him another hundred. He went to the king's son, Murdoch Mac Brian, and he got another hundred from him. He got food and drink at the king's; and when he was going away he said, " Now I am very much obliged to you. This will set me very well on my feet. After all that I have got there is another thing that I want."

" What is it ? " said the king.

" It is the lap-dog that is in and out after the queen that I wish for."

" Ha ! " said the king, " it is your mightiness and pride that has caused the loss of your means; but if you become a good man you shall get this along with the rest."

O'Cronicert bade the king good-by, took the lap-dog, leapt on the back of the old lame white horse, and went off at speed through wood, and over moss and rugged ground. After he had gone some distance through the wood a roebuck leapt up and the lap-dog went after it. In a moment the deer started up as a woman behind O'Cronicert, the handsomest that eye had ever seen from the beginning of the universe till the end of eternity. She said to him, " Call your dog off me."

" I will do so if you promise to marry me," said O'Cronicert.

" If you keep three vows that I shall lay upon you I will marry you," said she.

" What vows are they ? " said he.

" The first is that you do not go to ask your worldly king to a feast or a dinner without first letting me know," said she.

" Hoch ! " said O'Cronicert, " do you think that I cannot keep that vow? I would never go to invite my worldly king without informing you that I was going to do so. It is easy to keep that vow."

" You are likely to keep it ! " said she.

" The second vow is," said she, " that you do not cast

up to me in any company or meeting in which we shall be together, that you found me in the form of a deer."

"Hoo!" said O'Cronicert, "you need not to lay that vow upon me. I would keep it at any rate."

"You are likely to keep it!" said she.

"The third vow is," said she, "that you do not leave me in the company of only one man while you go out." It was agreed between them that she should marry him.

They reached the old tumble-down black house. Grass they cut in the clefts and ledges of the rocks; a bed they made and laid down. O'Cronicert's wakening from sleep was the lowing of cattle and the bleating of sheep and the neighing of mares, while he himself was in a bed of gold on wheels of silver, going from end to end of the Tower of Castle Town.

"I am sure that you are surprised," said she.

"I am indeed," said he.

"You are in your own room," said she.

"In my own room," said he. "I never had such a room."

"I know well that you never had," said she; "but you have it now. So long as you keep me you shall keep the room."

He then rose, and put on his clothes, and went out. He took a look at the house when he went out; and it was a palace, the like of which he had never seen, and the king himself did not possess. He then took a walk round the farm; and he never saw so many cattle, sheep, and horses as were on it. He returned to the house, and said to his wife that the farm was being ruined by other people's cattle and sheep. "It is not," said she: "your own cattle and sheep are on it."

"I never had so many cattle and sheep," said he.

"I know that," said she; "but so long as you keep me you shall keep them. There is no good wife whose tocher does not follow her."

He was now in good circumstances, indeed wealthy. He had gold and silver, as well as cattle and sheep. He went about with his gun and dogs hunting every day, and was a great man. It occurred to him one day that he would go to invite the King of Erin to dinner, but he did not tell his wife that he was going. His first vow was now broken. He sped away to the King of Erin, and invited him and his great court to dinner. The King of Erin said to him, " Do you intend to take away the cattle that I promised you ? "

" Oh ! no, King of Erin,' said O'Cronicert ; " I could give you as many to-day."

" Ah ! " said the king, " how well you have got on since I saw you last ! "

" I have indeed," said O'Cronicert ! " I have fallen in with a rich wife who had plenty of gold and silver, and of cattle and sheep."

" I am glad of that," said the King of Erin.

O'Cronicert said, " I shall feel much obliged if you will go with me to dinner, yourself and your great court."

" We will do so willingly," said the king.

They went with him on that same day. It did not occur to O'Cronicert how a dinner could be prepared for the king without his wife knowing that he was coming. When they were going on, and had reached the place where O'Cronicert had met the deer, he remembered that his vow was broken, and he said to the king, " Excuse me ; I am going on before to the house to tell that you are coming."

The king said, " We will send off one of the lads."

" You will not," said O'Cronicert ; " no lad will serve the purpose so well as myself."

He set off to the house ; and when he arrived his wife was diligently preparing dinner. He told her what he had done, and asked her pardon. " I pardon you this time," said she : " I know what you have done as well as you do yourself. The first of your vows is broken."

The king and his great court came to O'Cronicert's house ; and the wife had everything ready for them as befitted a king and great people ; every kind of drink and food. They spent two or three days and nights at dinner, eating and drinking. They were praising the dinner highly, and O'Cronicert himself was praising it; but his wife was not. O'Cronicert was angry that she was not praising it and he went and struck her in the mouth with his fist and knocked out two of her teeth. "Why are you not praising the dinner like the others, you contemptible deer?" said he.

"I am not," said she: "I have seen my father's big dogs having a better dinner than you are giving to-night to the King of Erin and his court."

O'Cronicert got into such a rage that he went outside of the door. He was not long standing there when a man came riding on a black horse, who in passing caught O'Cronicert by the collar of his coat, and took him up behind him: and they set off. The rider did not say a word to O'Cronicert. The horse was going so swiftly that O'Cronicert thought the wind would drive his head off. They arrived at a big, big palace, and came off the black horse. A stableman came out, and caught the horse, and took it in. It was with wine that he was cleaning the horse's feet. The rider of the black horse said to O'Cronicert, "Taste the wine to see if it is better than the wine that you are giving to Brian Boru and his court to-night."

O'Cronicert tasted the wine, and said, "This is better wine."

The rider of the black horse said, "How unjust was the fist a little ago! The wind from your fist carried the two teeth to me."

He then took him into that big, handsome, and noble house, and into a room that was full of gentlemen eating and drinking, and he seated him at the head of the table, and gave him wine to drink, and said to him, "Taste that wine to see if it is better than the wine that you are giving to the King of Erin and his court to-night."

"This is better wine," said O'Cronicert.

"How unjust was the fist a little ago!" said the rider of the black horse.

When all was over the rider of the black horse said, " Are you willing to return home now ? "

" Yes," said O'Cronicert, " very willing."

They then rose, and went to the stable : and the black horse was taken out; and they leaped on its back, and went away. The rider of the black horse said to O'Cronicert, after they had set off, " Do you know who I am ? "

" I do not," said O'Cronicert.

" I am a brother-in-law of yours," said the rider of the black horse; and though my sister is married to you there is not a king or knight in Erin who is a match for her. Two of your vows are now broken; and if you break the other vow you shall lose your wife and all that you possess."

They arrived at O'Cronicert's house ; and O'Cronicert said, " I am ashamed to go in, as they do not know where I have been since night came."

" Hoo ! " said the rider, " they have not missed you at all. There is so much conviviality among them, that they have not suspected that you have been anywhere. Here are the two teeth that you knocked out of the front of your wife's mouth. Put them in their place, and they will be as strong as ever."

" Come in with me," said O'Cronicert to the rider of the black horse.

" I will not: I disdain to go in," said the rider of the black horse.

The rider of the black horse bade O'Cronicert good-bye, and went away.

O'Cronicert went in ; and his wife met him as she was busy waiting on the gentlemen. He asked her pardon, and put the two teeth in the front of her mouth, and they were as strong as ever. She said, " Two of your vows are now broken." No one took notice of him when he went in, or said " Where have you been ? " They spent the night in eating and drinking, and the whole of the next day.

In the evening the king said, " I think that it is time for us to be going," and all said that it was. O'Croni-

cert said, "You will not go to-night. I am going to get
up a dance. You will go to-morrow."

"Let them go," said his wife.

"I will not," said he.

The dance was set a-going that night. They were
playing away at dancing and music till they became
warm and hot with perspiration. They were going out
one after another to cool themselves at the side of the
house. They all went out except O'Cronicert and his
wife, and a man called Kayn Mac Loy. O'Cronicert himself went out, and left his wife and Kayn Mac Loy in the
house, and when she saw that he had broken his third
vow she gave a spring through a room, and became a big
filly, and gave Kayn Mac Loy a kick with her foot, and
broke his thigh in two. She gave another spring, and
smashed the door and went away, and was seen no more.
She took with her the Tower of Castle Town as an armful on her shoulder and a light burden on her back, and
she left Kayn Mac Loy in the old tumble-down black house
in a pool of rain-drip on the floor.

At daybreak next day poor O'Cronicert could only see
the old house that he had before. Neither cattle nor
sheep, nor any of the fine things that he had was to be
seen. One awoke in the morning beside a bush, another
beside a dyke, and another beside a ditch. The king
only had the honor of having O'Cronicert's little hut over
his head. As they were leaving, Murdoch Mac Brian remembered that he had left his own foster-brother Kayn
Mac Loy behind, and said there should be no separation
in life between them and that he would go back for him.
He found Kayn in the old tumble-down black house. in
the middle of the floor, in a pool of rain-water. with his
leg broken; and he said the earth should make a nest in
his sole and the sky a nest in his head if he did not find
a man to cure Kayn's leg.

They told him that on the Isle of Innisturk was a herb
that would heal him.

So Kayn Mac Loy was then borne away, and sent to

the island, and he was supplied with as much food as would keep him for a month, and with two crutches on which he would be going out and in as he might desire. At last the food was spent, and he was destitute, and he had not found the herb. He was in the habit of going down to the shore, and gathering shell-fish, and eating it.

As he was one day on the shore, he saw a big, big man landing on the island, and he could see the earth and the sky between his legs. He set off with the crutches to try if he could get into the hut before the big man would come upon him. Despite his efforts, the big man was between him and the door, and said to him, "Unless you deceive me, you are Kayn Mac Loy."

Kayn Mac Loy said, "I have never deceived a man: I am he."

The big man said to him:

"Stretch out your leg, Kayn, till I put a salve of herbs and healing to it. Salve and binding herb and the poultice are cooling; the worm is channering. Pressure and haste hard bind me, for I must hear Mass in the great church at Rome, and be in Norway before I sleep.

Kayn Mac Loy said:

"May it be no foot to Kayn or a foot to any one after one, or I be Kayn the son of Loy, if I stretch out my foot for you to put a salve of herbs and healing on it, till you tell me why you have no church of your own in Norway, so as, as now, to be going to the great church of Rome to Rome to-morrow.

Unless you deceive me you are Machkan-an-Athar, the son of the King of Lochlann."

The big man said, "I have never deceived any man: I am he. I am now going to tell you why we have not a church in Lochlann. Seven masons came to build a church, and they and my father were bargaining about the building of it. The agreement that the masons wanted was that my mother and sister would go to see the interior of the church when it would be finished. My

father was glad to get the church built so cheaply. They
agreed accordingly ; and the masons went in the morning
to the place where the church was to be built. My father
pointed out the spot for the foundation. They began to
build in the morning, and the church was finished before
the evening. When it was finished they requested my
mother and sister to go to see its interior. They had no
sooner entered than the doors were shut ; and the church
went away into the skies in the form of a tuft of mist.

Stretch out your leg, Kayn, till I put a salve of herbs and healing to it. Salve and binding herb and the poultice are cooling ;
the worm is channering. Pressure and haste hard bind me, for
I must hear Mass in the great church at Rome, and be in Norway
before I sleep.

Kayn Mac Loy said :

"May it be no foot to Kayn or a foot to any one after one, or I
be Kayn son of Loy, if I stretch out my foot for you to put a
salve of herbs and healing on it, till you tell me if you heard what
befell your mother and sister."

"Ah!" said the big man, "the mischief is upon you; that tale is long to tell; but I will tell you a short tale about the matter. On the day on which they were working at the church I was away in the hill hunting game; and when I came home in the evening my brother told me what had happened, namely, that my mother and sister had gone away in the form of a tuft of mist. I became so cross and angry that I resolved to destroy the world till I should find out where my mother and sister were. My brother said to me that I was a fool to think of such a thing. 'I'll tell you,' said he, 'what you'll do. You will first go to try to find out where they are. When you find out where they are you will demand them peaceably, and if you do not get them peaceably you will fight for them.'

"I took my brother's advice, and prepared a ship to set off with. I set off alone, and embraced the ocean. I was overtaken by a great mist, and I came upon an island, and there was a large number of ships at anchor near it; I went in amongst them, and went ashore. I saw there a big, big woman reaping rushes; and when she would raise her head she would throw her right breast over her shoulder and when she would bend it would fall down between her legs. I came once behind her, and caught the breast with my mouth, and said to her, ' You are yourself witness, woman, that I am the foster-son of your right breast.' 'I perceive that, great hero,' said the old woman, ' but my advice to you is to leave this island as fast as you can.' ' Why ?' said I. ' There is a big giant in the cave up there,' said she, 'and every one of the ships that you see he has taken in from the ocean with his breath, and he has killed and eaten the men. He is asleep at present, and when he wakens he will have you in a similar manner. A large iron door and an oak door are on the cave. When the giant draws in his breath the doors open, and when he emits his breath the doors shut; and they are shut as fast as though seven small bars, and seven large bars, and seven locks were on them. So fast are they that seven

crowbars could not force them open.' I said to the old
woman, 'Is there any way of destroying him?' 'I'll tell
you,' said she, 'how it can be done. He has a weapon
above the door that is called the short spear : and if you
succeed in taking off his head with the first blow it will
be well; but if you do not, the case will be worse than it
was at first.'

"I set off, and reached the cave, the two doors of which
opened. The giant's breath drew me into the cave; and
stools, chairs, and pots were by its action dashing against
each other, and like to break my legs. The door shut
when I went in, and was shut as fast as though seven
small bars, and seven large bars, and seven locks were on
it; and seven crowbars could not force it open; and I was
a prisoner in the cave. The giant drew in his breath
again, and the doors opened. I gave a look upwards, and
saw the short spear, and laid hold of it. I drew the short
spear, and I warrant you that I dealt him such a blow with
it as did not require to be repeated; I swept the head off
him. I took the head down to the old woman, who was
reaping the rushes, and said to her, 'There is the giant's
head for you.' The old woman said, 'Brave man! I
knew that you were a hero. This island had need of your
coming to it to-day. Unless you deceive me, you are
Mac Connachar son of the King of Lochlann.' 'I have
never deceived a man. I am he,' said I. 'I am a soothsayer,' said she, 'and know the object of your journey.
You are going in quest of your mother and sister.' 'Well,'
said I, 'I am so far on the way if I only knew where to
go for them.' I'll tell you where they are,' said she;
'they are in the kingdom of the Red Shield, and the King
of the Red Shield is resolved to marry your mother, and
his son is resolved to marry your sister. I'll tell you how
the town is situated. A canal of seven times seven paces
breadth surrounds it. On the canal there is a drawbridge,
which is guarded during the day by two creatures that no
weapon can pierce, as they are covered all over with scales,
except two spots below the neck in which their death-

wounds lie. Their names are Roar and Rustle. When
night comes the bridge is raised, and the monsters sleep.
A very high and big wall surrounds the king's palace.'

" Stretch out your leg, till I put a salve of herbs and healing to
it . Salve and binding herb and the poultice are cooling; the
worm is channering. Pressure and haste hard bind me, for I must
hear Mass in the great church at Rome, and be in Norway before
I sleep.

Kayn Mac Loy said :

" May it be no foot to Kayn or a foot to any one after one, or I
be Kayn son of Loy, if I stretch out my foot for you to put a
salve of herbs and healing on it, till you tell me if you went
farther in search of your mother and sister, or if you returned
home, or what befell you."

" Ah ! " said the big man, " the mischief is upon you;
that tale is long to tell ; but I will tell you another tale.
I set off, and reached the big town of the Red Shield ; and
it was surrounded by a canal, as the old woman told me ;
and there was a drawbridge on the canal. It was night
when I arrived, and the bridge was raised, and the monsters were asleep. I measured two feet before me and a
foot behind me of the ground on which I was standing,
and I sprang on the end of my spear and on my tiptoes,
and reached the place where the monsters were asleep ;
and I drew the short spear, and I warrant you that I dealt
them such a blow below the neck as did not require to be
repeated. I took up the heads and hung them on one of
the posts of the bridge. I then went on to the wall that
surrounded the king's palace. This wall was so high that
it was not easy for me to spring over it ; and I set to work
with the short spear, and dug a hole through it, and got
in. I went to the door of the palace and knocked ; and
the doorkeeper called out, ' Who is there ? ' ' It is I,' said
I. My mother and sister recognized my speech; and my
mother called, ' Oh ! it is my son ; let him in.' I then
got in, and they rose to meet me with great joy. I was
supplied with food, drink, and a good bed. In the morn-

ing breakfast was set before us; and after it I said to my mother and sister that they had better make ready, and go with me. The King of the Red Shield said, ' it shall not be so. I am resolved to marry your mother, and my son is resolved to marry your sister.' ' If you wish to marry my mother, and if your son wishes to marry my

sister, let both of you accompany me to my home, and you shall get them there.' The King of the Red Shield said, ' So be it.'

"We then set off, and came to where my ship was, went on board of it, and sailed home. When we were passing a place where a great battle was going on, I asked the King of the Red Shield what battle it was, and the cause of it. ' Don't you know at all?' said the King of the Red Shield. 'I do not,' said I. The King of the Red Shield said, 'That is the battle for the daughter of the King of the Great Universe, the most beautiful woman in the world; and whoever wins her by his heroism shall get her in marriage. Do you see yonder castle?' 'I do,' said I. 'She is on the top of that castle, and sees from it the hero that wins her,' said the King of the Red Shield. I requested to be put on shore, that I might win her by my swiftness and strength, They put me on shore; and I got a sight of her on the top of the castle. Having measured two feet behind me and a foot before me, I sprang on the end of my spear and on my tiptoes, and reached the top of the castle; and I caught the daughter of the King of the Universe in my arms and flung her over the castle. I was with her and intercepted her before she reached the ground, and I took her away on my shoulder, and set off to the shore as fast as I could, and delivered her to the King of the Red Shield to be put on board the ship. Am I not the best warrior that ever sought you? said I. 'You can jump well' said she, 'but I have not seen any of your prowess.' I turned back to meet the warriors, and attacked them with the short spear, and did not leave a head on a neck of any of them. I then returned, and called to the King of the Red Shield to come in to the shore for me. Pretending not to hear me, he set the sails in order to return home with the daughter of the King of the Great Universe, and marry her. I measured two feet behind me and a foot before me, and sprang on the end of my spear and on my tiptoes and got on board the ship. I then said to the King of the Red Shield, 'What were you going to do? Why did you not wait for me?' 'Oh!' said the king, 'I was only making the ship ready and setting the sails to her before going on shore for you. Do you know what I am thinking of?' 'I do not,' said I. 'It is,' said the King, 'that I will return home with the daughter of the King of the Great Universe, and that you shall go home with your mother and sister.' 'That is not to be the way of it," said I. 'She whom I have won by my prowess neither you nor any other shall get.'

"The king had a red shield, and if he should get it on, no weapon could make an impression on him. He began to put on the red shield, and I struck him with the short spear in the middle of his body, and cut him in two, and threw him overboard. I then struck the son, and swept his head off, and threw him overboard.

"Stretch out your leg, Kayn, till I put a salve of herbs and healing to it. Salve and binding herb and the poultice are cooling; the worm is channering. Pressure and haste hard bind me, for I must hear Mass in the great church at Rome, and be in Norway before I sleep.

Kayn Mac Loy said:

"May it be no foot to Kayn or a foot to any one after one, or I be Kayn son of Loy, if I stretch out my foot for you to put a salve of herbs and healing on it, till you tell me whether any search was made for the daughter of the king of the Universe.

"Ah! the mischief is upon you," said the big man; "I will tell you another short tale. I came home with my mother and sister, and the daughter of the King of the Universe, and I married the daughter of the King of the Universe. The first son I had I named Machkan-na-skaya-jayrika (son of the red shield). Not long after this a hostile force came to enforce compensation for the King of the Red Shield, and a hostile force came from the King of the Universe to enforce compensation for the daughter of the King of the Universe. I took the daughter of the King of the Universe with me on the one shoulder and Machkan-na-skaya-jayrika on the other, and I went on board the ship and set the sails to her, and I placed the ensign of the King of the Great Universe on the one mast, and that of the King of the Red Shield on the other, and I blew a trumpet, and passed through the midst of them, and I said to them that here was the man, and that if they

were going to enforce their claims, this was the time. All
the ships that were there chased me; and we set out on
the expanse of ocean. My ship would be equalled in
speed by but few. One day a thick dark mist came on,
and they lost sight of me. It happened that I came to
an island called The Wet Mantle. I built a hut there;
and another son was born to me, and I called him Son of
the Wet Mantle.

"I was a long time in that island; but there was
enough of fruit, fish, and birds in it. My two sons had
grown to be somewhat big. As I was one day out killing birds, I saw a big, big man coming towards the island,
and I ran to try if I could get into the house before him.
He met me, and caught me, and put me into a bog up to
the armpits, and he went into the house, and took out on
his shoulder the daughter of the King of the Universe,
and passed close to me in order to irritate me the more.
The saddest look that I ever gave or ever shall give was
that I gave when I saw the daughter of the King of the
Universe on the shoulder of another, and could not take
her from him. The boys came out where I was; and I
bade them bring me the short spear from the house.
They dragged the short spear after them, and brought it
to me; and I cut the ground around me with it till I got
out.

"I was a long time in the Wet Mantle, even till my
two sons grew to be big lads. They asked me one day if
I had any thought of going to seek their mother. I told
them that I was waiting till they were stronger, and that
they should then go with me. They said they were
ready to go with me at any time. I said to them that
we had better get the ship ready, and go. They said, 'Let
each of us have a ship to himself.' We arranged accordingly; and each went his own way.

"As I happened one day to be passing close to land I
saw a great battle going on. Being under vows never to
pass a battle without helping the weaker side, I went on
shore, and set to work with the weaker side, and I knocked

the head off every one with the short spear.   Being tired,
I lay myself down among the bodies and fell asleep.

"Stretch out your leg, Kayn, till I put a salve of herbs and
healing to it.   Salve and binding herb and the poultice are cool-
ling; the worm is channering.   Pressure and haste hard bind
me, for I must hear Mass in the great church at Rome, and be in
Norway before I sleep.

Kayn Mac Loy said:

"May it be no foot to Kayn or a foot to any one after one, or
I be Kayn son of Loy, if I stretch out my foot for you to put a
salve of herbs and healing on it, till you tell me if you found the
daughter of the King of the Universe, or if you went home, or
what happened to you."

"The mischief is upon you," said the big man; that
tale is long to tell, but I will tell another short tale.
When I awoke out of sleep I saw a ship making for the
place where I was lying, and a big giant with only one
eye dragging it after him: and the ocean reached no
higher than his knees.   He had a big fishing-rod with a

big strong line hanging from it on which was a very big
hook.   He was throwing the line ashore, and fixing the
hook in a body, and lifting it on board, and he continued
this work till the ship was loaded with bodies.   He fixed
the hook once in my clothes; but I was so heavy that
the rod could not carry me on board.   He had to go on
shore himself, and carry me on board in his arms.   I was
then in a worse plight than I ever was in.   The giant set
off with the ship, which he dragged after him, and reached
a big, precipitous rock, in the face of which he had a large
cave: and a damsel as beautiful as I ever saw came out,
and stood in the door of the cave.   He was handing the
bodies to her, and she was taking hold of them and putting them into the cave.   As she took hold of each body
she said, 'Are you alive?'   At last the giant took hold of
me, and handed me in to her, and said, 'Keep him apart;
he is a large body, and I will have him to breakfast the
first day that I go from home.'   My best time was not
when I heard the giant's sentence upon me.   When he
had eaten enough of the bodies, his dinner and supper, he
lay down to sleep.   When he began to snore the damsel
came to speak to me; and she told me that she was a
king's daughter the giant had stolen away and that she
had no way of getting away from him.   'I am now,' she
said, 'seven years except two days with him, and there
is a drawn sword between us.   He dared not come nearer
me than that till the seven years should expire.'   I said
to her, 'Is there no way of killing him?'   'It is not easy
to kill him, but we will devise an expedient for killing
him,' said she,   'Look at that pointed bar that he uses
for roasting the bodies.   At dead of night gather the embers of the fire together, and put the bar in the fire till it
be red.   Go, then, and thrust it into his eye with all your
strength, and take care that he does not get hold of you,
for if he does he will mince you as small as midges.'   I
then went and gathered the embers together, and put the
bar in the fire, and made it red, and thrust it into his eye;
and from the cry that he gave I thought that the rock

When the giant began to snore, the damsel came and told me she was a
king's daughter, and had been stolen by him.—Page 318.

Irish Fairy Tales.

had split. The giant sprang to his feet and chased me through the cave in order to catch me; and I picked up a stone that lay on the floor of the cave, and pitched it into the sea; and it made a plumping noise. The bar was sticking in his eye all the time. Thinking it was I that had sprung into the sea, he rushed to the mouth of the cave, and the bar struck against the doorpost of the cave, and knocked off his brain-cap. The giant fell down cold and dead, and the damsel and I were seven years and seven days throwing him into the sea in pieces.

"I wedded the damsel, and a boy was born to us. After seven years I started forth again.

"I gave her a gold ring, with my name on it, for the boy, and when he was old enough he was sent out to seek me.

"I then set off to the place where I fought the battle, and found the short spear where I left it; and I was very pleased that I found it, and that the ship was safe. I sailed a day's distance from that place, and entered a pretty bay that was there, hauled my ship up above the shore, and erected a hut there, in which I slept at night. When I rose next day I saw a ship making straight for the place where I was. When it struck the ground, a big, strong champion came out of it, and hauled it up; and if it did not surpass my ship it was not a whit inferior to it; and I said to him, 'What impertinent fellow are you that has dared to haul up your ship alongside of my ship?' 'I am Machkan-na-skaya-jayrika,' said the champion, 'going to seek the daughter of the King of the Universe for Mac Connachar, son of the King of Lochlann.' I saluted and welcomed him, and said to him, 'I am your father: it is well that you have come.' We passed the night cheerily in the hut.

"When I arose on the following day I saw another ship making straight for the place where I was; and a big, strong hero came out of it, and hauled it up alongside of our ships; and if it did not surpass them it was not a whit inferior to them. "What impertinent fellow are you that has dared to haul up your ship alongside of our ships?' said I. 'I am,' said he, 'the son of the Wet Mantle, going to seek the daughter of the King of the Universe for Mac Connachar, son of the King of Lochlann.' 'I am your father, and this is your brother: it is well that you have come,' said I. We passed the night together in the hut, my two sons and I.

"When I rose next day I saw another ship coming, and making straight for the place where I was. A big, strong champion sprang out of it, and hauled it up alongside of our ships; and if it was not higher than they, it was not lower. I went down where he was, and said to him, 'What impertinent fellow are you that has dared to haul up your ship alongside of our ships?' 'I am the Son of the Wet Mantle,' said he, 'going to seek the daughter of the King of the Universe for Mac Connachar, son of the King of Lochlann. 'Have you any token in proof of that?' said I. 'I have,' said he: 'here is a ring that my mother gave me at my father's request.' I took hold of the ring, and saw my name on it: and the matter was beyond doubt. I said to him, 'I am your father, and here are two half-brothers of yours. We are now stronger for going in quest of the daughter of the King of the Universe. Four piles are stronger than three piles.' We spent that night cheerily and comfortably together in the hut.

"On the morrow we met a soothsayer, and he spoke to us: 'You are going in quest of the daughter of the King of the Universe. I will tell you where she is: she is with the Son of the Blackbird.

"Machkan-na-skaya-jayrika then went and called for combat with a hundred fully trained heroes, or the sending out to him of the daughter of the King of the Universe. The hundred went out; and he and they began on each other, and he killed every one of them. The Son of the Wet Mantle called for combat with another hundred, or the sending out of the daughter of the King of the Universe. He killed that hundred with the short spear. The Son of Secret called for combat with another hundred, or the daughter of the King of the Universe. He killed every one of these with the short spear. I then went out to the field, and sounded a challenge on the shield, and made the town tremble. The Son of the Blackbird had not a man to send out: he had to come out himself; and he and I began on each other, and I drew the short spear, and swept his head off. I then went into the castle, and took out the daughter of the King of the Universe. It was thus that it fared with me.

"Stretch out your leg, Kayn, till I put a salve of herbs and healing to it. Salve and binding herb and the poultice are cooling; the worm is channering. Pressure and haste hard bind me, for I must hear Mass in the great church at Rome, and be in Norway before I sleep."

Kayn Mac Loy stretched his leg; and the big man applied to it leaves of herbs and healing ; and it was healed. The big man took him ashore from the island, and allowed him to go home to the king.

Thus did O'Cronicert win and lose a wife, and thus befell the Leeching of the leg of Kayn, son of Loy.

THE DEVIL.

THE DEMON CAT.*

LADY WILDE.

THERE was a woman in Connemara, the wife of a fisherman; as he had always good luck, she had plenty of fish at all times stored away in the house ready for market. But, to her great annoyance, she found that a great cat used to come in at night and devour all the best and finest fish. So she kept a big stick by her, and determined to watch.

One day, as she and a woman were spinning together, the house suddenly became quite dark ; and the door was burst open as if by the blast of the tempest, when in walked a huge black cat, who went straight up to the fire, then turned round and growled at them.

"Why, surely this is the devil," said a young girl, who was by, sorting fish.

* *Ancient Legends of Ireland.* In Ireland one hears much of Demon Cats. The father of one of the present editors of the *Fortnightly* had such a cat, say county Dublin peasantry. One day the priest dined with him, and objecting to see a cat fed before Christians, said something over it that made it go up the chimney in a flame of fire. "I will have the law on you for doing such a thing to my cat," said the father of the editor. "Would you like to see your cat?" said the priest. "I would," said he, and the priest brought it up, covered with chains, through the hearth-rug, straight out of hell. The Irish devil does not object to these undignified shapes. The Irish devil is not a dignified person. He has no whiff of sulphureous majesty about him. A centaur of the ragamuffin, jeering and shaking his tatters, at once the butt and terror of the saints !

"I'll teach you how to call me names," said the cat; and, jumping at her, he scratched her arm till the blood came. "There, now," he said, "you will be more civil another time when a gentleman comes to see you." And with that he walked over to the door and shut it close, to prevent any of them going out, for the poor young girl, while crying loudly from fright and pain, had made a desperate rush to get away.

Just then a man was going by, and hearing the cries, he pushed open the door and tried to get in; but the cat stood on the threshold, and would let no one pass. On this the man attacked him with his stick, and gave him a sound blow; the cat, however, was more than a match in the fight, for it flew at him and tore his face and hands so badly that the man at last took to his heels and ran away as fast he could.

"Now, it's time for my dinner," said the cat, going up to examine the fish that was laid out on the tables. "I hope the fish is good to-day. Now, don't disturb me, nor make a fuss; I can help myself." With that he jumped up, and began to devour all the best fish, while he growled at the woman.

"Away, out of this, you wicked beast," she cried, giving it a blow with the tongs that would have broken its back, only it was a devil; "out of this; no fish shall you have to-day."

But the cat only grinned at her, and went on tearing and spoiling and devouring the fish, evidently not a bit the worse for the blow. On this, both the women attacked it with sticks, and struck hard blows enough to kill it, on which the cat glared at them, and spit fire; then, making a leap, it tore their heads and arms till the blood came, and the frightened women rushed shrieking from the house.

But presently the mistress returned, carrying with her a bottle of holy water; and, looking in, she saw the cat still devouring the fish, and not minding. So she crept over quietly and and threw holy water on it without a word.

No sooner was this done than a dense black smoke filled the place, through which nothing was seen but the two red eyes of the cat, burning like coals of fire. Then the smoke gradually cleared away, and she saw the body of the creature burning slowly till it became shriveled and black like a cinder, and finally disappeared. And from that time the fish remained untouched and safe from harm, for the power of the evil one was broken, and the demon cat was seen no more.

THE LONG SPOON.*

PATRICK KENNEDY.

The devil and the hearth-money collector for Bantry set out one summer morning to decide a bet they made the night before over a jug of punch. They wanted to see which would have the best load at sunset, and neither was to pick up anything that wasn't offered with the good-will of the giver. They passed by a house, and they heard the poor ban-a-t'yee † cry out to her lazy daughter; " Oh, musha, —— take you for a lazy sthronsuch ‡ of a girl ! do you intend to get up to-day ? " " Oh, oh," says the taxman, " there's a job for you, Nick." " Ovock," says the other, " it wasn't from her heart she said it ; we must pass on." The next cabin they were passing, the woman was on the bawnditch § crying out to her husband that was mending one of his brogues inside : " Oh, tattheration to you, Nick ! you never rung them pigs, and there they are in the potato drills rootin' away ; the —— run to Lusk with them." " Another windfall for you," says the man of the ink-horn, but the old thief only shook his

* *Legendary Fictions of the Irish Celts.*
† Woman of the house.
‡ Ir. *strŏinse—i. e.*, a lazy thing.
§ Ir. *bádhun—i. e.* enclosure, or wall round a house. From *ba*, cows and *dún*, a fortress. Properly, cattle-fortress,

horns and wagged his tail. So they went on, and ever so many prizes were offered to the black fellow without him taking one. Here it was a gorsoon playing *marvels* when he should be using his clappers in the corn-field; and then it was a lazy drone of a servant asleep with his face to the sod when he ought to be weeding. No one thought of offering the hearth-money man even a drink of butter-milk, and at last the sun was within half a foot of the edge of Colliagh. They were just then passing Monamolin, and a poor woman that was straining her supper in a skeeoge outside her cabin-door, seeing the two standing at the bawn gate, bawled out, " Oh, here's the hearth-money man —— run away wid him." " Got a bite at last," says Nick. " Oh, no, no ! it wasn't from her heart," says the collector. " Indeed, an' it was from the very foundation-stones it came. No help for misfortunes ; in with you," says he, opening the mouth of his big black bag ; and whether the devil was ever after seen taking the same walk or not, nobody ever laid eyes on his fellow-traveler again.

THE COUNTESS KATHLEEN O'SHEA.*

A very long time ago, there suddenly appeared in old Ireland two unknown merchants of whom nobody had ever heard, and who nevertheless spoke the language of the country with the greatest perfection. Their locks were black, and bound round with gold, and their garments were of rare magnificence.

Both seemed of like age ; they appeared to be men of fifty, for their foreheads were wrinkled and their beards tinged with gray.

In the hostelry where the pompous traders alighted it was sought to penetrate their designs ; but in vain—they

* This was quoted in a London-Irish newspaper. I am unable to find out the original source.

led a silent and retired life. And whilst they stopped there, they did nothing but count over and over again out of their money-bags pieces of gold, whose yellow brightness could be seen through the windows of their lodging.

"Gentlemen," said the landlady one day, "how is it that you are so rich, and that, being able to succor the public misery, you do no good works?"

"Fair hostess," replied one of them, "we didn't like to present alms to the honest poor, in dread we might be deceived by make-believe paupers. Let want knock at our door, we shall open it."

The following day, when the rumor spread that two rich strangers had come, ready to lavish their gold, a crowd besieged their dwelling; but the figures of those who came out were widely different. Some carried pride in their mien; others were shame-faced.

The two chapmen traded in souls for the demon. The souls of the aged were worth twenty pieces of gold, not a penny more; for Satan had had time to make his valuation. The soul of a matron was valued at fifty, when she was handsome, and a hundred when she was ugly. The soul of a young maiden fetched an extravagant sum; the freshest and purest flowers are the dearest.

At that time there lived in the city an angel of beauty, the Countess Kathleen O'Shea. She was the idol of the people and the providence of the indigent. As soon as she learned that these miscreants profited to the public misery to steal away hearts from God, she called to her butler.

"Patrick," said she to him, "how many pieces of gold in my coffers?"

"A hundred thousand."

"How many jewels?"

"The money's worth of the gold."

"How much property in castles, forests, and lands?"

"Double the rest."

"Very well, Patrick; sell all that is not gold; and bring

me the account. I only wish to keep this mansion and
the demesne that surrounds it."

Two days afterwards the orders of the pious Kathleen
were executed, and the treasure wss distributed to the
poor in proportion to their wants. This, says the tradition, did not suit the purposes of the Evil Spirit who
found no more souls to purchase. Aided by an infamous
servant, they penetrated into the retreat of the noble
dame, and purloined from her the rest of her treasure.
In vain she struggled with all her strength to save the
contents of her coffers; the diabolical thieves were the
stronger. If Kathleen had been able to make the sign of
the Cross, adds the legend, she would have put them to
flight, but her hands were captive. The larceny was
effected.

Then the poor called for aid to the plundered Kathleen,
alas, to no good: she was able to succor their misery no
longer; she had to abandon them to the temptation.

Meanwhile, but eight days had to pass before the grain
and provender would arrive in abundance from the western lands. Eight such days were an age. Eight days required an immense sum to relieve the exigencies of the
dearth, and the poor should either perish in the agonies
of hunger, or, denying the holy maxims of the Gospel,
vend, for base lucre, their souls, the richest gift from the
bounteous hand of the Almighty. And Kathleen hadn't
anything, for she had given up her mansion to the unhappy. She passed twelve hours in tears and mourning,
rending her sun-tinted hair, and bruising her breast, of
the whiteness of the lily; afterwards she stood up reso-
lute, animated by a vivid sentiment of despair.

She went to the traders in souls.

" What do you want? " they said.

" You buy souls ? "

" Yes, a few still, in spite of you. Isn't that so, saint,
with the eyes of sapphire ? "

" To-day I am come to offer you a bargain," replied
she.

"What?"

"I have a soul to sell, but it is costly."

"What does that signify if it is precious? The soul, like the diamond, is appraised by its transparency."

"It is mine."

The two emissaries of Satan started. Their claws were clutched under their gloves of leather; their gray eyes sparkled; the soul, pure, spotless, virginal of Kathleen—it was a priceless acquisition!

"Beauteous lady, how much do you ask?"

"A hundred and fifty thousand pieces of gold."

"It's at your service," replied the traders, and they tendered Kathleen a parchment sealed with black, which she signed with a shudder.

The sum was counted out to her.

As soon as she got home she said to the butler, "Here, distribute this: with this money that I give you the poor can tide over the eight days that remain, and not one of their souls will be delivered to the demon."

Afterwards she shut herself up in her room, and gave orders that none should disturb her.

Three days passed; she called nobody, she did not come out.

When the door was opened, they found her cold and stiff; she was dead of grief.

But the sale of this soul, so adorable in its charity, was declared null by the Lord; for she had saved her fellow-citizens from eternal death.

After the eight days had passed, numerous vessels brought into famished Ireland immense provisions in grain. Hunger was no longer possible. As to the traders, they disappeared from their hotel without any one knowing what became of them. But the fishermen of the Blackwater pretend that they are enchained in a subterranean prison by order of Lucifer, until they shall be able to render up the soul of Kathleen, which escaped from them.

THE THREE WISHES.

W. CARLETON.

IN ancient times there lived a man called Billy Dawson, and he was known to be a great rogue. They say he was descended from the family of the Dawsons, which was the reason, I suppose, of his carrying their name upon him.

Billy, in his youthful days, was the best hand at doing nothing in all Europe; devil a mortal could come next or near him at idleness; and, in consequence of his great practice that way, you may be sure that if any man could make a fortune by it he would have done it.

Billy was the only son of his father, barring two daughters; but they have nothing to do with the story I'm telling you. Indeed it was kind father and grandfather for Billy to be handy at the knavery as well as at the idleness; for it was well known that not one of their blood ever did an honest act, except with a roguish intention. In short, they were altogether a *dacent* connection, and a credit to the name. As for Billy, all the villainy of the family, both plain and ornamental, came down to him by way of legacy; for it so happened that the father, in spite of all his cleverness, had nothing but his roguery to *lave* him.

Billy, to do him justice, improved the fortune he got: every day advanced him farther into dishonesty and poverty, until, at the long run, he was acknowledged on all hands to be the completest swindler and the poorest vagabond in the whole parish.

Billy's father, in his young days, had often been forced to acknowledge the inconvenience of not having a trade, in consequence of some nice point in law, called the "Vagrant Act," that sometimes troubled him. On this account he made up his mind to give Bill an occupation, and he accordingly bound him to a blacksmith; but whether Bill was to *live* or *die* by *forgery* was a puzzle to his father,—though the neighbors said that *both* was most likely. At all events, he was put apprentice to a smith for seven years, and a hard card his master had to play in managing him. He took the proper method, however, for Billy was so lazy and roguish that it would vex a saint to keep him in order.

"Bill," says his master to him one day that he had been sunning himself about the ditches, instead of minding his business, "Bill, my boy, I'm vexed to the heart to see you in such a bad state of health. You're very ill with that complaint called an *All-overness ;* however," says he, "I think I can cure you. Nothing will bring you about but three or four sound doses every day of a medicine called ' the oil o' the hazel.' Take the first dose now," says he; and he immediately banged him with a hazel cudgel until Bill's bones ·ached for a week afterwards.

"If you were my son," said his master, "I tell you that, as long as I could get a piece of advice growing convenient in the hedges, I'd have you a different youth from what you are. If working was a sin, Bill, not an innocenter boy ever broke bread than you would be. Good people's scarce, you think; but however that may be, I throw it out as a hint, that you must take your medicine till you're cured, whenever you happen to get unwell in the same way."

From this out he kept Bill's nose to the grinding-stone; and whenever his complaint returned, he never failed to give him a hearty dose for his improvement.

In the course of time, however, Bill was his own man and his own master; but it would puzzle a saint to know whether the master or the man was the more precious youth in the eyes of the world.

He immediately married a wife, and devil a doubt of it, but if *he* kept *her* in whisky and sugar, *she* kept *him* in hot water. Bill drank and she drank; Bill fought and she fought; Bill was idle and she was idle ; Bill whacked her and she whacked Bill. If Bill gave her one black eye, she gave him another ; *just to keep herself in countenance.* Never was there a blessed pair so well met; and a beautiful sight it was to see them both at breakfast-time, blinking at each other across the potato basket, Bill with his right eye black, and she with her left.

In short, they were the talk of the whole town : and to see Bill of a morning staggering home drunk, his shirt sleeves rolled up on his smutted arms, his breast open, and an old tattered leather apron, with one corner tucked up under his belt singing one minute, and fighting with his wife the next; she, reeling beside him, with a discolored eye, as aforesaid, a dirty ragged cap on one side of her head, a pair of Bill's old slippers on her feet, a squalling child on her arm—now cuffing and dragging Bill, and again kissing and hugging him! Yes, it was a pleasant picture to see this loving pair in such a state!

This might do for a while, but it could not last. They were idle, drunken, and ill-conducted ; and it was not to be supposed that they would get a farthing candle on their words. They were, of course, *dhruv* to great straits ; and faith, they soon found that their fighting, and drinking and idleness made them the laughing-sport of the neighbors, but neither brought food to their *childhre,* put a coat upon their backs, nor satisfied their landlord when he came to look for his own. Still, the never a one of Bill but was a funny fellow with strangers, though, as we said, the greatest rogue unhanged.

One day he was standing against his own anvil, completely in a brown study—being brought to his wit's end how to make out a breakfast for the family. The wife was scolding and cursing in the house, and the naked creatures of childhre squalling about her knees for food. Bill was fairly at an amplush, and knew not where or how to turn himself, when a poor, withered old beggar came into the forge, tottering on his staff. A long white beard

fell from his chin, and he looked as thin and hungry that
you might blow him, one would think, over the house.
Bill at this moment had been brought to his senses by
distress, and his heart had a touch of pity towards the
old man; for, on looking at him a second time, he clearly
saw starvation and sorrow in his face.

"God save you, honest man!" said Bill.

The old man gave a sigh, and raising himself with great
pain, on his staff, he looked at Bill in a very beseeching
way.

"Musha, God save you kindly!" says he; "maybe you
could give a poor, hungry, helpless ould man a mouthful
of something to ait? You see yourself I'm not able
to work; if I was, I'd scorn to be behoulding to any
one."

"Faith, honest man," said Bill, "if you knew who
you're speaking to, you'd as soon ask a monkey for a
churn-staff as me for either mate or money. There's
not a blackguard in the three kingdoms so fairly on
the *shaughran* as I am for both the one and the
other. The wife within is sending the curses thick and
heavy on me, and the childhre's playing the cat's
melody to keep her in comfort. Take my word for
it, poor man, if I had either mate or money I'd help
you, for I know particularly well what it is to want
them at the present spaking; an empty sack won't stand,
neighbor."

So far Bill told him truth. The good thought was in his
heart, because he found himself on a footing with the
beggar; and nothing brings down pride, or softens the
heart, like feeling what it is to want.

"Why, you are in a worse state than I am," said the
old man; "you have a family to provide for, and I have
only myself to support."

"You may kiss the book on that, my old worthy," replied Bill; "but come, what I can do for you I will; plant
yourself up here beside the fire, and I'll give it a blast or
two of my bellows that will warm the old blood in your

body. It's a cold, miserable, snowy day, and a good heat will be of service."

"Thank you kindly," said the old man; "I *am* cold, and a warming at your fire will do me good, sure enough. Oh, it *is* a bitter, bitter day; God bless it!"

He then sat down, and Bill blew a rousing blast that soon made the stranger edge back from the heat. In a short time he felt quite comfortable, and when the numbness was taken out of his joints, he buttoned himself up and prepared to depart.

"Now," says he to Bill, "you hadn't the food to give me, but *what you could you did*. Ask any three wishes you choose, and be they what they may, take my word for it, they shall be granted."

Now, the truth is, that Bill, though he believed himself a great man in point of 'cuteness, wanted, after all, a full quarter of being square; for there is always a great difference between a wise man and a knave. Bill was so much of a rogue that he could not, for the blood of him, ask an honest wish, but stood scratching his head in a puzzle.

"Three wishes!" said he. "Why, let me see—did you say *three?*"

"Ay," replied the stranger, "three wishes—that was what I said."

"Well," said Bill, "here goes,—aha!—let me alone, my old worthy!—faith I'll overreach the parish, if what you say is true. I'll cheat them in dozens, rich and poor, old and young: let me alone, man—I have it here;" and he tapped his forehead with great glee. "Faith, you're the sort to meet of a frosty morning, when a man wants his breakfast; and I'm sorry that I have neither money nor credit to get a bottle of whisky, that we might take our *morning* together."

"Well, but let us hear the wishes," said the old man; "my time is short, and I cannot stay much longer."

"Do you see this sledge-hammer?" said Bill; "I wish, in the first place, that whoever takes it up in their hands

may never be able to lay it down till I give them lave ;
and that whoever begins to sledge with it may never stop
sledging till it's my pleasure to release him."

" Secondly—I have an arm-chair, and I wish that whoever sits down in it may never rise out of it till they have
my consent."

" And, thirdly—that whatever money I put into my
purse, nobody may have power to take it out of it but
myself ! "

" You devil's rip ! " says the old man in a passion,
shaking his staff across Bill's nose, " why did you not ask
something that would sarve you both here and hereafter ?
Sure it's as common as the market-cross, that there's not
a vagabone in his Majesty's dominions stands more in
need of both."

" Oh ! by the elevens," said Bill, " I forgot that altogether ! Maybe you'd be civil enough to let me change
one of them ? The sorra purtier wish ever was made than
I'll make, if you'll give me another chance."

" Get out, you reprobate," said the old fellow, still in a
passion. " Your day of grace is past. Little you knew
who was speaking to you all this time. I'm St. Moroky,
you blackguard, and I gave you an opportunity of doing
something for yourself and your family ; but you neglected
it, and now your fate is cast, you dirty, bog-trotting
profligate. Sure, it's well known what you are ! Aren't
you a by-word in everybody's mouth, you and your scold
of a wife ? By this and by that, if ever you happen to
come across me again, I'll send you to where you won't
freeze, you villain ! "

He then gave Bill a rap of his cudgel over the head,
and laid him at his length beside the bellows, kicked a
broken coal-scuttle out of his way, and left the forge in a
fury.

When Billy recovered himself from the effects of the
blow, and began to think on what had happened, he
could have quartered himself with vexation for not asking
great wealth as one of the wishes at least ; but now the

die was cast on him, and he could only make the most of
the three he pitched upon.

He now bethought him how he might turn them to the
best account, and here his cunning came to his aid.   He
began by sending for his wealthiest neighbors on pretence of business; and when he got them under his roof,
he offered them the arm-chair to sit down in.   He now
had them safe, nor could all the art of man relieve them
except worthy Bill was willing.   Bill's plan was to make
the best bargain he could before he released his prisoners;
and let him alone for knowing how to make their purses
bleed.   There wasn't a wealthy man in the country he
did not fleece.   The parson of the parish bled heavily;
so did the lawyer; and a rich attorney, who had retired
from practice, swore that the Court of Chancery itself
was paradise compared to Bill's chair.

This was all very good for a time.   The fame of his
chair, however, soon spread; so did that of his sledge.
In a short time neither man, woman, nor child would
darken his door; all avoided him and his fixtures as they
would a spring-gun or man-trap.   Bill, so long as he
fleeced his neighbors, never wrought a hand's turn; so
that when his money was out, he found himself as badly
off as ever.   In addition to all this, his character was
fifty times worse than before; for it was the general belief that he had dealings with the old boy.   Nothing now
could exceed his misery, distress, and ill-temper.   The
wife and he and their children all fought among one
another.   Everybody hated them, cursed them, and
avoided them.   The people thought they were acquainted
with more than Christian people ought to know.   This,
of course, came to Bill's ears, and it vexed him very
much.

One day he was walking about the fields, thinking of
how he could raise the wind once more; the day was dark,
and he found himself, before he stopped, in the bottom of
a lonely glen covered by great bushes that grew on each
side.   " Well," thought he, when every other means of

raising money failed him, " it's reported that I'm in league with the old boy, and as it's a folly to have the name of the connection without the profit, I'm ready to make a bargain with him any day ;—so," said he, raising his voice, " Nick, you sinner, if you be convenient and willing, why stand out here ; show your best leg—here's your man."

The words were hardly out of his mouth when a dark, sober-looking old gentleman, not unlike a lawyer, walked up to him. Bill looked at the foot and saw the hoof.— " Morrow, Nick," says Bill.

" Morrow, Bill," says Nick. " Well, Bill, what's the news ? "

" Devil a much myself hears of late," says Bill ; " is there anything *fresh* below ? "

" I can't exactly say, Bill ; I spend little of my time down now ; the Tories are in office, and my hands are consequently too full of business here to pay much attention to anything else."

" A fine place this, sir," says Bill, " to take a constitutional walk in ; when I want an appetite I often come this way myself—hem ! *High* feeding is very bad without exercise."

" High feeding ! Come, come, Bill, you know you didn't taste a morsel these four-and-twenty hours."

" You know that's a bounce, Nick. I eat a breakfast this morning that would put a stone of flesh on you, if you only smelt at it."

" No matter ; this is not to the purpose. What's that you were muttering to yourself awhile ago ? If you want to come to the brunt, here I'm for you."

" Nick," said Bill, " you're complate ; you want nothing barring a pair of Brian O'Lynn's breeches."

Bill, in fact, was·bent on making his companion open the bargain, because he had often heard that, in that case, with proper care on his own part, he might defeat him in the long run. The other, however, was his match.

" What was the nature of Brian's garment," inquired Nick. " Why, you know the song," said Bill—

> " ' Brian O'Lynn had no breeches to wear,
>   So he got a sheep's skin for to make him a pair;
>   With the fleshy side out and the woolly side in,
>   They'll be pleasant and *cool*, says Brian O'Lynn.'

"A *cool* pare would sarve you, Nick."

"You're mighty waggish to-day, Misther Dawson."

"And good right I have," said Bill; "I'm a man snug and well to do in the world; have lots of money, plenty of good eating and drinking, and what more need a man wish for?"

"True," said the other; "in the meantime it's rather odd that so respectable a man should not have six inches of unbroken cloth in his apparel. You are as naked a tatterdemalion as I ever laid my eyes on; in full dress for a party of scare-crows, William."

"That's my own fancy, Nick; I don't work at my trade like a gentleman. This is my forge dress, you know."

"Well, but what did you summon me here for?" said the other; "you may as well speak out, I tell you; for, my good friend, unless *you* do, *I* shan't. Smell that."

"I smell more than that," said Bill; "and by the way, I'll thank you to give me the windy side of you—curse all sulphur, I say. There, that's what I call an improvement in my condition. But as you *are* so stiff," says Bill, "why, the short and long of it is—that—hem—you see I'm—tut—sure you know I have a thriving trade of my own, and that if I like I needn't be at a loss; but in the meantime I'm rather in a kind of a so—so—don't you *take?*"

And Bill winked knowingly, hoping to trick him into the first proposal.

"You must speak above-board, my friend," says the other. "I'm a man of a few words, blunt and honest. If you have anything to say, be plain. Don't think I can be losing my time with such a pitiful rascal as you are."

"Well," says Bill, "I want money, then, and am ready

to come into terms. What have you to say to that, Nick?"

"Let me see—let me look at you," says his companion, turning him about. "Now, Bill, in the first place, are you not as finished a scare-crow as ever stood upon two legs?"

"I play second fiddle to you there again," says Bill.

"There you stand, with the blackguards' coat of arms quartered under your eye, and——"

"Don't make little of *black*guards," said Bill, "nor spake disparagingly of *your own* crest."

"Why, what would you bring, you brazen rascal, if you were fairly put up at auction?"

"Faith, I'd bring more bidders than you would," said Bill, "if you were to go off at auction to-morrow. I tell you they should bid *downwards* to come to your value, Nicholas. We have no coin *small* enough to purchase you."

"Well, no matter," said Nick. "If you are willing to be mine at the expiration of seven years, I will give you more money than ever the rascally breed of you was worth."

"Done!" said Bill; "but no disparagement to my family, in the meantime; so down with the hard cash, and don't be a *neger*."

The money was accordingly paid down! but as nobody was present, except the giver and receiver, the amount of what Bill got was never known.

"Won't you give me a luck-penny?" said the old gentleman.

"Tut," said Billy, "so prosperous an old fellow as you cannot want it; however, bad luck to you, with all my heart! and it's rubbing grease to a fat pig to say so. Be off now, or I'll commit suicide on you. Your absence is a cordial to most people, you infernal old profligate You have injured my morals even for the short time you have been with me; for I don't find myself so virtuous as I was."

" Is that your gratitude, Billy ? "

" Is it gratitude *you* speak of, man ? I wonder you don't blush when you name it. However, when you come again, if you bring a third eye in your head you will see what I mane, Nicholas, ahagur."

The old gentleman, as Bill spoke, hopped across the ditch, on his way to *Downing*-street, where of late 'tis thought he possesses much influence.

Bill now began by degrees to show off ; but still wrought a little at his trade to blindfold the neighbors. In a very short time, however he became a great man. So long indeed as he was a *poor* rascal, no decent person would speak to him ; even the proud serving-men at the " Big House " would turn up their noses at him. And he well deserved to be made little of by others, because he was mean enough to make little of himself. But when it was seen and known that he had oceans of money, it was wonderful to think, although he was *now* a greater black-guard than ever, how those who despised him before began to come round him and court his company. Bill, however, had neither sense nor spirit to make those sun-shiny friends know their distance ; not he—instead of that he was proud to be seen in decent company, and so long as the money lasted, it was, " hail fellow, well met," between himself and every fair-faced *spunger* who had a horse under him, a decent coat to his back, and a good appetite to eat his dinners. With riches and all, Bill was the same man still ; but, somehow or other, there is a great difference between a rich profligate and a poor one, and Bill found it so to his cost in *both* cases.

Before half the seven years was passed, Bill had his carriage, and his equipages ; was hand and glove with my Lord This, and my Lord That ; 'kept hounds and hunters; was the first sportsman at the Curragh; patronized every boxing ruffian he could pick up; and betted night and day on cards, dice, and horses. Bill, in short, *should* be a blood, and except he did all this, he could not presume to mingle with the fashionable bloods of his time.

It's an old proverb, however, that "what is got over the devil's back is sure to go off under it;" and in Bill's case this proved true. In short, the old boy himself could not supply him with money so fast as he made it fly; it was "come easy, go easy," with Bill, and so sign was on it, before he came within two years of his time he found his purse empty.

And now came the value of his summer friends to be known. When it was discovered that the cash was no longer flush with him—that stud, and carriage, and hounds were going to the hammer—whish! off they went, friends, relations, pot-companions, dinner-eaters, black-legs, and all, like a flock of crows that had smelt gun-powder. Down Bill soon went, week after week, and day after day, until at last he was obliged to put on the leather apron, and take to the hammer again; and not only that, for as no experience could make him wise, he once more began his tap-room brawls, his quarrels with Judy, and took to his "high feeding" at the dry potatoes and salt. Now, too, came the cutting tongues of all who knew him, like razors upon him. Those that he scorned because they were poor and himself rich, now paid him back his own with interest; and those that he measured himself with, because they were rich, and who only coun-tenanced him in consequence of his wealth, gave him the hardest word in their cheeks. The devil mend him! He deserved it all, and more if he had got it.

Bill, however, who was a hardened sinner, never fretted himself down an ounce of flesh by what was said to him, or of him. Not he; he cursed, and fought, and swore, and schemed away as usual, taking in every one he could; and surely none could match him at villainy of all sorts, and sizes.

At last the seven years became expired, and Bill was one morning sitting in his forge, sober and hungry, the wife cursing him, and the childhre squalling as before; he was thinking how he might defraud some honest neighbor out of a breakfast to stop their mouths and his own too, when who walks in to him but old Nick, to demand his bargain.

"Morrow, Bill!" says he with a sneer.

"The devil welcome you!" says Bill: "but you have a fresh memory."

"A bargain's a bargain between two *honest* men, any day," says Satan; "when I speak of *honest* men, I mean *yourself* and *me*, Bill;" and he put his tongue in his cheek to make game of the unfortunate rogue he had come for.

"Nick, my worthy fellow," said Bill, "have bowels; you wouldn't do a shabby thing; you wouldn't disgrace your own character by putting more weight upon a falling man. You know what it is to get a *come down* yourself, my worthy; so just keep your toe in your pump, and walk off with yourself somewhere else. A *cool* walk will sarve you better than my company, Nicholas."

"Bill, it's no use in shirking," said his friend; "your swindling tricks may enable you to cheat others, but you won't cheat *me*, I guess. You want nothing to make you perfect in your way but to travel; and travel you shall under my guidance, Billy. No, no—*I'm* not to be swindled, my good fellow. I have rather a—a—better opinion of myself, Mr. D., than to think that you could outwit one Nicholas Clutie, Esq.—ahem!"

"You may sneer, you sinner," replied Bill; "but I tell you that I have outwitted men who could buy and sell you to your face. Despair, you villain, when I tell you that *no attorney* could stand before me.

Satan's countenance got blank when he heard this; he wriggled and fidgeted about, and appeared to be not quite comfortable.

"In that case, then," says he, "the sooner I *deceive* you the better; so turn out for the *Low Countries*."

"Is it come to that in earnest?" said Bill, "and are you going to act the rascal at the long run?"

"'Pon honor, Bill."

"Have patience, then, you sinner, till I finish this horseshoe—it's the last of a set I'm finishing for one of your

friend the attorney's horses. And here, Nick, I hate idleness, you know it's the mother of mischief; take this
sledge-hammer, and give a dozen strokes or so, till I get it
out of hands, and then here's with you, since it must be
so."

He then gave the bellows a puff that blew half a peck
of dust in Club-foot's face, whipped out the red-hot iron,
and set Satan sledging away for bare life.

" Faith," says Bill to him, when the shoe was finished,
" it's a thousand pities ever the sledge should be out of your
hand; the great *Parra Gow* was a child to you at sledging, you're such an able tyke. Now just exercise yourself
till I bid the wife and childhre good-by, and then I'm
off.

Out went Bill, of course, without the slightest notion of
coming back; no more than Nick had that he could not
give up the sledging, and indeed neither could he, but was
forced to work away as if he was sledging for a wager.
This was just what Bill wanted. He was now compelled
to sledge on until it was Bill's pleasure to release him;
and so we leave him very industriously employed, while
we look after the worthy who outwitted him.

In the meantime, Bill broke cover, and took to the
country at large; wrought a little journey-work wherever
be could get it, and in this way went from one place to
another, till, in the course of a month, he walked back
very coolly into his own forge, to see how things went on
in his absence. There he found Satan in a rage, the perspiration pouring from him in torrents, hammering with
might and main upon the naked anvil. Bill calmly
leaned his back against the wall, placed his hat upon the
side of his head, put his hands into his breeches pockets,
and began to whistle *Shaun Gow's* hornpipe. At length
he says, in a very quiet and good-humored way—

" Morrow, Nick! "

" Oh! " says Nick, still hammering away—" Oh! you
double-distilled villain (hech!), may the most refined,
ornamental (hech!), doubled-rectified, super-extra, and

original (hech!) collection of curses that ever was gathered (hech!) into a single nosegay of ill-fortune (hech!) shine in the button-hole of your conscience (hech!) while you name is Bill Dawson! I denounce you (hech!) as a double-milled villain, a finished, hot-pressed knave (hech!), in comparison of whom all the other knaves I ever knew (hech!), attorneys included, are honest men. I brand you (hech!) as the pearl of cheats, a tip-top take-in (hech!) I denounce you, I say again, for the villainous treatment (hech!) I have received at your hands in this most untoward (hech!) and unfortunate transaction between us; for (hech!) unfortunate, in every sense, is he that has anything to do with (hech!) such a prime and finished impostor."

"You're very warm, Nicky, says Bill; "what puts you into a passion, you old sinner? Sure if it's your own will and pleasure to take exercise at my anvil, *I'm* not to be abused for it. Upon my credit, Nicky, you ought to blush for using such blackguard language, so unbecoming your grave character. You cannot say that it was I set you a hammering at the empty anvil, you profligate. However, as you are so industrious, I simply say it would be a thousand pities to take you from it. Nick, I love industry in my heart, and I always encourage it; so work away, it's not often you spend your time so creditably. I'm afraid if you weren't at that you'd be worse employed."

"Bill, have bowels," said the operative; "you wouldn't go to lay more weight on a falling man, you know; you wouldn't disgrace your character by such a piece of iniquity as keeping an inoffensive gentleman, advanced in years, at such an unbecoming and rascally job as this, Generosity's your top virtue, Bill; not but that you have many other excellent ones, as well as that, among which, as you say yourself, I reckon industry; but still it is in generosity you *shine*. Come, Bill, honor bright, and release me."

"Name the terms, you profligate."

" You're above terms, William ; a generous fellow like
you never thinks of terms."

" Good-by, old gentleman ! " said Bill, very coolly ; " I'll
drop in to see you once a month."

" No, no, Bill, you infern—a—a—you excellent, worthy,
delightful fellow, not so fast ; not so fast. Come, name
your terms, you sland——my dear Bill, name your terms."

" Seven years more."

" I agree ; but——"

" And the same supply of cash as before, down on the
nail here."

" Very good ; very good. You're rather simple, Bill ;
rather soft, I must confess. Well, no matter. I shall
yet turn the tab—a—hem ! You are an exceedingly
simple fellow, Bill ; still there will come a day, my *dear*
Bill—there will come——"

" Do you grumble, you vagrant ? Another word, and I
double the terms."

" Mum, William ; *tace* is Latin for a candle."

" Seven years more of grace, and the same measure of
the needful that I got before. Ay or no ? "

" Of grace, Bill ! Ay ! ay ! ay ! There's the cash. I
accept the terms. Oh blood ! the rascal—of grace ! !
Bill ! "

" Well, now drop the hammer, and vanish," says Billy ;
" but what would you think to take this sledge, while
you stay, and give me a——eh ! why in such a hurry ? " he
added, seeing that Satan withdrew in double-quick time.

" Hollo ! Nicholas ! " he shouted, " come back ; you
forgot something ! " and when the old gentleman looked
behind him, Billy shook the hammer at him, on which
he vanished altogether.

Billy now got into his old courses ; and what shows the
kind of people the world is made of, he also took up with
his old company. When they saw that he had the money
once more, and was sowing it about him in all directions,
they immediately began to find excuses for his former
extravagance.

" Say what you will," said one, " Bill Dawson's a spirited fellow, and bleeds like a prince."

" He's a hospitable man in his own house, or out of it, as ever lived," said another.

" His only fault is " observed a third, " that he is, if anything, too generous, and doesn't know the value of money; his fault's on the right side, however."

" He has the spunk in him," said a fourth; "keeps a capital table, prime wines, and a standing welcome for his friends."

" Why," said a fifth, " if he doesn't enjoy his money while he lives, he won't when he's dead ; so more power to him, and a wider throat to his purse."

Indeed, the very persons who were cramming themselves at his expense despised him at heart. They knew very well, however, how to take him on the weak side. Praise his generosity, and he would do anything; call him a man of spirit, and you might fleece him to his face. Sometimes he would toss a purse of guineas to this knave, another to that flatterer, a third to a bully, and a fourth to some broken-down rake—and all to convince them that *he* was a sterling friend—a man of mettle and liberality But never was he known to help a virtuous and struggling family—to assist the widow or the fatherless, or to do any other act that was *truly* useful. It is to be supposed the reason of this was, that as he spent it, as most of the world do, in the service of the devil, by whose aid he got it, he was prevented from turning it to a good account. Between you and me, dear reader, there are more persons acting after Bill's fashion in the same world than you dream about.

When his money was out again, his friends played him the same rascally game once more. No sooner did his poverty become plain, than the knaves began to be troubled with small fits of modesty, such as an unwillingness to come to his place when there was no longer anything to be got there. A kind of virgin bashfulness prevented them from speaking to him when they saw him getting out

on the wrong side of his clothes. Many of them would
turn away from him in the prettiest and most delicate
manner when they thought he wanted to borrow money
from them—all for fear of putting him to the blush by
asking it. Others again, when they saw him coming towards their houses about dinner hour, would become so
confused, from mere gratitude, as to think themselves in
another place ; and their servants, seized, as it were, with
the same feeling, would tell Bill that their masters were
" not at home."

At length, after traveling the same villainous round as
before, Bill was compelled to betake himself, as the last
remedy, to the forge ; in other words, he found that there
is, after all, nothing in this world that a man can rely on
so firmly and surely as his own industry. Bill, however,
wanted the organ of common sense ; for his experience—
and it was sharp enough to leave an impression—ran off
him like water off a duck.

He took to his employment sorely against his grain ;
but he had now no choice. He must either work or
starve, and starvation is like a great doctor—nobody tries
it till every other remedy fails them. Bill had been twice
rich ; twice a gentleman among blackguards, but always
blackguard among gentlemen ; for no wealth or acquaintance with decent society could rub the rust of his native
vulgarity off him. He was now a common blinking sot
in his forge ; a drunken bully in the tap-room, cursing
and brow-beating every one as well as his wife ; boasting
of how much money he had spent in his day ; swaggering
about the high doings he carried on ; telling stories about
himself and Lord This at the Curragh ; the dinners he
gave—how much they cost him, and attempting to extort
credit upon the strength of his former wealth. He was
too ignorant, however, to know that he was publishing
his own disgrace, and that it was a mean-spirited thing
to be proud of what ought to make him blush through a
deal board nine inches thick.

He was one morning industriously engaged in a quarrel

with his wife, who, with a three-legged stool in her hand, appeared to mistake his head for his own anvil ; he, in the meantime, paid his addresses to her with his leather apron, when who steps in to jog his memory about the little agreement that was between them, but old Nick. The wife, it seems, in spite of all her exertions to the contrary, was getting the worst of it ; and Sir Nicholas, willing to appear a gentleman of great gallantry, thought he could not do less than take up the lady's quarrel, particularly as Bill had laid her in a sleeping posture Now Satan thought this too bad ; and as he felt himself under many obligations to the sex, he determined to defend one of them on the present occasion ; so as Judy rose, he turned upon the husband, and floored him by a clever facer.

" You unmanly villain," said he, " is this the way you treat your wife ? 'Pon honor, Bill, I'll chastise you on the spot. I could net stand by, a spectator of such ungentlemanly conduct without giving up all claim to gallant——" Whack ! the word was divided in his mouth by the blow of a churn-staff from Judy, who no sooner saw Bill struck, than she nailed Satan, who " fell " once more.

" What, you villain ! that's for striking my husband like a murderer behind his back," said Judy, and she suited the action to the word, " that's for interfering between man and wife. Would you murder the poor man before my face, eh ? If *he* bates me, you shabby dog you, who has a better right ? I'm sure it's nothing out of your pocket. Must you have your finger in every pie ? "

This was anything but *idle* talk ; for at every word she gave him a remembrance, hot and heavy. Nicholas backed, danced and hopped ; she advanced, still drubbing him with great perseverance, till at length he fell into the redoubtable arm-chair, which stood exactly behind him. Bill, who had been putting in two blows for Judy's one, seeing that his enemy was safe, now got between the devil and his wife, *a situation that few will be disposed to envy him.*

"Tenderness, Judy," said the husband, " I hate cruelty.
Go put the tongs in the fire, and make them red hot.
Nicholas, you have a nose," said he.

Satan began to rise, but was rather surprised to find
that he could not budge.

"Nicholas," says Bill, "how is your pulse? you don't
look well; that is to say, you look worse than usual."

The other attempted to rise, but found it a mistake.

"I'll thank you to come along," said Bill. "I have a
fancy to travel under your guidance, and we'll take the
Low Countries in our way, won't we? Get to your legs,
you sinner; you know a bargain's a bargain between two
honest men, Nicholas; meaning *yourself* and *me*. Judy,
are the tongs hot?"

Satan's face was worth looking at, as he turned his eyes
from the husband to the wife, and then fastened them on
the tongs, now nearly at a furnace heat in the fire, conscious at the same time that he could not move out of
the chair.

"Billy," said he, "you won't forget that I rewarded
your generosity the last time I saw you, in the way of
business." "Faith, Nicholas, it fails me to remember any
generosity I ever showed you. Don't be womanish. I
simply want to see what kind of stuff your nose is made
of, and whether it will stretch like a rogue's conscience.
If it does, we will flatter it up the *chimly* with red-hot
tongs, and when this old hat is fixed on the top of it, let
us alone for a weather-cock." "Have a *fellow-feeling*, Mr.
Dawson; you know *we* ought not to dispute. Drop the
matter, and I give you the next seven years." "We
know all that,' says Billy, opening the red-hot tongs very
coolly. "Mr. Dawson," said Satan, "if you cannot remember my friendship to yourself, don't forget how often
I stood your father's friend, your grandfather's friend, and
the friend of all your relations up to the tenth generation.
I intended, also, to stand by your children, after you, so
long as the name of Dawson, and a respectable one it is,
might last." Don't be blushing, Nick," says Bill, " you

are too modest; that was ever your failing; hould up your head, there's money bid for you. I'll give you such a nose, my good friend, that you will have to keep an outrider before you, to carry the end of it on his shoulder." "Mr. Dawson, I pledge my honor to raise your children in the world as high as they can go; no matter whethery the desire it or not." "That's very kind of you," says the other, "and I'll do as much for your nose."

He gripped it as he spoke, and the old boy immediately sung out; Bill pulled, and the nose went with him like a piece of warm wax. He then transferred the tongs to Judy, got a ladder, resumed the tongs, ascended the chimney, and tugged stoutly at the nose until he got it five feet above the roof. He then fixed the hat upon the top of it, and came down.

"There's a weather-cock," said Billy; "I defy Ireland to show such a beauty. Faith, Nick, it would make the purtiest steeple for a church, in all Europe, and the old hat fits it to a shaving."

In this state, with his nose twisted up the chimney, Satan sat for some time, experiencing the novelty of what might be termed a peculiar sensation. At last the worthy husband and wife begun to relent.

"I think," said Bill, "that we have made the most of the nose, as well as the joke; I believe, Judy, it's long enough." "What is?" says Judy.

"Why, the joke," said the husband.

"Faith, and I think so is the nose," said Judy."

"What do you say yourself, Satan?" said Bill.

"Nothing at all, William," said the other; "but that— ha! ha!—it's a good joke—an excellent joke, and a goodly nose, too, as it *stands*. You were always a gentlemanly man, Bill, and did things with a grace; still, if I might give an opinion on such a trifle——"

"It's no trifle at all," says Bill, "if you spake of the nose." "Very well, it is not," says the other; "still, I am decidedly of opinion, that if you could shorten both the joke and the nose without further violence, you would lay

me under very heavy obligations, which I shall be ready
to acknowledge and *repay* as I ought." "Come," said
Bill, "shell out once more, and be off for seven years.
As much as you came down with the last time, and
vanish."

The words were scarcely spoken, when the money was
at his feet, and Satan invisible. Nothing could surpass
the mirth of Bill and his wife at the result of this adventure. They laughed till they fell down on the floor.

It is useless to go over the same ground again. Bill
was still incorrigible. The money went as the devil's
money always goes. Bill caroused and squandered, but
could never turn a penny of it to a good purpose. In this
way, year after year went, till the seventh was closed and
Bill's hour come. He was now, and had been for some
time past, as miserable a knave as ever. Not a shilling
had he, nor a shilling's worth, with the exception of his
forge, his cabin, and a few articles of crazy furniture. In
this state he was standing in his forge as before, straining
his ingenuity how to make out a breakfast, when Satan
came to look after him. The old gentleman was sorely
puzzled how to get at him. He kept skulking and sneak-
ing about the forge for some time till he saw that Bill
hadn't a cross to bless himself with. He immediately
changed himself into a guinea, and lay in an open place
where he knew Bill would see him. "If," said he, "I once
get into his possession, I can manage him." The honest
smith took the bait, for it was well gilded; he clutched
the guinea, put it into his purse, and closed it up. "Ho!
ho!" shouted the devil out of the purse, "you're caught,
Bill; I've secured you at last, you knave you. Why don't
you despair, you villain, when you think of what's before
you?" "Why, you unlucky ould dog," said Bill, "is it
there you are? Will you always drive your head into
every loophole that's set for you? Faith, Nick achora, I
never had you bagged till now."

Satan then began to tug and struggle with a view of
getting out of the purse, but in vain.

" Mr. Dawson," said he, " we understand each other.
I'll give the seven years additional, and the cash on the
nail." " Be aisey, Nicholas. You know the weight of the
hammer, that's enough. It's not a whipping with feathers
you're going to get, anyhow. Just be aisey." " Mr. Dawson, I grant I'm not your match. Release me, and I double the cash. I was merely trying your temper when I
took the shape of a guinea."

" Faith and I'll try yours before I lave it, I've a notion."
He immediately commenced with the sledge, and Satan
sang out with a considerable want of firmness. " Am I
heavy enough ! " said Bill.

" Lighter, lighter, William, if you love me. I haven't
been well latterly, Mr. Dawson—I have been delicate—my
health, in short, is in a very precarious state, Mr.
Dawson." " I can believe *that*," said Bill, " and it will be
more so before I have done with you. Am I doing it
right ? " " Bill," said Nick, " is this gentlemanly treatment
in your own respectable shop ? Do you think, if you
dropped into my little place, that I'd act this rascally
part towards you ? Have you no compunction ? " " I
know," replied Bill, sledging away with vehemence, " that
you're notorious for giving your friends a *warm* welcome.
Divil an ould youth more so ; but you must be daling in
bad coin, must you ? However, good or bad, you're in
for a sweat now, you sinner. Am I doin' it purty ? "

" Lovely, William—but, if possible, a little more delicate."

" Oh, how delicate you are ! Maybe a cup o' tay would
sarve you, or a little small gruel to compose your
stomach."

" Mr. Dawson," said the gentleman in the purse, " hold
your hand and let us understand one another. I have a
proposal to make." " Hear the sinner anyhow," said the
wife. " Name your own sum," said Satan, " only set me
free." " No, the sorra may take the toe you'll budge till
you let Bill off," said the wife ; " hould him hard, Bill,
barrin' he sets *you* clear of your engagement. " There it

is, my posy," said Bill; "that's the condition. If you don't give *me up*, here's at you once more—and you must double the cash you gave the last time, too. So, if you're of that opinion, say *ay*—leave the cash and be off."

The money again appeared in a glittering heap before Bill, upon which he exclaimed—" The *ay* has it, you dog. Take to your pumps now, and fair weather after you, you vagrant; but Nicholas—Nick—here, here——" The other looked back, and saw Bill, with a broad grin upon him, shaking the purse at him—"Nicholas come back," said he. "I'm short a guinea." Nick shook his fist, and disappeared.

It would be useless to stop now, merely to inform our readers that Bill was beyond improvement. In short, he once more took to his old habits, and lived on exactly in the same manner as before. He had two sons—one as great a blackguard as himself, and who was also named after him; the other was a well-conducted, virtuous young man, called James, who left his father, and having relied upon his own industry and honest perseverance in life, arrived afterwards to great wealth, and built the town called Castle Dawson; which is so called from its founder until this day.

Bill, at length, in spite of all his wealth, was obliged, as he himself said, "to travel,"—in other words, he fell asleep one day, and forgot to awaken; or, in still plainer terms, he died.

Now, it is usual, when a man dies, to close the history of his life and adventures at once; but with our hero this cannot be the case. The moment Bill departed, he very naturally bent his steps towards the residence of St. Moroky, as being, in his opinion, likely to lead him towards the snuggest berth he could readily make out. On arriving, he gave a very humble kind of a knock, and St. Moroky appeared.

"God save your Reverence!" said Bill, very submis. sively.

"Be off; there's no admittance here for so poor a youth as you are," said St. Moroky.

He was now so cold and fatigued that he cared little where he went, provided only, as he said himself, "he could rest his bones, and get an air of the fire." Accordingly, after arriving at a large black gate, he knocked, as before, and was told he would get *instant* admittance the moment he gave his name.

"Billy Dawson," he replied.

"Off, instantly," said the porter to his companions, "and let his Majesty know that the rascal he dreads so much is here at the gate."

Such a racket and tumult were never heard as the very mention of Billy Dawson created.

In the meantime, his old acquaintance came running towards the gate with such haste and consternation, that his tail was several times nearly tripping up his heels.

"Don't admit that rascal," he shouted; "bar the gate —make every chain, and lock and bolt, fast—I won't be safe—and I won't stay here, nor none of us need stay here, if he gets in—my bones are sore yet after him. No, no—begone, you villain—you'll get no entrance here —I know you too well."

Bill could not help giving a broad, malicious grin at Satan, and, putting his nose through the bars, he exclaimed—"Ha! you ould dog, I have you afraid of me at last, have I?"

He had scarcely uttered the words, when his foe, who stood inside, instantly tweaked him by the nose, and Bill felt as if he had been gripped by the same red-hot tongs with which he himself had formerly tweaked the nose of Nicholas.

Bill then departed, but soon found that in consequence of the inflammable materials which strong drink had thrown into his nose, that organ immediately took fire, and, indeed, to tell the truth, kept burning night and day, winter and summer, without ever once going out, from that hour to this.

Such was the sad fate of Billy Dawson, who has been walking without stop or stay, from place to place, ever since; and in consequence of the flame on his nose, and his beard being tangled like a wisp of hay, he has been christened by the country folk Will-o'-the-Wisp, while, as it were, to show the mischief of his disposition, the circulating knave, knowing that he must seek the coldest bogs and quagmires in order to cool his nose, seizes upon that opportunity of misleading the unthinking and tipsy night travelers from their way, just that he may have the satisfaction of still taking in as many as possible.

GIANTS.

WHEN the pagan gods of Ireland—the *Tuath-De-Danān* —robbed of worship and offerings, grew smaller and smaller in the popular imagination, until they turned into the fairies, the pagan heroes grew bigger and bigger, until they turned into the giants.

THE GIANT'S STAIRS.*

T. CROFTON CROKER.

ON the road between Passage and Cork there is an old mansion called Ronayne's Court. It may be easily known from the stack of chimneys and the gable-ends, which are to be seen, look at it which way you will. Here it was that Maurice Ronayne and his wife Margaret Gould kept house, as may be learned to this day from the great old chimney-piece, on which is carved their arms. They were a mighty worthy couple, and had but one son, who was called Philip, after no less a person than the King of Spain.

Immediately on his smelling the cold air of this world the child sneezed, which was naturally taken to be a good sign of his having a clear head; and the subsequent rapidity of his learning was truly amazing, for on the very first day a primer was put into his hands he tore out the A, B, C page and destroyed it, as a thing quite beneath his notice. No wonder, then, that both father and mother were proud of their heir, who gave such indisputable proofs of genius, or, as they called it in that part of the world, " *genus.*"

* *Fairy Legends of the South of Ireland.*

355

One morning, however, Master Phil, who was then just seven years old, was missing, and no one could tell what had become of him: servants were sent in all directions to seek him, on horseback and on foot, but they returned without any tidings of the boy, whose disappearance altogether was most unaccountable. A large reward was offered, but it produced them no intelligence, and years rolled away without Mr. and Mrs. Ronayne having obtained any satisfactory account of the fate of their lost child.

There lived at this time, near Carrigaline, one Robert Kelly, a blacksmith by trade. He was what is termed a handy man, and his abilities were held in much estimation by the lads and the lasses of the neighborhood; for, independent of shoeing horses, which he did to great perfection, and making plow-irons, he interpreted dreams for the young women, sung " Arthur O'Bradley " at their weddings, and was so good-natured a fellow at a christening, that he was gossip to half the country round.

Now it happened that Robin had a dream himself, and young Philip Ronayne appeared to him in it, at the dead hour of the night. Robin thought he saw the boy mounted upon a beautiful white horse, and that he told him how he was made a page to the giant Mahon Mac-Mahon, who had carried him off and who held his court in the hard heart of the rock. " The seven years—my time of service—are clean out, Robin," said he, " and if you release me this night I will be the making of you for ever after."

" And how will I know," said Robin—cunning enough, even in his sleep—" but this is all a dream ? "

" Take that," said the boy, " for a token "—and at the word the white horse struck out with one of his hind legs, and gave poor Robin such a kick in the forehead that, thinking he was a dead man, he roared as loud as he could after his brains, and woke up, calling a thousand murders. He found himself in bed, but he had the mark of the blow, the regular print of a horse-shoe, upon his forehead as red as blood; and Robin Kelly, who never before found himself puzzled at the dream of any other person, did not know what to think of his own.

Robin was well acquainted with the Giant's Stairs—as, indeed, who is not that knows the harbor? They consist of great masses of rock, which, piled one above another, rise like a flight of steps from very deep water, against the bold cliff of Carrigmahon. Nor are they badly suited for stairs to those who have legs of sufficient length to stride over a moderate-sized house, or to enable them to clear the space of a mile in a hop, step, and jump. Both these feats the giant MacMahon was said to have performed in the days of Finnian glory; and the common tradition of the country placed his dwelling within the cliff up whose side the stairs led.

Such was the impression which the dream made on Robin, that he determined to put its truth to the test. It occurred to him, however, before setting out on this adventure, that a plow-iron may be no bad companion, as, from experience, he knew it was an excellent knockdown argument, having on more occasions than one settled a little disagreement very quietly; so, putting one on his shoulder, off he marched, in the cool of the evening, through Glaun a Thowk (the Hawk's Glen) to Monkstown. Here an old gossip of his (Tom Clancey by name) lived, who, on hearing Robin's dream, promised him the use of his skiff, and, moreover, offered to assist in rowing it to the Giant's Stairs.

After a supper, which was of the best, they embarked. It was a beautiful still night, and the little boat glided swiftly along. The regular dip of the oars, the distant song of the sailor, and sometimes the voice of a belated traveler at the ferry of Carrigaloe, alone broke the quietness of the land and sea and sky. The tide was in their favor, and in a few minutes Robin and his gossip rested on their oars under the dark shadow of the Giant's Stairs. Robin looked anxiously for the entrance to the Giant's palace, which, it was said, may be found by any one seeking it at midnight; but no such entrance could he see. His impatience had hurried him there before that time, and after waiting a considerable space in a state of suspense not to be described, Robin, with pure vexation, could not help exclaiming to his companion, " 'Tis a pair of fools we are, Tom Clancey, for coming here at all on the strength of a dream."

" And whose doing is it," said Tom, " but your own ? "

At the moment he spoke they perceived a faint glimmering of light to proceed from the cliff, which gradually increased until a porch big enough for a king's palace unfolded itself almost on a level with the water. They pulled the skiff directly towards the opening, and Robin Kelly, seizing his plow-iron, boldly entered with a strong hand and a stout heart. Wild and strange was that entrance, the whole of which appeared formed of grim and grotesque faces, blending so strangely each with the other that it was impossible to define any : the chin of one formed the nose of another ; what appeared to be a fixed and stern eye, if dwelt upon, changed to a gaping mouth ; and the lines of the lofty forehead grew into a majestic and flowing beard. The more Robin allowed himself to contemplate the forms around him, the more terrific they became ; and the stony expression of this crowd of faces assumed a savage ferocity as his imagination converted feature after feature into a different shape and character. Losing the twilight in which these indefinite forms were visible, he advanced through a dark and devious passage, whilst a deep and rumbling noise sounded as if the rock was about to close upon him, and swallow him up alive forever. Now, indeed, poor Robin felt afraid.

" Robin, Robin," said he, " if you were a fool for coming here, what in the name of fortune are you now? " But, as before, he had scarcely spoken, when he saw a small light twinkling through the darkness of the distance, like a star in the midnight sky. To retreat was out of the question ; for so many turnings and windings were in the passage that he considered he had but little chance of making his way back. He, therefore, proceeded towards the bit of light, and came at last into a spacious chamber, from the roof of which hung the solitary lamp that had guided him. Emerging from such profound gloom, the single lamp afforded Robin abundant light to discover several gigantic figures seated round a massive stone table, as if in serious deliberation, but no word disturbed the breathless silence which prevailed. At the head of this table sat Mahon MacMahon himself, whose majestic beard had taken root, and in the course of ages grown into the stone slab. He was the first who perceived Robin; and instantly starting up, drew his long beard from out the huge piece of rock in such haste and with so sudden a jerk that it was shattered into a thousand pieces.

"What seek you?" he demanded in a voice of thunder.

"I come," answered Robin, with as much boldness as he could put on, for his heart was almost fainting within him; "I come," said he, "to claim Philip Ronayne, whose time of service is out this night."

"And who sent you here?" said the giant.

"'Twas of my own accord I came," said Robin.

"Then you must single him out from among my pages," said the giant; "and if you fix on the wrong one, your life is the forfeit. "Follow me." He led Robin into a hall of vast extent, and filled with lights; along either side of which were rows of beautiful children, all apparently seven years old, and none beyond that age, dressed in green, and every one exactly dressed alike.

"Here," said Mahon, "you are free to take Philip Ronayne if you will; but, remember, I give but one choice."

Robin was sadly perplexed; for there were hundreds upon hundreds of children; and he had no very clear recollection of the boy he sought. But he walked along the hall, by the side of Mahon, as if nothing was the matter, although his great iron dress clanked fearfully at every step, sounding louder than Robin's own sledge battering on his anvil.

They had nearly reached the end without speaking, when Robin, seeing that the only means he had was to make friends with the giant, determined to try what effect a few soft words might have.

" 'Tis a fine wholesome appearance the poor children carry," remarked Robin, " although they have been here so long shut out from the fresh air and the blessed light of heaven. 'Tis tenderly your honor must have reared them ! "

" Ay," said the giant, " that is true for you ; so give me your hand; for you are, I believe, a very honest fellow for a blacksmith."

Robin at the first look did not much like the huge size of the hand, and, therefore, presented his plow-iron, which the giant seizing, twisted in his grasp round and round again as if it had been a potato stalk. On seeing this all the children set up a shout of laughter. In the midst of their mirth Robin thought he heard his name called ; and all ear and eye, he put his hand on the boy who he fancied had spoken, crying out at the same time, " Let me live or die for it, but this is young Phil Ronayne."

" It is Philip Ronayne—happy Philip Ronayne," said his young companions ; and in an instant the hall became dark. Crashing noises were heard, and all was in strange confusion ; but Robin held fast his prize, and found himself lying in the gray dawn of the morning at the head of the Giant's Stairs with the boy clasped in his arms.

Robin had plenty of gossips to spread the story of his wonderful adventure : Passage, Monkstown, Carrigaline— the whole barony of Kerricurrihy rung with it.

" Are you quite sure, Robin, it is young Phil Ronayne you have brought back with you ? " was the regular question ; for although the boy had been seven years away, his appearance now was just the same as on the day he was missed. He had neither grown taller nor older in look, and he spoke of things which had happened before he was carried off as one awakened from sleep, or as if they had occurred yesterday.

"Am I sure? Well, that's a queer question," was Robin's reply; seeing the boy has the blue eyes of the mother, with the foxy hair of the father; to say nothing of the *purty* wart on the right side of his little nose."

However Robin Kelly may have been questioned, the worthy couple of Ronayne's Court doubted not that he was the deliverer of their child from the power of the giant MacMahon; and the reward they bestowed on him equalled their gratitude.

Philip Ronayne lived to be an old man; and he was remarkable to the day of his death for his skill in working brass and iron, which it was believed he had learned during his seven years' apprenticeship to the giant Mahon MacMahon.

A LEGEND OF KNOCKMANY.

WILLIAM CARLETON.*

WHAT Irish man, woman, or child has not heard of our renowned Hibernian Hercules, the great and glorious Fin M'Coul? Not one, from Cape Clear to the Giant's Cause-

---

* Carleton says—"Of the gray stone mentioned in this legend, there is a very striking and melancholy anecdote to be told. Some twelve or thirteen years ago, a gentleman in the vicinity of the site of it was building a house, and, in defiance of the legend and curse connected with it, he resolved to break it up and use it. It was with some difficulty, however, that he could succeed in getting his laborers to have anything to do with its mutilation. Two men, however, undertook to blast it, but, somehow, the process of ignition being mismanaged, it exploded prematurely, and one of them was killed. This coincidence was held as a fulfilment of the curse mentioned in the legend. I have heard that it remains in that mutilated state to the present day, no other person being found who had the hardihood to touch it. This stone, be-

way, nor from that back again to Cape Clear. And, by-
the-way, speaking of the Giant's Causeway brings me at
once to the beginning of my story. Well, it so happened
that Fin and his gigantic relatives were all working at the
Causeway, in order to make a bridge, or what was still
better, a good stout pad-road, across to Scotland; when
Fin, who was very fond of his wife Oonagh, took it into his
head that he would go home and see how the poor woman
got on in his absence. To be sure, Fin was a true Irishman, and so the sorrow thing in life brought him back, only
to see that she was snug and comfortable, and, above all
things, that she got her rest well at night; for he knew that
the poor woman, when he was with her, used to be subject
to nightly qualms and configurations, that kept him very
anxious, decent man, striving to keep her up to the good
spirits and health that she had when they were first married.
So, accordingly, he pulled up a fir-tree, and, after lopping
off the roots and branches, made a walking-stick of it, and
set out on his way to Oonagh.

Oonagh, or rather Fin, lived at this time on the very
tip-top of Knockmany Hill, which faces a cousin of its
own called Cullamore, that rises up, half-hill, half-moun-
tain, on the opposite side—east-east by south, as the
sailors say, when they wish to puzzle a landsman.

Now, the truth is, for it must come out, that honest
Fin's affection for his wife, though cordial enough in
itself, was by no manner of means the real cause of his
journey home. There was at that time another giant,
named Cucullin—some say he was Irish, and some say he
was Scotch—but whether Scotch or Irish, sorrow doubt
of it but he was a *targer*. No other giant of the day could
stand before him; and such was his strength, that, when
well vexed, he could give a stamp that shook the country

fore it was disfigured, exactly resembled that which the country
people term a miscaun of butter, which is precisely the shape of
a complete prism, a circumstance, no doubt, which, in the fertile
imagination of the old Senachies, gave rise to the superstition
annexed to it."

about him. The fame and name of him went far and
near ; and nothing in the shape of a man, it was said, had
any chance with him in a fight. Whether the story is
true or not, I cannot say, but the report went that, by one
blow of his fists he flattened a thunderbolt, and kept it in
his pocket, in the shape of a pancake, to show to all his
enemies, when they were about to fight him. Undoubtedly
he had given every giant in Ireland a considerable beating,
barring Fin M'Coul himself ; and he swore, by the solemn
contents of Moll Kelly's Primer, that he would never rest,
night or day, winter or summer, till he would serve Fin
with the same sauce, if he could catch him. Fin, however, who no doubt was the cock of the walk on his own
dunghill, had a strong disinclination to meet a giant who
could make a young earthquake, or flatten a thunderbolt
when he was angry ; so he accordingly kept dodging about
from place to place, not much to his credit as a Trojan, to
be sure, whenever he happened to get the hard word that
Cucullin was on the scent of him. This, then, was the
marrow of the whole movement, although he put it on
his anxiety to see Oonagh ; and I am not saying but there
was some truth in that too. However, the short and long
of it was, with reverence be it spoken, that he heard
Cucullin was coming to the Causeway to have a trial of
strength with him ; and he was naturally enough seized,
in consequence, with a very warm and sudden fit of affection for his wife, poor woman, who was delicate in her
health, and leading, besides, a very lonely, uncomfortable
life of it (he assured them) in his absence. He accordingly pulled up the fir-tree, as I said before, and having
snedded it into a walking-stick, set out on his affectionate
travels to see his darling Oonagh on the top of Knockmany, by the way.

In truth, to state the suspicions of the country at the
time, the people wondered very much why it was that
Fin selected such a windy spot for his dwelling-house,
and they even went so far as to tell him as much.

" What can you mane, Mr. M'Coul," said they, " by

pitching your tent upon the top of Knockmany, where you never are without a breeze, day or night, winter or summer, and where you're often forced to take your nightcap * without either going to bed or turning up your little finger; ay, an' where, besides this, there's the sorrow's own want of water?"

"Why," said Fin, "ever since I was the height of a round tower, I was known to be fond of having a good prospect of my own; and where the dickens, neighbors, could I find a better spot for a good prospect than the top of Knockmany? As for water, I am sinking a pump,† and, plase goodness, as soon as the Causeway's made, I intend to finish it."

Now, this was more of Fin's philosophy; for the real state of the case was, that he pitched upon the top of Knockmany in order that he might be able to see Cucullin coming toward the house, and, of course, that he himself might go to look after his distant transactions in other parts of the country, rather than—but no matter—we do not wish to be too hard on Fin. All we have to say is, that if he wanted a spot from which to keep a sharp lookout—and, between ourselves, he did want it grievously—barring Slieve Croob, or Slieve Donard, or its own cousin, Cullamore, he could not find a neater or more convenient situation for it in the sweet and sagacious province of Ulster.

"God save all here!" said Fin, good-humoredly, on putting his honest face into his own door.

"Musha, Fin, avick, an' you're welcome home to your own Oonagh, you darlin' bully." Here followed a smack that is said to have made the waters of the lake at the bottom of the hill curl, as it were, with kindness and sympathy.

"Faith," said Fin, "beautiful; an' how are you, Oonagh

* A common name for the cloud or rack that hangs, as a forerunner of wet weather, about the peak of a mountain.

† There is upon the top of this hill an opening that bears a very strong resemblance to the crater of an extinct volcano.

—and how did you sport your figure during my absence my bilberry?"

" Never a merrier—as bouncing a grass widow as ever there was in sweet ' Tyrone among the bushes.' "

Fin gave a short, good-humored cough, and laughed most heartily, to show her how much he was delighted that she made herself happy in his absence.

" An' what brought you home so soon, Fin?" said she.

" Why, avourneen," said Fin, putting in his answer in the proper way, " never the thing but the purest of love and affection for yourself. Sure you know that's truth, anyhow, Oonagh."

Fin spent two or three happy days with Oonagh, and felt himself very comfortable, considering the dread he had of Cucullin. This, however, grew upon him so much that his wife could not but perceive something lay on his mind which he kept altogether to himself. Let a woman alone, in the meantime, for ferreting or wheedling a secret out of her good man, when she wishes. Fin was a proof of this.

"It's this Cucullin," said he, " that's troubling me. When the fellow gets angry, and begins to stamp, he'll shake you a whole townland; and it's well known that he can stop a thunderbolt, for he always carries one about him in the shape of a pancake, to show to any one that might misdoubt it."

As he spoke, he clapped his thumb in his mouth, which he always did when he wanted to prophesy, or to know anything that happened in his absence; and the wife, who knew what he did it for, said, very sweetly,

" Fin, darling, I hope you don't bite your thumb at me, dear?"

" No," said Fin; " but I bite my thumb, acushla," said he.

" Yes, jewel; but take care and don't draw blood," said she. " Ah, Fin! don't, my bully—don't."

" He's coming," said Fin; "I see him below Dungannon."

"Thank goodness, dear! an' who is it, avick? Glory be to God!"

"That baste, Cucullin," replied Fin; "and how to manage I don't know. If I run away, I am disgraced; and I know that sooner or later I must meet him, for my thumb tells me so."

"When will he be here?"

"To-morrow, about two o'clock," replied Fin, with a groan.

"Well, my bully, don't be cast down," said Oonagh; "depend on me, and maybe I'll bring you better out of this scrape than ever you could bring yourself, by your rule o' thumb."

This quieted Fin's heart very much, for he knew that Oonagh was hand and glove with the fairies; and, indeed, to tell the truth, she was supposed to be a fairy herself. If she was, however, she must have been a kind-hearted one, for by accounts, she never did anything but good in the neighborhood.

Now it so happened that Oonagh had a sister named Granua, living opposite them, on the very top of Cullamore, which I have mentioned already, and this Granua was quite as powerful as herself. The beautiful valley that lies between them is not more than about three or four miles broad, so that of a summer's evening, Granua and Oonagh were able to hold many an agreeable conversation across it, from the one hill-top to the other. Upon this occasion Oonagh resolved to consult her sister as to what was best to be done in the difficulty that surrounded them.

"Granua," said she, "are you at home?"

"No," said the other; "I'm picking bilberries in Al-thadhawan" (*Anglicé*, the Devil's Glen).

"Well," said Oonagh, "get up to the top of Cullamore, look about you, and then tell us what you see."

"Very well," replied Granua; after a few minutes, "I am there now."

"What do you see?" asked the other.

"Goodness be about us!" exclaimed Granua, "I see the biggest giant that ever was known coming up from Dungannon."

"Ay," said Oonagh, "there's our difficulty. That giant is the great Cucullin; and he's now commin' up to leather Fin. What's to be done?"

"I'll call to him," she replied, "to come up to Cullamore and refresh himself, and maybe that will give you and Fin time to think of some plan to get yourselves out of the scrape. But," she proceeded, "I'm short of butter, having in the house only half-a-dozen firkins, and as I'm to have a few giants and giantesses to spend the evenin' with me, I'd feel thankful, Oonagh, if you'd throw me up fifteen or sixteen tubs, or the largest miscaun you have got, and you'll oblige me very much."

"I'll do that with a heart and a-half," replied Oonagh; "and, indeed, Granua, I feel myself under great obligations to you for your kindness in keeping him off of us till we see what can be done; for what would become of us all if anything happened Fin, poor man."

She accordingly got the largest miscaun of butter she had—which might be about the weight of a couple a dozen mill-stones, so that you may easily judge of its size —and calling up to her sister, "Granua," said she, "are you ready? I'm going to throw you up a miscaun, so be prepared to catch it."

"I will," said the other; "a good throw now, and take care it does not fall short."

Oonagh threw it; but, in consequence of her anxiety about Fin and Cucullin, she forgot to say the charm that was to send it up, so that, instead of reaching Cullamore, as she expected, it fell about half-way between the two hills, at the edge of the Broad Bog near Augher.

"My curse upon you!" she exclaimed; "you've disgraced me. I now change you into a gray stone. Lie there as a testimony of what has happened; and may evil betide the first living man that will ever attempt to remove or injure you!"

And, sure enough, there it lies to this day, with the mark of the four fingers and thumb imprinted in it, exactly as it came out of her hand.

"Never mind," said Granua, "I must only do the best I can with Cucullin. If all fail, I'll give him a cast of heather broth to keep the wind out of his stomach, or a panada of oak-bark to draw it in a bit; but, above all things, think of some plan to get Fin out of the scrape he's in, otherwise he's a lost man. You know you used to be sharp and ready-witted; and my own opinion, Oonagh, is, that it will go hard with you, or you'll outdo Cucullin yet."

She then made a high smoke on the top of the hill, after which she put her finger in her mouth, and gave three whistles, and by that Cucullin knew he was invited to Cullamore—for this was the way that the Irish long ago gave a sign to all strangers and travelers, to let them know they were welcome to come and take share of whatever was going.

In the meantime, Fin was very melancholy, and did not know what to do, or how to act at all. Cucullin was an ugly customer, no doubt, to meet with; and, moreover, the idea of the confounded " cake " aforesaid flattened the very heart within him. What chance could he have, strong and brave though he was, with a man who could, when put in a passion, walk the country into earthquakes and knock thunderbolts into pancakes? The thing was impossible; and Fin knew not on what hand to turn him. Right or left—backward or forward—where to go he could form no guess whatsoever.

"Oonagh," said he, "can you do nothing for me? Where's all your invention? Am I to be skivered like a rabbit before your eyes, and to have my name disgraced forever in the sight of all my tribe, and me the best man among them? How am I to fight this man-mountain— this huge cross between an earthquake and a thunderbolt?—with a pancake in his pocket that was once——"

" Be easy, Fin," replied Oonagh; " troth, I'm ashamed

of you. Keep your toe in your pump will you? Talking of pancakes, maybe we'll give him as good as any he brings with him—thunderbolt or otherwise. If I don't treat him to as smart feeding as he's got this many a day, never trust Oonagh again. Leave him to me, and do just as I bid you."

This relieved Fin very much; for, after all, he had great confidence in his wife, knowing, as he did, that she had got him out of many a quandary before. The present, however, was the greatest of all; but still he began to get courage, and was able to eat his victuals as usual. Oonagh then drew the nine woollen threads of different colors, which she always did to find out the best way of succeeding in anything of importance she went about. She then platted them into three plats with three colors in each, putting one on her right arm, one round her heart, and the third round her right ankle, for then she knew that nothing could fail with her that she undertook.

Having everything now prepared, she sent round to the neighbors and borrowed one-and-twenty iron griddles, which she took and kneaded into the hearts of one-and-twenty cakes of bread, and these she baked on the fire in the usual way, setting them aside in the cupboard according as they were done. She then put down a large pot of new milk, which she made into curds and whey, and gave Fin due instructions how to use the curds when Cucullin should come. Having done all this, she sat down quite contented, waiting for his arrival on the next day about two o'clock, that being the hour at which he was expected—for Fin knew as much by the sucking of his thumb. Now, this was a curious property that Fin's thumb had; but, notwithstanding all the wisdom and logic he used, to suck out of it, it could never have stood to him here were it not for the wit of his wife. In this very thing, moreover, he was very much resembled by his great foe, Cucullin; for it was well known that the huge strength he possessed all lay in the middle finger of his right hand, and that, if he happened by any mischance to lose it, he was no more, notwithstanding his bulk, than a common man.

At length, the next day, he was seen coming across the valley, and Oonagh knew that it was time to commence operations. She immediately made the cradle, and desired Fin to lie down in it, and cover himself up with the clothes.

"You must pass for you own child," said she; "so just lie there snug, and say nothing, but be guided by me." This, to be sure, was wormwood to Fin—I mean going into the cradle in such a cowardly manner—but he knew Oonagh well ; and finding that he had nothing else for it, with a very rueful face he gathered himself into it, and lay snug, as she had desired him.

About two o'clock, as he had been expected, Cucullin came in. "God save all here !" said he; "is this where the great Fin M'Coul lives ? "

"Indeed it is, honest man," replied Oonagh; "God save you kindly—won't you be sitting ? "

"Thank you, ma'am," says he, sitting down ; "you're Mrs. M'Coul I suppose ? "

"I am," said she ; "and I have no reason, I hope, to be ashamed of my husband."

"No," said the other, "he has the name of being the strongest and bravest man in Ireland ; but for all that, there's a man not far from you that's very desirous of taking a shake with him. Is he at home ? "

"Why, then, no," she replied ; "and if ever a man left his house in a fury, he did. It appears that some one told him of a big basthoon of a giant called Cucullin being down at the Causeway to look for him, and so he set out there to try if he could catch him. Troth, I hope, for the poor giant's sake, he won't meet with him, for if he does, Fin will make paste of him at once."

"Well," said the other, "I am Cucullin, and I have been seeking him these twelve months, but he always kept clear of me ; and I will never rest night or day till I lay my hands on him."

At this Oonagh set up a loud laugh, of great contempt, by-the-way, and looked at him as if he was only a mere handful of a man.

"Did you ever see Fin?" said she, changing her manner all at once.

"How could I?" said he; "he always took care to keep his distance."

"I thought so," she replied; "I judged as much; and if you take my advice, you poor-looking creature, you'll pray night and day that you may never see him, for I tell you it will be a black day for you when you do. But, in the meantime, you perceive that the wind's on the door, and as Fin himself is from home, maybe you'd be civil enough to turn the house, for it's always what Fin does when he's here."

This was a startler even to Cucullin; but he got up, however, and after pulling the middle finger of his right hand until it cracked three times, he went outside, and getting his arms about the house, completely turned it as she had wished. When Fin saw this, he felt a certain description of moisture, which shall be nameless, oozing out through every pore of his skin; but Oonagh, depending upon her woman's wit, felt not a whit daunted.

"Arrah, then," said she, "as you are so civil, maybe you'd do another obliging turn for us, as Fin's not here to do it himself. You see, after this long stretch of dry weather we've had, we feel very badly off for want of water. Now, Fin says there's a fine spring-well somewhere under the rocks behind the hill here below, and it was his intention to pull them asunder; but having heard of you, he left the place in such a fury, that he never thought of it. Now, if you try to find it, troth I'd feel it a kindness."

She then brought Cucullin down to see the place, which was then all one solid rock; and, after looking at it for some time, he cracked his right middle finger nine times, and, stooping down, tore a cleft about four hundred feet deep, and a quarter of a mile in length, which has since

been christened by the name of Lumford's Glen. This
feat nearly threw Oonagh herself off her guard; but what
won't a woman's sagacity and presence of mind accomplish?

"You'll now come in," said she, "and eat a bit of such
humble fare as we can give you. Fin, even although he
and you are enemies, would scorn not to treat you kindly
in his own house; and, indeed, if I didn't do it even in
his absence, he would not be pleased with me."

She accordingly brought him in, and placing half-a-dozen
of the cakes we spoke of before him, together with a can
or two of butter, a side of boiled bacon, and a stack of
cabbage, she desired him to help himself—for this, be it
known, was long before the invention of potatoes.
Cucullin, who, by the way, was a glutton as well as a hero,
put one of the cakes in his mouth to take a huge whack
out of it, when both Fin and Oonagh were stunned with
a noise that resembled something between a growl and a
yell. "Blood and fury!" he shouted; "how is this?
Here are two of my teeth out! What kind of bread is
this you gave me?"

"What's the matter?" said Oonagh coolly.

"Matter!" shouted the other again; "why, here are the
two best teeth in my head gone."

"Why," said she, "that's Fin's bread—the only bread he
ever eats when at home; but, indeed, I forgot to tell you
that nobody can eat it but himself, and that child in the
cradle there. I thought, however, that, as you were
reported to be rather a stout little fellow of your size, you
might be able to manage it, and I did not wish to affront
a man that thinks himself able to fight Fin. Here's another cake—maybe it's not so hard as that."

Cucullin at the moment was not only hungry, but rav-
enous, so he accordingly made a fresh set at the second
cake, and immediately another yell was heard twice as
loud as the first. "Thunder and giblets!" he roared,
"take your bread out of this, or I will not have a tooth in
my head; there's another pair of them gone!"

" Well, honest man," replied Oonagh, " if you're not able to eat the bread, say so quietly, and don't be wakening the child in the cradle there. There, now, he's awake upon me."

Fin now gave a skirl that startled the giant, as coming from such a youngster as he was represented to be. " Mother," said he, " I'm hungry—get me something to eat." Oonagh went over, and putting into his hand a cake *that had no griddle in it*, Fin, whose appetite in the meantime was sharpened by what he saw going forward, soon made it disappear. Cucullin was thunderstruck, and secretly thanked his stars that he had the good fortune to miss meeting Fin, for, as he said to himself, I'd have no chance with a man who could eat such bread as that, which even his son that's but in his cradle can munch before my eyes.

" I'd like to take a glimpse at the lad in the cradle," said he to Oonagh; " for I can tell you that the infant who can manage that nutriment is no joke to look at, or to feed of a scarce summer."

" With all the veins of my heart," replied Oonagh; " get up, acushla, and show this decent little man something that won't be unworthy of your father, Fin M'Coul."

Fin, who was dressed for the occasion as much like a boy as possible, got up, and bringing Cucullin out, " Are you strong?" said he.

" Thunder an' ounds!" exclaimed the other, " what a voice in so small a chap!"

" Are you strong?" said Fin again; " are you able to squeeze water out of that white stone?" he asked, putting one into Cucullin's hand. The latter squeezed and squeezed the stone, but to no purpose; he might pull the rocks of Lumford's Glen asunder, and flatten a thunderbolt, but to squeeze water out of a white stone was beyond his strength. Fin eyed him with great contempt, as he kept straining and squeezing and squeezing and straining, till he got black in the face with the efforts.

" Ah, you're a poor creature!" said Fin. " You a

giant! Give me the stone here, and then I'll show what
Fin's little son can do; you may then judge of what my
daddy himself is."

Fin then took the stone, and slyly exchanging it for the
curds, he squeezed the latter until the whey, as clear as
water, oozed out in a little shower from his hand.

"I'll now go in," said he "to my cradle; for I scorn to
lose my time with any one that's not able to eat my
daddy's bread, or squeeze water out of a stone. Bedad,
you had better be off out of this before he comes back;
for if he catches you, it's in flummery he'd have you in
two minutes."

Cucullin, seeing what he had seen, was of the same
opinion himself; his knees knocked together with the
terror of Fin's return, and he accordingly hastened in to
bid Oonagh farewell, and to assure her, that from that
day out, he never wished to hear of, much less to see, her
husband. "I admit fairly that I'm not a match for him,"
said he, "strong as I am; tell him I will avoid him as I
would the plague, and that I will make myself scarce in
this part of the country while I live."

Fin, in the meantime, had gone into the cradle, where
he lay very quietly, his heart at his mouth with delight
that Cucullin was about to take his departure, without
discovering the tricks that had been played off on him.

"It's well for you," said Oonagh, "that he doesn't happen to be here, for it's nothing but hawk's meat he'd
make of you."

"I know that," says Cucullin; "devil a thing else he'd
make of me; but before I go, will you let me feel what
kind of teeth they are that can eat griddle-bread like
that?"—and he pointed to it as he spoke.

"With all pleasure in life," said she; "only, as they're
far back in his head, you must put your finger a good
way in."

Cucullin was surprised to find such a powerful set of
grinders in one so young; but he was still much more so
on finding, when he took his hand from Fin's mouth, that

he had left the very finger upon which his whole strength depended, behind him. He gave one loud groan, and fell down at once with terror and weakness. This was all Fin wanted, who now knew that his most powerful and bitterest enemy was completely at his mercy. He instantly started out of the cradle, and in a few minutes the great Cucullin, that was for such a length of time the terror of him and all his followers, lay a corpse before him. Thus did Fin, through the wit and invention of Oonagh, his wife, succeed in overcoming his enemy by stratagem, which he never could have done by force: and thus also is it proved that the women, if they bring us *into* many an unpleasant scrape, can sometimes succeed in getting us *out* of others that are as bad.

KINGS, QUEENS, PRINCESSES, EARLS, ROBBERS.

THE TWELVE WILD GEESE.*

PATRICK KENNEDY.

THERE was once a King and Queen that lived very happily together, and they had twelve sons and not a single daughter. We are always wishing for what we haven't, and don't dare for what we have, and so it was with the Queen. One day in winter, when the bawn was covered with snow, she was looking out of the parlor window, and saw there a calf that was just killed by the butcher, and a raven standing near it. " Oh," says she, " if I had only a daughter with her skin as white as that snow, her cheeks as red as that blood, and her hair as black as that raven, I'd give away every one of my twelve sons for her." The moment she said the word, she got a great fright, and a shiver went through her, and in an instant after, a severe-looking old woman stood before her. " That was a wicked wish you made," said she, "and to punish you it will be granted. You will have such a daughter as you desire, but the very day of her birth you will lose your other children." She vanished the moment she said the words.

And that very way it turned out. When she expected her delivery, she had her children all in a large room of the palace, with guards all around it, but the very hour her daughter came into the world, the guards inside and outside heard a great whirling, and whistling and the twelve princes were seen flying one after another out through the

* The Fireside Stories of Ireland.

376

open window, and away like so many arrows over the woods. Well, the king was in great grief for the loss of his sons, and he would be very enraged with his wife if he only knew that she was so much to blame for it.

Every one called the little princess Snow-white-and-Rose-red on account of her beautiful complexion. She was the most loving and lovable child that could be seen anywhere. When she was twelve years old she began to be very sad and lonely, and to torment her mother, asking her about her brothers that she thought were dead, for none up to that time ever told her the exact thing that happened them. The secret was weighing very heavy on the Queen's conscience, and as the little girl persevered in her questions, at last she told her. "Well, mother," said she, "it was on my account my poor brothers were changed into wild geese, and are now suffering all sorts of hardship; before the world is a day older, I'll be off to seek them, and try to restore them to their own shapes."

The King and Queen had her well watched, but all was no use. Next night she was getting through the woods that surrounded the palace, and she went on and on that night, and till the evening of next day. She had a few cakes with her, and she got nuts, and *mugoreens* (fruit of the sweet briar), and some sweet crabs, as she went along. At last she came to a nice wooden house just at sunset. There was fine garden round it, full of the handsomest flowers, and a gate in the hedge. She went in, and saw a table laid out with twelve plates, and twelve knives and forks, and twelve spoons, and there were cakes, and cold wild fowl, and fruit along with the plates, and there was a good fire, and in another long room there were twelve beds. Well, while she was looking about her she heard the gate opening, and footsteps along the walk, and in came twelve young men, and there was great grief and surprise on all their faces when they laid eyes on her. "Oh, what misfortune sent you here?" said the eldest. "For the sake of a girl we were obliged to leave our father's court, and be in the shape of wild geese all day.

That's twelve years ago, and we took a solemn oath that
we would kill the first young girl that came into our
hands. It's a pity to put such an innocent and handsome
girl as you are out of the world, but we must keep our
oath." "But," said she, "I'm your only sister, that
never knew anything about this till yesterday; and I
stole away from our father's and mother's palace last
night to find you out and relieve you if I can." Every
one of them clasped his hands, and looked down on the
floor, and you could hear a pin fall till the eldest cried
out, "A curse light on our oath! what shall we do?"
"I'll tell you that," said an old woman that appeared at
the instant among them. "Break your wicked oath,
which no one should keep. If you attempted to lay an
uncivil finger on her I'd change you into twelve *booliaun
buis* (stalks of ragweed), but I wish well to you as well as
to her. She is appointed to be your deliverer in this way.
She must spin and knit twelve shirts for you out of bog-
down, to be gathered by her own hands on the moor just
outside of the wood. It will take her five years to do it,
and if she once speaks, or laughs, or cries the whole time,
you will have to remain wild geese by day till you're
called out of the world. So take care of your sister; it is
worth your while." The fairy then vanished, and it was
only a strife with the brothers to see who would be first
to kiss and hug their sister.

So for three long years the poor young princess was occupied pulling bog-down, spinning it, and knitting it into
shirts, and at the end of the three years she had eight made.
During all that time, she never spoke a word, nor laughed
nor cried; the last was the hardest to refrain from. One
find day she was sitting in the garden spinning, when in
sprung a fine greyhound and bounded up to her, and laid
his paws on her shoulder, and licked her forehead and her
hair. The next minute a beautiful young prince rode up to
the little garden gate, took off his hat, and asked for leave
to come in. She gave him a little nod, and in he walked.
He made ever so many apologies for intruding, and asked

her ever so many questions, but not a word could he get out of her. He loved her so much from the first moment, that he could not leave her till he told her he was king of a country just bordering on the forest, and he begged her to come home with him, and be his wife. She couldn't help loving him as much as he did her, and though she shook her head very often, and was very sorry to leave her brothers, at last she nodded her head, and put her hand in his. She knew well enough that the good fairy and her brothers would be able to find her out. Before she went she brought out a basket holding all her bog-down, and another holding the eight shirts. The attendants took charge of these, and the prince placed her before him on his horse. The only thing that disturbed him while riding along was the displeasure his stepmother would feel at what he had done. However, he was full master at home, and as soon as he arrived he sent for the bishop, got his bride nicely dressed, and the marriage was celebrated, the bride answering by signs. He knew by her manners she was of high birth, and no two could be fonder of each other.

The wicked stepmother did all she could to make mischief, saying she was sure she was only a woodman's daughter; but nothing could disturb the young king's opinion of his wife. In good time the young queen was delivered of a beautiful boy, and the king was so glad he hardly knew what to do for joy. All the grandeur of the christening and the happiness of the parents tormented the bad woman more than I can tell you, and she determined to put a stop to all their comfort. She got a sleeping posset given to the young mother, and while she was thinking and thinking how she could best make away with the child, she saw a wicked-looking wolf in the garden, looking up at her, and licking his chops. She lost no time, but snatched the child from the arms of the sleeping woman, and pitched it out. The beast caught it in his mouth, and was over the garden fence in a minute. The wicked woman then pricked her own fingers, and dabbled the blood round the mouth of the sleeping mother.

Well, the young king was just then coming into the big bawn from hunting, and as soon as he entered the house, she beckoned to him, shed a few crocodile tears, began to cry and wring her hands, and hurried him along the passage to the bedchamber.

Oh, wasn't the poor king frightened when he saw the queen's mouth bloody, and missed his child? It would take two hours to tell you the devilment of the old queen, the confusion and fright, and grief of the young king and queen, the bad opinion he began to feel of his wife, and the struggle she had to keep down her bitter sorrow, and not give way to it by speaking or lamenting. The young king would not allow any one to be called, and ordered his stepmother to give out that the child fell from the mother's arms at the window, and that a wild beast ran off with it. The wicked woman pretended to do so, but she told underhand to everybody she spoke to what the king and herself saw in the bed-chamber.

The young queen was the most unhappy woman in the three kingdoms for a long time, between sorrow for her child, and her husband's bad opinion; still she neither spoke nor cried, and she gathered bog-down and went on with the shirts. Often the twelve wild geese would be seen lighting on the trees in the park or on the smooth sod, and looking in at her windows. So she worked on to get the shirts finished, but another year was at an end, and she had the twelfth shirt finished except one arm, when she was obliged to take to her bed, and a beautiful girl was born.

Now the king was on his guard, and he would not let the mother and child be left alone for a minute; but the wicked woman bribed some of the attendants, set others asleep, gave the sleepy posset to the queen, and had a person watching to snatch the child away, and kill it. But what should she see but the same wolf in the garden looking up, and licking his chops again! Out went the child, and away with it flew the wolf, and she smeared the sleeping mother's mouth and face with blood, and then roared, and bawled, and cried out to the king and to everybody she met, and the room was filled, and every one was sure the young queen had just devoured her own babe.

The poor mother thought now her life would leave her. She was in such a state she could neither think nor pray, but she sat like a stone, and worked away at the arm of the twelfth shirt.

The king was for taking her to the house in the wood where he found her, but the stepmother, and the lords of the court, and the judges would not hear of it, and she was condemned to be burned in the big bawn at three o'clock the same day. When the hour drew near, the king went to the farthest part of his palace, and there was no more unhappy man in his kingdom at that hour.

When the executioners came and led her off, she took the pile of shirts in her arms. There was still a few stitches wanted, and while they were tying her to the stakes she still worked on. At the last stitch she seemed over-come and dropped a tear on her work, but the moment after she sprang up, and shouted out, " I am innocent; call my husband!" The executioners stayed their hands, ex-cept one wicked-disposed creature, who set fire to the faggot next him, and while all were struck in amaze, there was a rushing of wings, and in a moment the twelve wild geese were standing around the pile. Before you could count twelve, she flung a shirt over each bird, and there in the twinkling of an eye were twelve of the finest young men that could be collected out of a thousand. While some were untying their sister, the eldest, taking a strong stake in his hand, struck the busy executioner such a blow that he never needed another.

While they were comforting the young queen, and the king was hurrying to the spot, a fine-looking woman ap-peared among them holding the babe on one arm and the little prince by the hand. There was nothing but crying for joy, and laughing for joy, and hugging and kissing, and when any one had time to thank the good fairy, who in the shape of a wolf, carried the child away, she was not to be found. Never was such happiness enjoyed in any palace that ever was built, and if the wicked' queen and her helpers were not torn by wild horses, they richly deserved it.

THE LAZY BEAUTY AND HER AUNTS.

PATRICK KENNEDY'S " FIREIDE STORIES OF IRELAND."

THERE was once a poor widow woman, who had a daughter that was as handsome as the day, and as lazy as a pig, saving your presence. The poor mother was the most industrious person in the townland, and was a particularly good hand at the spinning wheel. It was the wish of her heart that her daughter should be as handy as herself ; but she'd get up late, eat her breakfast before she'd finish her prayers, and then go about dawdling, and anything she handled seemed to be burning her fingers. She drawled her words as if it was a great trouble to her to speak, or as if her tongue was as lazy as her body. Many a heart-scald her poor mother got with her, and still she was only improving like dead fowl in August.

Well, one morning that things were as bad as they could be, and the poor woman was giving tongue at the rate of a mill-clapper, who should be riding by but the king's son. " Oh dear, oh dear, good woman ! " said he, " you must have a very bad child to make you scold so terribly. Sure it can't be this handsome girl that vexed you ! " " Oh, please your Majesty, not at all," says the old dissembler. " I was only checking her for working herself too much. Would your majesty believe it? She spins three pounds of flax in a day, weaves it into linen the

next, and makes it all into shirts the day ofter. " My
gracious," says the prince, "she's the very lady that will
just fill my mother's eye, and herself's the greatest spinner
in the kingdom.   Will you put on your daughter's bonnet
and cloak, if you please, ma'am, and set her behind me?
Why, my mother will be so delighted with her, that perhaps she'll make her her daughter-in-law in a week, that
is, if the young woman herself is agreeable."

Well, between the confusion, and the joy, and the fear
of being found out, the women didn't know what to do;
and before they could make up their minds, young Anty
(Anastasia) was set behind the prince, and away he and
his attendants went, and a good heavy purse was left behind with the mother.   She *pullillued* a long time after
all was gone, in dread of something bad happening to the
poor girl.

The prince couldn't judge of the girl's breeding or wit
from the few answers he pulled out of her.   The queen
was struck in a heap when she saw a young country girl
sitting behind her son, but when she saw her handsome
face, and heard all she could do, she didn't think she could
make too much of her.   The prince took an opportunity
of whispering her that if she didn't object to be his wife
she must strive to please his mother.   Well, the evening
went by, and the prince and Anty were getting fonder
and fonder of one another, but the thought of the spinning used to send the cold to her heart every moment.
When bed-time came, the old queen went along with her
to a beautiful bedroom, and when she was bidding her
good-night, she pointed to a heap of fine flax, and said,
" You may begin as soon as you like to-morrow morning,
and I'll expect to see these three pounds in nice thread
the morning after."   Little did the poor girl sleep that
night.   She kept crying and lamenting that she didn't
mind her mother's advice better.   When she was left
alone next morning, she began with a heavy heart; and
though she had a nice mahogany wheel and the finest flax
you ever saw, the thread was breaking every moment,

One while it was as fine as a cobweb, and the next as
coarse as a little boy's whipcord. At last she pushed
her chair back, let her hands fall in her lap, and burst
out a-crying.

A small, old woman with surprising big feet appeared
before her at the same moment, and said, "What ails
you, you handsome colleen?" "An' haven't I all that
flax to spin before to-morrow morning, and I'll never be
able to have even five yards of fine thread of it put together." "An' would you think bad to ask poor *Colliach
Cushmōr* (Old woman Big-foot) to your wedding with
the young prince? If you promise me that, all your
three pounds will be made into the finest of thread while
you're taking your sleep to-night." "Indeed, you must
be there and welcome, and I'll honor you all the days of
your life." "Very well; stay in your room till tea-time,
and tell the queen she may come in for her thread as early
as she likes to-morrow morning." It was all as she said;
and the thread was finer and evener than the gut you see
with fly-fishers. "My brave girl you were!" says the
queen. "I'll get my own mahogany loom brought into
you, but you needn't do anything more to-day. Work
and rest, work and rest, is my motto. To-morrow you'll
weave all this thread, and who knows what may
happen?"

The poor girl was more frightened this time than the
last, and she was so afraid to lose the prince. She didn't
even know how to put the warp in the gears, nor how to
use the shuttle, and she was sitting in the greatest grief,
when a little woman, who was mighty well-shouldered
about the hips, all at once appeared to her, told her her
name was *Colliach Cromanmōr*, and made the same bargain with her as Colliach Cushmōr. Great was the
queen's pleasure when she found early in the morning a
web as fine and white as the finest paper you ever saw.

"The darling you were!" says she. "Take your ease
with the ladies and gentlemen to-day, and if you have all
this made into nice shirts to-morrow you may present

one of them to my son, and be married to him out of hand."

Oh, wouldn't you pity poor Anty the next day, she was now so near the prince, and, maybe, would be soon so far from him. But she waited as patiently as she could with scissors, needle, and thread in hand, till a minute after noon. Then she was rejoiced to see the third old woman appear. She had a big red nose, and informed Anty that people called her *Shron Mor Rua* on that account. She was up to her as good as the others, for a dozen fine shirts were lying on the table when the queen paid her an early visit.

Now there was nothing talked of but the wedding, and I needn't tell you it was grand. The poor mother was there along with the rest, and at the dinner the old queen could talk of nothing but the lovely shirts, and how happy herself and the bride would be after the honeymoon, spinning, and weaving, and sewing shirts and shifts without end. The bridegroom didn't like the discourse, and the bride liked it less, and he was going to say something, when the footman came up to the head of the table and said to the bride, " Your ladyship's aunt, Colliach Cushmōr, bade me ask might she come in." The bride blushed and wished she was seven miles under the floor, but well became the prince. " Tell Mrs. Cushmōr," said he, " that any relation of my bride's will be always welcome wherever she and I are." In came the woman with the big foot, and got a seat near the prince. The old queen didn't like it much, and after a few words she asked rather spitefully, " Dear ma'am, what's the reason your foot is so big ? " " *Musha,* faith, your majesty, I was standing almost all my life at the spinning-wheel, and that's the reason." " I declare to you, my darling," said the prince, " I'll never allow you to spend one hour at the same spinning-wheel." The same footman said again, " Your ladyship's aunt, Colliach Cromanmōr, wishes to come in, if the genteels and yourself have no objection." Very *sharoose* (displeased) was Princess Anty, but the prince sent her welcome, and she took her seat, and drank healths apiece to the company. "May I ask, ma'am?" says the old queen, "why you're so wide half-way between the head and the feet?" "That, your majesty, is owing to sitting all my life at the loom." "By my sceptre," says the prince, "my wife shall never sit there an hour." The footman again came up. "Your ladyship's aunt, Colliach Shron Mor Rua, is asking leave to come into the banquet." More blushing on the bride's face, but the bridegroom spoke out cordially, "Tell Mrs. Shron Mor Rua she's doing us an honor." In came the old woman, and great respect she got near the top of the table, but the people down low put up their tumblers and glasses to their noses to hide the grins. "Ma'am," says the old queen, "will you tell us, if you please, why your nose is so big and red?" "Throth, your majesty, my head was bent down over the stitching all my life, and all the blood in my body ran into my nose." "My darling," said the prince to Anty, "if ever I see a needle in your hand, I'll run a hundred miles from you."

"And in troth, girls and boys, though it's a diverting story, I don't think the moral is good; and if any of you *thuckeens* go about imitating Anty in her laziness, you'll find it won't thrive with you as it did with her. She was beautiful beyond compare, which none of you are, and she had three powerful fairies to help her besides. There's no fairies now, and no prince or lord to ride by, and catch you idling or working; and maybe, after all, the prince and herself were not so very happy when the cares of the world or old age came on them."

Thus was the tale ended by poor old *Shebale* (Sybilla), Father Murphy's housekeeper, in Coolbawn, Barony of Bantry, about half a century since.

THE HAUGHTY PRINCESS.

BY PATRICK KENNEDY

THERE was once a very worthy king, whose daughter was the greatest beauty that could be seen far or near, but she was as proud as Lucifer, and no king or prince would she agree to marry. Her father was tired out at last, and invited every king, and prince, and duke, and earl that he knew or didn't know to come to his court to give her one trial more. They all came, and next day after breakfast they stood in a row in the lawn, and the princess walked along in the front of them to make her choice. One was fat, and says she, " I won't have you, Beer-barrel! " One was tall and thin, and to him she said, " I won't have you, Ramrod! " To a white-faced man she said, " I won't have you, Pale Death ; " and to a red-cheeked man she said, " I won't have you, Cockscomb! " She stopped a little before the last of all, for he was a fine man in face and form. She wanted to find some defect in him, but he had nothing remarkable but a ring of brown curling hair under his chin. She admired him a little, and then carried it off with, " I won't have you, Whiskers! "

So all went away, and the king was so vexed, he said to her, " Now to punish your *impedence*, I'll give you to the first beggarman or singing *sthronshuch* that calls ; " and, as sure as the hearth-money, a fellow all over rags, and hair that came to his shoulders, and a bushy red beard all over his face, came next morning, and began to sing before the parlor window.

When the song was over, the hall-door was opened, the singer asked in, the priest brought, and the princess married to Beardy. She roared and she bawled, but her father didn't mind her. " There," says he to the bride-

Fireside Stories of Ireland.

groom, " is five guineas for you. Take your wife out of my sight, and never let me lay eyes on you or her again."

Off he led her, and dismal enough she was. The only thing that gave her relief was the tones of her husband's voice and his genteel manners. " Whose wood is this ? " said she, as they were going through one. " It belongs to the king you called Whiskers yesterday." He gave her the same answer about meadows and corn-fields, and at last a fine city. " Ah, what a fool I was ! " said she to herself. " He was a fine man, and I might have him for a husband." At last they were coming up to a poor cabin. " Why are you bringing me here ? " says the poor lady. " This was my house," said he, " and now it's yours." She began to cry, but she was tired and hungry, and she went in with him.

Ovoch! there was neither a table laid out, nor a fire burning, and she was obliged to help her husband to light it, and boil their dinner, and clean up the place after ; and next day he made her put on a stuff gown and a cotton handkerchief. When she had her house readied up, and no business to keep her employed, he brought home *sallies* [willows], peeled them, and showed her how to make baskets. But the hard twigs bruised her delicate fingers, and she began to cry. Well, then he asked her to mend their clothes, but the needle drew blood from her fingers, and she cried again. He couldn't bear to see her tears, so he bought a creel of earthenware, and sent her to the market to sell them. This was the hardest trial of all, but she looked so handsome and sorrowful, and such a nice air about her, that all her pans, and jugs, and plates, and dishes were gone before noon, and the only mark of her old pride she showed was a slap she gave a buckeen across the face when he *axed* her to go in an' take share of a quart.

Well, her husband was so glad, he sent her with another creel the next day ; but faith ! her luck was after deserting her. A drunken huntsman came up riding, and his beast got in among her ware, and made *brishe* of

every mother's son of 'em. She went home cryin', and
her husband wasn't at all pleased. "I see," said he,
"you're not fit for business. Come along, I'll get you a
kitchen-maid's place in the palace. I know the cook."

So the poor thing was obliged to stifle her pride once
more. She was kept very busy, and the footman and the
butler would be very impudent about looking for a kiss,
but she let a screech out of her the first attempt was
made, and the cook gave the fellow such a lambasting
with the besom that he made no second offer. She went
home to her husband every night, and she carried broken
victuals wrapped in paper in her side pockets.

A week after she got service there was great bustle in
the kitchen. The king was going to be married, but no
one knew who the bride was to be. Well, in the evening
the cook filled the princess's pockets with cold meat and
puddings, and, says she, "Before you go, let us have a
look at the great doings in the big parlor." So they came
near the door to get a peep, and who should come out but
the king himself, as handsome as you please, and no
other but King Whiskers himself. "Your handsome
helper must pay for her peeping," said he to the cook,
"and dance a jig with me." Whether she would or no,
he held her hand and brought her into the parlor. The
fiddlers struck up, and away went *him* with *her*. But
they hadn't danced two steps when the meat and the
puddens flew out of her pockets. Every one roared out,
and she flew to the door, crying piteously. But she was
soon caught by the king, and taken into the back parlor.
"Don't you know me, my darling?" said he. "I'm both
King Whiskers, your husband the ballad-singer, and the
drunken huntsman. Your father knew me well enough
when he gave you to me, and all was to drive your pride
out of you." Well, she didn't know how she was with
fright, and shame, and joy. Love was uppermost anyhow, for she laid her head on her husband's breast and
cried like a child. The maids-of-honor soon had her
away and dressed her as fine as hands and pins could do

it; and there were her mother and father, too; and while
the company were wondering what end of the handsome
girl and the king, he and his queen, *who* they didn't know
in her fine clothes, and the other king and queen, came
in, and such rejoicings and fine doings as there was,
one of us will never see, any way.

THE ENCHANTMENT OF GEAROIDH IARLA.

BY PATRICK KENNEDY.*

IN old times in Ireland there was a great man of the
Fitzgeralds. The name on him was Gerald, but the Irish,
that always had a great liking for the family, called him
Gearoidh Iarla (Earl Gerald). He had a great castle or
rath at *Mullymast* (Mullaghmast); and whenever the
English Government were striving to put some wrong on
the country, he was always the man that stood up for it.
Along with being a great leader in a fight, and very skilful at all weapons, he was deep in the *black art*, and could
change himself into whatever shape he pleased. His
lady knew that he had this power, and often asked him
to let her into some of his secrets, but he never would
gratify her.

She wanted particularly to see him in some strange
shape, but he put her off and off on one pretense or other.
But she wouldn't be a woman if she hadn't perseverance;
and so at last he let her know that if she took the least
fright while he'd be out of his natural form, he would
never recover it till many generations of men would be
under the mould. "Oh! she wouldn't be a fit wife for
Gearoidh Iarla if she could be easily frightened. Let him
but gratify her in this whim, and he'd see what a hero she
was!"—So one beautiful summer evening, as they were
sitting in their grand drawing-room, he turned his face

* *Legendary Fiction of the Irish Celts.*

away from her and muttered some words, and while you'd wink he was clever and clean out of sight, and a lovely *goldfinch* was flying about the room.

The lady, as courageous as she thought herself, was a little startled, but she held her own pretty well, especially when he came and perched on her shoulder, and shook his wings, and put his little beak to her lips, and whistled the delightfulest tune you ever heard.   Well, he flew in circles round the room, and played *hide and go seek* with his lady, and flew out into the garden, and flew back again, and lay down in her lap as if he was asleep, and jumped up again.

Well, when the thing had lasted long enough to satisfy both, he took one flight more into the open air; but by my word he was soon on his return.   He flew right into his lady's bosom, and the next moment a fierce hawk was after him.   The wife gave one loud scream, though there was no need, for the wild bird came in like an arrow, and struck against a table with such force that the life was dashed out of him.   She turned her eyes from his quivering body to where she saw the goldfinch an instant before, but neither goldfinch nor Earl Gerald did she ever lay eyes on again.

Once every seven years the Earl rides round the Curragh of Kildare on a steed, whose silver shoes were half an inch thick the time he disappeared; and when these shoes are worn as thin as a cat's ear, he will be restored to the society of living men, fight a great battle with the English, and reign king of Ireland for two-score years.*

Himself and his warriors are now sleeping in a long cavern under the Rath of Mullaghmast.   There is a table running along through the middle of the cave.   The Earl is sitting at the head, and his troopers down along in complete armor both sides of the table, and their heads resting on it.   Their horses, saddled, and bridled, are standing behind their masters in their stalls at each side;

* The last time *Gearoidh Iarla* appeared the horse-shoes were as thin as a sixpence.

and when the day comes, the miller's son that's to be born
with six fingers on each hand, will blow his trumpet, and
the horses will stamp and whinny, and the knights awake
and mount their steeds, and go forth to battle.

Some night that happens once in every seven years,
while the Earl is riding round the Curragh, the entrance
may be seen by any one chancing to pass by.   About a
hundred years ago, a horse-dealer that was late abroad
and a little drunk, saw the lighted cavern, and went in.
The lights, and the stillness, and the sight of the men in
armor, cowed him a good deal, and he became sober.
His hands began to tremble, and he let a bridle fall on the
pavement.   The sound of the bit echoed through the
long cave, and one of the warriors that was next him
lifted his head a little, and said, in a deep hoarse voice,
"Is it time yet?"   He had the wit to say, "Not yet but
soon will," and the heavy helmet sunk down on the table.
The horse-dealer made the best of his way out, and
I never heard of any other one having got the same
opportunity.

MUNACHAR AND MANACHAR.

TRANSLATED LITERALLY FROM THE IRISH BY

DOUGLAS HYDE.

THERE once lived a Munachar and a Manachar, a long
time ago, and it is a long time since it was, and if they
were alive then they would not be alive now.   They went
out together to pick raspberries, and as many as Munachar
used to pick Manachar used to eat.   Munachar said he
must go look for a rod to make a gad (a withy band, to
hang Manachar, who ate his raspberries every one; and
he came to the rod.   "God save you," said the rod.   "God
and Mary save you." "How far are you going?"   "Going

looking for a rod, a rod to make a gad, a gad to hang Manachar, who ate my raspberries every one."

"You will not get me," said the rod, "until you get
an axe to cut me." He came to the axe. "God save
you," said the axe. "God and Mary save you." "How
far are you going?" "Going looking for an axe, an axe
to cut a rod, a rod to make a gad, a gad to hang Manachar,
who ate my raspberries every one."

"You will not get me," said the axe, "until you get a
flag to edge me." He came to the flag. "God save you,"
says the flag." "God and Mary save you." "How far
are you going?" "Going looking for an axe, axe to cut
a rod, a rod to make a gad, a gad to hang Manachar, who
ate my raspberries every one."

"You will not get me," says the flag, "till you get
water to wet me." He came to the water. "God save
you," says the water. "God and Mary save you." "How
far are you going?" "Going looking for water, water to
wet flag to edge axe, axe to cut a rod, a rod to make a gad,
a gad to hang Manachar, who ate my raspberries every
one."

"You will not get me," said the water, "until you get
a deer who will swim me." He came to the deer. "God
save you," says the deer. "God and Mary save you."
"How far are you going?" "Going looking for a deer,
deer to swim water, water to wet flag, flag to edge axe,
axe to cut a rod, a rod to make a gad, a gad to hang
Manachar, who ate my raspberries every one."

"You will not get me," said the deer, "until you get a
hound who will hunt me." He came to the' hound.
"God save you," says the hound. "God and Mary save
you. "How far are you going?" "Going looking for a
hound, hound to hunt deer, deer to swim water, water to
wet flag, flag to edge axe, axe to cut a rod, a rod to make
a gad, a gad to hang Manachar, who ate my raspberries
every one.

"You will not get me," said the hound, "until you get
a bit of butter to put in my claw." He came to the butter.

" God save you," says the butter. " God and Mary save you." " How far are you going?" " Going looking for butter, butter to go in claw of hound, hound to hunt deer, deer to swim water, water to wet flag, flag to edge axe, axe to cut a rod, a rod to make a gad, a gad to hang Manachar, who ate my raspberries every one."

" You will not get me," said the butter, " until you get a cat who will scrape me." He came to the cat. " God save you," said the cat. " God and Mary save you." " How far are you going?" " Going looking for a cat, cat to scrape butter, butter to go in claw of hound, hound to hunt deer, deer to swim water, water to wet flag, flag to edge axe, axe to cut a rod, a rod to make a gad, gad to hang Manachar, who ate my raspberries every one."

" You will not get me," said the cat, " until you will get milk which you will give me." He came to the cow. " God save you," said the cow. " God and Mary save you." " How far are you going?" " Going looking for a cow, cow to give me milk, milk I will give to the cat, cat to scrape butter, butter to go in claw of hound, hound to hunt deer, deer to swim water, water to wet flag, flag to edge axe, axe to cut a rod, a rod to make a gad, a gad to hang Manachar, who ate my raspberries every one."

" You will not get any milk from me," said the cow, " until you bring me a whisp of straw from those threshers yonder." He came to the threshers. " God save you," said the threshers. " God and Mary save ye." " How far are you going?" " Going looking for a whisp of straw from ye to give to the cow, the cow to give me milk, milk I will give to the cat, cat to scrape butter, butter to go in claw of hound, hound to hunt deer, deer to swim water, water to wet flag, flag to edge axe, axe to cut a rod, a rod to make a gad, a gad to hang Manachar, who ate my raspberries every one."

" You will not get any whisp of straw from us," said the threshers, " until you bring us the makings of a cake from the miller over yonder." He came to the miller. " God save you." " God and Mary save you." How far are you going?" "Going looking for the makings of a cake, which I will give to the threshers, the threshers to give me a whisp of straw, the whisp of straw I will give to the cow, the cow to give me milk, milk I will give to the cat, cat to scrape butter, butter to go in claw of hound, hound to hunt deer, deer to swim water, water to wet flag, flag to edge axe, axe to cut a rod, a rod to make a gad, a gad to hang Manachar, who ate my raspberries every one.

"You will not get any makings of a cake from me," said the miller, "till you bring me the full of that sieve of water from the river over there."

He took the sieve in his hand and went over to the river, but as often as ever he would stoop and fill it with water, the moment he raised it the water would run out of it again, and sure, if he had been there from that day till this, he never could have filled it. A crow went flying by him, over his head. "Daub! daub!" said the crow. "My soul to God, then," said Munachar, "but it's the good advice you have," and he took the red clay and the daub that was by the brink, and he rubbed it to the bottom of the sieve, until all the holes were filled, and then the sieve held the water, and he brought the water to the miller, and the miller gave him the makings of a cake, and he gave the makings of the cake to the threshers, and the threshers gave him a whisp of straw, and he gave the whisp of straw to the cow, and the cow gave him milk, the milk he gave to the cat, the cat scraped the butter, the butter went into the claw of the hound, the hunted the deer, the deer swam the water, the water wet the flag, the flag sharpened the axe, the axe cut the rod, and the rod made a gad, and when he had it ready—I'll go bail that Manachar was far enough away from him.

There is some tale like this in almost every language, It resembles that given in that splendid work of industry and patriotism, Campbell's *Tales of the West Highlands* under the name of *Moonachug and Meenachug.* "The English House that Jack built," says Campbell, "has eleven steps, the Scotch Old Woman with the Silver Penny has twelve, the Novsk Cock and Hen

A-nutting has twelve, ten of which are double. The German story in Grimm has five or six, all single ideas." This, however, is longer than any of them. It sometimes varies a little in the telling, and the actors' names are sometimes *Suracha* and *Muracha* and the crow is sometimes a gull, who, instead of *daub! daub!* says *cuir cré rua lesh!*

DONALD AND HIS NEIGHBORS.

*From Hibernian Tales.**

HUDDEN and Dudden and Donald O'Nery were near neighbors in the barony of Balinconlig, and plowed with three bullocks; but the two former, envying the present prosperity of the latter, determined to kill his bullock, to prevent his farm being properly cultivated and labored, that going back in the world he might be induced to sell his lands, which they meant to get possession of. Poor Donald finding his bullock killed, immediately skinned it, and throwing the skin over his shoulder, with the fleshy side, out, set off to the next town with it, to dispose of it to the best of his advantage. Going along to road a magpie flew on the top of the hide, and began picking it, chattering all the time. The bird been taught to speak, and imitate the human voice, and Donald, thinking he understood some words it was saying, put round his hand and caught hold of it. Having got possession of it, he put it under his great-coat, and so went on to town. Having sold the hide, he went into an inn to take a dram, and following the landlady into the cellar, he gave the bird a squeeze which made it chatter some broken accents that surprised her very much. "What is that I hear?" said she to Donald. "I think it is talk, and yet I do not understand." "Indeed," said Donald, "it is a bird I have that tells me everything, and I always carry it with me to know when there is any

* A chap-book mentioned by Thackeray in his *Irish Sketch Book*.

danger. Faith," says he, " it says you have far better liquor
than you are giving me." "That is strange," said she,
going to another cask of better quality, and asking him if
he would sell the bird. "I will," said Donald, "if I get
enough for it." "I will fill your hat with silver if you leave
it with me." Donald was glad to hear the news, and taking
the silver, set off, rejoicing at his good luck. He had not
been long at home until he met with Hudden and Dudden.
"Mr." said he, "you thought you had done me a bad turn,
but you could not have done me a better ; for look here,
what I have got for the hide," showing them a hatful of
silver ; "you never saw such a demand for hides in your
life as there is at present." Hudden and Dudden that
very night killed their bullocks, and set out the next
morning to sell their hides. On coming to the place
they went through all the merchants, but could only
get a trifle for them; at last they had to take what they
could get, and came home in a great rage, and vowing
revenge on poor Donald. He had a pretty good guess
how matters would turn out, and he being under the
kitchen window, he was afraid they would rob him, or
perhaps kill him when asleep, and on that account when
he was going to bed he left his old mother in his place,
and lay down in her bed, which was in the other side of the
house, and they taking the old woman for Donald, choked
her in her bed, but he making some noise, they had to
retreat, and leave the money behind them, which grieved
them very much. However, by daybreak, Donald got
his mother on his back, and carried her to town. Stopping at a well, he fixed his mother with her staff, as if
she was stooping for a drink, and then went into a public-
house convenient and called for a dram. "I wish," said
he to a woman that stood near him, "you would tell my
mother to come in ; she is at yon well trying to get a
drink, and she is hard of hearing ; if she does not observe
you, give her a little shake and tell her that I want her."
The woman called her several times, but she seemed to
take no notice; at length she went to her and shook her

by the arm, but when she let her go again, she tumbled on her head into the well, and, as the woman thought, was drowned. She, in her great surprise and fear at the accident, told Donald what had happened. " O mercy," said he, " what is this ? " He ran and pulled her out of the well, weeping and lamenting all the time, and acting in such a manner that you would imagine that he had lost his senses. The woman, on the other hand, was far worse than Donald, for his grief was only feigned, but she imagined herself to be the cause of the old woman's death. The inhabitants of the town hearing what had happened, agreed to make Donald up a good sum of money for his loss, as the accident happened in their place, and Donald brought a greater sum home with him than he got for the magpie. They buried Donald's mother, and as soon as he saw Hudden he showed them the last purse of money he had got. " You thought to kill me last night," said he, " but it was good for me it happened on my mother, for I got all that purse for her to make gunpowder."

That very night Hudden and Dudden killed their mothers, and the next morning set off with them to town. On coming to the town with their burthen on their backs, they went up and down crying, " Who will buy old wives for gunpowder," so that every one laughed at them, and the boys at last clotted them out of the place. They then saw the cheat and vowed revenge on Donald, buried the old women, and set off in pursuit of him. Coming to his house, they found him sitting at his breakfast, and seizing him, put him in a sack, and went to drown him in a river at some distance. As they were going along the highway they raised a hare, which they saw had but three feet, and throwing off the sack, ran after her, thinking by her appearance she would be easily taken. In their absence there came a drover that way, and hearing Donald singing in the sack, wondered greatly what could be the matter. " What is the reason," said he, " that you are singing, and you confined ? " " O, I am going to heaven," said Donald, "and in a short time I

expect to be free from trouble." "O dear," said the
drover, "what will I give you if you let me to your
place?" "Indeed, I do not know," said he, "it would
take a good sum." "I have not much money," said the
drover, "but I have twenty head of fine cattle, which I
will give you to exchange places with me." "Well," says
Donald, "I do not care if I should loose the sack, and I
will come out." In a moment the drover liberated him,
and went into the sack himself, and Donald drove home
the fine heifers, and left them in his pasture.

Hudden and Dudden having caught the hare, returned,
and getting the sack on one of their backs, carried Donald,
as they thought, to the river and threw him in, where he
immediately sank. They then marched home, intending
to take immediate possession of Donald's property, but how
great was their surprise when they found him safe at home
before them, with such a fine herd of cattle, whereas they
knew he had none before. "Donald," said they, "what is
all this? We thought you were drowned, and yet you
are here before us." "Ah!" said he, "if I had but help
along with me when you threw me in, it would have been
the best job ever I met with, for of all the sight of cattle
and gold that ever was seen is there, and no one to own
them, but I was not able to manage more than what you
see, and I could show you the spot where you might get
hundreds." They both swore they would be his friend,
and Donald accordingly led them to a very deep part of the
river, and lifted up a stone. "Now," said he, "watch
this," throwing it into the stream; "there is the very
place, and go in, one of you first, and if you want help,
you have nothing to do but call." Hudden, jumping in,
and sinking to the bottom, rose up again, and making a
bubbling noise, as those do that are drowning, attempted
to speak, but could not. "What is that he is saying
now?" says Dudden. "Faith," says Donald, "he is calling for help; don't you hear him? Stand about," said
he, running back, "till I leap in. I know how to do it
better than any of you." Dudden, to have the advantage

of him, jumped in off the bank, and was drowned along with Hudden, and this was the end of Hudden and Dudden.

THE JACKDAW.

Tom Moor was a linen draper in Sackville Street. His father, when he died, left him an affluent fortune, and a shop of excellent trade.

As he was standing at his door one day a countryman came up to him with a nest of jackdaws, and accosting him, says, "Master, will you buy a nest of daws?" "No, I don't want any," "Master," replied the man, "I will sell them all cheap; you shall have the whole nest for ninepence." "I don't want them," answered Tom Moor, "so go about your business."

As the man was walking away one of the daws popped out his head, and cried "Mawk, mawk." "Damn it," says Tom Moor, "that bird knows my name; halloo, countryman, what will you take for the bird?" "Why, you shall have him for threepence." Tom Moor bought him, had a cage made, and hung him up in the shop.

The journeymen took much notice of the bird, and would frequently tap at the bottom of the cage, and say, "Who are you? Who are you? Tom Moor of Sackville Street."

In a short time the jackdaw learned these words, and if he wanted victuals or water, would strike his bill against the cage, turn up the white of his eyes, cock his head, and cry, "Who are you? Who are you? Tom Moor of Sackville Street."

Tom Moor was fond of gaming, and often lost large sums of money; finding his business neglected in his absence, he had a small hazard table set up in one corner of his dining-room, and invited a party of his friends to play at it.

The Jackdaw had by this time become familiar; his cage was left open, and he hopped into every part of the house; sometimes he got into the dining-room, where the gentlemen were at play, and one of them being a constant winner, the others would say, "Damn it, how he nicks them." The bird learned these words also, and adding them to the former, would call, "Who are you? who are you? Tom Moor of Sackville Street. Damn it, how he nicks them."

Tom Moor, from repeated losses and neglect of business, failed in trade, and became a prisoner in the Fleet; he took his bird with him, and lived on the master's side, supported by friends, in a decent manner. They would sometimes ask what brought you here? when he used to lift up his hands and answer, "Bad company, by G—." The bird learned this likewise, and at the end of the former words, would say, "What brought you here? Bad company, by G—."

Some of Tom Moor's friends died, others went abroad, and by degrees he was totally deserted, and removed to the common side of the prison, where the jail distemper soon attacked him: and in the last stage of life lying on a straw bed; the poor bird had been for two days without food or water, came to his feet, and striking his bill on the floor, calls out, "Who are you? Tom Moor of Sackville Street; damn it, how he nicks them, damn it, how he nicks them. What brought you here? bad company, by G—, bad company, by G—."

Tom Moor, who had attended to the bird, was struck with his words, and reflecting on himself, cried out, "Good God, to what a situation am I reduced! my father, when he died, left me a good fortune and an established trade. I have spent my fortune, ruined my business, and am now dying in a loathsome jail; and to complete all, keeping that poor thing confined without support. I will endeavor to do one piece of justice before I die, by setting him at liberty."

He made a struggle to crawl from his straw bed, opened

the casement, and out flew the bird.   A flight of jackdaws
from the Temple were going over the jail, and Tom Moor's
bird mixed among them.   The gardener was then laying
the plats of the Temple gardens, and as often as he placed
them in the day the jackdaws pulled them up by night.
They got a gun and attempted to shoot some of them ;
but, being cunning birds, they always placed one as a
watch in the stump of a hollow tree ; who, as soon as the
gun was leveled cried " Mawk," and away they flew.

The gardeners were advised to get a net, and the first
night it was spread they caught fifteen ; Tom Moor's
bird was amongst them.   One of the men took the net
into a garret of an uninhabited house, fastens the doors
and windows, and turns the birds loose.   " Now," said he,
" you black rascals, I will be revenged of you."   Taking
hold of the first at hand, he twists her neck, and throwing him down, cries, " There goes one."   Tom Moor's bird,
who had hopped up to a beam at one corner of the room
unobserved, as the man lays hold of the second, calls out,
" Damn it, how he nicks them."   The man alarmed, cries,
" Sure I heard a voice, but the house is uninhabited, and
the door is fast ; it could only be imagination."   On laying
hold of the third, and twisting his neck, Tom's bird again
says, " Damn it, how he nicks them."   The man dropped
the bird in his hand, and turning to where the voice came
from, seeing the other with his mouth open, cries out,
" Who are you ? " to which the bird answered, " Tom Moor
of Sackville Street, Tom Moor of Sackville Street."   " The
devil you are ; and what brought you here."   Tom Moor's
bird, lifting up his pinions, answered, " Bad company, by
G—, bad company, by G—."   The fellow, frightened almost out of his wits, opened the door, ran down stairs, and
out of the house, followed by all the birds, who by this
means regained their liberty.

THE STORY OF CONN-EDA; OR, THE GOLDEN APPLES OF LOUGH ERNE.*

Translated from the original Irish of the Story-teller,
ABRAHAM McCoy, *by* NICHOLAS O'KEARNEY.

IT was long before the time the western districts of *Innis Fodhla* † had any settled name, but were indiscriminately called after the person who took possession of them, and whose name they retained only as long as his sway lasted, that a powerful king reigned over this part of the sacred island. He was a puissant warrior, and no individual was found able to compete with him either on land or sea, or question his right to his conquest. The great king of the west held uncontrolled sway from the island of Rathlin to the mouth of the Shannon by sea, and far as the glittering length by land. The ancient king of the west, whose name was Conn, was good as well as great, and passionately loved by his people. His queen was a *Breaton* (British) princess, and was equally beloved and esteemed, because she was the great counterpart of the king in every respect; for whatever good qualification was wanting in the one, the other was certain to indemnify the omission. It was plainly manifest that heaven approved of the career in life of the virtuous couple; for during their reign the earth produced exuberant crops, the trees fruit ninefold commensurate with their usual bearing, the rivers, lakes, and surrounding sea teemed with abundance of choice fish, while herds and flocks were unusually prolific, and kine and sheep yielded such abundance of rich milk that they shed it in torrents upon the pastures; and furrows and cavities were always filled with the pure lacteal produce of the dairy.

* Printed first in the *Cambrian Journal*, 1855; reprinted and re-edited in the *Folk-Lore Record*, vol. ii.

† *Innis Fodhla*—Island of Destiny, an old name for Ireland,

All these were blessings heaped by heaven upon the western districts of *Innis Fodhla*, over which the benignant and just Conn swayed his scepter, in approbation of the course of government he had marked out for his own guidance. It is needless to state that the people who owned the authority of this great and good sovereign were the happiest on the face of the wide expanse of earth. It was during his reign, and that of his son and successor, that Ireland acquired the title of the "happy isle of the west" among foreign nations. Conn Mór and his good Queen Eda reigned in great glory during many years; they were blessed with an only son, whom they named Conn-eda, after both his parents, because the Druids foretold at his birth that he would inherit the good qualities of both. According as the young prince grew in years, his amiable and benignant qualities of mind, as well as his great strength of body and manly bearing, became more manifest. He was the idol of his parents, and the boast of his people; he was beloved and respected to that degree that neither prince, lord, nor plebeian swore an oath by the sun, moon, stars, or elements, except by the head of Conn-eda. This career of glory, however, was doomed to meet a powerful but temporary impediment, for the good Queen Eda took a sudden and severe illness, of which she died in a few days, thus plunging her spouse, her son, and all her people into a depth of grief and sorrow from which it was found difficult to relieve them.

The good king and his subjects mourned the loss of Queen Eda for a year and a day, and at the expiration of that time Conn Mór reluctantly yielded to the advice of his Druids and counsellors, and took to wife the daughter of his Arch-Druid. The new queen appeared to walk in the footsteps of the good Eda for several years, and gave great satisfaction to her subjects. But, in course of time, having had several children, and perceiving that Conn-eda was the favorite son of the king and the darling of the people, she clearly foresaw that he would become suc-

cessor to the throne after the demise of his father, and
that her son would certainly be excluded. This excited
the hatred and inflamed the jealousy of the Druid's daughter against her step-son to such an extent that she resolved in her own mind to leave nothing in her power undone to secure his death, or even exile from the kingdom,
She began by circulating evil reports of the prince; but,
as he was above suspicion, the king only laughed at the
weakness of the queen ; and the great princes and chieftains, supported by the people in general, gave an unqual-
ified contradiction ; while the prince himself bore all his
trials with the utmost patience, and always repaid her bad
and malicious acts towards him with good and benevolent
ones. The enmity of the queen towards Conn-eda knew
no bounds when she saw that the false reports she circulated could not injure him. As a last resource, to carry
out her wicked projects, she determined to consult her
Cailleach-chearc (hen-wife), who was a reputed enchantress.

Pursuant to her resolution, by the early dawn of morning she hied to the cabin of the *Cailleach- Chearc,* and di-
vulged to her the cause of her trouble. " I cannot render
you any help," said the *Cailleach,* " until you name the
duais " (reward). " What *duais* do you require," asked
the queen, impatiently. " My *duais,*" replied the enchantress, " is to fill the cavity of my arm with wool, and the
hole I shall bore with my distaff with red wheat." " Your
duais is granted, and shall be immediately given you," said
the queen. The enchantress thereupon stood in the door of
her hut, and bending her arm into a circle with her side,
directed the royal attendants to thrust the wool into her
house through her arm, and she never permitted them to
cease until all the available space within was filled with
wool. She then got on the roof of her brother's house,
and, having made a hole through it with her distaff,
caused red wheat to be spilled through it, until that was
filled up to the roof with red wheat, so that there was no
room for another grain within. " Now," said the queen,

" since you have received your *duais*, tell me how I can accomplish my purpose." " Take this chess-board and chess and invite the prince to play with you; you shall win the first game. The condition you shall make is, that whoever wins a game shall be at liberty to impose whatever *geasa* (condition) the winner pleases on the loser. When you win, you must bid the prince, under the penalty either to go into *ionarbadh* (exile), or procure for you, within the space of a year and a day, the three golden apples that grew in the garden, the *each dubh* (black steed), and *cuileen con na mbuadh* (hound of supernatural powers), called Samer, which are in the possession of the king of the Firbolg race, who resides in Lough Erne.* Those two things are so precious, and so well guarded, that he can never attain them by his own power; and if he would rashly attempt to seek them, he should lose his life."

The queen was greatly pleased at the advice, and lost no time in inviting Conn-eda to play a game at chess, under the conditions she had been instructed to arrange by the enchantress. The queen won the game, as the enchantress foretold, but so great was her anxiety to have the prince completely in her power, that she was tempted to challenge him to play a second game, which Conn-eda, to her astonishment, and no less mortification, easily won. " Now," said the prince, " since you won the first game, it is your duty to impose your *geis* first." " My *geis*," said the queen, " which I impose upon you, is to procure me the three golden apples that grow in the garden, the *each dubh* (black steed), and *cuileen con na mbuadh* (hound of supernatual powers), which are in keeping of the king of the Firbolgs, in Lough Erne, within the space of a year and a day ; or, in case you fail, to go into *ionarbadh* (exile). and never return, except you surrender yourself to lose your head and *comhead beatha* (preservation of life).

* The Firbolgs believed their elysium to be under water. The peasantry still believe many lakes to be peopled. See section on *T'yeer-na-n-Oge.*

"Well, then," said the prince, "the *geis* which I bind
you by, is to sit upon the pinnacle of yonder tower until
my return, and to take neither food nor nourishment of
any description, except what red-wheat you can pick up
with the point of your bodkin ; but if I do not return, you
are at perfect liberty to come down at the expiration of
the year and a day."

In consequence of the severe *geis* imposed upon him,
Conn-eda was very much troubled in mind ; and, well knowing he had a long journey to make before he would reach
his destination, immediately prepared to set out on his
way, not, however, before he had the satisfaction of wit-
nessing the ascent of the queen to the place where she was
obliged to remain exposed to the scorching sun of the summer and the blasting storms of winter, for the space of one
year and a day, at least.   Conn-eda being ignorant of what
steps he should take to procure the *each dubh* and *cuileen
con na mbuadh*, though he was well aware that human
energy would prove unavailing, thought proper to consult
the great Druid, Fionn Dadhna, of Sleabh Badhna, who
was a friend of his before he ventured to proceed to Lough
Erne.   When he arrived at the bruighean of the Druid,
he was received with cordial friendship, and the *failte* (welcome), as usual, was poured out before him, and when he
was seated, warm water was fetched, and his feet bathed,
so that the fatigue he felt after his journey was greatly
relieved.   The Druid, after he had partaken of refreshments, consisting of the newest of food and oldest of liquors,
asked him the reason for paying the visit, and more particularly the cause of his sorrow ; for the prince appeared
exceedingly depressed in spirit.   Conn-eda told his friend
the whole history of the transaction with his stepmother
from the beginning to end.   "Can you not assist me ? "
asked the Prince, with downcast countenance.   " I cannot,
indeed, assist you at present," replied the Druid ; " but I
will retire to my *grianan* (green place) at sun-rising on
the morrow, and learn by virtue of my Druidism what
can be done to assist you."   The Druid, accordingly, as

the sun rose on the following morning, retired to his *grianan*, and consulted the god he adored, through the power of his *draoidheacht*.* When he returned, he called Conn-eda aside on the plain, and addressed him thus : ' My dear son, I find you have been under a severe—an almost impossible—*geis* intended for your destruction ; no person on earth could have advised the queen to impose it except the Cailleach of Lough Corrib, who is the greatest Druidess now in Ireland, and sister to the Firbolg, King of Lough Erne. It is not in my power, nor in that of the Deity I adore, to interfere in your behalf ; but go directly to Sliabh Mis, and consult *Eánchinn-duine* (the bird of the human head), and if there be any possibility of relieving you, that bird can do it, for there is not a bird in the western world so celebrated as that bird, because it knows all things that are past, all things that are present and exist, and all things that shall hereafter exist. It is difficult to find access to his place of conceal-ment, and more difficult still to obtain an answer from him ; but I will endeavor to regulate that matter for you ; and that is all I can do for you at present."

The Arch-Druid then instructed him thus :—" Take," said he, " yonder little shaggy steed, and mount him im-mediately, for in three days the bird will make himself visible, and the little shaggy steed will conduct you to his place of abode. But lest the bird should refuse to reply to your queries, take this precious stone (*leag lorgmhar*), and present it to him, and then little danger and doubt exist but that he will give you a ready answer." The prince returned heartfelt thanks to the Druid, and, having saddled and mounted the little shaggy horse without much delay, received the precious stone from the Druid, and, after having taken his leave of him, set out on his journey. He suffered the reins to fall loose upon the neck of the horse according as he had been instructed, so that the animal took whatever road he chose.

* *Draoidhèacht, i.e.*, the Druidic worship ; magic, sorcery, divination.

It would be tedious to relate the numerous adventures he had with the little shaggy horse, which had the extraordinary gift of speech, and was a *draoidheacht* horse during his journey.

The Prince having reached the hiding-place of the strange bird at the appointed time, and having presented him with the *leag lorgmhar*, according to Fionn Badhna's instructions, and proposed his questions relative to the manner he could best arrange for the fulfilment of his *geis*, the bird took up in his mouth the jewel from the stone on which it was placed, and flew to an inaccessible rock at some distance, and, when there perched, he thus addressed the prince, " Conn-eda, son of the King of Cruachan," said he, in a loud, croaking human voice, " remove the stone just under your right foot, and take the ball of iron and *corna* (cup) you shall find under it; then mount your horse, cast the ball before you, and having so done, your horse will tell you all the other things necessary to be done." The bird, having said this, immediately flew out of sight.

Donn-eda took great care to do everything according to the instructions of the bird. He found the iron ball and *corna* in the place which had been pointed out. He took them up, mounted his horse, and cast the ball before him. The ball rolled on at a regular gait, while the little shaggy horse followed on the way it led until they reached the margin of Lough Erne. Here the ball rolled in the water and became invisible. " Alight now," said the *draoidheacht* pony, " and put your hand into mine ear; take from thence the small bottle of *ice* (all-heal) and the little wicker basket which you will find there, and remount with speed, for just now your great dangers and difficulties commence." Conneda, ever faithful to the kind advice of his *draoidheacht* pony, did what he had been advised. Having taken the basket and bottle of *ice* from the animal's ear, he remounted and proceeded on his journey, while the water of the lake appeared only like an atmosphere above his head. When he entered the lake the ball again appeared, and rolled along until it came to the margin, across which was a causeway, guarded by three frightful serpents; the hissings of the monsters was heard at a great distance, while, on a nearer approach, their yawning mouths and formidable fangs were quite sufficient to territy the stoutest heart. "Now," said the horse, "open the basket and cast a piece of the meat you find in it into the mouth of each serpent; when you have done this, secure yourself in your seat in the best manner you can, so that we may make all due arrangements to pass those *draoidheacht peists*. If you cast the pieces of meat into the mouth of each *peist* unerringly, we shall pass them safely, otherwise we are lost." Conn-eda flung the pieces of meat into the jaws of the serpents with unerring aim. "Bare a benison and victory," said the *draoidheaeht* steed, "for you are a youth that will win and prosper." And, on saying these words, he sprang aloft, and cleared in his leap the river and ford, guarded by the serpents, seven measures beyond the margin. "Arc you still mounted, prince Conn-eda?" said the steed. "It has taken only half my exertion to remain so," replied Conn-eda. "I find," said the pony, "that you are a young prince that deserves to succeed; one danger is now over, but two others remain." They proceeded onwards after the ball until they came in view of a great mountain flaming with fire. "Hold yourself in readiness for another dangerous leap," said the horse. The trembling prince had no answer to make, but seated himself as securely as the magnitude of the danger before him would permit. The horse in the next instant sprang from the earth, and flew like an arrow over the burning mountain. "Are you still alive, Conn-eda, son of Conn-mór?" inquired the faithful horse. "I'm just alive, and no more, for I'm greatly scorched," answered the prince. "Since you are yet alive, I feel assured that you are a young man destined to meet supernatural success and benisons," said the Druidic steed. "Our greatest dangers are over," added he, "and there is hope that we shall overcome the next and last danger." After they had proceeded a short distance, his faithful steed, addressing Conn-eda, said, " Alight, now, and apply a portion of the little bottle of *ice* to your wounds." The prince immediately followed the advice of his monitor, and, as soon as he rubbed the *ice* (all-heal) to his wounds, he became as whole and fresh as ever he had been before. After having done this, Conn-eda remounted, and following the track of the ball, soon came in sight of a great city surrounded by high walls. The only gate that was visible was not defended by armed men, but by two great towers that emitted flames that could be seen at a great distance. " Alight on this plain," said the steed, "and take a small knife from my other ear; and with this knife you shall kill and flay me. When you have done this, envelop yourself in my hide, and you can pass the gate unscathed and unmolested. When you get inside you can come out at pleasure; because when once you enter there is no danger, and you can pass and repass whenever you wish; and let me tell you that all I have to ask of you in return is that you, when once inside the gates, will immediately return and drive away the birds of prey that may be fluttering round to feed on my carcass; and more, that you will pour any drop of that powerful *ice*, if such still remain in the bottle, upon my flesh, to preserve it from corruption. When you do this in memory of me, if it be not too troublesome, dig a pit, and cast my remains into it."

" Well," said Conn-eda, " my noblest steed, because you have been so faithful to me hitherto, and because you still would have rendered me further service, I consider such a proposal insulting to my feelings as a man, and totally in variance with the spirit which can feel the value of gratitude, not to speak of my feelings as a prince. But as a prince I am able to say, Come what may—come death itself in its most hideous forms and terrors—I never will sacrifice private friendship to personal interest. Hence, I am, I swear by my arms of valor, prepared to meet the worst—even death itself—sooner than violate the principles of hu-

manity, honor, and friendship! What a sacrifice do you
propose!" "Pshaw, man! heed not that; do what I ad-
vise you, and prosper." "Never! never!" exclaimed the
prince. "Well, then, son of the great western monarch,"
said the horse, with a tone of sorrow, "if you do not follow
my advice on this occasion, I tell you that both you and
I shall perish, and shall never meet again; but, if you act
as I have instructed you, matters shall assume a happier
and more pleasing aspect than you may imagine. I have
not misled you heretofore, and, if I have not, what need
have you to doubt the most important portion of my
counsel? Do exactly as I have directed you, else you
will cause a worse fate than death to befall me. And,
moreover, I can tell you that, if you persist in your resolution, I have done with you forever."

When the prince found that his noble steed could not
be persuaded from his purpose, he took the knife out of
his ear with reluctance, and with a faltering and trembling
hand essayed experimentally to point the weapon at his
throat. Conn-eda's eyes were bathed in tears; but no
sooner had he pointed the Druidic *scian* to the throat of
his good steed, than then dagger, as if impelled by some
Druidic power, stuck in his neck, and in an instant the
work of death was done, and the noble animal fell dead
at his feet. When the prince saw his noble steed fall
dead by his hand, he cast himself on the ground, and cried
aloud until his consciousness was gone. When he recovered, he perceived that the steed was quite dead; and,
as he thought there was no hope of resuscitating him, he
considered it the most prudent course he could adopt to
act according to the advice he had given him. After
many misgivings of mind and abundant showers of tears,
he essayed the task of flaying him, which was only that
of a few minutes. When he found he had the hide
separated from the body, he, in the derangement of the
moment, enveloped himself in it, and proceeding towards
the magnificent city in rather a demented state of mind,
entered it without any molestation or opposition. It was

a surprisingly populous city, and an extremely wealthy place ; but its beauty, magnificence, and wealth had no charms for Conn-eda, because the thoughts of the loss he sustained in his dear steed were paramount to those of all other earthly considerations.

He had scarcely proceeded more than fifty paces from the gate, when the last request of his beloved *draoidheacht* steed forced itself upon his mind, and compelled him to return to perform the last solemn injunctions upon him. When he came to the spot upon which the remains of his beloved *draoidheacht* steed lay, an appalling sight presented itself ; ravens and other carnivorous birds of prey were tearing and devouring the flesh of his dear steed. It was but short work to put them to flight ; and having uncorked his little jar of *ice,* he deemed it a labor of love to embalm the now mangled remains with the precious ointment. The potent *ice* had scarcely touched the inanimate flesh, when, to the surprise of Conn-eda, it commenced to undergo some strange change, and in a few minutes, to his unspeakable astonishment and joy, it assumed the form of one of the handsomest and noblest young men imaginable, and in the twinkling of an eye the prince was locked in his embrace, smothering him with kisses, and drowning him with tears of joy. When one recovered from his ecstasy of joy, the other from his surprise, the strange youth thus addressed the prince: " Most noble and puissant prince, you are the best sight I ever saw with my eyes, and I am the most fortunate being in existence for having met you ! Behold in my person, changed to the natural shape, your little shaggy *draoidheacht* steed ! I am brother of the king of the city ; and it was the wicked Druid, Fion Badhna, who kept me so long in bondage ; but he was forced to give me up when you came to *consult* him, for my *geis* was then broken ; yet I could not recover my pristine shape and appearance unless you had acted as you have kindly done. It was my own sister that urged the queen, your stepmother, to send you in quest of the steed and powerful

puppy hound, which my brother has now in keeping.
My sister, rest assured, had no thought of doing you the
least injury, but much good, as you will find hereafter;
because, if she were maliciously inclined towards you,
she could have accomplished her end without any trouble.
In short, she only wanted to free you from all future
danger and disaster, and recover me from my relentless
enemies through your instrumentality. Come with me,
my friend and deliverer, and the steed and the puppy-
hound of extraordinary powers, and a golden apple shall
be yours and a cordial welcome shall greet you in my
brother's abode; for you will deserve all this and much
more."

The exciting joy felt on the occasion was mutual, and
they lost no time in idle congratulations, but proceeded
on to the royal residence of the King of Lough Erne.
Here they were both received with demonstrations of joy
by the king and his chieftains; and, when the purpose
of Conn-cda's visit became known to the king, he gave a
free consent to bestow on Conn-eda the black steed, the
cuileen con-na-mbuadh, called Samer, and the three apples
of health that were growing in his garden, under the
special condition, however, that he would consent to remain as his guest until he could set out on his journey in
proper time, to fulfil his *geis*. Conn-eda, at the earnest
solicitation of his friends, consented, and remained in the
royal residence of the Firbolg, King of Lough Erne, in the
enjoyment of the most delicious and fascinating pleasures
during that period.

When the time of his departure came, the three golden
apples were plucked from the crystal tree in the midst
of the pleasure-garden, and deposited in his bosom; the
puppy-hound, Samer, was leashed, and the leash put into
his hand; and the black steed, richly harnessed, was got
in readiness for him to mount. The king himself helped
him on horseback, and both he and his brother assured
him that he might not fear burning mountains or hissing
serpents, because none would impede him, as his steed

was always a passport to and from his subaqueous kingdom. And both he and his brother extorted a promise
from Conn-eda, that he would visit them once every year
at least.

Conn-eda took leave of his dear friend, and the king
his brother. The parting was a tender one, soured by
regret on both sides. He proceeded on his way without
meeting anything to obstruct him, and in due time came
in sight of the *dún* of his father, where the queen had
been placed on the pinnacle of the tower, in full hope
that, as it was the last day of her imprisonment there,
the prince would not make his appearance, and thereby
forfeit all pretensions and right to the crown of his father
forever. But her hopes were doomed to meet a disappointment, for when it had been announced to her by her
couriers, who had been posted to watch the arrival of the
prince, that he approached, she was incredulous; but
when she saw him mounted on a foaming black steed,
richly harnessed, and leading a strange kind of animal by
a silver chain, she at once knew he was returning in
triumph, and that her schemes laid for his destruction
were frustrated. In the excess of grief at her disappointment, she cast herself from the top of the tower, and was
instantly dashed to pieces. Conn-eda met a welcome
reception from his father, who mourned him as lost to
him forever, during his absence; and, when the base
conduct of the queen became known, the king and his
chieftains ordered her remains so be consumed to ashes
for her perfidy and wickedness.

Conn-eda planted the three golden apples in his garden,
and instantly a great tree, bearing similar fruit, sprang
up. This tree caused all the district to produce an ex-
uberance of crops and fruits, so that it became as fertile
and plentiful as the dominions of the Firbolgs, in consequence of the extraordinary powers possessed by the
golden fruit. The hound Samer and the steed were of the
utmost utility to him; and his reign was long and prosperous, and celebrated among the old people for the great

abundance of corn, fruit, milk, fowl, and fish that prevailed during this happy reign. It was after the name Conn-eda the province of Connaucht, or *Conneda*, or *Connacht*, was so called.